I0584137

The Vatican Ruby

Craig Godfrey

Black Rose Writing | Texas

©2023 by Craig Godfrey
All rights reserved. No part of this book may be reproduced, stored in a retrieval system or transmitted in any form or by any means without the prior written permission of the publishers, except by a reviewer who may quote brief passages in a review to be printed in a newspaper, magazine or journal.

The author grants the final approval for this literary material.

First printing

This is a work of fiction. Names, characters, businesses, places, events, and incidents are either the products of the author's imagination or used in a fictitious manner. Any resemblance to actual persons, living or dead, or actual events is purely coincidental.

ISBN: 978-1-68513-109-8
PUBLISHED BY BLACK ROSE WRITING
www.blackrosewriting.com

Printed in the United States of America
Suggested Retail Price (SRP) $21.95

The Vatican Ruby is printed in Calluna

*As a planet-friendly publisher, Black Rose Writing does its best to eliminate unnecessary waste to reduce paper usage and energy costs, while never compromising the reading experience. As a result, the final word count vs. page count may not meet common expectations.

For Sebastian Godfrey,
creative artist and *a chip off the old block.*

The Vatican Ruby

PROLOGUE

Jameson Rowley and Elspeth Poole can't seem to avoid adventure. Some would say trouble. Jameson, the head chef of the Hook, Line and Sinker seafood restaurant on Hobart's waterfront, and Elspeth, assistant curator and conservator at the Tasmanian Museum, met when Elspeth waited tables at the restaurant to put herself through university. They shared a passion for travel and history, especially Tasmanian history. But Jameson's enthusiasm as a private collector occasionally grated against Elspeth's ethics and her dedication to the museum's public collections.

A year earlier the couple became involved in the search for a missing cache of gold bullion deserted by Napoleon's retreating army, after the devastating battle near a village called Waterloo in Belgium in 1815.

After the ingots of gold were hidden at the bottom of a well by the Duke of Wellington's retreating Royal Engineers, the treasure disappeared only to be found a century later, in 1916, by Australian sappers excavating trenches on the battlefields of Tromelles, on the Western Front.

A chance purchase of a World War I soldier's personal papers and possessions, by Jameson at a Hobart antique action, hinted at the existence of the trove. This led Jameson and Elspeth to France where they encountered the wrath of drug lords and modern-day gangsters pursuing the same treasure.

All hell broke loose.

Later Jameson and Elspeth found themselves on the trail of missing art works collected by the mysterious German businessman Herr von Gaunt. This search led them into life threatening circumstances – following clues found diving on the rusted wreck of the *Lake Illawarra* lying below the Tasman Bridge – to the West Coast towns of Queenstown and Zeehan in Tasmania. lspeth had made a poor choice of company in her a few years earlier. With ex-boyfriend Hawk following their every move, the lives of the two adventurers were once again in peril.

Fool's Hoard was totally unexpected. Just as Jameson returned to the kitchen and Elspeth settled back in the downstairs corridors of the Tasmanian Museum, along came a baffling mystery and an irresistible challenge. It all started in 1692 when the wicked Pirate Port of Port Royal sank into the ocean after a devastating earthquake.

With Elspeth invited to work with the Institute of Jamaica for two weeks on the sunken city Jameson was not prepared to miss out. This led to the couple once again becoming involved in an intriguing mystery involving a lost hoard of looted Spanish treasure, a corrupt Jamaican politician, a drug cartel and a retired maritime archaeologist with a taste for adventure.

More recently Elspeth and Jameson found themselves in Italy. Once again Elspeth travelled on museum business, this time to Rome. Excited at having discovered valuable high-end antiquities at a local house sale in Hobart – that turned out to be proof of a forgery racket from the 1950s in Naples – Jameson tagged along. Neither expected to discover evidence for the existence of Vataea, Pompeii's lost sister city. Nor did they expect Vesuvius, south of Rome to erupt during their visit. Against all odds they infiltrate a modern-day antiquities gang which leads them to Poveglia Island on the Lagoon of Venice from where the billionaire criminal Cambino and his beautiful, yet ruthless accomplice Drishya operate their world-wide antiquities racket.

The race was then set: to find the Lance of Destiny, said to be lost in Vataea. The same lance that pierced the side of Jesus of Nazareth – a powerful artefact said to have supernatural powers.

CHAPTER ONE

The siege of Cadiz...

1812. With the seat of power in Seville occupied by the French, the port city of Cadiz – hosting Spain's large navy – became the political capital immediately attracting Napoleon's attention. He determined to take control of the Iberian Peninsula in the Mediterranean. From February 1810 to August 1812 seventy thousand French soldiers, struggling to advance on the port city from inland, were held at bay by ten thousand Spanish troops, assisted by British and Portuguese forces, in and around Cadiz. For over two years Cadiz was a fortress city under siege and for some this dilemma created opportunities to gain riches that was simply too tempting.

Cadiz, Spain. August 1812...

Septimus Tilley clamped his pipe with vice-like teeth. If he bit down any harder, he would crush the fired clay stem. The tobacco, of course, had burnt out hours earlier, but his favourite pipe, with its bowl the shape of a young nymph's head, gave him comfort. Outside on the cobbles of Calle de San Pedro the hobnailed boots of the night guard were heard lingering close by. Too close by. Standing inside the doorway, Septimus looked back to his colleagues working in the soft light of a masked lantern. Anwyn Blizzard was a comely thirty-nine-year-old, fearless, determined woman toughened by a Moroccan prison. She stood with Captain Alexander Ramsay Fate who'd taken charge. Accompanying them was First Mate Ambrose Smith and ship's cook Walter Grubb. They stared back at Septimus; their faces caked with sweat and rock dust, their eyes wide and aware. Septimus, an overweight forty-seven-year-old shipping clerk – short and squat like a hogshead they jested – and the most unlikely in the group to be persuaded into a life of crime, pushed his ear harder against the inside of the huge wooden door of the apothecary. His sensitive nose recognised the bouquet of Turkish tobacco, a sun-cured highly aromatic tobacco popular with many Spanish soldiers. Although he couldn't speak Spanish, Septimus recognised the slurred words of an inebriate. The group waited silently. Outside, the voices dissipated. Shortly after, stillness returned to the street once more, a street already veiled in semi-darkness under a quarter moon and a wartime curfew.

Acknowledging a nod from Septimus, Captain Fate, the fifty-one-year-old gang leader – who had been quartermaster to the Royal Engineers in the British Army – resumed drilling. The group had shared the drilling for hours now, their hands calloused from turning the brace and their shoulders pained from pressuring the head. It was hard work drilling into a bank vault, but the rewards stood to be staggering.

Somewhere outside a town guard cried. It was two hours past midnight, Sunday morning, and the Banco de Cadiz was deserted, and would remain so until early Monday. The group was almost through the wall but there was no time for complacency. This heist, the brainwave of Captain Fate, would see all involved publicly executed should they be caught; executed by garrotting –

strangulation with an iron collar affixed to a post and tightened with a screw.

One week earlier, Captain Alexander Ramsay Fate, masquerading as a British merchant, had managed to arrange a short lease on a vacant building next door to the bank. Their story was that the property would be an outlet for Spanish and imported medicines. Medicines were in high demand during this time of war. This was no easy task in a city under siege by the French the past two years. With the aid of gold to grease the palm of certain authorities the captain was given permission to wholesale his apothecaries from the site. The premises were duly stocked with crates, with labels labelled such as *Dr. Lignum and Son's Herbal Apothecary. For the cure of all kinds of sores and wounds.* Others were convincingly in Spanish; like *Peruvian calaguala,* chests of the purgative mechoacán or smilax hailed as an anti-syphilis treatment. Sample products in glass bottles and stoneware jars were displayed on shelves in the small shop window. The ruse was complete. However, the merchant had made it clear to the civic authority they would not be in a position to trade for another week.

The doors remained locked.

Meanwhile, inside, during the past five nights, the crew carefully chiselled away and removed the limestone blocks of both the merchant premises and then the adjoining Banco de Cadiz. Here, the bank's vault with its iron walls, backed onto the wall of the importers. Now, at two hours after midnight, Sunday, the group shared the long and tedious task of drilling dozens of holes through the steel plate. Each hole – made by one-inch diameter auger drill bits – connected side by side like a series of dots until a section of twenty inches by twelve was completed.

Sometime after the 4AM. Ambrose Smith, the second youngest of the group at thirty-seven, drilled the final hole.

'We're through,' his hushed words barely audible from the dark and dusty opening in the stonework. Cap'n Fate slapped Smith on the back and pushed into the space with the lantern. He inspected the holes. Twenty one-inch holes horizontal, top and bottom, and twelve vertical holes each side.

Fate noticed there was very little holding the drilled section of the one-and-a-half-inch thick steel plate in place. He cast the light over the serration, squinting to peer inside but could see very little. Only the musty smell of the stale vault air kindled his enthusiasm.

'Hammer,' he hissed back into the blackness, his hand outstretched behind him like a surgeon might ask an assistant for a scalpel. The next manoeuvre would be the most dangerous. They had no option but to pummel at the weakened plate with a twenty-pound sledgehammer. Fate gripped the tool and positioned himself.

'Check the door!'

Septimus shuffled across the flagstones through the darkness back to the front door of the apothecary. He listened. All was quiet. Turning the key, he twisted the huge iron bolt and poked his head out into the street.

'All clear,' he called back in a loud whisper.

It took ex-quartermaster Fate several hefty blows, when the serrated plate fell inwards crashing to the vault floor. Everyone froze. Fate waited for confirmation. Septimus Tilley gave the *all clear* a second time, re-locked the door and joined the others at the entrance to the breached wall.

'What can you see?' he asked, his croaky parched voice high and excited. The wait seemed endless.

Fate leant into the gap as well as possible for a man his size. It was always agreed Walter Grubb, the lean twenty-eight-year-old cook, would do the hard yards inside the vault.

'Cap'n,' Anwyn Blizzard said. 'Don't keep us in suspense.'

Fate crawled back out of the opening, dusting himself down.

'Well?' Blizzard persisted.

'Mates, we have our work cut out,' the quartermaster grinned. 'There must be forty chests of coin in there, not to mention locker after locker of private deposits.'

'Devil's blood, we done it,' Ambrose Smith slapped Anwyn on the back.

'Don't dilly-dally lad,' Fate ordered the cook. 'Get yer skinny arse in there.'

With the aid of a purpose-built wooden sill placed over the jagged steel, Walter Grubb was man-handled through the narrow gap. He was handed a small crowbar and another lantern. From inside Walter fought claustrophobia as he stared back at the dimly lit faces of his nefarious cohort. They all relied on *him* now.

He would have to work fast as the chests were too large to feed through the opening and the sun would cast its hard dawn shadows across the port in less than two hours. Walter stared at the task ahead briefly. *Where to start?* The chests, stacked neatly in the centre of the vault, were of heavy iron, all with the crest of the bank in relief on the lids with solid iron handles each end. He attacked the first chest. The lock pulled away from the latch. He threw the lid open.

'Jesus!'

Captain Fate. 'What?'

'Gold?' Anwyn Blizzard cried out louder than she intended.

Walter lifted the hefty chest for the others to see. 'It's empty!' he hissed.

A sudden fear of failure bristled amongst the gang. No one had ever considered for a moment the vault could be empty.

'What? Can't be ...'

'Look for yourself.' Walter tipped the chest upside down.

'No! It can't be. It's impossible,' Fate barked through the gap. 'Check them others.'

But Walter was already jemmying the next chest. 'Empty!' Chest after chest were forced open. Each chest was the same. The bank's coffers were either moved to another hiding place due to the siege or the bank was broke.

'Lord help us!' Fate sat back heavily on the pile of limestone, his battle-scarred face taut with failure. His fists balled. His knuckles whitened. Anger brewed.

Septimus pushed his ruddy round face into the opening. 'What's in the lockers?'

Walter turned on the wooden lockers built across two walls, each with individual locks. These, the gang knew, were private citizen holdings. The first locker revealed paperwork, bundles of what looked to be legal documents, deeds written on vellum and the like. The second was more forthcoming. Holding his lantern in his left hand, Walter reached in and removed a bag of coin.

'This's more like it,' he tossed the satchel of specie to a waiting hand.

'Gold!' someone cheered from the other side.

Capt'n Fate snatched the bag spilling the coins into his palm. There were no more than twenty coins, mixed denominations of escudos. Not much, but better than nothing. Encouraged, Walter attacked the remaining lockers with the energy of a sacking looter. Coin was lean, ten small purses of gold and silver only. Jewellery was even leaner. It appeared the wealthy residents of Cadiz weren't prepared to trust their bank in these volatile times.

'What's that?' Captain Fate's arm appeared through the gap and he waved a finger impatiently at what appeared to be stacked boxes draped with a dark sail cloth. They were barely discernible in the blackness beside the looted lockers. Walter swung his lantern over the waist-high boxes.

'Well?' Fate snapped.

The cook sat his lantern on the top locker and peeled back the sail.

'Chests!'

Chests Walter hadn't noticed in their urgency. 'There's four wooden crates capt'n.'

'Damn your eyes man. There's writin' on them crates. What's them words?'

'I think it's Italian.'

'Open one and be bloody quick about it.' Fate's wounded eye twitched. Walter wasted no time cracking open the top crate. Throwing straw aside he hoisted a heavy parcel wrapped in velvet cloth. 'Well?'

'I think it's a statue.'

'Jesus lad. What kind of statue?'

'Well, I'll be blowed.' Walter revealed a statue of Madonna at least eighteen inches tall, her head bowed in prayer. She stood on what appeared to be clouds holding the sceptre in her right hand with baby Jesus in her left arm. Both Madonna and child wore a crown, and the baby held the *Globus Cruciger*, an orb that represented the world.

'It's bloody heavy.'

'Give it 'ere lad. Quick now.' Fate snatched at the statue, but at a dozen pounds in weight it took both hands to lift it through the opening. Walter watched from the vault awaiting the captain's appraisal.

'Is it gold?' he asked.

'It be gold alright. And solid.' Fate lowered the statue into the light of the apothecary lantern, the better to inspect the religious artefact. 'Them be rubies too ... and emeralds,' he noted the gemstones in the crown and the *Rays from Heaven* backdrop to support the statue.

'It's wood, right?' Anwyn Blizzard asked, hesitant. 'I mean gold leaf on wood?'

'Nay lass, feel its weight. Thart's solid gold and at least a hundred years old. More maybe.' Captain Fate twisted back to Walter. 'Well don't stand there lad, get on with it. What's in them other boxes?'

Walter said nothing. He simply stood, staring back like the village idiot, his lean dust covered face and bloodshot eyes gaping back at the others with the widest grin.

'Now what?'

Walter remained silent. While the others were gloating over Madonna Walter *had* been busy. He held something else in his hand.

'What is it then?'

Walter. 'Here, take it.'

Blizzard reached through snatching the ten-inch-long ingot. She recognised the weight immediately.

'Gold! Hell's teeth, that's a gold bar.' She passed it on, turning back to Walter. 'Is there more?' Her face brightened as gold fever threatened all caution.

'Maybe a hundred or more,' he said sharing Anwyn's enthusiasm.

'What?'

'Stacked under Madonna ... gold bars.'

'Hazzah, hazzah,' Fate cheered as loud as he dared. 'At last, something for our trouble.'

Walter passed bar after bar to Anwyn where the others formed a line. Ten minutes later the bullion was stacked on the apothecary floor.

Quartermaster Fate's scarred face re-appeared, framed in the opening. The glint of greed had returned to those cold dark eyes. 'What's in them other crates?'

Walter threw the empty box aside and tackled the second. 'Jesus Christ!' he jumped backwards, crossing himself. The lantern teetered, creating ghoulish shadows shifting on the vault wall.

'What is it for Christ sake?' Fate hissed, frustrated he could not fit through the gap. Walter stepped up to the crate once more, reaching out cautiously. He studied the contents under the weak light before gingerly lifting a human skull from its velvet cocoon.

Fate. 'Is that what I think it is?'

'Aye.' Walter positioned the skull for the Cap'n to see.

'Hold it to the light for Christ's sake.' The eye sockets were filled with what appeared to be rubies and the head was bejewelled with precious gemstones held with gold inlay.

'Oh, dear Lord. Will yer look at thart? Pass it 'ere.'

Fate passed the skull back to the others. 'Well?' he twisted back to Walter, the excitement and an old duelling scar to his mouth causing the man to dribble. 'What else is there?'

'Bones, skeletons, skulls, all decorated with gems,' Walter's tone was one of reverence, almost a fear of superstition. Knowing a little of Spain's history in the New World, the wiry cook asked. 'Do you reckon it's Inca gold cap'n, stuff the Spanish purloined from them natives in Peru like?'

'Inca? Don't be a fool. These are Papal treasures. But how the bloody hell they got here is anyone's business. Get on with it lad, time is deserting us.'

Twenty minutes later...

'We done good lads,' Fate turned to Anwyn Blizzard. 'An' you too me lovely. Better than I 'oped a moment ago.' Captain Fate ran a greedy tongue over parched lips, greedy for gold. Outside the day was warming, besides, the mercury hadn't dropped that much overnight either. He drank greedily from a water canteen. With the robbery over they were all keen to leave the mess behind them before the vault was opened – as much as Fate would've liked to be a fly on the wall when they did.

Quartermaster Fate, given the sobriquet Capt'n by his partners in crime, pushed back into the hollowed wall. 'Yer ready to come out lad?' he asked Walter, already standing at the opening, reliant on the others to lift him back through to the apothecary over the jagged steel.

'Aye cap'n, good an' ready.'

'Yer certain there ain't no more?'

'No. Look for yerself.' Walter stepped back, holding the lantern head high to cast the flame across every inch of the fifteen-foot square vault. Fate pushed an arm and head in as far as the gap allowed, his good eye searching about. Carefully Walter pivoted on the spot, spilling the light into every dark corner.

Fate was fast.

He struck like a cobra. Burying his pocket pistol in Walter's back directly behind the heart, he fired. The shot was muffled with the flintlock's muzzle hard against the cook's body. The eleven-millimetre lead ball passed directly through the man's vital organ, splintering a rib on exit. Walter fell to the vault floor, his body lying across the discarded chests, dying instantly.

'Jesus Lord cap'n, what yer done?' First Mate Ambrose squeezed alongside Fate. 'Yer killed him.'

'Aye, and I'd shoot the thievin' bastard again too if'n he were to blink them eyes once more.'

The others gathered around the demolished wall, incredulous at what in all appearances was cold-blooded murder. Fate backed away to allow the others access. 'He were stealin' from us mates. There ain't no place but honour amongst thieves, right.'

Walter's body lay twisted across bullion chests on his back, blood pooling from the exit wound in his heart with his eyes wide open and his mouth in a silent scream. A gold ingot poked out from the top of his trousers where he had hidden it. Quartermaster Alexander Ramsey Fate didn't miss a trick. That's why he was the cap'n.

Fate gathered the others around the ingots and reliquary treasures, packaged ready in carpet bags.

'Anyone,' Fate scowled in a low voice, 'anyone steals from us receives the same, savvy.' Anwyn, Ambrose and Septimus looked to the Quartermaster, their faces wary. 'Savvy?'

Silence.

'I said ... savvy?'

'Aye ... aye cap'n.'

'Good. An' thart rule goes for me too, we're all in this together.'

Fair enough, they all thought. *It was the code of pirates' past.*

And if one wanted to label them, they *had* turned pirate, in a sense, especially after this plunder.

Immediately overhead from the first floor, fine dust filtered through cracks in the floorboards. The fine particles sparkled, floating through a beam of early morning sun entering from a narrow slit of a window above the front door. Fate signalled for silence, but the others were already alert. Someone was afoot on the floor above but how they entered was the real worry. Fate quickly, silently, reloaded his pocket pistol. Ambrose drew his dagger while Anwyn rushed to the stair. She threw her back hard to the wall, searching the top of the staircase for the intruder. Drawing her stiletto from its scabbard, Anwyn took to the treads. The century-old boards creaked. More dust particles dictated the intruder was aware and made their move, away from the stair. With the agility of an alley cat Ambrose hurried to the back staircase. He moved smartly, quietly, up the stairs bursting onto the deserted first floor.

'Jaysuz!'

Anwyn met him halfway, her stiletto pricking his chest in the semi-darkness. 'Where is he?'

'Christ. I don't know.'

Instantly they heard a window crash closed on its lead-weighted sash. Anwyn and Ambrose raced to the scene, but their trespasser had bolted.

Somewhere outside a cockerel crowed. Dawn was upon them and the curfew would be lifted, but now was a dangerous time to leave when passing guards would query their presence in the deserted streets. The wise thing to do would be to sit it out for an hour or two until the city came alive and they could load their wagon without attracting attention, blend in with passing traffic. But with the advent of the intruder upstairs, Fate thought it prudent to move sooner rather than later, to make good their escape.

'We'll have to risk it,' Capt'n Fate was worried, and rightly so. 'We need to leave, now.' He turned to Septimus who looked anxious. 'You know what to do.' Fate opened the main door and peered out, blinking as the blinding early morning sun poured through the gap. 'Go. Go man go. And for god's sake, make haste.'

'What about Walter?' Anwyn Blizzard sheathed her stiletto, jerking her head back to the breached bank wall. The lantern in the vault flickered in its last throws casting dancing shadows like demonic images.

'He can greet the bankers when they open the vault temorrer mornin'.'

Anwyn returned a wry smile, a smile that threatened to weaken the cold heartedness of Fate. But gold appeared to be the man's only mistress. Yet Anwyn Christina Blizzard from Carlisle really was a most desirable woman. Long auburn hair plaited down her back, her green eyes glinted like emeralds with her clothing exposing her feline figure leaving little to the imagination. But pity help any man who took advantage. The woman was a fire cat, deft with both dagger and fists.

Fate met Anwyn Blizzard masquerading as a young man at the Marrakesh waterfront in Morocco. She was imprisoned alongside nineteen men about to be chained to the oars of a galley. Anwyn had been caught stealing food in the market, forced to do so through hunger. Prior to the chain gang, Anwyn and the other prisoners had been held at the notorious and mysterious Prison of Qara, an underground prison in the Imperial northern central Moroccan city of Meknes. Qara was a frightful place. Said to have no door, prisoners were dropped through holes in the ceiling ... and fed the same way.

The gaol was a labyrinth of corridors, hallways and mazes designed to lose one forever. It was said once one was imprisoned here there was no escape. Imprisonment was for life. Four months Anwyn Blizzard languished there. Fortunately, she had already learnt lifesaving skills aboard a privateer, the *Blackbird*, captained by Thomas Schoeman – known as Black Tom. The same man whose persistent advances she terminated by pinning his hand to the cabin wall with her stiletto; the same man who marooned her at Marrakesh.

Anwyn was one of the rare few to leave Qara Prison behind her. The only reason her life was saved being the shortage of slave rowers for the ruler Mohammed IV's galleys.

It had been a matter of good fortune, right place at the right time. Between the unshackling of the prison irons and the re-shackling at the oars of the galley, Anwyn's gang managed to riot. They escaped their guard, scattering into the market crowds gathered at the souk near the waterfront. Anwyn took shelter in a provedore where Quartermaster Fate was negotiating provisions. Recognising a countryman, and being short of crew himself, Fate paid extra for the merchant's silence and Anwyn Blizzard was smuggled on board the *El Delfin*.

The *El Delfin* was a decommissioned Royal Navy topsail schooner, once HMS *Sting*. Built in 1799 the two-masted gaff rig had a square topsail on her foremast. She was a 73-foot, 127-ton ship, 20 feet in the beam. Her navy ship's company had been forty. Now the *El Delfin*'s crew was twenty-five. As a merchant vessel the gundeck, which once had eight twelve-pounder cannons, now carried only four. Now *El Delfin* was as much an opportunistic privateer as she was merchant ship.

The next twenty minutes at the apothecary were nerve racking. The bells of the nearby cathedral at the Plaza de la Cathedral pealed six in the morning. Fate paced the flagstones of the apothecary when the coded knock came at the door. Septimus had returned with a two-horse passenger carriage and another crew member.

'Move it, move fast lads.' Captain Fate kept an eye out. The city of Cadiz was waking to a new day. Soon the streets would be filled with soldiers. The loaded carpet bags were eased into the carriage, stacked floor to ceiling in the passenger compartment. Fate took the livery driver's seat and Septimus, the more respectable accomplice in appearance, squeezed alongside. With the cabin full, Anwyn Blizzard rode on the carriage step. Ambrose followed on foot as rear guard, twenty paces behind, watching for trouble.

The carriage trundled over the cobblestones of Calle de San Pedro towards Calle Gral Luque, finally arriving at Avenida del Puerto where the remaining crew waited nervously on board the *El Delfin*, docked at the Cadiz port.

The morning had warmed considerably, and the overweight accountant Septimus ran a handkerchief over his lathered brow.

'Steady as she goes,' Fate forced a smile at Septimus.

'Do you think we've been watched?' Septimus's voice was anxious.

'So far so good. Just keep smilin' fer Christ's sake. Look cheerful.'

A gunshot rang out.

The half-ounce lead ball sizzled by Fate's right ear shattering against a limestone wall as the cart cornered into Avenida del Puerto. Anwyn leapt from the step and rolled across the narrow lane with the agility of a cat, diving behind an archway. Fate cracked the whip. The horses broke from a trot to a canter. Septimus turned awkwardly. Two watchmen on foot made chase.

'Are they soldiers?' Fate asked.

'Watchmen I'd say.'

'One of them must have been our intruder.'

'Which places them on the wrong side of the law.'

'That's what I was thinking. They want a piece of the pie.'

The second pursuer stopped suddenly. He levelled his musket. At fifty yards he had a clear shot at his target … Fate's head.

And a well-aimed round shot at this distance would split the captain's head like a melon. Anwyn stepped from the archway and Septimus watched a ten-inch blade penetrate the musketeer's side. His gun discharged. The bullet whistled off towards the clouds. The shooter collapsed to the ground, dead. The other assailant turned as Anwyn attacked. He threw his arm in the air masking his body with his cape. Briefly blinded, Anwyn groped to secure hermark, but the man was fast. With his left hand he wielded a swordsman's dagger. In his right, a three-foot rapier. The cape settled and Anwyn's attacker leapt forward. The dagger pierced her below her breast and as the rapier stabbed forward, Anwyn parried with her stiletto. The two blades locked. With a flick of the attacker's wrist Anwyn's stiletto spiralled into the air. The assailant stepped in for the kill, not suspecting Ambrose reaching from a doorway. The first mate took Anwyn's attacker by the hair. He jerked the killer's head back before slicing his dagger across the man's throat. Anwyn and Ambrose's faces were dotted with jetting blood and the body collapsed to the cobbles. Anwyn snatched up her stiletto. 'Thanks.'

'Don't mention it.'

Somewhere close by excited shouting had the two on the run. The gunshots had woken the docks. 'Soldiers?'

'No doubt ... run!'

The carriage disappeared from the lane onto the main thoroughfare along the waterfront.

'We need to create a decoy.' The moment these words emerged from Anwyn's lips a knot of regular Spanish guards appeared at the double, all uniformed by the British in blue with black shakos and white gaiters. They were armed with Brown Bess muskets.

'Jaysus!' Ambrose looked to Anwyn. 'I'll take the plaza and circle back to the ship.'

'See you there.'

Ambrose careened off down a lane adjacent to the waterfront. The guards picked up speed. They closed in from fifty yards to forty. But running in boots on cobbles was fraught with difficulty. Anwyn wasted no time running in the opposite direction. She hit steep steps, a stone stairway leading to church gardens and to Oratorio de la Santa Cueva.

At the corner the guards split into two groups.

Ambrose ran into Plaza de Espana dissolving into a market crowd. At the far side of the plaza, he dared turn. His three pursuers had split up again. But comfortable he had lost them he circled back towards the docks.

The great wood and iron doors to the church were open. Anwyn entered. Inside early worshippers prayed silently where the atmosphere was dim and cool. She hurried through the nave, positioning herself behind a colossal column. To the worshippers, piety took precedence and Anwyn's behaviour attracted little attention. The south transept door opened; a door normally locked. A priest entered. Anwyn pushed past the clergy, stepping back into the bright sunlight.

'Halt!'

Accented English.

'Halt I say!'

The order reached Anwyn the moment the door slammed behind her. She'd been spotted. Anwyn bolted. Shouting followed, Spanish words, angry, determined. Anwyn crossed the manicured garden, barely noticing oranges trees in full blossom. She ran down the first lane, ducking right, ducking left. Anwyn feared she would be lost in the maze of alleys but anything was better than being captured … Or even worse, tortured.

Hobnailed boots clattered along the cobbles close behind her. Anwyn rounded another corner. She dived into an entrance. She unsheathed the stiletto. A blue uniform rushed by …

One second … two seconds …

Peering out, the lane was empty. Anwyn hurried in the opposite direction. For a brief moment anxiety struck. But early morning shadows pointed west. The *port* was to the west. Another frantic scramble, another plaza, several more lanes and Anwyn saw blue water at the end of an alley. She burst into the open on Avenida del Puerto. Before her it seemed a hundred ships were either moored in the bay or docked along the wharves. All were Spanish Navy, escaping the French occupiers inland, and the area was swarming with the military preparing for a new day under siege. Anwyn melded into the crowd best she could, walking calmly at as fast a pace as she dared. Near the end of the main port, Anwyn hurried east to a smaller merchant port where *El Delfin* was docked.

Ambrose was already on board, catching carpetbags thrown from the carriage. Men were aloft on the yards, unfurling the sails while others loosened the ropes from the wharf bollards.

The favourable tide was running out.

Fate scanned the docks as Anwyn boarded. 'Have you got company?' He stood at the top of the companionway to the quarterdeck supervising the loot stored in his stern cabin.

'I think I lost them.'

'Good. Hurry.' Fate saw blood under Anwyn's arm. 'You're wounded.'

'It's nothing.'

'See to it.' The last thing Fate wanted was a crew member dying of lockjaw.

Within minutes *El Delfin* was passing the rocky shoals of the harbour under full sail and offering a farewell salute to the guard on the ramparts of San Sebastian Castle, built at the end of the long stone causeway, the Paseo Fernando Quinones. Fate ran his eyeglass back along the causeway. Anwyn climbed the quarterdeck steps, following his eye line. Men could be seen running towards the fortress. 'Anything we should be concerned about?' she asked the quartermaster.

'Soldiers headin' to the castle. But to answer yer question? Nay lass, by the time they inform the guard we'll be well outa the range o' even their biggest cannon.'

Ambrose cast an eye back to the two British ships, HMS *Nautilus* and HMS *Rigid*, anchored offshore and now a mile away. With the *El Delfin's* Union Jack fluttering proudly from her stern, their departure attracted no more than a friendly wave from the warship's watch. When suddenly ...

'Devils teeth! Will yer look at thart? The castle's signalling the Navy.'

Fate spun on his heels fixing the two Royal Navy ships in focus. 'Jesus Christ!'

Anwyn. 'What is it?'

'Look fer yourself.' Fate pressed the spyglass into Anwyn's hand and peered into the rigging. 'Mr Smith!' He barked into the first mate's ear. 'Unfurl the top gallant and studding sails. We need all the wind up our arse we can get.'

'Aye sar.'

While Ambrose whistled down to the bosun, Anwyn framed the big ships in the spy glass. 'Damn their eyes,' she muttered. Anwyn watched half a dozen Royal Navy tars cranking the capstan to weigh anchor. 'That's not good.'

'No it ain't,' Fate grumbled. 'I'm thinkin' they want to know why we terminated them coves what was chasing us.'

'What are our chances?'

'I'm not worried lass. Those great gunships may 'ave firepower but nuthin'll catch the *El Delfin*. All the same we'll take no risks.'

Cap'n Fate slipped a silver fob from his waistcoat pocket. For two hours exactly HMS *Nautilus* had pursued the *El Delfin*. But Fate proved himself right. The heavily armed battleship was no match for the topsail schooner. By late morning she turned back to *huzzahs* all round and dancing to the hornpipe along with a lively fiddler, amidships. Another hour passed and Fate felt he could relax. He held the spyglass firm against his good eye focussing on three sets of sail he guessed were French, progressing lazily, north on the horizon. First mate Ambrose Smith, still with cutlass at his side and wearing a brace of pistols, joined Fate on the quarterdeck. None of the shore party had eaten in twenty-four hours and now they were free of Cadiz the mate's belly growled, but the ship's cook had been 'left behind'.

'We'll be needin' a new cook cap'n.'

'Aye, thart we will.' Fate swigged a flask of rum before stroking his chin in thought. He always seemed to be nursing a headache lately and his scarred face pained him no end, especially here in the tropics. 'Young Ben helped Walter in the past,' Fate finally decided. 'See to it that *he's* in charge o' the galley now.'

'Ben?' Ambrose queried of the fifteen-year-old gunner's mate.

'Aye, Ben. He can boil pork can he not?'

'Aye.'

'Then see to it. At least 'til we sail well clear to the south of the Canaries. Then we might pick up a good Negro cook, savvy. One o' them Moors maybe, what can give them vittles' a bit o' spice.' If nothing else about their sojourn in Cadiz, Fate had enjoyed the food.

'Canaries cap'n. Aren't we headed to Italy? I mean we could make a good deal with the Vatican could we not?'

'We'll never get through the Strait,' Fate spoke of the Strait of Gibraltar. 'Too risky with all this shite goin' on.' Fate panned his spyglass back over the horizon where the French sails were vanishing. 'No. We'll sail south around to the Indian Ocean and up the coast.'

'To Madagascar?'

'Aye.'

'We'll pay a visit to our old friend Maharaja.'

Ambrose knew the self-titled Maharaja to be no more than a pirate living on the west coast of the island off the east coast of Africa. Indian-born Abdur al-Rahman, the freebooter, rarely risked his neck at sea; instead he purchased stolen property and sold it on for huge profits. And Ambrose knew Quartermaster Fate wanted to unload the papal treasure smartly as once the theft was discovered and the British merchant ship *El Delfin* suspected of the crime, they would have several governments in pursuit.

'Madagascar it is then. You're probably right cap'n.'

'Probably!' Fate collapsed his spyglass, securing it in a leather sheath about his neck and fixed his mate with a murderous eye. Although Ambrose stood his ground Fate recognised a twinge of fear in the man's demeanour. Fate knew his strengths. He knew he was superior. The mate had good reason to be scared, so this made the quartermaster feel slightly generous. '*Probably* ... ain't the right word matey. I knows I'm right.'

With a liberal wind beating down from north east off the Moroccan coast *El Delfin* made good speed sailing south under full sail.

'Packard,' Fate ordered the helmsman. 'Keep them sails full and steady as she goes.'

'Aye cap'n.'

Fate called to Francis Crisp the second mate. 'Keep an eye out.' The quartermaster turned back to Ambrose, the heel of his hand resting on the handgrip of his cutlass. 'Fetch Septimus and meet me in me cabin. We'll take a rum and inspect our prize.'

In the main cabin young Ben, the newly appointed ship's cook, nervously brought a plate of cold salted pork to the captain's table. Fate cast an eye over the grey-brown salted meat boiled for hours, two days ago. 'What the firk!'

'Sir?' Ben was justifiably terrified of his new position. After all Walter's fate in the bank vault travelled faster than any fly on-board ship. Fate spat vitriol at the boy. 'Would you eat that?' On closer inspection the lad now saw what angered the quartermaster. 'Maggots!' Fate snatched up the wriggling joint and heaved it out the stern window, pewter charger included. And the ships biscuits didn't fare any better, being home to hundreds of weevils.

'Is there no bread left?'

'Yes cap'n.'

'Then fetch me bread and cheese.'

Septimus met the boy in the doorway where there was barely room for the overweight clerk and the skinny runt to pass. The door squealed on its rusting hinge and the bookkeeper stood under the first beam, contemplating the Quartermaster's mood. Ambrose and Anwyn were already positioned at the table, inspecting a skull with a gold and pearl crown atop a skeletal torso adorned with precious stones.

'Well don't stand there like a great blancmange man,' Fate barked at Septimus. 'Get yer fat arse over 'ere and bring a bottle o' rum from the grog cupboard.'

Septimus stood one end of the table, Fate the other, first mate and Anwyn in the middle. Together they studied the macabre bejewelled remains.

'Any thoughts bookkeeper?' the quartermaster asked. Septimus ground his teeth silently. He hated being titled bookkeeper, he was an accountant for Christ's sake. Once a revered naval accountant at Greenwich, until he fell foul of the law and joined this lot.

'Actually,' Septimus conceded. 'I *do* have some idea.'

'Well now,' the capt'n's gnarly face brightened. 'Don't keep us in suspense.'

'Before us here is Saint Valerius in Weyarn.'

'You can read Italian then?' Anwyn asked.

'Latin actually. I know a little, yes. See there,' and Septimus pointed out a gold cartouche fastened to the breastplate. 'Valerius apud S Weyarn,' he read aloud.

'Jesus!' Fate crossed himself. 'Are you saying these are the remains of a saint?'

'Yes. Yes I am.' Two of the stolen crates lay open, exposing their haunting contents; mostly skulls and torsos all inlayed, embellished and festooned with rare and precious gems, gold, silver and pearls. 'They are all saints. Every single bone in our presence.'

'Are you certain, I mean you haven't looked at them all?'

'I have read of these revered remains before. They are kept at the Vatican. They are sacred Vatican treasures in fact, but I can't understand how they ended up in a bank vault in Cadiz.'

Ambrose. 'The Spanish must have looted them.'

'Spain and Italy are allies,' Anwyn said. 'Impossible.'

To say Quartermaster Fate was worried was an understatement. He had always been a superstitious man and the fear of god darkened the cabin.

'I suggest we collect the gems, the gold, silver and pearls,' Ambrose said. 'An' commit them bones to Davey Jones.'

'Do yer knows what you're sayin' man?' Fate roared. 'Can you hear your folly? You heard the bookkeeper, they's sacred.'

'We could give 'em a proper burial ... at sea like.'

'We'll do no such thing. We'll stick to the plan and let the Maharaja decide their fate. He is Muslim after all, and I should imagine he does not fear the wrath of our Christian god.'

Four and a half weeks later off Cape Town...

First mate Ambrose Smith watched the canoes and small tenders, loaded high with fresh fruits and vegetables, race to meet the *El Delfin* anchored in Cape Town bay. Under British sovereignty since 1806, Cape Town was not where the first mate wanted to be right now. The port was swarming with Royal Naval men with five ships of the line in the bay. There were also three convict transports on their voyage to New South Wales, all loaded with their wretched cargo of fellow humans. But as Quartermaster Fate pointed out, as long as they kept a low profile, they were safe. As there was no chance news from Cadiz could have arrived in Cape Town as yet.

'Two days, three,' Fate ordered. 'We resupply, and then sail round the cape and north to Madagascar, savvy.'

But news from Madagascar had travelled down the African east coast to the inns of Cape Town and Septimus was first to reach Fate with the news. 'Maharaja has been captured.'

'What? When?'

'Five weeks past.'

'By the Royal Navy?'

'No, the East India Company. They say he put up one hell of a fight. Most of his men were killed and the ones that weren't were captured and hanged.'

'Devil's blood.' Fate stared out the stern window. The bay seemed so tranquil. So peaceful. Yet now it felt dangerous. 'So what did they do with Abdur al-Rahman?' he asked of the Maharaja.

'They say he was chained in the brig of an east Indiaman and taken to Bassein in the Maharashtra state.'

'India?'

'Aye. They plan to make an example of him, a spectacle if you like, of his public execution.'

'Then he's a dead man already.'

Ambrose bit down on his lip. 'So, what will we do now, cap'n?'

Fate watched young Ben fussing about arranging fresh fruits on a salver. He twisted the boy's ear. 'Stop fussin' so.' Ben's face twisted with pain. 'Now bugger off and fetch Miss Blizzard. Tell 'er the cap'n requests 'er presence at the double.'

With Anwyn joining the others in the stern cabin Fate unfurled a chart of the Indian Ocean, weighting the stiffened vellum corners with whatever he had in reach upon the table. 'As you well know, Septimus 'ere and my good self 'ave made a detailed inventory of the Cadiz loot,' Fate said with a level of pride. 'An' with my knowledge of gem values, and the bookkeeper's abacus skills we come up with a moderate valuation o' one hundred and sixty thousand pounds.'

'Jaysus!' Ambrose whistled. 'As high as thart.'

'Jaysus, as high as thart. Aye.'

Anwyn. 'Then what will we do?'

'We can't sail back north either coast o' Africa. India's out o' the question. This 'ere treasure is hotter than we could ever expect,' Fate said. 'To be honest with yer I ain't prepared to separate the gems from them bones. Them remains are Christian Martyrs, saints for Christ's sake. We're gonna have to secure 'em safe somewhere and send a message to the Vatican. They can come fetch 'em.'

'Then why in the Devil's name did we steal 'em?'

'That's what I asked meself. However, what's done is done.'

'But cap'n ...'

'But nuthin'. We have a hundred an' three bars o' gold worth about twenty thousand guineas and ten wee bags o' coin, mostly silver reales, but there are ninety gold escudos of various denominations. We'll sail to the Orient and maybe trade.' Fate rest his hands on his hips a moment standing by the open window to allow a refreshing breeze caress his open blouse. 'We may even encounter a rich prize while we're there,' he said watching the swell roll out from under the stern. 'I 'ear them frogs 'ave been sailin' the Pacific of late.'

'Trade?'

'Aye. There's plenty o' money to be made in tea and porcelain or even indigo, for starters. Plenty for everyone, you mark my words.'

'Trade where, cap'n? Canton?'

'We have no choice but to sail the Indian Ocean and I'm suggesting we base ourselves at Manilla.'

'In the Philippines?'

'Aye. It's Spanish. Britain is Spain's ally.'

'For now.'

'We'll be well out of harm's way for a year or two. We'll change identities, re-name the ship.'

'Are you suggesting we sail through the Timor Sea?' Anwyn said. 'Through the Dutch East Indies? Any Hollander East Indiaman would blow us out of the water.'

'Don't be daft.' Fate drew his finger across the map. Eyes followed. 'We sail south of New Holland and through the strait north o' Van Diemen's Land, then north through the Coral Sea, the Solomons and north-west to the Philippines.'

'That's a long voyage cap'n.'

'Aye. Five months maybe, but we have the Roarin' Forties up our arse,' Fate spoke of the powerful westerly winds that rage in the Southern Hemisphere between latitudes 40 degrees and fifty degrees south. 'And, what's more, time's on our side.'

'Cap'n Fate,' Ambrose said quietly. 'Alexander,' he added trusting on the personal approach for clemency. 'I got a wife and three bairns in Liverpool. I cannot ...'

'Cannot or will not,' The Quartermaster seethed. 'Which is it to be?'

'Cap'n, I ...'

Fate rounded on his first mate, his face inches from Ambrose's. 'We just pulled off the biggest robbery since Christ knows when. Inadvertently I agree. However, it is what it is. We'll all be stinkin' rich when this is over. Go back now an' you'll hang within a week. Trust me, there's plenty o' bastards what'll shop yer once they knows what's for.'

'We have one problem,' Anwyn said.

Fate's scarred face twitched. 'Now what?'

'The gold bars were mined in Columbia,' Anwyn told the gathering. 'And are stamped with the Spanish Royal Treasury hallmark including, I noticed, the official assayers chisel marks where samples have been removed for testing.'

'She's right you know,' Septimus sighed.

'Then we melt 'em down and make our own ingots.'

'It could look suspicious to some authorities.'

Fate looked at the others, his face smug. 'I don't think so. Not where we're goin'.' Fate already had a plan, but for the moment he thought it best kept to himself.

Fifteen weeks since Cadiz...

With a twenty-foot swell rolling beneath them the *El Delfin* had thousands of miles of Indian Ocean ahead to look forward to. The storms seemed endless. It was cold and wet and terrifying. Terrifying for the crew, bar Cap'n Alexander Ramsay Fate. Admittedly he sought courage in rum. If it wasn't the spyglass levelled at the horizon it was a bottle.

December 1812. Somewhere near 41 degrees south and 143 degrees east...

The rogue wave rolled across the port bow like a thunderous mountain tipping the *El Delfin* on a perilous list. Fate swore the top yards dipped into the boiling ocean. He witnessed at least four crew lost overboard. There was nothing anyone could do to save them. Survivors on deck heard the mainmast snap, like a branch would fracture under the foot of a heavy boot. By the time the seventy-three-foot schooner righted herself she was disabled. Although the rudder was damaged slightly, the helmsman managed to keep her nose-first into the waves.

'Cut it loose,' Fate screamed over the crashing waves and the gale force winds. Several men leapt into action, hacking at the stays with axes wielded like foresters. Fearful minutes later Fate watched the mainsail and rigging follow the severed mast into the sea. Fate's last reckoning had their position on the forty-first parallel, somewhere between the southern tip of King Island and Hunter Island off the coast of Van Diemen's Land.

'Land,' Ambrose shouted, pointing frantically south-east. Fate had seen the north-west coast of Van Diemen's Land earlier, before the storm worsened. With the ship in dire straits, they had no choice other than attempt to beach the ship on the coast. Admiralty charts purchased second-hand in Cape Town showed expansive beaches marked where the coast should be, if the captain's reckoning was accurate. But the swells, the tide and the wind had other plans. Although the storm dissipated somewhat the sea remained rough and it proved a long sleepless night.

Late the next day...

Progress had been slow and nerve-racking, as they drifted helplessly miles offshore. With the mainmast gone they relied on the foremast with its damaged gaff topsails hanging loose like sheets on washing day. Sometime during the night, the last of the damaged pintles holding the rudder in place broke free, sinking to the seabed.

Cap'n Fate braced himself against the damaged mast stump, focussing through his spyglass the best he could. A new night threatened, and his vision was poor. He figured they were three miles off the coast and drifting hard for their rendezvous with destiny. They were truly at the mercy of the elements. The beach ahead was vast and as Fate pressed his better eye against the lens, he watched tempestuous waves exploding onto the sand. *At least there are no rocks,* he thought; not that he could identify any in the spray and mist-blurred vista of approaching doom. The surf was high, the water turbulent, but the wind was in their favour at last. They had no choice. *El Delfin* was carried landward with a westerly blowing into her ragtag foremast topsails.

Half a mile offshore Fate identified an estuary, a river running into the ocean. And if his mind wasn't playing tricks, he thought the water looked brown where it ran into the sea, Fate determined the tide was ebbing and a disturbing current boiled, almost like a vortex. Scanning the coast, he hoped this did not herald a reef, but then he determined it to be a sandbar.

Cap'n Fate collapsed his spyglass and secured it. Then, to no one in particular, he muttered,

'We may survive this after all.'

Late 1814. Two years later. Parramatta, New South Wales...

Anwyn sat at her walnut secretaire in the warders' quarters of the Parramatta Female Factory. Captain Fate may have deserted her, yet good fortune kissed her brow. She sat in silence a moment, contemplating her correspondence, planning her sequence of events. Outside Anwyn heard the laughing kingfisher bird – the native bird the Aborigines named kookaburra – making its call from high in a gumtree. She dipped her goose quill into the stone ink pot. It was time to write her letter.

To Mr Archibald Mullens
Ivy Cottage
Melville Street
Hobart Town

Dear Mr Mullens,

In 1812, I was aboard the schooner El Delfin sailing
to Port Jackson from England via Cape Town when
the ship wrecked on the west coast of Van Diemen's
Land and was grounded in the estuary of a river on
the wild coast. I was amongst a handful of survivors.
The captain, Alexander Ramsay Fate, and most of the
crew drowned. I was travelling with Mrs Veronica
Lambert from Cape Town, as governess to her two
daughters, Scarlett and Cleo whom I schooled while
they travelled out from England. Desperate for the
remuneration this employment offered me I left
behind my four-year-old son, Thomas, with his
father, in Plymouth.

Mrs Lambert, a wealthy grazier's wife, was sailing
ahead of her husband who was to join her in the
following months and settle in Parramatta to raise
sheep. Alas, neither Scarlett, Cleo nor Mrs Lambert
survived the wreck.

On board the ship, and unbeknown to me at the
time, was a treasure stolen from the vault of the Bank
of Cadiz. This treasure was made up of sacred Vatican
reliquary jewels along with the skeletal remains of
martyred saints. This property has since been
returned to the Vatican, but a large amount of gold
was also stolen, and I was witness to this cache being
buried, before myself and the few survivors were
rescued, firstly by the natives of the island who helped
us survive on fish, shellfish and vegetation, before
walking us to the north of the island where we

encountered an American whale ship. We were taken by this ship to Sydney Cove in New South Wales.

Unfortunately, I was arrested with the El Delfin's first and second mates, the ship's purser and three crew. (The ones who salvaged and buried the gold after hiding the Vatican treasures in another location where they could be salvaged by Vatican representatives. Something that was done eighteen months later I heard.)

Sadly, I am still a prisoner, an innocent soul sentenced to five years' imprisonment for conspiracy to defraud the Vatican. A charge I vehemently deny. I am held in the Female Factory at Parramatta.

Now I have received a letter from Plymouth that my husband has been killed in a coach accident and that my son is living with a neighbour. But my neighbour is poor and there is a chance my son will be taken to an orphanage. I am desperate sir and am appealing to your mercy to help me reunite with my son.

I am offering to exchange a map of the whereabouts of the buried gold for the expense of my neighbour and her two children's fare (her husband deserted her) to sail with my son to New South Wales. To return the frightened boy back to his mother.

For security reasons I ask you not to write to me directly at the Female Factory where I am incarcerated, as all correspondence is monitored by the warden. Can you please correspond through the prison chaplain who can be contacted through the very respectable landlord Jonathan Greenway at the Feather Inn at Darlinghurst?

Signed Your most obedient and humble servant
Jane Foderingham
Parramatta
February 1815

Anwyn speared the quill back into to its pewter stand and rolled the blotter over her last paragraph, imagining any ink smudge could be misconstrued as widow's tears. This was her ninth such letter and three in the past seventeen months had been successful. Gullible, wanting, greedy old men; sending her sums of money from three hundred to five hundred guineas. But the ruse could not last forever. At least not from her current address. She would need to relocate before the law caught up with her. Already one pursuer, having failed to find the gold, had sent a curt letter, and she had to respond with reassuring dialogue that her co-ordinates to the lost gold could be a little out since landslides were not uncommon in the area and sandbars shifted. Anwyn gave herself another month in the hope her last suitor would not fail her.

Of course, all the above was a lie, but cleverly and carefully planned, selecting her prey carefully from government gazettes at her disposal in the clerk's office in the township of Parramatta. The plan was always to write to people of means living in the recently settled colony of Hobart Town. And the north-west coast of Van Diemen's Land was not too distant from Hobart Town, which made the excursion to look for gold all that more attractive. Besides, most educated citizens had read of the Vatican treasures and their recovery. It was big news in Europe. So why should the gold not be hidden along the coast as well? It was a win-win situation.

December 1812...

Quartermaster Alexander Ramsay Fate, Septimus Tilley, Ambrose Smith and twenty-one of the *El Delfin's* crew had actually survived. Four others had died at sea during the damaging storm and two others died of their wounds, ashore. As a gesture of sacrament to those crew who died ashore, the bodies were buried along with the Vatican relics, which were left in a cave a mile south of the estuary from where the *El Delfin* broke up; its remains were eventually lost in the shifting sands of the area.

However, Anwyn was never party to hiding the treasure. She actually didn't have a clue where it lay. While Septimus, herself and most of the crew hid the priceless Vatican reliquaries in a cave, Fate and Ambrose hid their other treasure; keeping with them a bag of Spanish dollars and gold escudos, to tide them all over. The rescue by an American whaler was true however Fate's plan was to return from Sydney Town with a ship, retrieve the treasure and sail to the Orient.

Twenty-five-year-old Sydney Cove was a military settlement, and the crew of the *El Delfin* were duly arrested and interrogated. News of the robbery in Cadiz was still to reach the New South Wales colony. However, Governor Macquarie was a suspicious man, believing the men to be privateers and held the crew in custody. Anwyn, being the only woman on board, was exempted. She could act the lady when necessary and to avoid being imprisoned she took up a position as overseer at the Female Factory in Parramatta.

Months passed. Quartermaster Fate, who before capture had sent word to the Vatican about the whereabouts of the sacred remains, believed he had received forgiveness. Cardinal Antonius Francis Traglia sailed to Van Diemen's Land and collected the martyred saints' remains, adorned in riches enough to feed a starving continent like Africa. It would take eighteen months, but the saints' relics were finally returned to Rome. The gold of course was never recovered.

About a year later Anwyn heard news of a mass breakout in Sydney. Fate along with his cohorts had escaped. Fate, it seemed, managed to convince the owner of a Yankee whaler, *Siren*, to sail them back to the west coast of Van Diemen's Land to retrieve the treasure. However, the ship disappeared, and it would be another year before Anwyn received word that wreckage had been found on Flinders Island along with the ship's name plate, *Siren, Nantucket.*

Anwyn mourned. Not for her fellow crew but for the lost treasure. It was now gone forever. But what better idea than to capitalise on the rumours whispered around New South Wales. Anwyn met Jonathon Greenway, innkeeper of the Feather Inn, and the swindling letter ruse was born.

CHAPTER TWO

One Hundred and thirty-seven years later. Gordon River. Macquarie Harbour. July 18th 1952...

Jackie Ingles leant over the chrome bow rail of their seventy-eight-foot MV *Diligent*, admiring her reflection in the ancient tannin-stained smooth waters of the wide river. She was in her late forties, but age had been kind. Only the slightest of salty whiteness dotted her silky long black pepper hair, tumbling past her shoulders. And her tanned skin, the legacy of enjoying the adventurous outdoors, was smooth and blemish free, a fact Jackie attributed to her nightly ritual of applying Astral skin cream. Pleased with what she saw, Jackie tossed back her head, thrusting her face to the warm midday sun, high in a cloudless sky. These moments could be sparse here in the wilderness that was Macquarie Harbour. The weather was typically unpredictable with the Indian Ocean crashing ashore a few miles west. But it was the loneliness of the area Jackie and her husband Guy loved most. One did not have to travel far from where the two lived aboard the *Diligent*, docked in Strahan Harbour, a seaside fishing village half an hour cruise north-west, to be alone.

Jackie leant into the bow rail looking back to husband Guy in the lacquered teak wheelhouse as the slight westerly whipped her hair about her face. The same westerly worked the twin Perkins diesels that little harder. Guy smiled back, the smile of a happy and contented man. He raised a glass of rum and Coca Cola in salute. The sun was well past the yardarm; besides Guy enjoyed his Rum and Cola, and it helped take his mind off the atrocities of war he had witnessed less than a decade earlier.

Jackie had met Guy late in life; her first husband had been killed in New Guinea in 1944. She had been a nurse based in Sydney when she met Guy, a US marine on *R and R* from the aftermath of war in the Pacific. That was in 1946. He was a line officer on board the USS *Hornet* with many stories to tell about fighting the Japanese at sea. The two found they had so much in common, fell in love and married in '48. Now here they were, masters of their own destiny, designing their future together, a future which at the moment looked most fortuitous.

The saturated ten-ton log reared up from the fast-flowing water like a Japanese submarine on the attack. Its gnarly branches, severed close to the trunk rammed the wooden cruiser, shattering the hull and exposing its interior to the elements.

Jackie was tossed overboard.

It happened so quickly.

With a face torn with anguish Guy watched his wife's body rush by the port side. She was like a rag doll. There was nothing he could do to save her. Instinctively Guy steered the MV *Diligent* to starboard to the shoreline, less than fifty feet away. The luxury cruiser ploughed into the dense vegetation of the unforgiving landscape. *Diligent* struck the river bank. Travelling at seven knots, large overhead branches made light work of the superstructure. Guy was thrown forward, smashing his head against the control panel. He collapsed unconscious to the wheelhouse deck where the freezing, snow-melt water off the western mountains, quickly surrounded him. The river rushed aboard, seeking the empty spaces of the cruiser with relentless speed. The *Diligent* sank quickly. Here she settled keel first on a horizontal ledge twenty feet below the surface, wedging between great tree trunks that had met a similar fate centuries earlier. Twenty feet north and the cruiser would have slipped into deep water.

Guy hadn't a clue how long he had been unconscious. Ten seconds, ten minutes? But his consciousness flooded back faster than the craft filled with water. He was trapped. Open and closing his mouth like a landed fish, Guy swallowed a lot of water, but he was also trapped in an air pocket. Somehow, he had fallen down the companion way and the stateroom door jammed shut behind him. Now he floated beneath a convex skylight where the smallest of air pockets kept him alive. Guy was terrified. He gasped at the precious air. Through the skylight he could see blue sky, sunlight, salvation. But there was no way out. A vision of Jackie being swept away tormented him. *Maybe she made it safely ashore. Yes. Jackie would find him.*

Minutes passed. Guy fought hard to battle his fear. He could feel his heart pounding.

Jackie, save me. I know you're out there.

Guy took deep breaths. He tried to ration his breathing, slow his heart rate. But panic was never far off. As minutes passed so did Guy's confidence. He surrendered to his fate. Taking a pocketknife from its sheath on his belt he scratched into the Perspex skylight ...

Jackie, I'm sorry. I love you.

Finally, his own carbon dioxide overcame him and he mercifully drifted back into unconsciousness once again, finally sinking to the stateroom deck where his lungs filled with water.

CHAPTER THREE

Two hundred or so years since the siege of Cadiz.
Hook, Line and Sinker Seafood restaurant. Hobart Waterfront...

It was every chef's nightmare. Diners' food orders mounted like debts to a bankrupt. And they weren't just tables of two; they were tables of eight, ten, fifteen even, all ordering à la carte from an extensive seafood menu. And we aren't talking just fish and chips - dropped into boiling oil, crispy fried and served within minutes. We're talking serious complex dishes cooked to order, pan dishes they're called in the trade. Each dish with its convoluted ingredients and seasoned to perfection for an ever-critical public – thanks, in part, to 'reality' cooking television shows.

The restaurant was full by 7PM and the bar was packed with hungry diners waiting for a table.

Queues formed on the street. It seemed no end. Everyone was famished, ordering complex entrées and appetisers followed by intricate mains involving a library of recipes demanding perfect balance and precision. Jameson's brow dotted with sweat. His headband was saturated. Salty dampness stung his eyes. The kitchen was roasting like the Pilbara Desert in January.

And that's bloody hot.

The extractor fans struggled with broiling grills, deep fryers, bain-maries, ovens, chargrills, steamers and a twelve-burner stove top crammed with frypans. Off to one side of the stove more pans stood by the flames, like passenger jets awaiting take-off amongst a shimmering mirage on a Dubai tarmac.

The orders backed up while challenging diners made a normal gruelling shift a nightmare ...

I want this without that and that with extra this, sauce on the side, no roe on the scallops, no octopus but extra prawns, gluten free, vegan, kosher ...

Compounding the complicated.

There is no light at the end of the tunnel. Waiters yelled. Cooks cursed. Customers grumbled.

We have to be at the theatre,
We have a plane to catch.
We've been waiting an hour.

Jameson's head spun. The bar overflowed. The queue outside snaked along the docks. Food was running low. Yet still the orders came.

Then a waiter dropped a meal ...

Cook another.

Another meal is sent back ...

I said this without that.

The apprentice cut her hand. The larder cook walked off the job. The fry cook burnt his arm. The cook's skin blistered ...

The kitchen-hand dropped a stack of plates.

More orders.

This without that and that without this ...

We've sold out of tuna. Oysters have finished. One serve of crayfish left ...

This without that and that without this ...

It was every chef's nightmare.

Jameson's eyes sprung open. He sat up in bed and took a long drink of water from the glass on his bedside table. Although the nightmare had dissolved into darkness the sweat was real. Jameson looked at his clock. 5.10AM. It would be light soon. He crashed back onto his pillow, exhausted from his dream. Afraid at first to fall back asleep, Jameson finally dozed off, whiffling softly. A new dream. A fresh day.

Jameson woke two hours later. The nightmare was a vague memory. What really mattered was it was the chef's day off. In fact, he had the weekend off to relax before the huge week ahead. A week that would see him working long hours for eight days straight during the Tasmanian Wooden Boat Festival.

The bi-annual event demanded one hundred per cent effort. Jameson looked at the alarm clock. Just after seven. Immediately he heard soft footsteps out on the landing and caught the aroma of Vittoria Italian Blend hitching a ride on a draught up the spiral stairs from the kitchen.

'You're awake, great.' Elspeth sat a brew next to the bed and jumped playfully on the mattress. 'What were you dreaming about? You woke me at five shouting something incoherent.'

'Did I?'

'Yes. Swearing like you were in the kitchen.'

'I think I *was* in the kitchen.' Jameson pulled Elspeth to him, rolling her onto her back. He stole a kiss.

Elspeth screwed up her nose. 'Not till you clean your teeth buddy.'

'Really?'

'Or at least drink some coffee.'

'Is that a promise?'

'For a kiss, yes.'

'A kiss!' Jameson caressed her breast. Elspeth pushed his hand away. 'Have you forgotten something?'

Jameson was fixated on romance. 'Ah ...' he thought hard, his face suitably querulous.

Elspeth mouthed. 'Calvino!'

'Damn. What time is it?'

'Shower time.'

'Not quite.' Jameson threw Elspeth effortlessly back onto the bed. She squealed. He manoeuvred his naked body on top of hers when a heavy fist thumped on the back door downstairs.

'Calvino!' Jameson groaned. 'He's early.' Elspeth wriggled from under Jameson, fetching up her night gown and wrapping it about her slender olive-skinned body, an inheritance from her Lebanese grandmother. 'He's never early!' Jameson stepped into the shower. 'Bastard!'

Elspeth unlatched the door and Jameson's mate Calvino Marchesi barged in, lively as a one-man band. He pecked Elspeth on the cheek before she had time to duck. *Got her every time.* Elspeth reeled back, too late. She closed the door. 'Jam's in the shower, want a coffee.'

'Please.' He noted the red button flashing on the Breville espresso machine. 'Espresso.'

Calvino scrolled an eye down Elspeth's silk nightgown. He meant to be discreet. *Christ, I don't think she's wearing knickers!* Elspeth tightened the wrap around. Calvino felt his face flush. 'Beautiful day for it,' he said trying to climb out of the hole he just dug for himself.

Beautiful day for what?

'Beautiful day in paradise,' Elspeth agreed. Tasmania *was* paradise, no question. For a moment there Elspeth thought he was being suggestive. No. It was typical Calvino opening his mouth to change feet. She hit the half pour button, smiling to herself. Elspeth didn't mind Calvino; he had a heart of gold really. He was just clumsy with women, yet he fancied himself as a Romeo. Typical hot blooded Italian male really. And it wasn't as if he was unattractive. He liked to wear shorts, even in winter. Why? Well, he'd paid over five hundred dollars to have a dragon tattooed, knee to ankle, wrapping around his calf. He also tied his long goatee beard like a man bun giving him a piratical look. Twice Elspeth had set him up with a blind date and twice he stuffed up. 'Cream?' she asked.

'Are you kiddin' me? Cream in espresso, that's like ... that's like meatballs with gravy.'

Elspeth had heard that one before of course. She just kept forgetting his heritage. Besides, second-generation *Italiano* Calvino sounded more Australian than Crocodile Dundee.

'So,' Elspeth leant her back against the sink and sipped her flat white (with cream). 'Where to first?' she asked. The reason Calvino and Jameson were up so early on a Saturday morning was garage sales.

'New Town. I checked the adverts and there's a couple of older addresses there that I reckon could be worth a go.' Calvino tipped back his shot of espresso and shuddered. 'Speaking of which, I'll go and rouse Jam up, otherwise we'll miss the bargains.'

The garage sales were a regular for Jameson and his mate. Every fortnight they met early on Saturday and went on the hunt, never knowing what might turn up when old properties, their sheds, cellars and attics were cleaned out. Although if they were honest with themselves, the pickings had become leaner over the years.

Calvino barged into the bedroom. Jameson was naked, drying himself.

'Jesus man,' Calvino feigned shock. 'Put some clothes on for Christ's sake.'

'Haven't you ever heard of knocking?'

'You haven't got a door mate.'

Jameson slipped into his Bonds. For a thirty-year-old he was still trim. Sure he had a slight gut, but it was tight; when he held his breath and sucked in.

Calvino. 'Nearly ready?'

'Yeh, yeh. Let me clean my teeth will you, I'll be right down.'

Downstairs Calvino was back behind the wheel of his Jeep Grand Cherokee. He played tunes on the radio and, humming, he watched the back door. Calvino loved Jameson's cottage. He was envious even, and contemplated buying a block of land at Storm Bay himself.

Mind you Jameson was grateful he hadn't. Too close for comfort. The shack, for that's what Jameson called his home, was situated at the southern end of the beach at Storm Bay, forty minutes' drive from Hobart's CBD. It was left to Jameson by his Granddad, an eccentric old bugger, who built a lighthouse – fire engine red – in the middle of the shanty and fixed a swinging barrel over the front door that read ... wait for it.

Melanoma Cottage.

'Why *Melanoma Cottage?* visitors would query.

'Well,' Granddad would answer, 'everyone kept telling me this property was a great spot.'

Nestled on a small rocky ledge, part of a headland, the other shacks weren't too close. With a builder mate, Jameson added another floor with a bedroom overlooking the water. Access to the upper floor and lighthouse was a spiral staircase wrapped about a huge dead tree trunk salvaged from his builder mate's farm in the north of the island state. The master bedroom and its en-suite occupied most of the second level. This was crammed with Jameson's collection of shipwreck artefacts, antique bottles and relics of historic importance, like his Great War relics. Junk to many. Overnight visitors slept on the couch or on blow-up mattresses.

Perfect.

Jameson and Calvino had been mates since school, but the boy with parents born in Naples, moved to Melbourne eight years ago and had only recently returned. Calvino had always chased a bargain and had a knack for making a dollar. Even at school he was shrewd, like earning cash collecting empty aluminium cans to sell at the scrap depot; until he was caught filling some of the cans with sand.

'Never get sick of that view mate,' Calvino said staring through the windscreen at the deserted beach and bay.

'I never take it for granted Cal. I wouldn't live anywhere else. So, where to?'

'New Town.'

'New Town,' Jameson approved. 'Good call. There's some nice old estates there.'

'That's what I thought. And there's three garage sales listed there today.'

Forty minutes later. New Town.,,

Calvino didn't see the speed hump. Teeth jarred. 'Sorry about that.' He unfolded the scrap of note-paper onehanded, slowed for the next hump, and managed to read the first address he had written down. 'Cross Street.'

'There, turn left'

Bargain hunters were already in the driveway fossicking through cardboard boxes, sorting clothes racks, inspecting useless ornaments; clutter mostly, like electrical gear that should have been left at the tip.

'Umbrella stand,' Calvino picked up the chrome stand. '1960s, four holding hoops plus drip tray. Good nick. Forty bucks.'

'What are you going to do with that?' Jameson asked, not that he was interested. Something else arrested his interest.

'Sell it on at a boot sale,' Calvino said. 'If I can get it for thirty, I reckon I could sell it for fifty.' That's why Calvino loved the garage sales, the chance to make a buck. Jameson reached across a trestle of women's shoes for a 1950s *Mackintosh's Quality Street* sweets tin. In the past he had scored a whale bone chess set inside an old tin. The owner had thought the set was plastic. Jameson was so excited he didn't even haggle her down on the five-dollar price tag.

'What's in the chocolate tin?' Calvino asked.

Jameson forced the lid open; rusted about the edges, it showed signs of being slightly damaged by fire sometime in the past. 'Letters, photos, old cards.' Jameson lifted the bundles of letters free, inspecting some of the cards. '*Happy Birthdays, Merry Christmases.*'

Calvino lost interest. 'Same old crap.'

'This one's dated 1956. When were you born?'

'Not in 1956!' Calvino saw a box of tools and disappeared under the table. Jameson lifted the *Season's Greetings* cards bundle. They were bound together with a rubber band and he noted the contents seemed to be in some kind of chronological order. The oldest card was 1940s, but the letters were much older. Some as early as the 19th century ...

19th century! *Bingo.*

Don't draw attention by reading them now. Ten bucks! Pay the lady.

'You bought them then?' Calvino never questioned *why* with his friend. Jameson was a discerning buyer and Calvino guessed there was something special in that corroded sweets tin. He tossed the umbrella stand onto the back seat of the Jeep.

Jameson. 'Did you get it for thirty bucks?'

'Got it for twenty-five.'

'Good work.' Back on the road Jameson opened his tin for a better inspection.

'What have you got?' Calvino asked.

'There's some early letters in here, really early.' Jameson fossicked through the tin, his voice trailing off. 'And a few sketches too ... and ... and ... interesting ...'

Calvino recognised his friend's vagueness. Jameson's mind was elsewhere. 'That's great then. So now where?'

No reply.

'Jam!'

'What?'

'Now where?'

'Oh ... ah,' Jameson checked Calvino's note. 'Flint Street,' he said, 'Wherever that is.'

Elspeth had met girlfriends at Salamanca Place on Hobart's waterfront for coffee. Now at 4PM she walked through the back door of the Storm Bay shack, dropping keys into the fruit bowl. Best mate Claire was right behind her, nursing a six pack of White Rabbit Dark Ale under her arm. Jameson sat at the kitchen table, in command of a magnifying glass which he hovered over a batch of yellowing paperwork, tattered photos and obscure scribblings.

'How was the garage hunt?' Elspeth asked.

'Great.'

Claire. 'Any bargains?'

'I don't know yet.'

Elspeth put an arm around Jameson and studied the pile. As a museum curator, old documents were always of interest. Claire opened the fridge to find room for the six pack, looked at the kitchen clock. *After four!* She tore three stubbies free from the cardboard cradle and stole a wedge of cold pizza.

'Well, what have we got then?' Elspeth spread family snapshots over the tabletop with her finger. 'Someone's memories?'

'Something like that.'

Elspeth's first impression of the tin's contents scored a three out of ten. 'One man's junk is another man's treasure huh?'

Jameson grunted.

'Salamanca and the docks were busy,' she said. 'Everyone's going crazy setting up for the Wooden Boat Festival next weekend.'

Jameson sighed. He had a tough week ahead and he'd be happy when the bi-annual event was over. The Hobart festival was the biggest in the Southern Hemisphere. Wooden craft, including tall ships, sailed in from around the globe and as much as Jameson enjoyed the spectacular sight, it meant nothing but hard work and extreme stress for him; being the chef of a busy waterfront restaurant.

'That's cute,' Claire passed Jameson a beer and crammed the last piece of pepperoni in her mouth before plucking a vintage Christmas card from an orderly pile. An adorable Shirley Temple-like *little miss* poked her head from the centre of a crusty pie with the caption around the pie dish, *A Christmas Greeting.* 'Cute and a little weird.'

Jameson agreed. Jameson liked Claire. She was Elspeth's oldest school friend, scatty, impulsive, crazy even. She said what was on her mind. No filter some would say. At medium height she was overweight in an appealing way, with red hair and winning smile.

'What else is there?'

'Letters, some photos, a mini book calendar for 1935 and a bunch of letters spanning a hundred years or more.'

'Family letters?'

'Some. But many aren't related. I haven't had a chance to read many of them, but there's one here that talks about a woman in prison in Parramatta writing to some bloke in Hobart Town asking for money to get her son out from England. She even mentions that if he helps her, she'll send him a map of where some gold was hidden, off a wrecked ship.'

Of course, Elspeth was of the opinion Jameson was playing one of his pranks and dismissed the thought outright. Claire was more pragmatic, gullible even. 'Gold! Yeh right!'

'I know it all sounds a con job,' Jameson said. 'But there it is.'

Claire picked up the tattered correspondence, yellow and brown from centuries of handling and slightly scorched with what appeared to be a smoke stain. '*To Mr Archibald Mullens,*' Claire read out aloud. '*Ivy Cottage, Melville Street, Hobart Town. In 1812 I was aboard the schooner* El Delfin *sailing to Port Jackson from England via Cape Town when the ship wrecked on the west coast of Van Diemen's Land...*'

Elspeth peered over Claire's shoulder. 'You serious?'

'Yes. Read it yourself.'

They read the rest of the letter together. '*Signed Your most obedient and humble servant, Jane Foderingham, Parramatta, February 1815.*'

'What's all that crap about Bank of Cadiz and Vatican jewels? Someone's trying one on,' Claire took a generous tug at her beer. 'What do you reckon El, a con job? Like those Nigerians wanting your bank details so they can send you the three-thousand-dollar interest owing on an old investment, or some shite like that.'

'Not quite.' Elspeth held the paper to the light looking for a watermark or anything that could help confirm it was actually a genuinely old letter. 'But this is fascinating all the same.'

'1815?' Claire was never the history buff. 'Was Hobart Town here then?'

'Of course. The township was eleven years old in 1815,' Elspeth said. 'But there weren't too many civilians, it was more a military presence as Van Diemen's Land was a penal colony.'

'This is really interesting, Jam,' Elspeth said, refolding the parchment. She fossicked through the tin. 'It certainly looks the real deal. I wonder who Jane Foderingham was?'

'I've already called Andre,' Jameson said of his historian friend. 'And I'm taking the tin to show him in the morning.'

Next morning,,,

The Risdon Road address was heritage registered, hidden by a hundred-year-old hedge and listed in several tourist publications as haunted. Jameson's good friend Andre encouraged this rumour, as he felt it kept undesirables at bay. Fifty-something Andre Peterson – academic, bibliophile, collector and sometimes antique dealer – lived with Cecil the pug in the Georgian sandstone cottage. Stepping through the solid wooden gate – its peeling paint heritage green – was like stepping back in time. The roof was Welsh slate, the narrow veranda a Victorian add-on and the brass door knocker was a grotesque gargoyle cast in the 1820s back in Birmingham. The pathway to the front door demanded to be negotiated with respect, as it was lined with unkempt, overgrown gnarly rosebushes, their thorns capable of shredding one's clothes.

'Come in, come in.'

Jameson was poised to knock but the door jarred open a few centimetres and Andre's face appeared, peering from the dark within like the tax man was standing on his threshold.

'I heard you open the gate old boy,' Andre chuckled, his Manchester accent clearly identifiable even after thirty or more years living in Australia.

Andre tugged at the door, opening it barely wide enough for Jameson to enter. Andre cursed. 'The bloody door's jammed on something.' He made a show of yanking the door back and forth for leverage. Jameson squeezed into the front passage and couldn't help but smile. A vintage Country Life magazine was caught up in the 'argument'. He muscled it free and the door swung open smoothly.

'Good work old chap.' Andre took one last peek out towards the street before closing the door.

Jameson read the magazine cover. '1963,' he handed the journal over.

'Yes, good read, those old Country Lifes.' Andre took the magazine and threw it back onto a pile behind the door stacked precariously to chest height. 'After you, and mind the boxes,' he warned. Three cartons almost blocked the entrance to his front living room. 'They arrived last week, and I haven't had a chance to unpack them yet.'

'You're still collecting then?'

Jameson's friend, whom he had met at an antique auction years earlier, was a collector and dealer. He was a hoarder really, when he wasn't selling the odd item to buy the less important things in his life, like food. His passion was arms and armour, particularly Japanese. The full Samurai warrior scowling from the shadows was testament to this interest.

'Still collecting? Of course, I'm still collecting,' Andre said. 'I'll be a squirrel till the day I die.'

Andre made room on the living room sofa and cleared an armchair for himself. 'I must say this garage sale discovery of yours sounds exciting.' Andre stared impatiently at the fire-stained chocolate tin, now resting on his friend's lap. 'You mentioned on the phone the name of a ship, *El Delfin*.'

'Yes. You said the name rang a bell.'

'It certainly did. And I've been up half the night reading.' Andre's passion outside Oriental armour was maritime history and his special interest besides the colonial period was the Napoleonic era. He also owned the finest private library on maritime history in Australia. Now, at the mention of the ship *El Delfin*, Andre's face was like a schoolboy given a month's pocket money in advance to spend on lollies. 'Here.' He passed Jameson a book on the Royal Navy, the relative page bookmarked with an antique post card.

'HMS *Sting*?' Jameson read aloud. 'What's this?'

'Keep reading,' Andre sat upright, animated, crossing one leg over the other, locking his fingers together around his knee.

'HMS *Sting* was a Royal Navy topsail schooner,' Jameson recited. '127 tons, 73 feet long, 20 feet in the beam, 9-foot 6 inches depth in the hold, gaff rig with topsail on her foremast. She was originally built in Bermuda in 1798 as a civilian vessel and named *Cricket*, of six guns, used by Lord Hugh Garland at his holdings in Jamaica. Lord Garland was forced to sell her, and the *Cricket* was purchased by the Royal Navy as a scout for two thousand five hundred pounds. Under order of the Admiralty, she was renamed HMS *Sting*. She carried a complement of forty. Forty!' Jameson whistled. 'And an armament of eight, twelve-pound carronades. A topsail schooner?" Jameson finally queried.

'A topsail schooner is fore-and-aft rigged on all of two or more masts with square sails above the foremast. But she was built as a sloop actually.'

'So, she had a second mast added by the Navy?'

'That's correct.'

Jameson read on. 'It says here *Sting* was involved as a lookout leading up to the Battle of Trafalgar.'

'Yes, but she was too small to be involved in the fighting. After Trafalgar she was decommissioned and sold off to a Captain Rodney Lowestoft in 1807. Lowestoft was ordered to rename her, and he called her *Cricket* once more. But he died at sea and the ship was sold on by his widow in 1809 to what in all appearances seems to be a privateer named Alexander Ramsay Fate ...'

'Fate!' Jameson interrupted. 'As mentioned in the letter, Fate?' he tapped his chocolate tin.

'Gosh, you are quick.' Andre fired off a derisive smile. 'Yes, as in the letter, Fate. This privateer Fate renamed her the *El Delfin* ...'

'Ah, now I see where we're going.'

'Good. Fate was given a commission, a letter of marque if you like, by King George III to harass French shipping. He was quite successful too.'

'Privateer huh?' Jameson knew privateers were still popular with the crown in the early 19th century. Captains were protected against arrest for piracy by this signed letter of marque from their monarch and were given carte blanche to commit robbery under arms on the high seas. They could attack vessels belonging to England's enemies, capture prisoners for exchange and the proceeds, the loot, was to be divided between the crown, the privateer's sponsors, ship owners, captains and crew.

'Legal piracy!'

'Exactly.'

'So, what on earth was the *El Delfin* doing getting herself wrecked on the west coast of Van Diemen's Land?'

'Glad you asked old chap.' Andre's smug demeanour returned. 'This is where you show me the letters you told me about on the phone last night.'

Jameson placed the chocolate tin on the coffee table already untidy with a dozen cigar boxes filled with old clock parts scattered about. He opened the tin. Andre leant forward. The anticipation was palpable. Research was his strength and he loved nothing more than such a challenge. Andre positioned his reading glasses further along his generous nose to read in silence a moment, to study the first correspondence. One by one he studied several letters. There followed a moment's silence, as Andre sat back, impressed. 'Amazing.'

Jameson. 'That's what I thought.'

'And they're genuine.'

'Well, I hoped so.'

'No doubt old man. The writing is a cursive style of the period, easy to follow, flamboyant curves. Orthography appears genuine.'

'Orthography?'

'The spelling and even spelling mistakes are of the era. In other words, true to the period. There is a naivety, dare I say originality, in the writing.' Andre studied other letters, weighing up the paper itself before reading further. 'The parchments are from different batches. What I mean by that is, they are not from the same supplier or manufacturer.' Some were frayed, nibbled by insects and others damaged by smoke and heat. Andre noted some pages still bore traces of the original stitching which would have held the pages together at one stage.

'Now, let us have a little read, see what mischief is afoot. *Dear Mr Mullens,*' Andre started aloud. '*In 1812, I was aboard the schooner* El Delfin *sailing to Port Jackson from England via Cape Town when the ship wrecked on the west coast of Van Diemen's Land and was lost in the estuary to a river on the wild coast. I was amongst a handful of survivors ...* that part's true,' Andre said.

Jameson was surprised at his friend's comment. 'Well, I would have thought so.'

'But most of it's a lie,' Andre said.

'Really?'

'Yes old chap. What you have here is rare to the extreme. Not many of these letters survive.'

'What do you mean?'

'Have you ever heard of the Spanish prisoner letters?'

'You mean the con?'

'Yes. A confidence trickster writes a sob story to a wealthy patron to send them money to bring their loved ones, usually children, back from another country. In exchange they offer the patron a map to lost gold or something of value – usually hidden close to the patron's address – but where the writer can't get to so easily – because they, the author of the letter, have been unfairly incarcerated. Nothing's changed since then. The Nigerians are still at it.'

Jameson coughed a laugh. 'They were Claire's thoughts exactly.'

'Yes, well. And they're succeeding I might add, catching wealthy gullible pensioners here in Australia.'

'Of course, Spanish prisoner letters, I've heard of them, but I never thought of this letter like that.'

'I'll stake my reputation on it old boy,' Andre read on '*The captain, Alexander Ramsay Fate, and most of the crew drowned. I was travelling with Mrs Veronica Lambert from Cape Town, as governess to her two daughters, Scarlett and Cleo of whom I schooled while they travelled out from England. Desperate for the remuneration this employment offered me I left behind my four-year-old son, Thomas, with his father, in Plymouth ...* Here we go, here comes the bullshit ... *Mrs Lambert, a wealthy grazier's wife, was sailing ahead of her husband who was to join her in the following months; settling in Parramatta to raise sheep. Alas, neither Scarlett, Cleo nor Mrs Lambert survived the wreck ...* and so on and so on.' Andre scanned the neat handwriting a second time. 'And here it is ... *I am offering to exchange a map of the whereabouts of the buried gold for the cost of my neighbour and her two children's fare (her husband deserted her) to sail with my son to New South Wales. To return the frightened boy back to his mother.*

For security reasons I ask you not to write to me directly at the Female Factory where I am incarcerated, as all correspondence is monitored by the warden. Can you please correspond through the prison chaplain ... blah, blah, blah ... *contacted through the very respectable landlord Jonathan Greenway ... respectable? Of course,* *... at the* **Feather Inn** *at Darlinghurst? Signed Your most obedient and humble servant. Jane Foderingham.'*

Andre found a plastic A4 pocket, delicately ironed the creases out of the frail two-hundred-year-old letter and sheathed it carefully. 'You'll have to take care of this, it's been well read and will fall apart if you don't. It is so typical of a Spanish prisoner letter.'

'Why *were* they called that?'

'Because it appears that the first letters came from Spain to England, and the writer claimed to be a prisoner in a Spanish prison.'

'This one's a prisoner in Parramatta. Then it's truly an historic document.'

'Yes ... well,' Andre had that glint of success in his eye, difficult to disguise. 'It'll prove even more valuable if we can confirm a few things, like the *El Delfin* for starters.'

'How do you mean?'

'I did a little research after you read me the letter over the phone yesterday. It appears the *El Delfin* wasn't registered at Lloyds in London. We know Fate was a privateer. By the way, his highest rank when in the Army was quartermaster, but he had the seafarer's experience and claimed the role of captain when he went rogue. What I did discover, however, was that there was an unusual robbery at Cadiz while the city was under siege by the French in 1812.'

'Unusual robbery? Go on.'

Andre went on to describe the unusual and original bank robbery via an adjoining wall of a warehouse next to the Bank of Cadiz. 'Not only was a substantial amount of gold bullion and some coin stolen, but also sacred religious artefacts belonging to the Vatican.'

'Vatican? How could that be?'

'Glad you asked old boy. Here,' Andre tossed four pages of handwritten notes scrawled in haste onto Jameson's lap. 'In twenty-five words or less I'll explain,' Andre continued. 'Napoleon looted Vatican treasures when he invaded Rome in 1796 and defeated the Papal troops of Pope Pius the Sixth. However, by the early years of the new century, t Napoleon had a change of heart and for political reasons he determined to encourage the Roman Catholic Church back into France to aid civil stability, following the turmoil of the French Revolution. Returning the sacred reliquary treasures would be seen as the responsible thing to do. But for some reason it took until 1809 for a truce to be signed and provision made for the return of the treasures. Diplomatic communication, it seems, hasn't changed much.

'In late 1809 the Vatican sent a ship to Paris to retrieve the treasures, but on its return voyage sailing down the west coast of southern Spain, the ship was damaged by a huge storm and was forced to limp into Cadiz for repairs. As these repairs were to take several weeks, the treasures were transferred into the vault of the Bank of Cadiz for safe keeping. By now it was February 1810 and France had occupied Spain and Cadiz was under siege. The Vatican treasures were deemed safer left in the bank vault. Wasn't that a mistake?'

'That was more like two hundred,' Jameson said.

'Pardon?'

'You said in twenty-five words or less. That was more like two hundred words.'

'Yes well. It was still the short version.'

'And a fascinating short version at that. So, this privateer, Alexander Ramsay Fate stole the Vatican treasures when, 1810?'

'1812 actually. Sometime before the siege ended.'

'Then how did he escape Cadiz?'

'The *El Delfin* masqueraded as a merchant, delivering medicines to the war-ravaged city. I need to do more research, but from what I can gather they leased the warehouse next to the bank and set it up as an apothecary.'

'And dug a hole through the wall into the bank.'

'Exactly.'

'Clever. But the letter mentions the treasures were finally returned to the Vatican. And the gold bullion?'

'That, dear boy, is where this story gets interesting.'

'Oh?'

'In this letter it says the Vatican treasures were finally returned to Rome. And I'm certain there is truth in that. It's something I need to research. The writer, false name Jane Foderingham, has alluded to a certain amount of truth in her letters.'

'Write about what you know, eh?'

'Exactly. It gave her pleas a certain amount of authenticity. This gives her credence should the recipient make enquiries. Don't forget this is an era when communication was slow and painstakingly difficult.'

'You said letters, plural?'

'I can only assume she would have sent out others. Your letter isn't a one only. At a guess I'd say this was a trial copy she wrote but kept for some reason. Another copy would have been sent. This kind of fraud was quite lucrative in the 19th century. People today aren't so gullible. Now, let's see what else you have in there.' Andre nodded at the chocolate tin.

Jameson started placing the contents on the table in some kind of order. Greeting cards, photos, other letters and assorted ephemera. There was even an invoice for gardening tools from a general store in Stanley, a fishing village on the north-west coast of Tasmania, dated 1923. Andre started with the photos and noted the latest as 1950s, but several images were taken with a Box Brownie and others sepia printed on thick card, pre-1900.

'This place I recognise,' Andre held up a small black and white photo. It showed an old man and a younger man, maybe thirties, standing on rocks with the estuary to a river behind them and what appeared to be a pleasant day by the sea with ocean waves crashing ashore. 'That's the Arthur River.'

'North-west Tassie?'

'That's right. I recognise those logs piled on the rocks by storms past. Quite unique to the area. They've washed down the river over the centuries and the Southern Ocean waves have tossed them back up on the shoreline like matchsticks.'

'Full sized trees, driftwood. Crazy.'

'Yes.' Andre flipped the photo over, but the back was blank. 'I've often wondered how many of those logs are King Billy or Huon Pine and asked myself why the locals don't salvage them?'

Jameson looked at the photo with renewed interest. 'What do you reckon, 1940s?'

'Bit earlier I'd say. 1930s. Note the rakish lean on the fedora hat and those trousers with braces, they look corduroy.'

The next photo showed the younger man alone, leaning on an early model Ute. He was clearly older but recognisable and the photo taken on the same bluff, but from a different position, again looking over the estuary entrance to the ocean. Once again, the logs helped identify the location.

'That's a 1934 Ford Utility,' Jameson said.

'1934?'

'Yes. A mate of mine is mad about vintage cars and was looking to buy one fully restored. It was Australia's first Ute with an all-metal cabin and a tray at the back for farmers to cart stuff about, like hay bales. It was designed to take the wife to church on Sundays and to take pigs to market Monday.'

'Huh! Makes sense. But that photo must be much later, like 1940. See how the man's aged?'

'Are you sure it's the same man?'

'Positive.'

Jameson put the two photos side by side. 'Yes, you're right. That's the same bloke, but older.'

'If I didn't know any better, I'd say this photo was the same bloke later still.' Jameson passed over a small black and white of a man in his late 50s, early 60s, next to a motor launch, 1950s model. The name of the boat was clear.

'*Diligent.*' Andre read. 'I wonder if there is a boat register still around.'

'If it was registered,' Jameson read the date on the back. 'It is 1957.'

One particular photo caught Jameson's eye. It was damaged, in fact one third was missing, apparently torn in half. Jameson pulled the black and white photo from the pack. It was also taken somewhere on the west coast Jameson imagined. The scene was desolate, unflattering and not that pictorial, so why take it? He flipped the photo to read *Dolphin Cove*. But of particular interest was a co-ordinate, 41° 40'13 S and the date July 2nd, 1952. Clearly the co-ordinate was a latitude reference, but the longitude was missing, presumably written on the missing piece.

'At some stage this photo was torn in two,' Andre said. 'It says Dolphin Cove. I've never heard of it, have you?'

'No. I searched *Dolphin Cove* in the Tasmanian atlas. Nothing. Google searched. Zero. But I searched the co-ordinate. It's the Pieman River.'

'Also on the west coast.'

'That's right. You mentioned gold bullion,' Jameson said. 'We know the Vatican treasures were returned but there is still the mention of gold bullion.'

Andre's smile was infectious. 'Okay. Are you ready for this?'

'Shoot!'

'I read last night that it appears a hundred or more gold bars were indeed buried somewhere along the coast near to where the ship wrecked. I've Googled newspapers and articles of the period and have searched my own database and library, although I need more time. But it seems locals have been searching for the gold for years and the persistent rumours have been handed down generation after generation. But I've got to say, old chap, this little box of tricks of yours seems to authenticate the rumour and those photos of Arthur River are a tantalising clue. The letter clearly states that the *El Delfin* wrecked where a river ran into the ocean and on the west coast of Van Diemen's Land. That area, of course wasn't settled until years later. By all accounts the survivors were aided by the indigenous people ...'

'Friendly!'

'Clearly. These Aborigines fed them shellfish and when they were fit enough, they led them to the north coast. Here they met up with a Yankee ship, the *Beaver*, whaling or sealing in Bass Strait.'

'But that's in her letter. Is it really true?'

'I can't see why that part would not be true. We know the missing bullion is true, I found reference to it in the records under the siege of Cadiz.'

'You found evidence.'

'Yes, didn't I mention, it was recorded as stolen along with the Vatican treasures,' Andre said. 'So that did actually happen. What I'd like to find out is, what is this Jane Foderingham's real name?'

As fascinating as all this was, it was still hearsay and Jameson had the busiest long weekend of the year approaching. An event that would see him working eighteen-hour days while the Hook, Line and Sinker restaurant catered for six to seven hundred diners daily.

'I'm looking forward to the festival,' Andre wouldn't miss the bi-annual event for anything. 'I'm sorry you're going to miss it old chap.'

'I'll just be glad when it's over,' Jameson said. 'Even now the restaurant's picking up with so many visitors arriving, event organisers, government officials. As a matter of fact, we have the Spanish ambassador booked on Wednesday, party of twenty.'

'Spanish huh?'

'And the French and the Russian tall ship *Shtan ... Shtan ...*'

'*Shtandart.* Eighteenth century frigate replica.'

'That's it. With its crew of maritime training cadets. But the Spanish ambassador's flying in early to meet the Spanish tall ship *San Sebastian Elcano*, which I believe left Perth three days ago for Hobart.'

'Hmm. Maybe you could ask him to help throw some light on this lot,' Andre quipped, nodding to the documents. Jameson bundled the items back into the decorative sweets tin with its picture on the lid of a British Army redcoat soldier wearing a shako flirting with a milkmaid holding a box of chocolates.

'At least the coming week will give me time to research your box of goodies,' Andre loved a challenge, especially old documents reeking of mould and secrets. 'I trust you'll leave them with me?'

'All yours Andre. Now I better get to work. Good luck.'

Storm Bay, late afternoon Sunday...

Jameson flicked the cap from a cold Boag's Premium with the blunt edge of bread knife and joined the girls on the balcony overlooking the bay. Elspeth and friend Claire had started without him, each with a chilled Jansz sparkling rosé in hand. Tonight would be Jameson's last free evening before the busy ten days straight. He necked his beer and sat with a gratifying sigh.

'So,' Elspeth started. 'What did Andre have to say?'

Jameson grinned, pausing for effect. Teasing. Elspeth had seen this grin before. Something positive was in the air. 'Well?'

Immediately they heard a car pull up on the gravel driveway at the front of the cottage. Jameson looked over his shoulder and recognised the Jeep Grand Cherokee through the kitchen window. 'Calvino! What's he doing here?'

'Ah yes,' Elspeth started. 'He invited himself to dinner.'

'He what?'

'He called me earlier to see if he left his sunglasses here yesterday and when I told him Claire was staying, he invited himself for dinner.'

'Cheeky bastard.'

'I think he's got the hots for you babe,' Elspeth slapped Claire playfully on the knee.

Claire feigned embarrassment. 'Stop it.' Secretly she was thrilled.

'Hey guys,' Calvino squeezed his six pack of pale ales into the fridge and joined the others. 'What's happening?'

Jameson clinked stubbies and Calvin took the spare seat, leant back hooking his feet on the balcony rail and drank half his beer in one mouthful.

'Thirsty mate?'

'You could say that. So, did you find out anything interesting about your tin of old photos and stuff.'

'I did actually.' Jameson shared a triumphant grin. He explained the situation so far. *The short story* as he told them.

'You've gotta be kidding. Vatican treasure?' Claire said. 'What is it with you Jameson Rowley, you're a tinny bastard.'

'I know, it all sounds a bit crazy huh?'

'Well,' Elspeth said. 'If anyone can throw some light on the story, Andre can.'

For the next half hour Jameson told what he knew so far.

'Where are these photos?' Claire asked. 'I know the west coast pretty well, I had an aunt I used to visit a bit, in Strahan, when I was younger.'

'I've left it all with Andre.'

'So,' Calvino finally swung his legs off the rail, tucking them under the seat. He leant forward with elbows on the table. 'Do you reckon it's all true? I mean Vatican treasure. Mate that's crazy.'

'I know that part's true. But like I explained, this Jane Foderingham was sending out dodgy letters to people she knew were cashed up to con money out of them. The Vatican treasures are worth millions ...'

'More like billions nowadays.'

'Yes well ... they were returned. But Andre seems to think there is some truth in the lost gold story.'

Jameson bar-b-qued meats while Elspeth prepared her brilliant Cypriot salad – a recipe of twenty-one ingredients found in a cooking magazine. The coming wooden boat festival was discussed, but the conversation did not travel far from the lost gold story.

'By the way,' Calvino said, finishing the last lamb cutlet on the platter. 'I volunteered to help old Clyde supervise visitors on *Maryanne.*' Calvino spoke of Captain Clyde's ketch *Maryanne* built in 1935. 'So, I'll see you around at the festival I reckon.'

'Not me mate,' Jameson said opening fresh beers. 'I'll be sweating it out in the restaurant.'

CHAPTER FOUR

The week could only be described as a blur. And this was the calm before the storm. The tall ships from several participating nations rendezvoused in Storm Bay near the estuary to the River Derwent on the days prior to the weekend. This was in preparation for the gathered fleet to sail spectacularly upriver en-masse, and to dock in Hobart to a huge welcome with media representatives from all over the globe. The news boasted Hobart would be host to two-hundred-thousand visitors over the following weeks; a massive boost to the economy.

Nothing quite prepares the visitors to Hobart, and locals for that matter, for the Wooden Boat Festival. Since 1994 this celebration of sail is the largest in the Southern Hemisphere, hosted by Hobart bi-annually in February. Supposedly one of the biggest events of its kind in the world, there was definitely no argument that this festival was the largest of its kind in the Southern Hemisphere.

Jameson and Elspeth leant on their waterfront cottage balcony rail, hot mugs of espresso coffee in hand, and watched the flotilla, an armada of mast and canvas sailing on a stiffening breeze up the River Derwent towards the Hobart waterfront. They picked out the larger or more famous of the tall ships; the 52 foot, 60 ton cutter *Lady Nelson* – Tasmania's own flag ship replica that brought the first settlers to Van Diemen's Land in 1803, the Danish *Yukon*, the schooner *Windward Bound*, the 88 foot 72 tonne *Enterprise*, the *Rhonda 11, Tenacious, Young Endeavour*. Five hundred wooden boats and nearly quarter of a million visitors were on their way towards Hobart.

'There's the *James Craig*,' Elspeth said of the 72 metre barque built in Scotland in 1874. 'Isn't that something?'

'Especially when you consider she was rusting in Research Bay here on the Derwent until the early seventies, when her hull was patched up and towed to Sydney where volunteers rebuilt her to be re-launched in all her glory in 1997.'

'She was originally launched as the *Clan MacLeod*,' Elspeth said.

'I'm impressed. You know your tall ships then.'

Elspeth grinned back. 'Can't lie, I just heard it on the news while you made the coffee.'

Later that morning. Constitution Dock. Hobart...

Reporter Michael Burns couldn't believe what he was hearing. *This is either the biggest story since Tutankhamen or bullshit*. Here he was interviewing an enthusiastic deckhand on board the *Maryanne* about the wooden-hulled ketch built in Hobart nearly a century ago, and the bloke starts ranting on about a shipwreck and lost treasure on the west coast of Tasmania. There was a story here, the journo could smell it, and he invited this Calvino Marchesi to nearby Lark's Distillery for a coffee and whisky.

Elspeth focussed Jameson's high powered binoculars on the tall ship, a magnificent sight under full sail. The ship's bow came into sharp focus and Elspeth read aloud, '*Il Corvo Nero*.'

'Really?' Jameson joined her on the balcony. 'Very impressive huh? That's *Il Corvo Nero*,

The Black Raven.'

'And what's so special about her, other than she's a magnificent ship with a weird name?'

'I've heard of her before.' Jameson searched the name on his mobile. 'Here. The three-masted barque *Il Corvo Nero*, 90.5 meters long including bowsprit, was built by the Bilbao Shipyards in Spain in 1980. She is 11.5 metres in the beam with a draught of 5.4 metres and a displacement of 1800 tons. Her 18 sails include squares, stays and jibs. She can manage twelve knots in a good wind. Her original name was *Veracruz*, but the present owners changed the name. And she has a carved black raven figure head,' Jameson paused. 'Ah, that's interesting.'

Elspeth. 'What is?'

'She is here as a guest only and not a part of the Wooden Boat Festival.'

'Why's that?'

'She has a steel hull.'

'Fair enough.'

'But what this doesn't tell us,' Jameson said holding his iPhone 11, 'is that she belongs to a drug cartel.'

'Are you serious?'

'Yes. I remember I read that somewhere else. It's owned by a Mexican billionaire, a woman called ...' Jameson scrolled down the mobile screen. 'Here we go ... a woman called Senora Maya Hidalgo.'

'A woman owning a great sail ship,' Elspeth was impressed. She refocussed the binoculars. 'Go girl. How did she make her money?'

'Don't know.' Jameson checked the data. 'Ah ... says here she is the biggest export of plastic products in Mexico and that her net wealth is 4.7 billion U.S dollars.'

'Nice.'

'Ah yes, here it is. She has been up on drug charges ... in 2007 she was arrested, charged with organised crime and conspiracy to drug trafficking and laundering money.'

'Wow, that's heavy. Why isn't she in prison?'

Jameson swiped the screen. Clearly there was plenty on the woman. 'Charges dropped in March 2008.'

'Is there a photo?'

'Here.' Jameson held out his mobile. A most attractive older woman with sharp features, chalk white teeth and coal black hair past her shoulders smiled back at Elspeth.

'She's pretty.'

'She's also sixty.'

'No?'

'Says here, Maya Hidalgo, born June 10th 1959.' Elspeth scrolled down even further. 'Although her legitimate income is from her plastics factories, she has family connections with the Sinaloa cartel and in particular the Leyva Brothers and she is a niece of Miguel Gallardo, the godfather and boss of bosses of the cocaine trade in Colombia.'

'I wonder if she's on board?'

Once again electronic media shined. 'Says here she flew in from Mexico last week, joining the ship in Melbourne for the sail to Hobart and the festivities.'

Elspeth. 'Huh! I'd like to see her.'

On board the barque Il Corvo Nero. Hobart Docks...

Jorge Diaz followed the steward and his trolley into the main cabin. 'Senora,' Diaz greeted Maya Hidalgo in her native tongue, Spanish. 'I trust you slept well.'

Maya had stepped from the bathroom, freshly showered and dressed only in a robe, her glossy black hair glistening like the feathers of a raven. The woman was unabashed about her appearance in front of her head of security. They had been intimate once, or maybe twice, but Maya discarded lovers like her favourite cigarette, *Treasurer Luxury Blacks.*

The billionaire dismissed the steward with a flick of the hand, lifting the cover on a silver salver of freshly prepared fruits. She forked a square of mango.

'I slept soundly enough.' She said, her emerald green eyes examining Jorge with passing interest. The suave, dark-haired and dangerously handsome Mexican was trim and fit, like a character in a James Bond movie, she fancied. But as a wealthy woman she could have any man she desired, and at sixty she liked a one-night stand to be around thirty-five. Jorge's use-by-date had expired, and the forty-six-year-old respected his position.

'I have brought you the local newspaper senora.' Maya took the folded paper. '*The Mercury*!' She noted how thin it appeared. 'Now what on earth would I want with ... *The Mercury*?'

'Page three senora. I think you will find it of some interest.'

Selma Hidalgo sat at the serving table where the steward had laid breakfast. She pushed the salver aside and spread the paper. 'Page three you say.'

'Si.'

Maya read the headline aloud. '*Spanish Gold Discovery. Vital clues found at garage sale.* What's this?'

'Read on Senora.'

Maya read in silence the article published by the journalist who interviewed Jameson's mate Calvino. Everything Calvino knew was in black and white for the world to see. Maya sat back deep in thought.

'Why this is crazy,' she finally spoke. 'We always suspected that gold was hidden somewhere on the west coast of this island, a few million dollars' worth on today's market maybe.' She puffed out her cheeks. 'Mere pocket money. But there is no mention of Saint Adamo Abate.' It was common knowledge that the remains of several saints, their bodies embedded with priceless gemstones and precious metals, were retrieved by the Vatican in the early 19th century. However, the skull of one particular saint, Saint Adamo Abate, was still missing.

'It has always been said that the skull of Saint Adamo Abate was never returned to the Vatican,' Diaz said.

'Yes, I know this.'

'And that those remains remained lost with the gold,' Jorge Diaz smiled proudly. If Senora was happy, he was happy, and this information could possibly see him regain her favour. For if Jorge had only one ambition, it was to return to the arms of Maya Hidalgo, and share her fortune.

Maya tapped her finger on the folded paper. 'Find where this man lives, the friend of this Calvino Marchesi who has this ... this chocolate tin, and bring it to me. You know what to do.'

Jorge retired from the boss's cabin a happy man. Maya poured herself coffee, forked a mouthful of scrambled eggs with smoked salmon and looked to a photo on the cabin wall of herself with her dead husband Alejandro in happier times, taken on deck aboard the *Il Corvo Nero.* The ship had been his baby and now Maya felt obliged to retain his legacy. She wasn't comfortable on the open seas; that's why she flew around the globe to meet the ship on occasions like this festival. And even now the memory of her husband's murder was fresh on her mind. Alejandro Hidalgo had been gunned down by a rival cartel twelve years ago now and Maya missed the man dearly, but life had to go on.

Less than two hundred metres away at the Hook, Line and Sinker, Jameson prepared for the second day of the festival. Both lunch and dinner bookings were already filled. In fact, there were very few reservations vacant on the pages of the reservation book. Simon, the maître d', was already working with the sommelier restocking the bar when Jameson helped himself to a double shot espresso to kick start the day.

'You're a dark horse Jam,' Simon said in greeting.

'What was that?'

'You didn't tell us you were onto a lost treasure.' Simon used a tone as if he was reading *Treasure Island* to a ten-year-old.

Jameson stood with cup poised to the lips, mouth open. He was incredulous. 'Pardon?'

'You're in the paper, *again*,' the maître d' nodded to the morning's *Mercury* on the bar. Jameson snatched up the paper.

Simon. 'Page three.'

Jameson read the headline *Spanish Treasure Discovery. Vital clues found at garage sale.* 'What the ...'

Jameson speedread the article. Said nothing and moved to the fire-escape where he phoned Calvino.

'Jam!' Calvino was in his usual good spirits. 'Mornin' mate, ready for another big day?'

'You bloody idiot!'

'Good mornin' to you too.'

'Can you give me one good reason why you would go to the newspaper and tell them about my discovery?'

'Oh, did they print it then?'

'So you did ...'

'Wait a sec. I didn't go to the paper; some journo was asking me questions on board the *Maryanne* yesterday and ...'

'And what?'

'Well somehow the subject came up and ...'

'And you blabbed a story about a lost treasure. You're a bloody idiot.' Jameson was too angry to talk further. He ended the call. Today of all days, he didn't need this stress.

5.45PM...

Elspeth let herself into Jameson's cottage. Although she spent most of her nights here at Storm Bay, she kept a flat in the Glebe, a quaint suburb with a stunning view of Mount Wellington - Hobart's guardian angel - and an easy walk to the museum where she worked as assistant curator.

Something was amiss.

Elspeth caught a whiff of aftershave and sweat. Feeling positively uncomfortable, Elspeth replaced her handbag with a meat mallet from the utensil stand. She crossed the open living area to the sliding doors opening onto the balcony. Locked. Elspeth studied the dresser briefly, and then the bookshelves. Items had been moved; she was certain of it. Elspeth gripped the mallet even firmer. She took to the spiral stairs leading up to the bedroom. The treads creaked. Elspeth's face tightened, but determined she hurried on. Upstairs, all clear. She rushed to the upper deck sliding doors. Locked. After checking the en-suite Elspeth studied the shelves weighted with Jameson's treasures; antiques collected since he was a teenager. And there were some valuable pieces, but nothing appeared missing. However, Elspeth could see that things had been moved.

With Jameson far too busy to bother right now Elspeth would have to settle down and wait, knowing he wouldn't be home until after midnight. It seemed a no-brainer; Jameson had called her in his afternoon break to tell her about Calvino, *idiot!* Someone who read the article was already up to mischief. '*This is exactly why you keep your mouth shut,*' Jameson had said over and over in the past. Returning to her handbag she called Andre.

Headlights flooded the kitchen. Car tires crunched gravel. Elspeth sat bolt upright, but the cottage immediately returned to darkness. Darkness but for the flickering light from late night telly. It was almost one o'clock in the morning and she had fallen asleep on the couch. Jameson walked in the backdoor wearing his checked pants and black double breasted cook's jacket. He reeked of fries, grills, smoking oils and sweat. He was exhausted. Elspeth broke the news of the break in and received the tirade she expected.

'Calvino. That stupid bastard. I've already given him a serve. Why? How could he be so dumb?' Elspeth shrugged. 'Anything missing?' he asked.

'Not that I can tell. They went to great pains to try and cover the fact they were even here. The doors were left locked. Clearly they were after the chocolate tin and nothing else.'

'That's crazy.'

'The scary thing is I think I only just missed them.'

'How's that?'

'I could smell aftershave ... and sweat for that matter.'

'Aftershave?'

'Yes. It smelt expensive too. Like *Spice and Wood* by *Creed* with cedarwood, cloves and lemon.'

'Oh, that's specific.'

'Yes well, I looked to buy you some for your last birthday, but it was, like, over five-hundred a bottle.'

'Jesus El.'

'They clearly know you're busy at the restaurant.'

'It's doubtful they know about you though, El. Bastards.' Jameson looked at his antique dresser groaning under the weight of old pewter, eighteenth century Delft ware and early porcelain. All valuable. Nothing amiss.

Elspeth. 'I'll get you a beer.'

'I had a traveller on the way home. I'm exhausted El and I've got to be up at six.' Jameson managed the briefest of showers and crashed onto the bed half wet. He was asleep in thirty seconds.

Coffee never tasted so good. Jameson was hungover from lack of sleep, nothing else. Elspeth spread Vegemite on two pieces of toast while Jameson called Andre.

'You awake?' he asked the historian.

'I am now,' the scholar sounded groggy. 'What time is it anyway?'

'Six thirty.'

'Oh, that late?' Andre attempted to be cheerful. 'That was bad news about the break in.'

'Yes, bloody Calvino, I don't understand him sometimes. Now Andre, I'm concerned about you mate. They might come after you next if they found out you have the tin.'

'But how could they find out about me?'

'It's not worth the risk. Hide the tin well.'

'Okay. I've actually found out some very exciting information. I wanted to call you yesterday, but I know you're very busy. Can we meet?'

'I'm flat out. Will be all week. What news?'

Andre really didn't want to talk over the phone. 'This is big my friend. Really big.'

'Damn it Andre, don't keep me in suspense.'

'Okay ...'

'Wait, Elspeth's here, I'll put you on speaker phone.'

'Hi El.'

'Hi Andre.'

'Okay then. You know the Vatican religious treasures were returned,' Andre started.

'Yes.'

'Well, I found out how. Captain Fate or Quartermaster Fate, whatever rank you want to give him, sent word to the Vatican from Sydney Town with a map of where the Vatican treasures were hidden and these were indeed collected by a trusted representative of the Vatican, a Venetian merchant, who returned the items to their rightful owners in February 1814. However, one item remained lost. Hidden at a different location from the jewelled saints' bones. Fate, you must understand, planned to sail to the west coast of Van Diemen's Land and retrieve the gold well before the Vatican even knew of the whereabouts of the treasure. But as we know from the letters, Fate and his crew, having been rescued by the Nantucket whaler *Siren*, were wrecked on Flinders Island and all lives lost ... almost.'

'Yes. But what was the one item never returned?'

'Wait for it.'

'There *was* one survivor of the wreck as far as I can ascertain.'

'Who?'

'Septimus Tilley the bookkeeper.'

'One survivor huh?'

'Yes. He was badly injured with a head wound from a loose spar, but he washed ashore. Now Flinders Island wasn't occupied in 1812, but sealers made occasional visits and Septimus was taken care of by some Aboriginal women, 'wives' of the sealers. He convalesced with these people for three months, when the government cutter *Albatross* called on the sealers. By then the sealers had heard rumours about a Royal Navy ship, *El Delfin*, escaping Cadiz and knew enough to suspect Septimus was involved. So, when confronted by a threatening government cutter they decided to shop Septimus. He was duly arrested and taken to Hobart Town where he was found guilty of crimes in war-time Spain and sentenced to fourteen years' imprisonment. It was now 1813. Apparently Septimus was a difficult prisoner. In 1822 he was sent to the recently established Sarah Island penal colony at Macquarie Harbour.'

'How did you find out about Septimus Tilley?' Elspeth asked. 'Tilley the bookkeeper?'

'He left a diary of sorts; it's a little vague, but I found a transcript on the net. The Archives post everything these days. It's a relative goldmine for people like me.'

'Okay, but what was this one item not returned to the Vatican?'

'A-ha. This is the juicy bit. Have you ever heard of Saint Adamo Abate? ... No of course you haven't. Well Abate was a Benedictine abbot who was all for the unification of Italy under Roger II, King of Sicily around 1060 I believe ...'

'Yes ... and?'

'Well, his skull was never returned. Missing until this day. His decorated torso has been identified amongst the other remains of the saints returned to the Vatican, but the skull of Abate is missing. It is almost certainly with the gold ingots that have never been located.'

'So what? Is it bejewelled?' Jameson said. 'A bit of gold leaf and a diamond in one of the teeth?'

'Hah!' Andre laughed at Jameson's suggestion. Jameson was impatient; he had a busy restaurant kitchen to run.

'Far more valuable than a diamond and gold leaf,' Andre paused for effect. 'Saint Adamo Abate's skull *was* bejewelled, yes,' Andre said. 'But the cranium was hinged and inside was, or rather is, the largest ruby ever found; an uncut 'pigeon blood' stone the size of a large grapefruit by all accounts.'

'No!'

'It's true. I have a sketch of it once published in the Illustrated London News.'

'What's a stone like that worth?'

'Priceless.'

On board Il Corvo Nero. Hobart Docks...

'Priceless. Hear that.' Jorge Diaz, Maya Hidalgo's head of security and personal bodyguard, shared a dark smile with his boss. It had been no problem bugging the cottage at Storm Bay; one voice-activated recording device under the kitchen table – held with chewing gum - and one in the bedroom. The highly sensitive microphone had a range of ten to twelve metres, more than enough. Now it paid off.

'Nothing is priceless,' Maya said in her Mexican-accented Spanish. 'It would fetch fifty million on the black market.'

It was late morning when Jorge brought Maya a copy of the recording and she was dressed for her first official luncheon at Government House. Mayo stood before Jorge, her face centimetres from his. 'You have done well Jorge,' she purred, straightening his tie. Jorge smelt fresh mint and imagined her body. She really was a seductress, even in her sixtieth year. He considered pushing her back on the chaise lounge and taking her there and then, but, well, she was dressed for lunch and may not react the way he hoped.

'So, do we know who this Andre is?' Maya said. 'The man clearly has the evidence and he clearly knows what he's talking about.'

'No, I don't know who he is, but I'll soon find out. I put a tracking device under the cook's car.'

'Jorge,' Maya's smile was positively bewitching. 'You really are a very clever man.' Maya tidied the bodyguard's shirt, tucking it tighter under his belt and deliberately brushing her hand against him. She caught the slight twitch and congratulated herself, confirming in her mind that men were still attracted to her. 'Now drive me to Government House.'

Orfeo De Luca stood in the doorway to the Hook, Line and Sinker Restaurant, turning heads. But he was used to turning heads with his Chris Hemsworth movie star looks; espresso brown tapered beard and gym-toned body conspicuous within a tailored indigo blue Armani silk suit, white shirt, powder blue bowtie and chalk white scarf looped about his neck, drooping over his shoulders. The devilishly charismatic and handsome forty-two-year-old adviser to the Italian Embassy in Australia did not have a reservation and immediately observed the busy restaurant was at full capacity.

'Good evening sir,' Simon the maître d' appeared from a party of happy diners seated within the bow of an old fishing boat – part of the restaurant décor – to greet the late arrivals. 'We are fully booked but there are one or two tables about to leave if you'd care to wait,' Simon advised the tall, personable gentleman with the strong accent. De Luca was happy to wait. Simon ushered the man and his female companion to the bar for a pre-dinner drink whilst they waited. It appeared the young woman on his arm was a recent acquaintance.

Orfeo De Luca ordered vodka martinis and took a moment to look about the popular seafood restaurant that had been highly recommended by the concierge at the Grand Chancellor Hotel, a hundred metres from the restaurant, where they were house guests. But recommended or not, De Luca was here on business.

The crayfish baked in its half shell with fresh Tasmanian scallops in a white wine shallot sauce was of remarkable standard, even for such a highly-awarded establishment. And the Bay of Fires Riesling – with its pristine aromatic and floral purity – was as an intoxicating accompaniment, as was the Italian man's date sitting opposite. After a final course, a plate of Hillwood Farm strawberries, the gentleman introduced himself to Simon.

'Signor Orfeo De Luca, adviser to the Italian Ambassador.' With so many luminaries visiting Hobart this week, De Luca's position meant little to Simon. 'Tell me, your chef, Signor Jameson Rowley I believe.'

'Yes, you're certainly well informed.'

'Oh, I make it my business. My crayfish was *deliziosa*.'

'Excellent.'

'This Jameson, I would like to meet him.'

'Oh, I'm terribly sorry. He's very busy.'

'I know thees ... thees is why I would like to invite the kitchen staff and yourself signor maître d' to breakfast on board the Italiano tall ship *Amerigo Vespucci*.'

This was totally unexpected. Simon was keen already. 'That's very kind sir.'

'Not at all. Call me Orfeo and this is my friend Amelia.' Amelia smiled. She wasn't Italian.

'Simon.' Simon offered his hand. 'I'll tell Jameson, I am certain he would love to come. What time?'

'Seven.' The man was persistent and had an air of authority about him, hard to ignore. 'Tell him I will not take *no* for an answer.'

Next Day. 7AM...

Jameson could see life at the end of the tunnel. The entire week had been a *madhouse* but today was day three of the festival itself, and what better way to start the morning than having someone else cook him breakfast in the stateroom of the Italian tall ship. Signor Orfeo

De Luca needn't have worried. Jameson would not miss this opportunity for anything.

Built at the Naval Shipyard of Castellammare di Stabia in Naples and launched in 1931, the *Amerigo Vespucci* was inspired by a late 18th century ship of the line. A fully rigged, three masted, wooden hull ship with overall length of 101 metres, seven metres draught and 15.5 metres in the beam. And the wood panelled stateroom did the magnificent ship proud.

Jameson waited dockside with sous chef, Stu, for the others to arrive, breathing in the Stockholm tar and the salty morning air of Hobart's Sullivan's Cove, whilst enjoying the sight of so much mast and sail and the flags of so many nations proudly exhibiting their wooden sea craft from the tall ships to hand-crafted canoes. So much history. So much romance. Stu's stomach rumbled.

'What do the Italian's eat for breakfast anyway, pizza?'

'Pizza! No, you ignoramus. Pastries.'

'For breakfast?'

'Yep. Maybe some crusty bread and cold meats if we're lucky.'

'I'd rather eat cold pizza.'

'*You* would.'

'So, we're not getting eggs and bacon either, then?'

'No Stu, no eggs and bacon.'

Breakfast was fast, fresh and generous. Hot bread rolls, sweet rusk-hard bread called fette biscottate, cold deli meats followed by chocolate pastries, and endless caffè latte.

'Typical Italiano, si,' Orfeo De Luca made a point of sitting next to Jameson. There was no sign of his lady friend, the *model* Simon had mentioned to Jameson, hanging off the envoy's arm the evening before.

'This was most kind of you to invite us all here this morning,' Jameson looked down the table at a dozen of his contented restaurant staff who managed the appointment.

'My plesh-ar. After break-fast, I will give you a tour of thees sheep.' Now that was music to Jameson's ears. 'But first, tell me, you are the man mentioned in the newspaper are you not, the man who found ze letters and photos that might lead to ze discovery of some ... how the romantics say, hidden tress-ar.'

Treasure! Jesus! Here we go.

Jameson replied with an evasive shrug. 'You read the local paper then?' he answered dryly.

'Yes, of course. I am Ambassador's adviser, si? Eet is my duty to stay up with ze affairs of ze ports I visit.'

'It's only hearsay, just rumours,' Jameson said, uncomfortable with the direction the conversation was headed. 'A few lost gold bars, maybe. Nothing more.'

De Luca turned bodily in his chair to face Jameson. He leant forward discreetly, staring into Jameson's eyes. 'I have a request ... a ... ah ... more an order really.'

'Order? From whom?'

De Luca looked about. Everyone at the table was in animated conversation. 'From ze Holy See,' he finally said so softly Jameson barely heard him.

'Holy See!' Jameson repeated in a loud whisper. 'As in *the* Pope?'

'Si, si. Pope Francis his-self, eet appears we have a ... ah ... how you say in Eengleesh ... window-of-opportunity, si, si ... window of opportunity to find and deliver back to the Vatican, the miss-een remains of Saint Adamo Abate.' Suddenly Jameson realised the connection. His face showed recognition. 'You know about thees things I am theenking?'

Jameson sighed. There seemed no point lying. 'Yes, actually I heard about the missing ... ah ... skull, yesterday.'

'Then you must help me ... help Italy return these sacred remains to ze Vatican. Ze church will reward you. God will reward you.'

Jameson coughed a laugh. *God will reward you.* He didn't mean to be rude, but it certainly sounded like it. Either way De Luca showed no sign of being insulted.

'I don't know,' Jameson pushed back his chair. 'I've just found an old tin full of letters, old photos, private stuff. I don't even know what I've got really.' This was a lie of course. Jameson had a sixth sense when he was onto something, past experiences had proven this. Now, only recently his house was entered by persons unknown ...

Persons unknown.

Jameson reddened. 'Was it you or any of your mob who broke into my house ... burgled me, looking for these letters and photos?'

'No! Certainly not.' De Luca was taken aback. 'You say someone ... how you say ... ah, burgle your house?'

'Yes, two days ago while I was at work.'

'Thees ees bad.'

'Bloody oath it's bad. I'm pissed. If my partner came home an hour earlier she may have walked into an ambush.'

'Mr Rowley, I no do thees thing.' De Luca grew serious, his face ashen. 'You still have thees tin, si?'

'Yes I do,' Jameson said defiantly. 'And it's well hidden ... and, I might add, it's not in my cottage.'

De Luca snatched Jameson's arm, squeezing tighter than he intended. 'Only bad persons would do thees thing. We must work together ...'

Jameson jerked his wrist free. 'I don't think so mate.'

'Ees for the Holy See, for our countries' relations.'

'Thanks for breakfast.' Jameson stood abruptly, suddenly realising the entire table had gone quiet. They all stood. Jameson turned his back on his staff to confront De Luca. He leant in close and said softly, 'I'll think about it. Right?'

'Your tour?' De Luca said, defeated.

Jameson turned. 'Tour?'

'Of thees sheep, I show you.'

'Another time.'

Back on the docks enthusiastic wooden boat lovers gathered. The early February morning was showing all signs of proving another day in paradise. Stu caught up with his chef, they were mates outside work and he knew his friend well. Something was amiss. 'What the hell was that all about?' Stu said.

'What?'

'De Looka, De Lucka, whatever his bloody name is?'

'Nothing.'

'Didn't sound like nothing.'

Jameson clamped his sous chef's arm dragging him away from the *Amerigo Vespucci* and undoubtedly, prying eyes. 'Look Stu. I've got urgent business. I need an hour. Can you go straight into work, see to the ordering, get the crew motivated? I'll be in by ten at the latest.'

'Sure thing. I was planning on going straight to work after brekky anyway.'

'Cheers.'

Stu watched Jameson disappear across the docks and make a call on his mobile. Seven minutes later Iyaan Bilal, Pakistani economic student and Uber driver, met Jameson on the GPO corner in his white, dented, 2010 Ford Mondeo and drove away, turning left, into Argyle Street. Both Iyaan and Jameson had no reason to notice the deep blue Jeep Wrangler hire car following.

'You like these sheeps mate?' Iyaan started idle conversation in his Pakistani-Aussie, as the festival disappeared in the rear-view mirror.

'Ships ... sure.' Jameson's mind was elsewhere.

Five minutes later at Tower Hill, Iyaan turned into New Town and started a zig zag of side streets heading to Jameson's destination - Risdon Road.

'You have friend?' the driver asked.

'Friend? Yes. Lots of friends, why?'

'He follow.'

'What? Jameson looked over his shoulder.

'That blue car, follow from sheeps.'

Jameson looked in his passenger side mirror, noting the not too subtle Jeep Wrangler. 'Are you certain it's following?'

'Sure I'm certain. You see.' And Iyaan turned right at the next street. The Jeep followed. Considering recent circumstances Jameson had no doubt his Uber driver was correct. 'Stop at the corner, I'll walk.'

'You sure?'

'I've only a short walk.'

The driver parked at the curb. The Jeep had no choice but to pass by, turning onto Risdon Road. With tinted windows it was impossible for Jameson to see the Jeep driver. Iyaan gave Jameson the thumbs up. 'See ya, mate,' the driver grinned in his best rendition of an Aussie.

Jameson crossed the busy road and walked briskly towards Andre's. There was no sign of the Jeep. Jameson walked past Andre's cottage thirty metres before pressing into a built-up driveway. He waited. Seconds later the blue Wrangler sped past. Jameson watched the Jeep turn into another side street. When he was certain the coast was clear he hurried back to Andre's cottage and disappeared behind the hedge. Across the street, a lone pedestrian walked casually in Jameson's footsteps and in the direction of the first street corner.

Andre was still in his pyjamas – with a sailing ship pattern – slippers and loosely tied dressing gown. 'Jameson! I wasn't expecting you.'

'I tried to call you from my Uber.'

'My phones on the charger ... what were you doing in an Uber?'

'Long story. Where's the tin?'

'On the coffee table. I've been working hard at it'

Jameson hurried to the living room casting an eye over Andre's eclectic collection of antiques on display in every corner. Floor to ceiling. Home comfort was not of importance to the academic hoarder. Jameson fell upon the *Mackintosh's Quality Street* sweets tin. He noted the photos bundled in some kind of order. 'We have to hide this and hide it well.' Jameson moved to the window and stole a glance out towards the road. But the huge heritage listed hedge blocked ninety per cent of the view.

Andre frowned. 'Everything alright?'

'No. I was followed here?'

'Followed? Who by?'

'Don't know.' Jameson brought Andre up to speed.

'That Calvino's more trouble than he's worth,' Andre muttered.

'You can say that again.'

'And you were definitely followed.'

'Yes. It must have been whoever broke into my cottage and at the moment the only suspect is the Italian embassy.'

'Is there something you've forgotten to tell me?'

'Didn't I mention, this Signor Orfeo De Luca is the Italian ambassador's right-hand man, on a mission from god too if you'd believe what he had to say. But we need to hide this stuff really well.' Jameson gathered the material placing it safely back in the tin. 'And I mean *really* well.'

'I found out all about *our* Spanish prisoner letter writer Anwyn Blizzard,' Andre said, helping stack the documents.

'Oh, and?'

'Her full name was actually Anwyn Christina Blizzard. She was thirty-nine when she arrived at Sydney Town on the Nantucket whaler *Siren*.'

'Wow! Where did you learn that.'

'Sydney Gazette, 1813. They're all online these days. All the survivors of that shipwreck are listed.'

'What else did you learn?'

'Well we know the crew under Captain Fate were wrecked on their way back to retrieve the gold. Clearly Fate cut the *Siren* captain in on the deal. But they all died. However, Anwyn stayed behind. For what reason I don't know, but later that year a woman who answers to Anwyn's description turns up at the Parramatta Female Factory.'

'As a prisoner?'

'No, she is registered as a warder at the prison and her name is Jasmin Bradenham.'

'Jasmin Bradenham? Why does that sound faintly familiar?'

'Because I'm certain Jasmin Bradenham and Jane Foderingham are one and the same.'

'Jane Foderingham of the Spanish Prisoner letters fame?'

'Exactly.'

'What makes you say that?'

'Here,' Andre opened his laptop to a page where two handwritten documents were displayed side by side. 'One is your prisoner letter signed by Jane and the other is a prison report about an unruly prisoner whom Jasmin Bradenham, the warder, reported on. Look at the writing. Identical.'

'You're right.'

'I certainly am. I need coffee,' Andre smacked his lips. 'I've made a pot, want one?'

'No thanks, I'm good.'

'The Parramatta women's prison opened in 1821. But when Anwyn, calling herself Jasmin Bradenham, worked there as a warder, or overseer, in 1814, the prison for women was just two very crowded rooms above the male prison. Here, the prisoners were made to work, spinning wool and linen and sleeping on the floor where they worked. This space was called the *factory above the gaol*.'

'In retrospect,' Jameson said, 'the information in her con letters was mainly true, I mean the parts about the hidden gold. If nothing else, it gives credence to the hidden gold story. But how do we know it hasn't already been found.'

'Good question.' Andre shuffled a pile of newspaper cuttings collected over the years. 'Here, read this.'

It was a yellowing page torn from a local 1967 Zeehan news circular. 'Roger DeGroot of Zeehan,' Jameson read out loud, 'has returned from his week-long search for the missing gold, often searched for along the north-west coast ... and?' Jameson looked for more information.

'There's bits missing,' Andre said. 'But there's other references in other paper cuttings up into the 70s, then it seems to have been forgotten about again.'

'Interesting.'

'We should take a road trip up the coast. When can you get some time off?'

'I've got two more big nights before it settles down.' Jameson noted the time on one of three antique clocks in the one room. The mantle clock chimed 9.45. 'I've gotta get to work.' He was about to call another Uber when Andre interrupted.

'I'll take you.'

'You're still in your pyjamas!'

'Give me two seconds, I'll put some clothes on.'

Five minutes passed. Jameson was by the door holding the *Mackintosh's* tin. 'Where are you going hide this?'

'Give it here.' Andre headed for his bedroom, returning empty handed.

'Hidden well?'

'Don't you worry.'

CHAPTER FIVE

Tuesday morning. The festival was over. And somewhat sadly, the fleet of visiting ships, one by one, departed Hobart heading into Storm Bay and out into the Tasman Sea. After a tough ten days straight Jameson finally had time to relax. He watched the ships sailing down the Derwent Estuary, enjoying the spectacle over coffee on his balcony. Strangely, Jameson suddenly felt lost. For a rare moment in his life he had no immediate plans. It was time to shower and meet the day head on.

Twenty minutes later Elspeth stepped into the bathroom offering Jameson a fresh towel in one hand and his mobile in the other. 'Andre,' she mouthed silently. 'He sounds upset.'

Jameson took the call. 'I don't know how to tell you this Jameson ...'

'Tell me what?'

'I've been burgled.'

Jameson felt light-headed. He imagined the worst. No ... he knew it to be the worst. 'The tin?' he shouted into the phone.

'Gone!'

'Jesus Christ Andre. How? How for god's sake? I told you. I warned you ...'

'I know, I know. I don't know how they managed to find it under the bed.'

'Un-under the what?'

'My bed. I hid it wrapped in a towel under my bed.'

Words couldn't describe Jameson's anger. He was incredulous. 'Under your friggin' bed! Jesus Christ. That's the first place I'd look.'

'Don't panic.'

'Don't panic! What do you mean don't panic?'

'I copied everything.'

'You did?'

'I scanned everything, photos, letters, cuttings ... the lot. It's all on my laptop.'

Instantly the day had renewed purpose. 'I'll be right over.'

Fifty-five minutes later Jameson and Elspeth parked around the back of Andre's Georgian cottage where the original stables still stood. Inside the front room Andre had his laptop booted and the file ready for inspection. The drive to town had mellowed Jameson. He gave Andre a man-hug. 'Sorry; I was pissed.'

Andre waved off any apology. 'It was nothing.'

'Then you don't want to hear what he called you earlier?' Elspeth shared a hug with their old friend.

Andre shrugged. 'Everything's on the laptop and I've already sent you the file.'

'Cool. But now the pressure's on. Those thieving bastards have as good a chance of finding the gold as we have.'

'Oh, so we are planning a road trip then?'

'Yep.'

'Excellent.' Andre shot Elspeth a wink. 'Exciting stuff eh?'

'Not if those thieving bastards beat us to it.'

'Maybe, maybe not,' on Andre's face appeared an overconfident smile. 'They may have the tin but they don't have this.' He held up a key, solid brass, older style.

'Where was that?'

'Well, when I emptied the tin to copy everything, late into the night I might add, I found a false bottom and this lone key stared back.'

Elspeth reached out. 'May I?' She took the key and rolled it about in her hand. 'I've seen keys like this before.' And a small card, fastened with a thread of leather, read ... '*Seek the darkness of a lonely smoker.*'

'What?'

'It says here, *Seek the darkness of a lonely smoker.*'

Jameson. 'What's that all about?

'Weird huh?' Andre said. 'I think it's a cryptic message.'

'Really?'

'What else could it be?'

'And a key to what?'

'It reminds me of a hotel room key,' Elspeth said. 'Jameson, remember when we were in Melbourne last year and we stayed at the Ship Hotel in Williamstown?'

'The one where you nearly fell headfirst down the stairs because the ancient carpet was all frayed.'

'That's the one. Well their room still had the original keys from the 1800s. This key is exactly the same.'

'You're right.'

'They don't make them like they used to. You can see it's quite intricate; it's not for a lock that would be easy to pick.'

'I'll find out,' Andre said. 'I have a good friend who does shoe repairs, and he has a key cutting business on the side.' Andre put the key in his waistcoat pocket and took out another object. 'I have something else.'

'Oh?'

'This was hidden with the key and it's either a piece of rubbish or very important.' He held up a crescent shaped object the size of a wagon wheel biscuit broken in half. 'It's made of plaster.' Elspeth and Jameson inspected the abstract geometric glyphs carved into it.

'What is it?'

'I honestly don't know. But in the context in which it was found, I'm sure it's important.'

Jameson studied the artefact and couldn't help it think he had seen the patterns before somewhere. 'Plaster you say?' It was certainly light in weight.

'Plaster, yes. And old. In the 19th century plaster of Paris figures were popular, especially votive figures, religious statues and the like. It was called chalkware.'

Late afternoon...

'That's the key for a Barnstead lock,' Shoe repairer Rodney informed Andre of the long-established Tasmanian locksmiths *Barnstead Security*. He loved the moment when his knowledge of locks and keys was recognised. 'I'd know their work anywhere.'

'What's it for?'

'That's an old hotel key for sure. It's got a number on it; that should make it easier to find out.'

'How can I find out for certain?'

'I know Harry Barnstead, fifth-generation Barnstead. I'll give you his number and you tell him you were talking to me.'

Later that afternoon, Harry Barnstead was waiting for Andre at the front counter of his store. 'There's only one place left in Tassie that still uses these old Pickering locks.'

'Pickering?'

'Yes. Been locksmiths in London since 1780.'

'And where might that one place be?'

'The Red Fox Inn in Hadspen, up north. We re-tweaked all the locks to their rooms and service areas when they did a full reno back in 2008. Your key was cut for room 5.'

'Oh?'

'Yes, you can just see the number there.' Barnstead pointed to a worn numeral, barely readable, before handing the key back. 'But this one's old, really old, where did you find it?'

'In a shoebox of old junk,' Jameson said in all honesty.

'I'll make a reservation,' Elspeth didn't hesitate, the moment they heard back from Andre.

Jameson. 'Make a reservation. What, the two of us?'

'Yes, unless you'd prefer to take Calvino.'

Elspeth didn't see the pillow fly across the room until it slapped her in the face. Jameson followed and the two dropped onto the bed giggling. They kissed, passionately. Elspeth pushed Jameson away, rolling onto her back looking at the fan in a lazy spin. The night was balmy and still, and the mosquitoes were out, forcing them to keep the sliding doors closed.

'The festival is over, the city's getting back to normal and you've earned a break,' Elspeth said. 'Let's drive up to Hadspen for a night at the Red Fox Inn.' Jameson wasn't as spontaneous as Elspeth. He thought a moment. 'It's only a two-and-a-half-hour drive,' she insisted. 'One night.'

'Okay. Call them.'

Minutes later. 'They have two rooms left, The Library, and the Hunting Suite.'

'The rooms all have a title?'

'Apparently. I booked the Library.'

'Good choice.'

'I thought you'd like that.'

The Red Fox Inn was built in the 1820s, almost two hundred years ago, old for Tasmania, settled by Europeans in 1804. The modern traveller must stoop beneath a door lintel off the tiny town's main street. All a part of the inn's charm. However, Jameson felt much of this charm vacated the premises when renovators moved in a dozen years earlier and the current owners opted for that French provincial décor sweeping the countryside.

'Are the rooms by chance still in their original numerical order?' Jameson asked the owner. The seventy-year-old widow with bright red lipstick and an unsettling wig looked at Jameson as if he'd asked for cup of tea in bed.

'What on earth do you mean?'

'Well, the inn is so old I was wondering how original its layout is.'

'I think what Jameson's asking,' Elspeth said, 'is, are the rooms exactly where they were two hundred years ago.'

'What a silly question, of course they are where they were originally. What do you think? They were in the middle of the orchard?'

Jameson sighed. 'I meant, is, say, room five two hundred years ago, still room five now?'

'Goodness me, I presume so. How would I know?'

'Then is room five available?'

'No, it's occupied actually.'

The owner smelt of ... Jameson couldn't quite nail it. Was it her perfume or were her clothes protected from insects? It wasn't mothballs. 'Why do you ask?' she demanded to know.

'Oh,' Elspeth lied. 'A friend said they stayed in Room Five and raved about it.'

'Really?' The woman shuffled. Jameson recognised a similarity to Basil Fawlty. 'You requested the Library when you made the reservation. Room nine.'

Did we?

The owner slid the solid antique brass key across the counter. It was exactly the same as the one from the chocolate tin. 'She's ready for retirement,' Jameson said quietly from the first-floor landing. Elspeth checked over the bannisters to make certain they were out of earshot. She agreed, smiling. 'Did you smell her perfume?' she said. 'It smelt like *Ant-rid.*'

'That's what it was. I was trying to pinpoint it. Yeh, *Ant-rid.*'

Elspeth pushed open the door to room nine. The room was neat and clean, the décor French provincial early 21st century. Jameson caught a subtle whiff of mothballs.

Two other couples enjoyed the peace and quiet of the small country village inn. After dinner, which was served in the original taproom – a four course all-inclusive affair which Jameson suggested represented local produce at its saddest – they retired to their room where Jameson crashed before Elspeth stepped from the shower. Still exhausted from the festival, Jameson slept through.

7AM. Energised, Jameson looked across at Elspeth. Clearly, she had been awake some time, quietly listening to Jameson's whiffling. 'You're awake then?'

'God, I didn't realise how tired I was,' Jameson stifled a yawn. 'What time's checkout?'

'Ten.'

'Ten,' Jameson grinned. 'What on earth can we do until then?'

Elspeth snuggled in closer. She was naked. 'I'll think of something,' she said, and her hand disappeared beneath the sheet.

A few minutes after nine.

They showered and dressed. Jameson took the brass key, apparently to room five and found in the chocolate tin. He stepped from room nine onto the first-floor landing where the landlady's activities downstairs in the kitchen echoed up the empty staircase. The other travellers had checked out. Jameson crossed the floor in his socks and knocked gently on door five.

'What if someone answers?' Elspeth whispered.

'Hadn't thought of that.'

'Well?'

'We'll ask them if they have any spare soap.'

Elspeth giggled. They waited. Jameson knocked a second time. Nothing. He slipped the key in the lock. The sound reverberated around the landing. But the key was an ill fit. 'Now what?'

'It was probably a long shot anyway Jam,' Elspeth said quietly. 'Our key must be a hundred and fifty years old, if not older.'

'Sure, but check the locks, they're all ancient.'

'Let me see,' Elspeth took the key. Jameson stepped aside. Elspeth inserted the shaft, jiggling around wards that clearly did not want to fit the key. She tried the doorknob. It turned. 'It's unlocked you idiot!'

'Hey, careful who you call idiot.' Jameson pushed the door open gently, hoping the guests *had* checked out. The curtains were still drawn but, in the darkness, they made out sheets thrown aside and used towels on the floor. The room had been vacated. Jameson took Elspeth by the hand, and they slipped into the room, closed the door and hit the light switch.

They took in their surroundings.

'Now I can see why Mrs Ant-rid wondered why we wanted to stay in this room.' It was pokey compared to their room nine and the bed, only a Queen, looked positively tiny after the king in their own room. One of the more unusual features was two chimneys, one filled in with a restored wood oven, the type used in a 19th century kitchen. It was décor only. But clearly a wall had been removed during renovations years ago, probably to make the room larger. In so doing the room now had two fireplaces, back-to-back.

Elspeth took the key from Jameson. 'Okay … *Seek the darkness of a lonely smoker*,' she read aloud in a whisper.

'*Lonely smoker … Lonely smoker …* No one smokes these days and even if they did they'd have to go outside.'

'But it's not *these days*, this message was written years ago when nearly everyone smoked, and wherever they liked.'

Jameson had a sudden memory of his late uncle Terry, a heavy smoker. He would refuse to smoke outside in winter and puff away blowing the smoke into the kitchen stove extractor or blow it up the chimney, if the room had one.

'The chimney!'

'That's what I said.'

'No. *Lonely smoker …*'

'Chimney!'

'Yes.'

Elspeth was thinking, no, it's not that simple Jam. But there are, for some crazy reason, two fireplaces in room five. Jameson was already on his knees with his hand up the flue. It was common knowledge lots of old folk in centuries past concealed valuables up the chimney. Elspeth shook her head. 'Jam, you are going to get so dirty.'

'It's clean El, there hasn't been a fire lit in here since the place was renovated.' Jameson's fingers danced blindly into the throat of the chimney and tapped into the smoke shelf above the fire plate. 'Nothing.'

'What did you expect?'

'I don't ... aha!'

'What is it?' Jameson's face twisted sideways, flush against the chimney, as his arm disappeared all the way, as far as possible. His tongue protruded in a vain attempt to lengthen his reach. 'Well?'

'Loose brick.' Jameson fished about in the blackness. He felt into a cavity. Pieces of brick crumbed into the grate. 'Nothing!' Jameson pulled a not so clean arm free. 'Damn it. It honestly felt like an empty space. The sort of gap for hiding loot, but nothing.'

Elspeth had resigned the search to failure but ...

'Oh well it was fun to have a night away anyhow.'

10.05AM. Check-out. Hotel foyer...

'Look out,' Jameson said a little louder than he should have. 'Here comes Mrs Ant-rid.' The landlady appeared to be blessed with a sixth sense. They watched through the thick handmade glass panels of the hotel's rear door as the woman crossed the manicured lawn from the orchard with the speed of a marathon walker, elbows high, arms pumping like a marionette.

'You're off then?' she said rather haughtily, short on breath, stepping through the back door. 'Sleep well I trust?'

'Yes, thank you.'

'Did you sign the visitors' book?' The landlady pointed to an open book with neatly headed columns, *Name, Address, Comments.* The leather-bound book sat on a glass topped counter. It was then that Jameson saw the artefacts beneath the glass.

'What the heck?'

Elspeth. 'What?'

The proprietor looked up, querulous lines forming on her brow.

'Oh,' Jameson said. 'I was just looking at this old stuff in the glass case.'

'Old stuff?' Elspeth knew something was amiss. Jameson never called an artefact *old stuff.* She joined him at the cabinet where Jameson surreptitiously pointed out a crescent shaped plaster cast with its geometric glyphs. Elspeth recognised it immediately.

'What's all this?' Jameson asked the owner, very matter-of-factly.

'Those, they're bits and pieces the builder found when they were doing renovations here years ago.'

Elspeth tried to look only mildly interested. She signed the visitors' book and joined Jameson, staring at the old bone buttons, 19th century coins, blacksmith-forged nails, a stoneware ink pot, shards of pottery bottles, clay pipe bowls and even a fragment of old lace. Nothing remarkable except for the cast.

'You-have-got-to-be-kidding,' Elspeth whispered. 'That's the other half of our plaster crescent thingie!'

It looked exactly the same, yet a mirror image.

'That piece there,' Jameson casually tapped a finger on the glass directly above the object. 'What is that?'

The landlady leaned over to see what on earth could possibly be so interesting. She bunched her lips. 'You tell me and we'll both know.' The woman chuckled to herself.

'Where was that found?'

'Well, I'll never forget because the builder said Father Christmas must have lost it.'

'In the chimney?'

'What? That was a good guess.'

'Well, you know, Father Christmas ... chimneys and all that.'

'What chimney?' Elspeth asked, struggling to contain her excitement.

'Room five ... huh! That's the room you asked about. Isn't that strange?'

As far as Jameson was concerned the artefact didn't belong in the case. 'Well thank you for a lovely stay,' Jameson said. He hoisted their shared overnight bag over his shoulder and shot out the door as if he couldn't wait to leave. Elspeth, taken aback, followed.

'Jameson!' Out in the back yard Elspeth rushed to catch up. 'Jameson!' She tugged at his sleeve. 'What are you doing?'

Jameson twisted about, whispering, 'Keep her busy.'

'What?'

'Keep her busy.'

'These trees,' Jameson called out to the landlady as the woman busied herself with paperwork at her reception counter under the stairs. 'These trees, what are they ... pears?'

'Pardon?' The landlady joined her strange guests in the yard. 'What was that?'

'These trees,' and Jameson waved his free arm towards the orchard twenty metres away, 'are they pears?' And before she could answer, he marched in their direction. Elspeth and the woman followed.

'They're quince actually.'

'Oh, quince as in cheese and quince paste?'

'That's right.'

'Elspeth has a wonderful recipe for quince paste, don't you?'

'Do I?' Elspeth answered, confused.

'Yes. You got it from an old copy of Mrs Beeton's cookery book remember, didn't you El?'

'I did? I mean *yes*, I did.'

Jameson positioned himself to discreetly send Elspeth another message.

Keep her busy.

'Yes. It's delicious.'

'Well,' the landlady was starting to doubt her guest's soundness of mind. 'It's simple enough. Just Quince and sugar.'

'Ah, but that's where you are wrong,' Jameson said. 'Do you mind if I have a closer look?'

'Please yourself.'

Jameson marched ahead into the orchard. The landlady and Elspeth followed.

'Oh, I left my slippers in the room,' Jameson lied. 'I'll be right back.' The owner was left open mouthed. 'Tell her about adding vanilla paste,' Jameson called out over his shoulder, before hurrying back into the inn leaving Elspeth struggling to explain the benefits of adding vanilla paste to the jam. The landlady listened politely, albeit confused. Jameson returned one and a half minutes later. One and a half minutes too long for Elspeth. 'I must have packed my slippers after all,' he said absentmindedly.

Elspeth knew now exactly what Jameson was up to. 'Did you get it?' she asked, nervously waving to their startled host through the windscreen, as Jameson backed from the carpark.

'Yep.'

'Oh my god Jameson Rowley, you are insane.'

'Thank you. You aren't too bad yourself.'

'What if she notices it missing?'

'She won't. I shuffled everything about to make the case look full.'

'Good work.' Elspeth had a moment of guilt. 'You know it's stealing.'

'Look at it as a loan El, we'll post it back to her later, anonymously.'

'Promise?'

'Promise.'

Next day. Andre's cottage. New Town Road.

Elspeth knocked. No answer. Jameson tried the door, it opened. He called out. 'Andre!' Still no answer. They entered. Without warning the hallway came alive. It sounded like a thousand empty cans had tumbled from a pile. 'Jesus!' Jameson recoiled putting his hands up to protect himself as Elspeth retreated back onto the veranda.

'Huh! Got you.' Andre appeared from around a doorway while two dozen rattling cans finally steadied. 'That's my burglar alarm,' And to prove a point Andre pulled the communal cord once more and the cans once again rattled. 'There's a trip wire at your foot.'

Jameson managed one word. 'Clever.' Otherwise, he was speechless.

'Well done,' Elspeth was more complimentary.

They brought Andre up to date with their find. He was impressed. 'I can't believe you actually found that,' he tut-tutted, shaking his head. Elspeth cleared a spot on the coffee table and slid the two crescent halves together. The segment from the chocolate tin and the fragment from the Red Fox Inn fitted together like the sections of a two-piece jigsaw. 'Now,' Andre's voice hinted at reverence. 'All we have to do is work out what it means.'

'You said it's made of plaster,' Elspeth said.

Plaster ware, or chalkware as it was called then, was popular in the 19th century,' Andre said. 'Chalkware was made from a fine white powder produced by heating the mineral gypsum, which was found in great quantities in Paris, at Montmartre actually, hence the name ...'

'Plaster of Paris.'

'Spot on. Occasionally it was mixed with glue to produce a hardened and shiny work surface. These two pieces have been mixed with a water-based glue.'

'Like what?'

'Well natural polymers made from vegetables heavy in starches.'

'Like spuds.'

'That's it. Others were protein sources like soybean or milk albumen.'

'Is that the same material the ancient Romans used in their frescos?'

'No, that was a lime plaster.'

Hook, Line and Sinker, Seafood Restaurant. Hobart's waterfront. Late that night ...

Jameson enjoyed a knock-off beer at the bar. The one night off in Hadspen had been short lived and he felt he needed a decent break after the past week. At least now he had time to analyse the crazy events surrounding his discovery of the *Mackintosh's Quality Street* sweets tin.

It was after midnight. The last diners for the evening were returning to their hotels, their homes and for a few, to their berths aboard the few remaining boats. Otherwise, the docks were deserted. Jameson bid Simon the maître d' good night and stepped out onto Hunter Street. The waterfront was eerily quiet after the festivities. More importantly the wooden boat festival had proven to be another hugely successful global event, guaranteed to be hosted by Hobart once again in two years' time.

Although still fatigued from the festival, Jameson managed a spring in his step along Old Wharf to where he leased a parking space for his Ute. Crossing in front of the old Art School into poorly lit Evans Street behind the restaurant, Jameson realised he was not alone. A black car crept across the docks. Jameson glanced over his shoulder. The car pulled to the curb fifty metres away. The headlights blinked out. Jameson sped up, crossing into the old railway yard, a deserted waterfront wasteland awaiting development. Jameson checked over his shoulder. The car had disappeared.

Overhead the only streetlamp flickered weakly, its globe dying a slow death. Looking about anxiously Jameson unlocked his Ute. He was about to climb behind the wheel when the black car reappeared at speed from another direction. The headlights switched to full beam. Jameson was blinded. The car braked hard alongside. Jameson balled his fists. He tensed, preparing for an altercation. Immediately he realised the driver was a cop; at least he wore a uniform.

'Jameson Rowley?' the driver said as the window scrolled down.

'Yes.' Jameson switched from self-defence to defensive. He knew he was below .05; he'd only had two beers, one in the kitchen and one at the bar. 'What do you want?'

'Get in.'

'What?'

The driver, a tall slender man, mid-forties, drinker's gut not helped by his shirt tucked tightly into his trousers, alighted. He swung the back passenger door open. 'He said get in.' Jameson noted a well-built figure in the back was of an older man, early fifties maybe.

'It's alright Mr Rowley.' The reassuring words resonated from darkness in a slow confident drawl. Jameson stooped to assess the situation. 'I'm Inspector Ray Wilson. Do get in,' he waved a hand across the seat beside him. Jameson took a breath, sighed, and stepped into the car. The driver closed the door behind him and stood sentry outside, his hands locked behind his back.

Enough illumination spilt from the dash for Jameson to recognise that this man had had surgery on a cleft lip as a child. The light caught his rather clumsy scar in a most unflattering manner. 'What's this all about?' Jameson asked.

'You've had a busy time of it lately.'

'Yes, well I'm head chef in the busiest restaurant in town during a huge event,' Jameson answered. 'Why do you ask?'

'I'm inspector Ray Wilson, and I'll not detain you too long Mr Rowley,' the man said with a slight lisp due to his deformity. 'Suffice to say you are biting off more than you can chew.'

'Pardon?' But Jameson now had a hint of what to expect.

'I said you are biting off more than you can chew.' There was an element of impatience in the inspector's tone. 'This treasure you seek ...'

'Ah ... treasure is it?'

'There is no such thing as lost treasure. It is some boyhood fantasy you are dreaming about.'

'What? You read the papers too huh?'

'More than that. I have an order from Canberra sent from the Vatican, from Pope Francis himself that any remains of the martyred saint are to be returned to Rome, to Vatican City.'

'You just said there *is* no treasure.'

'And you better believe it.'

Now he's talking in riddles!

Jameson shook his head. He had taken a disliking to this bloke already. 'Look, it's a free country, at least it was when I last voted, and I will spend my time doing whatever I want.'

'This is not advice Mr Rowley, I am warning you ...'

'Warning me!'

'You are treading on the feet of very important and determined people. I am ordering you ...'

'You finished?' Jameson put his hand on the door handle.

'You are playing with fire.'

'Ah well there you go,' Jameson said, opening the door and stepping back into the night. 'Playing with fire is something this cook is good at.'

The unmarked police car sat idling. They waited for Jameson to drive off. 'Bloody upstart,' Inspector Ray Wilson spat. 'Who does he think he is?'

The uniformed driver, Sergeant Jack Begley, eyeballed his boss in the rear view, 'I'm sure me and some mates could mock-up something, get him arrested ... on ... say drug charges. It wouldn't be too hard to stitch him up with a bag of pills.'

'He hasn't got a record Jack, he's clean as a whistle. It might cause more problems than we already have.' Wilson rubbed his scar. 'But I'll think about it.'

'I wouldn't leave it too long Ray,' the sergeant said informally. 'He and his mates have a background, they're not exactly novices at uncovering mysteries.'

'Don't you underestimate me either, Jack,' Wilson hissed. 'Need I remind you my relatives, distant and close, have been looking for these missing gold ingots for generations. It was my ancestor who was an accomplice of that crafty bitch Anwyn Blizzard who was party to the stashing of the treasure in the first place, for Christ's sake. And this is the closest any one in my family has ever come. Stuffed if I'll let them be found by his lot.'

'How did that old chocolate tin with the clues in it turn up at that garage sale anyhow?'

'All I could find out was the surname of the people who had the garage sale was Newham, so god knows how it wound up there.'

'What of the Vatican then?"

'What about the Vatican?'

'Well, they have the resources. They're determined to find this gem-studded skull of that saint. It's not just the value of the damned thing, it's sacred. And to top it off an Italian tall ship turns up with the Ambassador on board at the same time the discovery was made public.'

'Yeh. You wouldn't read about it.'

Jack. 'What's the plan then Ray? We know the Italians have already contacted Jameson, we found out he and some staff of his had breakfast on board the *Amerigo* what's it ...'

'*Amerigo Vespucci.*'

Yeh. Does that mean that cook's jumped into bed with the Vatican?'

'Christ knows. Call it a night. But first thing tomorrow get me an invite on that ship before it sails.'

Next day. Bar T-42. Hobart Waterfront...

Sleuth Andre was beside himself with excitement. Elspeth and Jameson were relaxing over drinks when Andre caught up with them. Andre loved the challenge, the research, delving into history books and dusting off old documents. He was clearly pleased with himself.

'What do you want to hear first? The plaster puzzle or where Saint Adamo Abate and his fellow martyrs came from?'

Elspeth sat straight. 'I'd like to know what ...'

'Saint Adamo, good choice,' Andre pre-empted. He loved the drama, the suspense. 'In the 1570s vineyard workers in southern Italy discovered a Roman catacomb full of thousands of skeletons dating back to the first three centuries after the emergence of Christianity. There were estimates of more than half a million people in the subterranean chambers. Now, when the Catholic Church heard of this discovery, they were convinced that many of the skeletons must belong to early Christians, martyrs. So, the powers that be in the church saw a marketing gold mine.'

Elspeth. 'Marketing?'

'Bear with me. You must understand in the decades prior to this discovery, early in the 16th century, Catholics in northern Europe and especially Germany had been persecuted by the Protestants, who had ransacked the Catholic Churches, plundering and vandalising, destroying their sacred relics. Now these bones of Christian *martyrs* suddenly had a purpose. They were cleaned and dressed in ornate costumes and bejewelled with precious gemstones. Every church and chapel wanted one or two to make a grandiose statement. They became village patrons. They became revered, sacred and most desirable ... with me so far?'

'I think so,' Jameson said. 'The words fanatical, gullible peasants come to mind.'

'Yes, well. Wealthy families wanted them for their chapels. They became valuable commodities. And not just anyone could purchase one. You needed connections in Rome, particularly one of the papal guards.'

'So, who decorated them?'

'Nuns in the convents prepared them. They spun a fine mesh gauze with which they delicately wrapped each bone which also acted as medium to attach the gemstones and gold leaf. Family heirlooms in the villages were donated and many personal pieces of jewellery, like rings, were placed on the finished martyr.'

'Well, that's fascinating,' Elspeth said. 'And our missing saint's skull is one of these?'

'Yes.'

'And what's your verdict on the plaster cast?'

'I know exactly what this is.' Andre held the two crescent-shaped pieces of the plaster puzzle.

'Okay,' Elspeth said. 'What is it?'

Andre was silenced a moment. Side-tracked by Claire who turned up to the bar late with a new coiffure and a streak of fire engine red through her hair. Andre had heard the others talk of Claire, but they had never met. Claire slid a chair over from a vacant table and sat heavily.

'I'm Andre.'

'Hi. I've heard all about you, I'm Claire.' Claire picked up one half of the plaster puzzle. 'So, this is what you were talking about on the phone El?'

'Yes, and Andre thinks he knows what it is,' Elspeth said. 'Andre, back to you.'

'It's a petroglyph.'

'Petra what?' Claire sat back.

'Petroglyph. This,' and Andre held the two pieces together, 'is a plaster model of a life size Aboriginal petroglyph. The original is on the west coast of Tasmania.'

'At Preminghana,' Elspeth said. 'South of Cape Grim.'

'That's correct. I was searching through books on the history of the north-west and found an article on the rock carvings. Then it hit me. This is a model of a petroglyph.'

Jameson. 'I think your right on the money Andre.'

'Then on closer inspection I noticed writing around the circumference.' Andre pointed out writing around the one-centimetre edge.

Elspeth focussed on the small but tidy cursive script scratched into the plaster and read aloud, '*Turn your back on the truth.*'

'What the hell does that mean?'

'It's a clue,' Andre said. 'Another riddle.'

Claire. 'It's weird.'

'And,' Andre added. 'Note there are three words on each piece ...'

'Meaning you need both to get the riddle.'

'Exactly.'

'There's something else Jameson has to tell you,' Elspeth said.

Jameson grew serious. 'Ah ... yes.' He went onto explain his clandestine meeting with Inspector Ray Wilson.

'On behalf of the Vatican eh?' Andre asked.

'Yes, Orfeo De Luca, that Italian dignitary, said the same thing.'

Claire. 'Well now what will we do?'

'Bugger 'em I say.' Jameson had enough beer on board to feel adventurous. 'I'm all for it.'

Claire. 'For what?'

Elspeth knew Jameson too well. 'I think Jameson's been itching for a road trip, especially after our night at Hadspen.'

'What about the police?' Andre asked. 'And the Vatican?'

'Oh come on, it's a free country.' Jameson's face flushed with enthusiasm. 'Well, who's in? I can manage a few days off now the festival's over. What about you El?'

'I'm owed time off and we are overstaffed at the museum this week with the new trainees.'

Jameson. 'Andre, you in?'

'Me?'

'Yes mate, why not. We can nail this together. Actually, we could all fit in your van.'

Elspeth. 'You'd love it Andre, it'd be fun.'

'You're hardly busy,' Jameson said. 'You're retired.'

'What about Cecil?' Andre said of his pug.

'Bring him along.'

'Ah no, that won't work.'

'Why not?'

'Cecil doesn't handle travelling too well and besides, he suffers from flatulence.'

'A farting dog in a van,' Claire pulled a face. 'Maybe it's not a great idea.'

'Andre?'

'I … I, well … I do have a cousin available, who moves in home and looks after Cecil on occasion.'

'There you go, Claire said. 'That's four of us.'

'Four,' Jameson said. 'Are you coming Claire?'

'Well, you're not going without me.'

Jameson's mate Calvino walked through the bar door on the tail of the excitement. 'There you all are, I've been looking all over for you guys.'

'Good,' Jameson grinned. 'You're just in time to have a shout.'

'What?'

Jameson scooped up three empty beer glasses and passed them to Calvino. 'What are you drinking Claire?' he asked on Calvino's behalf.

'I'll have the same as you guys.'

Calvino stared back. 'You have some redeeming to do Calvino,' Elspeth said. 'After talking to that journalist about treasure.'

Calvino's mouth dropped open. 'Better hurry,' Jameson said. 'Happy hour finishes in three minutes.'

Calvino rushed to the bar. Minutes later; 'Who's not going where without whom?' Calvino asked, sliding the tray of drinks onto their table.

'Pardon?'

'When I arrived, I heard Claire say, *you're not going without me.*'

Jameson looked at Elspeth.

'One tray of drinks does not redeem you Calvino,' she said, trying not to smile. 'You're coming too, you can be our steward.'

'Go where?'

'Looking for lost gold. The gold you blabbed to the whole world about.'

'But ... I ...'

Claire had always had an eye for Calvino. She kicked him under the table.

'Oh,' Calvino blushed. 'I suppose I could spare the time.'

CHAPTER SIX

Off the west coast of Tasmania...

Il Corvo Nero looked magnificent under full sail. Her three thousand square feet of black canvas captured every breath of wind, spearing her bowsprit into deep troughs and climbing her way out over mountainous waves. Waves rolling east, off the expanse of the Indian Ocean.

Cartel boss Maya Hidalgo watched her cigarettes and lighter slide across the cabin table like some supernatural entity was sitting with her. She cursed herself for not driving overland with Jorge Diaz and Emiliano, her heads of security. Although they had bugged the seaside cottage at Storm Bay, not a great deal of information had been forthcoming. Yet they learnt enough to know the small group of friends was onto something. They had booked accommodation at Stanley, a small village on the north-west coast of Tasmania. Now Maya was at the mercy of Mother Nature. She loved her ship. She enjoyed sailing on a reasonable ocean. But this swell was something else.

Maya called the bridge. Captain Gerardo Garcia was young for a tall ship captain at thirty-four, but he had the skills required. He had been contracted to the cartel three years now and although he was not involved in the nefarious operations of the organisation, he was no fool. He knew he would be under Maya Hidalgo's spell for as long as she demanded. But the pay was excellent, and she paid to send his four children to private boarding schools in the United States. All he had to do was keep his nose out of her business and captain her precious *Black Raven*.

'My apologies ma'am,' Captain Garcia, standing legs apart for stability, answered over the intercom from the bridge. 'But,' he warned his boss, 'we will endure this weather until at least King Island,'

'Are you still estimating a four-day sail?'

'If we can maintain the fourteen knots, yes mam.'

Maya looked at her lunch of Tasmania salmon. It truly was some of the finest salmon in the world, and she would know, she'd dined all over the globe. And Jose her chef had prepared today's salmon her favourite way; baked fillet over a salad of vine ripened tomatoes, coriander, red onion, avocado and freshly squeezed lime. Although the plate was weighted and the table had a fiddle rail to avoid accidents, the untouched meal followed the cigarettes from one side of the surface to the other. Maya had lost her appetite.

Taking her mind off the weather, the Mexican focussed on the lost skull of Saint Adamo Abate. History recorded the skull, with its articulated hinged cranium, contained the *Ratnaraj Ruby*, a gemstone the size of a grapefruit, nestled in the cranial cavity. This rare and indeed priceless pigeon-blood red ruby was thought to have been discovered in East Africa and was spoken reverently as the king of all precious stones. For all her billions of dollars, Maya Hidalgo had one ambition outside the cartel; to possess the finest gemstones in the world. So, when she sailed into Hobart, only to hear of circumstances she could never have foreseen, Maya just knew she was destined to possess the stone. Yes, she would possess the *Ratnaraj Ruby*.

Jorge Diaz and Emiliano enjoyed the five-hour drive north on the Midlands Highway, continuing north-west along the Bass Highway in their hired orange-gold Mitsubishi ASX SUV. They travelled light, except for a silver sports bag on the back seat, as they were to meet up with the *Il Corvo Nero* in Stanley. In the bag were automatic rifles and a hundred thousand in US cash. Bribe money. The plan? To find Jameson, his girlfriend and their fellow travellers in Stanley and find out what they knew. Although the Mexicans were in possession of the vintage sweets tin and its contents there were vital clues missing.

Failure was not an option.

Besides, Diaz and Emiliano had been promised half a million dollars bonus each, once they located the saint's skull.

Half a million!

Jorge Diaz daydreamed of what he would do with the money. Emiliano drove.

CHAPTER SEVEN

Marrawah. Population in 2016 Census, 121...

'*Tasmania's most westerly town with the purest air in the world,* so it says here,' Claire read aloud the blub on the tourist information panel erected next to the town store and petrol station. There wasn't much else about. '*In the 1800s Aboriginal people were forcibly moved from the lands around Marrawah.* Jesus, that sucks ... hey, listen to this. *The last Tasmanian tiger was captured near Marrawah in the 1920s.*'

Jameson, Elspeth and Claire stood about watching Andre fill the tank of his Mitsubishi seven-seater. It was great to stretch the legs after seven hours on the road with only one coffee break and one bathroom stop. Calvino reappeared. He had smashed his first National meat pie before he vacated the store and was into his second by the time he joined the others. 'Not bad guys, bloody hot an' all. Hey Jam,' Calvino told Jameson. 'There's a book swap in the shop, heaps o' second-hand books, yer might find a bargain.'

Jameson didn't need to be told twice and disappeared into the shop. Claire watched Calvino eat, like an insatiable pet hound hanging around the kitchen. The pie sure as hell smelt good. 'Bite?' Calvino offered Claire his steak and onion. Claire weakened and took a bigger bite than intended. Gravy ran down her chin and she wiped tomato sauce off her face. It was late afternoon, and they would set up camp within the hour.

'Can't you guys wait for dinner?' Elspeth said.

Minutes later Jameson stepped from the shop, book in hand. 'Orright, yer found something then,' Calvino grinned, dusting pasty flakes off the front of his footy jumper. 'Knew yer would.'

Andre recognised Jameson's bargain immediately; *Mrs Beeton's Household Management*, a cookbook that had been popular since 1861. 'Good for you,' Andre cheered. 'What issue?'

'1928,' Jameson said. 'But in ace condition.'

'How much?

'Ten bucks.'

Andre shook his head in admiration. The book would sell for over a hundred in an antiquarian book shop. Andre cast an eye towards the shop. 'Anything else?'

'Don't bother, there's nothing else worth buying.'

Andre, with all his contacts in all the right places, had sourced special permission through an old friend to visit the *Preminghana Indigenous Protected Area* on the coast, twenty odd kilometres north-west of Marrawah at an Aboriginal cultural property. Here, they could inspect the ancient petroglyphs on the shoreline. Andre's ten-year-old Mitsubishi van trundled over the rough dirt track like an elephant with a wounded knee. Passing through manuka thickets, tea-tree swamps, eucalyptus woodlands, coast wattle and honeysuckle, it wasn't difficult to imagine a tribe of indigenous inhabitants following the same route to the coast after a day on the hunt.

Ted Lanyard, an Aboriginal elder, met them on site. Parking at a headland with only sand dunes to protect them from the wild weather almost perpetually roaring in off the Southern Ocean, the crew finally stretched their legs. Greeted by a salty cool wind, it truly was a wild and beautiful, yet desolate and untamed place.

The Aboriginal elder's words arrived on the wind. 'Andy yer ol' bastard,' he called out, his head and shoulders appearing over the nearest dune like a mirage.

'Teddy!' Andre met the indigenous islander halfway. The two hugged, patting backs the way only old mates do. Ted was dedicated to his Aboriginal heritage.

'Come on then,' Ted Lanyard called out to the others over his shoulder. 'Better pull yer finger out, if you want to see the petroglyphs.' And he wandered off impatiently in the direction from where he had come.

Elspeth's long hair whipped about her face. The wind had picked up lashing the perennial grass of the dunes, creating mini vortexes of fine dry sand. Out at sea eternal waves charged the shore; each with its own personality, a perpetual armada of white caps, like the sails of an invading navy.

A short ten-minute stroll in soft sand led them into a low valley with a cliff face next to a narrow creek, protected from the wind. Here sand dunes gave way to a rocky landscape where the majority of the chiselled engravings were situated.

'Wow!' Elspeth had seen many photos but seeing the petroglyphs in situ was breathtaking. Especially when one considered the intricate carvings were created by people with such primitive tools.

'What did they use to carve these?' she asked the Aboriginal elder.

'We found a quarry love,' Ted said, 'for want of a better word, where they knapped tools out of quartzite and basalt.'

'Fascinating.'

Each slab of carved rock was predominately concentric circles, trellised lines and rows of dots and crosses. Nearby Ted pointed out large bird tracks carved into the stone. 'They reckon them tracks are emu.'

'And as we know,' Elspeth said, 'the emu on this island is now extinct.'

'That's right miss.'

'How long have they been here?' Calvino asked.

'These were first noted by shepherds from the nearby Van Diemen's Company farmlands inland from here,' Andre told the others. 'And they took schoolteacher and amateur archaeologist Archibald Meston to the site, who recognised them as important.'

'Yeh, that was 1933,' Ted said. 'Apparently a storm blew in uncovering them. They were hidden under the dunes.'

'At the time they were carbon dated. They are believed to have been abandoned to shifting sands, and then topped with soil, about 850 years ago.'

'Then whitefella come with his cattle,' Ted added. 'And this caused erosion.'

'So, if it wasn't for the whitefella's cows,' Calvino said, 'they wouldn't have been discovered.'

The Aboriginal elder shot Calvino a *who's this turkey* look. Calvino, often accused of opening his mouth to change feet, was unperturbed. 'Something else worries me.'

'Oh!' Elspeth was wary.

Jameson interrupted. 'And what might that be Cal?'

'Well, if these carvings were abandoned, as you said, eight hundred and something years ago, how could the abos ... sorry, Aborigines, have chiselled clues to a treasure lost in 1800s?'

'Treasure!' Ted Lanyard's shaggy eyebrows raised a few centimetres. 'What yer sayin' treasure?'

Elspeth, Jameson and Claire turned on Calvino, each with their individual brand of exasperation. Ted looked to Andre, 'What treasure Andy? You didn't say anything on the phone about treasure.'

Andre looked to the others. He would have to come clean, well at least give the elder some sort of explanation, as he hadn't exactly been one hundred per cent up-front with the man.

'We're actually on a bit of a mission Ted,' Andre started.

'Mission?'

'We are looking for a lost ship that sank off the coast here in 1812.'

'Jesus! Then what's them carvin's got to do with it?'

'Well, we believe there are petroglyphs carved by the original peoples of this land or by survivors of the wreck that give a clue to the whereabouts of the missing ship.'

'And treasure?' Ted's eyes sparkled.

'That's just hearsay,' Jameson said. 'We have no proof of any treasure.'

'What makes you think our carvin's are a clue, any'ow?'

'Let's head back to the van,' Andre suggested.

Andre unfolded the old T-towel protecting the separate pieces of the plaster cast. He placed it carefully on the open tailgate of his van, and joined the two halves together.

Ted studied the artefact. 'That's at Sundown Point eight k's south of Arthur River,' the elder said without hesitation.

'What?' Jameson said. 'You recognise it?'

'Sure I do. It's different to all the rest. There's forty of 'em yer know, found so far.'

'I've seen the photos and they all look the same to me,' Calvino said.

'That's 'cos yer a whitefella,' Ted Lanyard retaliated, his opinion of Calvino sinking even lower. 'Nar, think what yer like mate,' Ted carefully picked up the two halves, 'but this one's got a ship on it.'

'It has?'

They all studied the plaster mould carefully. 'It certainly looks a little different,' Andre said. 'And what appears at a stretch to look like a canoe with masts and sails could be miscued for a sailing ship.'

'There are two masts.'

'That is, *if* it's a ship.'

'Some elders reckon it was carved by whitefella,' Ted said. 'Years and years after them others.'

'Then we must take a look, Sundown Point you say.'

'Yeh, but yer can forget the carvin's for a mo, I got someone yer gotta meet first.'

'Oh?'

'Yeh, me old mate Bob at Arthur River.'

The Arthur River meanders through rainforest so dense you would not want to be lost amongst it, finally spilling into the Southern Ocean at the seaside village named after the River – Arthur River, population 121 and more in summer when the shack owners arrived for their fishing holidays. The tiny village was well situated at the mouth of the River. The coast here has to be respected, with angled, lichen-veneered slabs of flat rock – stacked like odd shaped fallen dominos – guarding either side of the river's mouth. Here the tannin-stained river escaped into the Southern Ocean. At the entrance, frothing breakers undulated and twisted, colliding with sunken rocks joining tidal rips like tormented demons from the deep. It was not a place to swim. Fallen trees from decades past; from rainforest trees of blackwood, sassafras, mighty eucalyptus, myrtle and ancient Huon Pines, washed down river only to stack in massive piles of driftwood on the rocks at either side of the estuary. At first glance for the more imaginative, they represented silver ghosts from the ancient forest. They piled higgledy-piggledy, strewn ashore and then deserted by the eternal surf. It was a rare and beautiful sight.

Eighty-nine-year-old Bob Mundy sat on his veranda drinking a long glass of his daughter's home-made ginger beer. He watched the van-load of 'city folk' pull into his driveway with a measure of curiosity and caution. That was until he recognised a familiar face. Ted Lanyard climbed from the front seat coughing a greeting. 'Bob.'

'Ted.'

'Got a mob 'ere up from 'obart what wanna talk to yer 'bout the good ol' days.'

Old Bob made an effort to stand to greet his visitors, offering a warm smile showing off teeth so white they had to be dentures. His baggy trousers were held up to his navel with braces over a sleeveless singlet. His feet were bare.

'Ted yer old bastard,' Bob put an arm around his friend's shoulder, first onto the front porch, while his other hand tweaked his privates.

'Yer right there Bob?' Ted grinned, watching his friend's less than subtle manoeuvre.

'Yeh mate, Sandy bought me jocks for Father's Day but they're a bit tight. I prefer boxers.'

The others filed up the wooden steps onto the veranda. Ted introduced them. 'Elspeth, Jameson and Claire ain't it?'

'Yep.'

'An' you've heard me talk about me brainy mate Andy before.' Bob nodded.

'It's Andre,' Andre smiled at Bob. 'But Andy'll do.'

Calvino shuffled awkwardly. 'And that's Calvert.' Ted leant over to whisper in Bob's ear, "e's the bright one.'

'Calvino,' Calvino corrected.

'Yeh, whatever.'

'Well, I never had so many visitors all at once.' Bob offered a calloused hand in greeting; a gnarly fist that hinted at years of hard work. Even at arm's length Jameson caught a whiff of rum on the old man's gingery breath. Artful by nature, Bob gave Elspeth's long legs a discretionary inspection the moment she took in the magnificent ocean view. Elspeth turned back ...

Bob eyes darted to Ted. 'The good ol' days yer say?'

'What?'

'You said they're here to talk about the good ol' days, Ted?'

'Well, I thought you might tell 'em about the ship's timbers found all them years back.'

'What's the interest in old timbers?' Bob was fishing. He knew the answer.

'They're looking for treasure,' Ted wanted to laugh but he settled for a smirk.

Bloody Calvino! Jameson and Elspeth cringed.

'We're serious historians really,' Elspeth spoke for the team. Andre nodded sagely.

'Grab a pew,' Bob told all and sundry. He sat himself back down heavily and took a long drink. Calvino had to satisfy himself sitting on the top step.

'You fellas like a ginger beer?' Bob asked Elspeth's legs. 'Me daughter Sandra makes a decent brew, same recipe the Cascade Brewery made back in the 1920s.'

Although a cool wind blew in off the ocean, it was quite warm on the sheltered balcony. Everyone could use a drink. 'Sandy's out back Ted, she'll rustle up some drinks.'

'Sure.'

Bob watched Ted open the fly wire over the front entrance. 'Don't let them damned flies in.'

The old man ran a hand through his snowy hair, receding from a weathered brow, and took in his audience with lazy hooded eyes.

'So, yer here for the treasure eh?'

'N-no!' Elspeth reiterated. 'We're historians trying to solve the mystery ship story.'

Bob didn't believe a word of it. These blokes weren't the first treasure hunters to come to town, and they wouldn't be the last. Bob Mundy sniffed loudly. 'The treasure were found years ago,' he said casually. 'It's gone.'

Calvino couldn't hold back. 'How do you know?'

'So, yer do know about the treasure then,' Bob licked his lips eyeing Calvino.

'We heard stories but it's irrelevant to our research,' Jameson offered.

'So, you're not interested in the gold bars, the iron chests of gold coins, the silver plate and the gemstones, enough to buy a city they said.'

Clearly this was all fanciful. 'Are you saying,' Jameson wore a serious face, playing along with the old fisherman, 'that someone *actually* found treasure?'

'Sure am?'

'Did you see it?'

'No lad, it was before my time.'

'Silver plate, gold coins and gems you said.'

'That's how the story goes.'

'Do you know who found it?'

'God no. It's not the kind o' thing you'd blab about, now is it. You'd take the money and run. At least I would.'

'Does anyone know *anything* about this find of the century?'

'You're a persistent bugger ain't yer? The answer's no. It's all rumours.

If anything, Jameson felt they were being handfed old wives' tales. He continued to fish. 'You mentioned old ship's timbers.'

'Yeh, it was me granddaddy, Fred Mundy. He found the ship exposed after a huge storm, before it disappeared once again.'

'Oh, go on.'

'Grandad moved here after the post office opened in Arthur River in 1910,' Bob started. 'He was in his thirties when 'e settled here. He was a shipwright see, like *his* daddy's daddy who was trained by the lags at the Port Arthur shipyard.'

'Port Arthur?'

'Yeh, so 'e reckoned. And there was a market for fishing boats in the area 'cos the fishin' was so good ya see. Still is. 'e used to go into the tea-tree swamps south o' here to get tea-tree knees for his boats see. 'e always said that tea-tree was the best. Strong fit bugger 'e were too. Used to go into the swamps, chop the knees out o' the trees an' carry 'em back on 'is lonesome 'e did.'

Elspeth. 'What do you mean by knees?'

'Natural bends in timber what made good framing … transoms and the like for 'is craft. Now it was on one o' these excursions that he told me he seen the mast of a ship, just the top like, pokin' above the trees. When he managed to beat a path to the spot, which wasn't easy on account o' the razor grass and tiger snakes, he said he saw the remains of a ship, just the superstructure mind. The rest was buried in the swamp and dunes.'

Elspeth. 'When would this be, roughly?'

'Roughly ... just after the war.'

'The Great War.'

'Yeh. 1919 ... twenty, maybe.'

'You said superstructure?' Jameson said. 'Like how much?'

"E didn't really say, but 'e said it reminded him of the *Endeavour*.'

'Captain Cook's ship?'

'That's the one. Exceptin' this ship only had two masts and was smaller 'e thought. So, me granddaddy went back to this 'ere wreck several times to collect planks of oak. It was in good nick see and 'e was recycling it in his own boats.'

'Really?'

'Yes, really.'

Jameson. 'Crazy!'

'Bloody clever more like,' Bob shuffled, defensive in his chair.

'No offense Mr Mundy,' Jameson replied. 'I meant crazy as in there are probably fishing boats out there still, today, with timber from a much older ship in their construction.'

'Yeh, well when yer put it like that ...'

'When exactly was this?' Elspeth asked. 'When your grandfather built the boats, that is?'

'As I said, after the war. But into the '20s and '30s ... into the '40s too I reckon.' The old man looked out across the sand bars to the Indian Ocean with its breakers crashing ashore. 'I remember 'im boilin' the new planks in real long tin troughs to bend 'em like. Lit fires underneath for the full length o' the trough, maybe fifteen foot or more.'

'Any idea how big this ship was, did he say?'

'Like I said, smaller than the *Endeavour*, seventy, eighty feet 'e reckoned. Twenty in the beam, two masts.'

Jameson knew this to be approximately the length of a schooner or frigate. 'And he never took you, when you were a young boy?'

'No. I actually grew up in New Norfolk and that's where I spent most o' me younger years workin' around the timber mills or the hop farms in season, like me own daddy. By the time I was old enough to be interested, the ship had disappeared?'

'Disappeared?'

Elspeth. 'How?'

'Bushfires swept up the coast, burnt through the swamps when it was dry one summer. 'e went back for more planks one year after the fires and said all the superstructure was gone. Burnt. Then when 'e went back a few years later 'e said the sand dunes had shifted due to the strong winds we get 'ere when the Roaring Forties blow through and 'e couldn't find any trace o' her.'

'Winds like the ones pickin' up now,' Sandra Mundy said, stepping out onto the porch with a tray of drinks while Ted held the fly wire open.

'This is Sandy,' Ted said. Sandy was Bob's sixty-one-year-old daughter. She passed drinks around and Jameson noted Ted Lanyard's eyes follow her. If he didn't know any better, he'd say Ted was keen on this country *girl*.

'You said south of here.' Elspeth said to Bob.

'What was that?'

'You said your grandad found this ship south of here. Where exactly?'

'Christ knows lovey. It's all a blur now-a-days. There's some pretty rough coast down the west o' Tassie.'

'Did ya tell 'em about the Aboriginal carvin's?' Sandy asked her father, leaning against the dodgy balcony rail with a frosted mug of ginger beer.

'We was getting' to that,' Bob said. 'Have you heard about the Aboriginal carvin's?'

'Yes, Ted took us to the Mount Cameron site.'

'Don't let no other elders hear yer call it that,' Ted spat. 'It's called Preminghana now since we took back the land from the invading whitefellas in the 1990s.'

'Sorry, Preminghana.'

'Rum anybody?' Bob floated a half bottle of Bundy before the gathering.

'Why not.' Jameson reached out with his glass.

Elspeth placed an open palm over her glass. 'Bit early for me. So, you were saying ... the carving?'

'Yeh. Down at Sundown Point eight kilometres south o' here,' Bob said, 'there's about forty of 'em on layered mudstone. Concentric and overlapping circles, straight lines and crosses. But there's one in particular that some say was carved by a white man. It shows distinctly the petroglyph of what could only be a sailing ship.'

'We were talking about it earlier with Ted.'

'Some academic types from the university come up and studied 'em years ago. They reckon it's a coincidence, that it's just crosses and lines carved into the stone but I'm tellin' ya it's a ship. It's the same academic types what refuse to believe any Europeans arrived here before Captain Cook. Ignorant sods. I know enough about me history to know it's quite possibly a Dutchie, a Spaniard, a Portuguese or a Chinese junk even, what got blown off course hundreds o' years before Cook came along.'

'Or an English privateer,' Calvino started before he was stared down by the others.

'Dad should know his history,' the daughter cut in. 'He watches enough documentaries on the telly.'

'Well, there's not much else to do these days with old age catchin' up. Anyways,' Bob continued, 'them carvings were discovered by some schoolteacher bloke in 1933. Now my daddy took me to see 'em the first time in the late thirties when I was eight or nine. They reckon they go back two thousand years.'

'But not the ship!'

'No, no. I told yer, that was chiselled by a whitefella for some reason, probably tryin' to copy the blackfellas work. That's one o' the later carvings, maybe a coupla hundred years old.'

Jameson. 'And you seriously think it represents a ship?'

'Yep. A full square-rigger. Go look for yourself. If yer know anything about ships, you'll recognise it the moment ya see it.'

Ted Lanyard looked at Calvino. 'Told yer,' he said, his smug smile exposing white teeth.

It was time to water the raspberries. Sandy grabbed the watering can and headed down the veranda steps to the tap. 'Have you still got that bolt?' she asked her father over her shoulder.

'Yeh that's right,' Bob leant forward on his seat. 'I've got a bolt off the ship 'ere somewhere.'

'A bolt!' Jameson tried to curb his interest. This was the first tangible clue of any description.

'Yes, copper I think it is,' Bob said. 'About a foot long. It's in the shed if I remember correctly, I'll go see.' The old man stood shakily. 'Bloody leg,' he cursed, snatching his walking stick. Bob opened the fly wire door turning back to Jameson inviting him to follow. 'Actually, I could use a hand.'

Jameson bounced to his feet. 'Lead the way.'

Inside, the weatherboard house was dark after the bright sun, cool, musty in places, otherwise it smelt of fresh baking and ginger beer. Bob caught Jameson looking into the lounge room in passing, and in particular at a double-barrelled shotgun proudly sitting on brackets over the mantelpiece. 'That was me daddy's,' Bob said. 'Yer like huntin'?'

'No. But I like old guns.'

'That's a Husqvarna break action twelve gauge made in 1912.'

'Does it still fire?'

'Bloody oath. Wanna shot?'

'Ah,' Jameson thought about it. 'Better not.'

Jameson stepped from the backdoor into a hectare of unattended fruit trees and hedge-thick blackberry bushes strangling a perimeter fence leaning on a twenty-degree angle. One supported the other. Poison the blackberries and the fence would fall. The shed was no better. On a fifteen-degree lean, the mill-sawn weatherboards leant precariously against the rusted chassis of what old Bob Mundy said was once his daddy's prized Dodge truck. "57 Dodge.' Bob said, noting Jameson's interest. Bob pushed the shed door open. It squealed on its one remaining hinge. For a workshop in disrepair Bob seemed to know what was where. He reached up to a shelf of paint tins for a rod of solid metal about three hundred millimetres long with a green patina.

"Ere it is. That's copper don't ya reckon?'

'Definitely.' And Jameson recognised the hull bolt immediately as off an early sailing ship.

'How did you end up with this?'

'Well like I said granddaddy took timbers from the ship's hull and 'e ended up with heaps o' these too. That's the only one left. Dad used 'em for one thing or another.'

Jameson rolled the two-kilo copper bolt over in his hand, thumbing brittle encrustations loose when he exposed a small mark. The broad arrow stamp of the British Empire. Jameson felt renewed excitement.

'Ya can have it if ya want,' Bob said.

'Really?'

'Yeh. It's no good to me. Take it. I'm glad it's found a home with someone what appreciates it.'

'Thank you. That's very kind of you Mr Mundy.'

'Call me Bob.' Old Bob screwed up his face as his leg gave him grief. 'There's somethin' else I remember ...'

'Oh.'

'Yeh. I remember me daddy tellin' me that granddaddy said there was a two-pronged tree growin' out of the middle of the ship.'

'Like a forked tree?'

'Yes. An oak he reckoned. An oak in the swamps o' west Tasmania ... strange eh. His thoughts were that the wood from the ship had grown a tree. Well we know that's impossible. But as I said ... an oak?'

'That was burnt too I guess, in the bushfires?'

'Yeh, apparently.'

Jameson backed out of the collapsing shed, itself a relic of another era, which he imagined would disappear soon, along with old Bob, when something caught his eye. 'Where did that come from?'

Bob looked at the metre roll of patinated copper sheeting, furled like a carpet with jagged edges. Holes were spaced in the metal every few inches or so. 'Ah yeh,' Bob grinned. 'Yer got a good eye lad. That's off a ship too.'

'Off this same ship?' Jameson asked, holding up his gift.

'No.' Bob was silent a moment, rubbing his chin. 'It's copper. I've had it for bloody years. Someone gave it to me. That come from 'round 'ere.'

'Oh?'

'Yeh, there's the remains of a smaller ship buried under all them logs in the estuary. There's always been talk of a shipwreck there, but there's a hundred ton o' logs on top of it.'

'It's copper sheathing off a ship's hull,' Jameson said. 'You can see the holes where it was nailed to timber.'

'Yeh, that's what I was told.' Bob stared at the artefact, valued for its copper and not it's history.

'It wouldn't be where the treasure rumour started would it?' Jameson asked.

'Nar, I don't think it's old enough, but as I said, if there is a ship there, it's well and truly buried. You may as well take that too if yer want it. I fancied usin' it for somethin' but it's been sittin' there since dad died.'

They left old Bob and daughter Sandra far richer in knowledge than they first expected. Sundown Point was only a short drive south of Arthur River. Now early evening, the February sun floated above the clear horizon, casting long shadows on what was proving to be a tantalising puzzle. The wind had died off, the sea had lost its wrath, and the deserted coast possessed a haunting charm. They parked at the edge of the dunes watching the approaching sunset.

Elspeth took a moment. 'Beautiful.'

Ted Lanyard almost whispered. 'Yeh, me ancestors called this place Laraturunawn.' Suddenly he grew animated severing the reverie. 'We better not stuff about, there's bugger all moon tonight an' it'll be black as me grandaddy's armpit 'ere in an hour.'

They followed Ted down an old animal track to the beach and rocks below, following single file like obedient children and shortly came upon the petroglyphs, displayed across the landscape, appearing and disappearing at natures bidding for millennia, a primitive gallery with each exhibit hiding ancient secrets. Many were carved where they had fallen, stacked neatly on a sharp angle where the rocks had formed, millions of years earlier.

Circles were predominant, lines criss-crossing, geometric patterns staring back like alien faces. They were spiritual. They demanded reverence. Like a landscape of ancient rune stones that only indigenous peoples from the dawn of mankind could possibly understand.

With Ted's permission, Jameson clambered from stone to stone, snapping photos on his mobile, searching for *ship rock*.

'Ever been to Stonehenge?' Elspeth asked no one in particular.

'I was there in the 90s,' Andre said. 'Fascinating.'

'Well, I feel these petroglyphs are equally significant in their own spiritual way.'

Ted Lanyard was impressed. 'Yes, us first peoples believe they was sacred to the ancients. Several elders have seen ghosts of their ancestors here.'

'Ghosts,' Claire stepped closer to Elspeth.

'Yeh, but them good ghosts, as long as they are respected. As long as this sacred place is respected.'

The final thread of fiery sunset blinked out beneath the horizon, like molten iron being quenched in a trough. The temperature dropped noticeably, and a gentle breeze picked up, wisping about them like spirits of the dead.

'Found it!' Jameson's excited voice broke the silence from where he stood twenty metres away, one foot hooked up on a large circular slab of layered mudstone one metre in diameter.

'It's not like the others,' Jameson said. 'It's sitting over here alone, and it doesn't appear to be a part of the larger collection,' Jameson flooded the stone with light from his mobile. The others circled about. 'And if that doesn't look like a ship with two masts I don't what else it could be.'

The stone had a natural flaw running through the middle on a five-minutes-to-four angle. Jameson used his hand to brush loose sand off its surface exposing more of the stone. Now they could all clearly see that the flaw was represented exactly in the same position as the join on the two halves of the miniature plaster cast.

'Oh-my-god,' Andre took the two half plaster casts from his safari coat pocket, unwrapping them with care. 'Will you look at that!' There was no mistaking the match between the cast and the petroglyph.

'Well, I'll be buggered,' Ted grinned scratching his chin. 'You'se were right after all.'

The crude carving of the hull of the *ship*, shaped more like an orange wedge, was demonstrated either side of the flaw in the petroglyph, with two masts, yard arms and ...

'They must be gunports,' Andre said, pointing out the obvious.

'What was the cryptic message?' Calvino asked. 'Something about turning your back?'

'*Turn your back on the truth*,' Claire said, turning her back to the petroglyph and looking back at the other carvings.

Elspeth. 'I can't imagine the meaning being literal, Claire.'

'The inscription around the edge of the plaster mould said *turn your back on the truth*, right?'

'Right.'

'So!' Claire scoured the distant dunes to the north. They all did likewise.

'Is it pointing a finger to another rock carving I wonder?' Andre suggested. They all gaped into the nearest dunes, but the approaching darkness was unrelenting.

Instantly a whistle reached them from a dune a hundred metres away. Ted Lanyard recognised the darkened figures. 'That's Wayne and Kev,' he said waving back. 'They're a coupla elders, cousins actually. They're on duty this week, lookin' out for idiots that come 'ere an' desecrate the site.'

'Really?'

'Yeh mate. We've had all sorts of shit go on 'ere, whitefellas taking souvenirs. Once, years ago, the bloody museum cut one of the carvings off the cliff face with a bloody great bushman's saw and carted it away to the museum. Bloody vandals. Now this site is *our* land again. *Our* responsibility.' A second whistle summoned Ted. 'Better go see 'em, tell 'em what yer up to, back in jiffy.'

While the others watched Ted clamber back over the rocks and climb the dune, Jameson stood transfixed staring into the glyph. 'We've got to turn it around, look at the back of it.'

'What?'

'*Turn your back on the truth*,' Jameson repeated. 'It's telling us to inspect the back of the stone. Look, it's not like the others, it's a separate ... it's different.'

'How are we going to flip it? It must weigh a ton.'

'Nah,' Calvino weighed in. It was time to redeem himself even if just a little – and he already had a large driftwood branch wedged behind the edge of it.

'Calvino!' Elspeth glanced back at Ted who was now a fading silhouette disappearing over the dune, .along with his cousins.

'It's shifting,' Calvino wheezed, putting his back into the leverage. 'Give us a hand.'

Jameson joined him. Andre joined Elspeth nervously watching for the return of the sacred site caretakers. Claire fetched another sturdy branch and, jamming that alongside Calvino's, she weighed in with her shoulder also. Thirty seconds later they had the metre-wide, five hundred kilo rock on its edge, propped in the sand like some great medallion. Jameson panned his mobile phone torch to the rear of the rock. It was flat, clearly a large laminate of mudstone like the other petroglyphs but a stand-alone specimen.

'Anything?'

Jameson brushed it down. 'Can't see a thing, it's clean. Jesus!'

'Try the edge,' Claire said. Calvino ran his own torch around the circumference. 'Nothing!'

Jameson inspected the indentation where, they assumed, it had been lodged for nearly two hundred years. There was nothing but compacted sand, a perfect mould of the rock. 'There's got to be something.'

Carefully the rock was dropped back into place and they stood around staring in silence.

'It has to be a clue.'

'What else could it be? Why would anyone make this plaster copy if it wasn't important?'

'True.'

'The more I look at it, the more I think it was carved by a white man,' Jameson said. 'Made to look like an indigenous carving.'

'I agree.'

'Now what?'

Elspeth looked at the time on her phone. 'It's nearly eight. We're supposed to be in Stanley by now,' she said of the four-bedroom Airbnb they had booked in the seaside township on the north-west coast.

'Anyone know how long it is to Stanley?' Calvino said, secretly pleased he had eaten a pie earlier.

'Google maps,' Elspeth said, 'says one hour four minutes.'

'Did anyone call to tell them we'd be late?' Claire asked stifling a yawn. It had been a long day with a deflating end.

'I did back at Arthurs' when we had a signal,' Elspeth said. 'And the owner's texted me the code to the key safe.'

With darkness came the wallabies and the pademelons, and eerie screams in the blackness warned them the Tasmanian devils were hungry. Sundown Point certainly was a spiritual and haunting place and Claire would swear later she saw wandering spirits.

'Maybe the treasure *was* found years ago,' Calvino said, joining the others waving to Ted and his cousins as they drove off.

Claire was sullen. 'Or maybe there wasn't any to find in the first place.'

'Listen guys,' Jameson said. 'We have evidence in the written word that the bullion was buried here on the west coast, and you heard old Bob when he said the discovery years ago was all hearsay, there's no proof it was found.'

CHAPTER EIGHT

Stanley – 403 kilometres by road north-west of Hobart ... 'Is the second-last major township on Tasmania's northwest. Population, less than 500,' Elspeth read aloud, floating her torch over a booklet on north-west Tasmania.

'What's the attraction?'

'Well, it's one of the most charming historic sea-side villages in Australia, that's the attraction. Settled by the Van Diemen's Land Company in 1826, and today,' Elspeth read on, 'it relies on tourism and commercial fishing and is under the jurisdiction of the Circular Head Council.'

'Circular Head,' Calvino laughed at the analogy.

'Circular Head as in head of land Cal, not that thing resting on your shoulders ... ah! And speaking of which, there's The Nut.'

Everyone took in the view through the windscreen. Driving north-west along the Bass Highway through some of Tasmania's prettiest rural countryside, Stanley's famous Nut, an impressive geological feature, stood proud and alone in the darkness, a silhouette in the night. Like an Egyptian sphinx, guarding the coastline against evil gods that may lurk in the wild unpredictable sea here – Bass Strait.

Andre eased his van off the Bass Highway and onto the Stanley main road where a four-kilometre country road led into the seaside village perched beneath The Nut on the waterfront of a seahorse-shaped spit of land.

'A volcanic plug,' Elspeth read aloud of The Nut. 'First discovered by Bass and Flinders when they explored the coast here in 1798.'

With the village nestled comfortably at its base, the Nut dominated the skyline with its steep sides rising 143 metres. The township was quiet. A few lamps lit the main street otherwise the village was in darkness.

'Shoot! The pub's even shut.'

'What have we got to eat?' Calvino muttered anxiously.

'You had a coupla pies earlier, you've done okay.'

'Claire ate one.'

'Half.'

'I've got a packet of Oreos,' Andre offered.

'And I've got two packets of chips.'

'We won't starve then.'

'Where are we staying?'

'Alexander Terrace. It runs from the town square to the waterfront ...'

'And there it is,' Claire leant over the driver's seat pointing out the signpost next to the statue of the lone soldier – a memorial to soldiers lost in The Great War. In such a quaint tiny town the street was easy to locate.

The cottage was picture perfect. Two front rooms overlooked Stanley's tranquil bay. The sign on the gate read *built mid 1840s.* Recently fully restored and now an Airbnb the stone residence with a rough render was a one floor cottage with two skylighted attic rooms squeezed into the roof space. Although the small house was originally built by Captain Fred Marshal, it was now named after the current owners, *Granny Ettie's Cottage.*

Andre managed to park the van up a narrow side lane built for a horse and cart, where activated security lights lit a quaint English cottage type garden of vegetables and herbs out the back.

It was 9.15PM.

Claire made straight for the larder cupboard. 'God I'm hungry.'

Calvino joined Claire at the sparsely stocked cupboard. 'Anything to eat?'

'Not unless you like split peas, bi-carb, flour or tomato paste. There's not even a tin of baked beans.'

Andre. 'Well, they're not obligated to stock the larder.'

Elspeth pushed the other two aside. 'There's a tin of mushrooms, arborio rice, chicken salt.'

'Chicken salt! Jesus!'

Elspeth looked about for Jameson who was already surveying the garden, fossicking about under giant leaves, searching for anything edible. He returned with a 300-centimetre zucchini and a handful or fresh oregano.

'They don't call me hunter and gatherer for nothing,' the chef grinned. 'Someone find me a decent sized pot.'

Twenty-five minutes later chicken salt seasoned zucchini risotto with tinned mushrooms, oregano and parsley never tasted better. Andre's Oreos went down a treat for dessert and Calvino supplied a warm six pack of Moo Brew Pale Ale.

After dinner it wasn't long before sated bellies turned to talk of gold. 'So,' Jameson said fondling his copper hull pin, courtesy of old Bob Mundy. 'We can safely say my stolen chocolate tin belonged to someone looking for the treasure.'

Elspeth. 'That's a no brainer.'

'How old's that tin anyway?' Calvino asked.

'1950s.'

Andre sighed. 'We've got more questions than answers.'

'Andre, can you show us what you have on your laptop?'

Andre flipped his Apple Mac open on the kitchen table and pulled the folder from *Dropbox* where he called the file *Mother's Rose Garden Photos*. 'No one would ever find it hidden there.'

'Unless the thief was fond of roses.'

'Yeh right.'

'Good work Andre.'

'So, I've filed the photos in what I ascertain is chronological order.'

Calvino pulled a face. 'Chronic what?'

'Chronological order. By date. I've listed the images according to the periods I think they were taken. Some were easy, like the Victorian photos and, up to the 1920s, then it became harder, as there are no dates on anything.'

Elspeth. 'That tells me that the accumulation was by one or two persons only, that they were so familiar they didn't write names, dates or addresses on them.'

'So, the tin turns up at a garage sale in 2019,' Claire said. 'Where was the address?'

'Cross Street, New Town,' Jameson said. 'I do remember the owner telling me the house belonged to a Mrs McCutchen and that she was her granddaughter.'

'Who was the granddaughter? The one having the sale?'

'Yes. She was helping granny clear out stuff as the house is to be put on the market.'

'Granddaughter huh. Was she a McCutchen?'

'Originally yes. But she married a Smith; her name was Tanya Smith.'

'How old is she, thereabouts?'

'Tanya? Late fifties.'

'McCutchen you say,' Andre pushed his glasses further up the bridge of his nose and scrolled the mouse down the screen. 'That name rings a bell. McCutchen ... McCutchen ...'

'Well, it should ring a bell. It came from McCutchen's house.'

'No, I seem to recall reading it ... aha ... there we go.'

'What have you got?'

'Skelton Henry McCutchen.'

'Bloody hell!' Calvino snorted. 'Who'd call their kid Skelton?'

Claire. 'Who'd call their kid Calvino?'

'Touché.'

'Captain Skelton Henry McCutchen,' Andre read on from letters and notes scanned onto his computer, 'was a master mariner who sailed schooners from Melbourne to Circular Head ...'

'That's here,' Claire said.

'Clever girl, you must have eaten your Weetabix this morning.'

'Ha!'

'Captain McCutchen married Eliza Hickey – nee Jones – in Melbourne in 1858. They had five children, oldest one a daughter, Maud. Her claim to fame was her impersonation of the Australian Magpie ... well, well ... By the 1860s Captain McCutchen was trading in New Zealand. He ... oh ...'

'What?'

'He drowned in a river along with his first mate and ship's boy at Tokatoka in New Zealand in 1871 aged 38. Thirty-eight, that was young.'

'And he had five kids.'

'It says here that the river punt he used was overloaded with Kauri logs.'

'Sad.'

'I wonder if whoever put this collection together in the 1950s found the gold.'

'If there ever was any gold.'

'Like I said before,' Andre said. 'We have more questions than answers.'

7AM. Stateroom aboard the Italian tall ship Amerigo Vespucci...

Inspector Ray Wilson found the cannoli a little rich. The deep-fried pastries filled with ricotta and candied orange peel were far too sweet for his taste; especially this hour of the morning. Wilson swallowed awkwardly and sipped his freshly poured espresso to rebalance the taste buds but gulped too much and burnt his mouth. *Jesus!* He was having a bad time of it.

Orfeo De Luca chose not to notice but was quietly amused at the policeman's discomfort. The inspector and his cronies at Police Headquarters had done little to help him. Not since the Second Word War had the Vatican come so close to possibly discovering the whereabouts of the missing skull of Saint Adamo Abate. De Luca glanced out the stern window of the ship's stateroom and noted the harbour-master pilot's tugboat slowly catching up in their wake. Soon the pilot boat would be alongside the Italian ship to take the inspector, who had invited himself aboard for the farewell cruise down river, back to port, along with the pilot.

For De Luca it was too little too late.

'They were at Arthur River today, you say,' Wilson was asking questions to answers he should have known, being the local law. 'How do you know this?' the inspector asked De Luca. 'My boys said nothing to me of this.'

My boys.

De Luca fidgeted; he was less than happy. 'Frankly, Inspector, you have been of little help.'

'I'm sorry I couldn't have been of more help Signor De Luca,' Wilson said. 'But we have no evidence that the group of treasure hunters, for that's all they are, treasure hunters, fossickers, have any real clues to go on.'

'Then why have they driven north to the Arthur River and last night booked accommodation at the village of Stanley?' This sharp reprimand came from the new arrival on board, flown in to assist De Luca. She was less diplomatic. As a Polish translator employed by the Vatican Magdalena Kowalski was wife to a Vatican Swiss Guard and one of the few women holding a Vatican City passport. Magdalena was forty-seven, an accomplished poet with a master's degree in Applied Archaeological Sciences from the International Telematic University in Rome. Growing up in Poland, a country with an advanced attitude to women's liberation, she was fiercely independent and soon came to the attention of the head of the *Dicastero per la Comunicazione* or Dicastery for Communication at the Vatican. She spoke fluent English and Italian as well as her native Polish. 'Can you explain why they would suddenly take a drive to the north of your island?'

'I ... um ... I'm not too sure really,' Wilson was feeling less than confident. He eyed the plate of savoury Ciambella di San Cataldos but his earlier confidence waned and he now felt uncomfortable. If he had learnt anything, it was the fact that he needed to make his own arrangements and get to Stanley himself.

'I don't think you realise, Inspector, just how important it is to the Vatican, to the faithful, to have this sacred relic returned to its rightful place,' Magdalena didn't suffer fools lightly. 'I have been privileged to have been shown the remains of Saint Adamo Abate. They are locked away beneath the Vatican, in the underground vaults beneath The Pinacoteca.'

Inspector Ray Wilson had recently read of the Pinacoteca in the Vatican's brief to the Hobart police department. He knew it to be an eighteen-room museum of some 42,000 square metres with more than 70,000 exhibits. It had one of the world's largest collections of artworks from medieval times to the 19th century. Gathered by Pope Pius XI, many works were retrieved from Paris after the Congress of Vienna, in 1815, when Napoleon lost to Wellington at Waterloo. Other collections contained the Gregorian Egyptian Museum and the Gallery of Geographic Maps.

'It is heart wrenching to think someone, even two hundred years ago, would sever the head from the saint's body for financial gain,' De Luca told Wilson. 'But now we have reason to believe the skull itself is intact, and still contains the sacred *Ratnaraj Ruby*.'

The inspector heard the commotion to starboard as the pilot pulled alongside. It was time to leave. But this determined Pole wasn't letting him off lightly. Magdalena Kowalski leant in close before the man had a chance to stand, leaning on both arms of his chair, her breath smelling strongly of coffee. She really was a most attractive older woman, with light brown hair to her shoulders, slim athletic body and sharp facial features. She allowed the slightest of smiles, yet her eyes were cold.

'The bejewelled remains of the saints,' Magdalena said. 'These precious reliquaries are of immense importance to the Catholic Church. They were once worshipped holy objects believed by 16th and 17th century Catholics to be protectors, personifications even, of the glory of the afterlife. They are as revered today as they were centuries past,' she said in her fluent accented English. 'Unfortunately for now, they are kept in vaults away from public view.'

Inspector Ray Wilson stood awkwardly while a steward stood by with his coat. 'As I said I'm sorry we were not of more help,' he said half-heartedly. 'What are your plans now, if you don't mind me asking?'

'Plans?' De Luca propped the stateroom door open. 'Our plan ees, to sail to Stanley, pick up the trail as you say in Engleesh. We sail the west coast I am thinkeen. More quicker.'

7AM. Stanley...

Elspeth was first to stir. 'Couldn't sleep.'

'Me neither,' Jameson pulled aside the thick woollen curtains flooding their bedroom with sunlight heralding a perfect morning. 'I've got too much on my mind.'

'Me too. I need a walk,' Elspeth said. 'Get some fresh air before the others get up.'

'I'll come with you.'

Like any visitor waking up in Stanley for the first time, Elspeth and Jameson headed to the waterfront. 'This has got to be one of the most picturesque seaside villages in Australia.'

'I wouldn't argue with that,' Elspeth conceded. Circling overhead a dozen noisy Pacific gulls seemed to agree. Almost hypnotically Jameson and Elspeth were drawn towards the fishing boats, where

Alexander Terrace terminated at a quaint wooden train station, decommissioned years ago. 'I didn't know trains stopped here?' Jameson said.

'It wasn't for passengers, it was for logging, 1913 'til the late 80s.'

'Logging huh?'

'Yes, I read about it recently. Taking logs from Black River and from here to Burnie. It was used to transport farm produce also.'

Shaded by The Nut were delightfully quaint seafarer cottages. The property boundaries here were determined by the Van Diemen's Land Company, who settled Stanley in the early 19th century. The cottages were similar but different, each unique with its own story, its own archive of past memories.

'Cute town,' Elspeth said. 'But I can't say I would like to live here. A bit quiet.'

'Sure. But what about when we retire? I can see you El, feet up on an ottoman knitting me a knee rug ...'

Elspeth grabbed Jameson's arm and spun him about with a serious smile. 'We!'

'What?'

'We. You said when *we* retire. You're thinking well ahead Jameson Rowley.' Elspeth smiled flirting with the thought. 'Are you trying to tell me something?'

Jameson feigned a serious face. 'That wasn't a marriage proposal.'

'Marry you!' Elspeth shot back without taking breath. 'Don't flatter yourself.'

Jameson deflated. It was time to revise. They passed a real estate advertisement board screwed to the picket fence of yet another delightful cottage.

'Here,' Jameson said cheerfully. 'For Sale ... Three bedrooms, one bathroom, large back yard ...'

'Even has a great view,' Elspeth studied the photos of the interior of the property displayed on the advertisement poster. 'I wonder how much a place like that would go for.'

Jameson stopped. 'You're kidding me!'

'What?'

Jameson stepped up to the placard, a board as tall as he was with clear digital photos of the master bedroom, the kitchen and the living room with its fireplace and, most importantly, the fireplace mantel.

'Will – you – look – at – that?' Jameson stared at the photos, his mouth wide open.

Elspeth stood at his side, cocking her head one way, then another. 'The master bedroom's nice, but the kitchen looks a bit small ... and I certainly don't like that wallpaper.'

'No! Look above the fireplace.'

'Oh!' Elspeth ran an eye over several framed family photos on the mantelpiece, a late Victorian marble cased clock and a rather ugly pair of pottery dogs, which she recognised as early 19th century Staffordshire. 'You mean the spaniels? They're hideous.'

'Not the dogs ... look carefully.'

Besides a deck of cards and the TV remote a large pewter plate propped on a stand. 'You mean the plate?'

'Yes El. It's an *officer's mess* plate. But not any old plate, look carefully.'

'Oh wow!' Now Elspeth shared Jameson's enthusiasm. Around the wide rim was an engraving of a two-masted ship and the words *Royal Navy* in a ribbon cartouche. On the opposite rim were the words *Mess No.7*, also within a ribbon cartouche. 'Trust you to notice that. It's nice.'

'Nice! It's nice alright. And rare as well. And if I didn't know any better, I'd say it's been under water, see the evidence of encrustation.'

'Like, off a shipwreck?'

'Exactly. And it's been cleaned. I've got to get a look at it.'

'What? Now?'

'Yes now.'

'But it's just after seven.'

Jameson swung the white picket gate open and was knocking on the door before Elspeth could protest. After three attempts, each knock rising in patience and volume Jameson hurried around the back of the cottage. Elspeth waited on the footpath.

'Bugger it,' Jameson re-joined Elspeth. 'No one home.' He slipped his mobile from his pocket and tapped in the estate agent's number.

Elspeth. 'What are you doing?'

Jameson held up his hand for silence the moment his call was answered. 'Morning. This is Jameson Rowley, I'm outside the cottage in Alexander Terrace ... the property you have listed ... and I am here with my wife and we would like to look through the property ...'

Elspeth. 'Wife!'

Jameson waved his hand at Elspeth and placed a finger to his lips. 'Yes, my wife, Elspeth Rowley ...' after a brief conversation. 'You could meet us here at nine. No sooner ... okay, nine it is. See you shortly then.'

'What have you done?'

'She'll be here to meet us at nine. Her office is only two hundred metres away on the main street.'

'We have no intention of buying this cottage. Jesus Jameson. All this just to get a look at that plate.'

'That's no ordinary plate El. Just play along. We'll tell her we've been looking at properties up the coast here.'

'Here you go again. We!'

Beyond the age of mid-life crisis, Barbara Hordern's Botox lips were unfortunately dominant, veneered liberally with candy red lipstick. Probably waxed onto her lips while she was driving. And any semblance of the business woman maintaining a moderate figure had been abandoned years ago. Jameson had an immediate image of Barbara sitting in one of the town's cafes enjoying cake and coffee or the extended lunch. After all there couldn't be a great deal to do in this seaside village, not for an older real estate agent anyhow.

Jameson forced his eyes away from the black roots of her beehive coiffure, where the peroxide was wearing thin, like the hair itself.

'Jameson Rowley,' he introduced himself and shook the woman's offered hand. 'And this is my wife Elspeth,' Jameson lay on the, *my wife,* line thick with an accentuated smile.

'Elspeth,' Barbara reiterated. 'What a lovely name.'

Once inside the inspection was cursory while Jameson made faces behind the agent's back for Elspeth to keep the woman preoccupied. He desperately wanted to inspect the plate. Once in the kitchen, Jameson excused himself *for another look at the living room*. He disappeared before Barbara knew what was happening.

'U-hum,' Barbara Hordern stood in the living room doorway uncomfortable at Jameson touching what did not belong to him, especially with the owners absent.

'Oh ... ah ... this old plate caught my eye,' Jameson smartly sat the pewter charger back on its stand on the mantle. Elspeth flushed. *He could be a little more subtle.* 'I love this room,' Jameson lied. 'Especially the wallpaper. Nobody wallpapers these days.'

The agent didn't know what to think, but wallpaper butterflies didn't seem, to her, to be to the young couple's taste.

'Yes, quite,' she said. 'It's ... ah ... different.'

Jameson continued the performance rolling his head in a wide arc up one wall of butterflies and down the other, then momentarily stopping at the plate.

'That's supposedly off an old shipwreck,' Barbara said.

'Sorry ... ah ... what was?' Jameson wasn't a good actor. 'Oh! The plate. Off a shipwreck huh? What? Around here?'

'Down Arthur River way apparently. The owner of this cottage is a friend of mine, well in a small place like Stanley everyone's friends really. Eve's father found that old thing in the sand dunes back in the seventies. It's off an English ship someone told her. Eve saw something similar on the Antique Road Show, so she dragged it down from the attic, scrubbed it up and sat it there as a conversation piece.'

'Oh.'

'Eve you said.'

'Sorry?'

'You said Eve was a friend of yours.'

'Yes.'

'Are they away?'

Now that question had Elspeth redden once more.

'No,' Barbara said. 'They went to Launceston for the night ... shopping. We don't have any department stores in Stanley, but I guess you know that.' If the real estate agent was uncomfortable with the stranger's questions, she didn't show it. 'They'll be back by lunch time if you want to make an offer on the cottage.'

Elspeth waited for the agent to walk out of sight. Once Barbara rounded the first corner into the main street she let loose. 'Don't you ever put me in that position again,' Elspeth was less than happy. 'You could have been a bit more subtle. What were you thinking? Picking up the plate!'

Elspeth's wrath washed over Jameson's infectious enthusiasm. 'HMS *Sting*, Elspeth. The plate was engraved HMS *Sting* under the Royal Navy cartouche. It was covered with encrustation, but I could just make out the ship's name.'

Elspeth was gobsmacked. 'Really ... I ... how?'

'Because it's off the wreck of the *El Delfin*. The *El Delfin* was once the HMS *Sting* remember?'

'Yes, yes, but ...'

'Clearly when the HMS *Sting* was decommissioned by the Royal Navy and changed hands much of the sundries were sold with it.'

'Like mess plate utensils,' Elspeth walked back up to the advertising placard to study the pewter plate in the photo.

'Exactly. Mess plate utensils, glassware, armaments,' Jameson went on. 'Probably even the old, salted pork in the barrels stored in the hold was sold on as well.'

'Are you certain it said HMS *Sting*?'

'As certain as I know I love you,' Jameson slapped his hands about Elspeth's cheeks and stole a kiss.

'Steady lover boy.' Elspeth looked back at the photo. She could read *Royal Navy* and *Mess No.7* and now the encrustation was clear. 'So, what have you got in mind?'

'I'm glad you asked.' Jameson was pleased to see a change in mood. 'We'll make ourselves known to Eve the owner, that's what I have in mind.'

Claire and Calvino had made a grocery store run and now Elspeth and Jameson walked into a haze of crispy bacon-infused fug. 'Jesus Claire, turn the stove fan on.'

'Oh yeh ... right.'

While the aroma of frying bacon and eggs and toast permeated the small cottage, the old-style percolator bubbled coffee. Jameson left the front door wedged open and repeated the process at the back door. 'It's a wonder the smoke alarm didn't go off.'

'You *have* been busy,' Elspeth said, watching Claire cook up a storm; a rare event indeed. She stood with Jameson at the rear door. Escaping smoke spiralled about them like inquisitive spectres. Jameson snatched a piece of buttered toast while Claire sliced the bacon onto kitchen paper.

'Where have you two been anyway?' Claire winked at Elspeth.

'We have just had the most extraordinary luck.'

'Oh?'

Jameson explained the discovery of the pewter plate. Claire and Calvino listened in silence. 'Are you kiddin' me?'

Elspeth. 'No. All true.'

Andre stepped from the bathroom, where he had heard their entire story also. 'That's crazy,' he said, still towelling a body best kept concealed. 'What were the chances of that?'

Calvino. 'So, what do we do now?'

'We ... maybe El and I, need to have a chat with the cottage owner,' Jameson said. 'Her name's Eve.'

'And how do you plan to do that without looking suspicious?'

'Yeh,' Claire said. 'Without drawing attention, or look like some fanatic treasure hunter?'

'Well,' Jameson said. 'Apparently they'll be home from Launceston in a few hours.'

'They've been to Lonnie shopping,' Elspeth added.

'So, I'm ...'

'We!'

'We ... are going to just rock up and knock on her door,' Jameson looked chuffed. 'And tell her I saw the photo out front. Simple as that.'

Late morning, Jameson made his fifth reconnaissance and finally noted a 2005 Mercedes in the driveway of the cottage for sale. He fetched Elspeth. With a spring in his step Jameson literally danced up the front steps and onto the porch. He rapped knuckles on the door. Eve proved a most amiable person. The retired florist lived with her second husband, Henry Eddystone, retired public servant and their two Shih Tzus, Cookie and Wiki, and weren't averse to a visitor or two. Jameson decided to be upfront about the house inspection.

'We love this cottage, really adore it, but for professional reasons we may have to settle in Burnie.'

'Burnie!' the Eddystones said in chorus, looking to each other. Their lips pinched. Eve made a round of instant coffees regardless. After all company was rare in Stanley and Eve thought they were such a sweet couple. Jameson watched Henry drop three sugar lumps into his cup before joining them on a floral-patterned couch with matching armchairs. Briefly lost for words they all studied the butterfly wallpaper.

'Jameson loves your wallpaper,' Elspeth broke the silence.

'Yes,' Jameson smiled. 'I have a thing about butterflies.'

'Really? Well, you'd be the only one. My mother and father hung that paper themselves twenty years ago.'

'Oh.'

'They passed several years back, and I inherited the cottage,' Eve looked at the wall. 'And that ghastly wallpaper.'

'Barbara told me your father found that old plate in the sand dunes,' Jameson said impatiently, pointing with his coffee mug to the pewter charger on the mantelpiece. 'Back in the seventies I think she said.'

'Well yes. Daddy came home with it after a fishing trip. Said he stubbed his foot on it walking over a dune.'

'Fascinating.'

'Henry thinks it was off a really old shipwreck lost down the coast ... don't you Henry?'

Henry nodded, eyeing the sugar bowl and considering another lump of sugar, if only Eve would look away. 'It was near Arthur River I believe.'

'Is that where your father found it,' Elspeth asked. 'Arthur River?'

'Somewhere there,' Barbara said vaguely. 'I think so.'

'I was cleaning out the workshop years ago,' Henry said, 'when the plate turned up and I showed it to Eve and she said, *golly, daddy found that in the dunes years and years ago*. Then she saw a similar piece on the Antiques Roadshow, and it was valued at fifty pounds.'

'Wow!'

'So, I cleaned off the white shell stuff stuck onto it, as best I could anyway,' Eve said proudly. 'And Henry made a stand for it and ... well ... voilà. There it is.'

'Did your father find anything else?' Jameson asked reining in his enthusiasm, struggling to keep a poker-face.

'No, he didn't. But Henry did,' Eve said. 'Tell them Henry.'

'Oh, some years back, probably late 90s, I used to help a friend who was an auctioneer who specialised in local house auctions, you know, entire estates, old farm properties selling up. And we'd find all sorts of interesting things in the outhouses, barns and cellars ...'

'Henry was the man holding up the item to be auctioned,' Eve smiled, her eyes filled with pride.

'Ross Brown Auctioneers he was,' Henry said. 'And ten or twelve years ago ...'

'More like fifteen,' Eve interrupted.

'Yes, well. Ross attended a deceased estate auction on the coast here. A lovely sandstone homestead in the Regency style, 1830s it was, a few miles north of Arthur River down the coast.'

'It belonged to a Captain Clifford Jeffrey of the British Army, didn't it Henry? He bred sheep. Good grazing country there, it's the sea air and all that.'

'So,' Henry won back the stage. 'Ross was completing the inventory with the deceased's only child and sole inheritor ...'

'Benjamin Jeffrey.'

'Yes. Benjamin Jeffrey, a man in his mid-seventies, when Ross said, 'That's about it then, isn't it?' And Benjamin Jeffrey said to Ross, 'Yes' ...'

'Except for the shipwreck stuff under the stairs,' Eve intervened, again.

Jameson's eyes widened.

'What shipwreck stuff? asked my husband. So, the homeowner takes Ross to a cupboard under the servant stairs at the rear of the property and blow me if it's not full of artefacts off an old ship. So Ross asked, 'Where did this come from?'' Eve stopped to look at her husband. 'You tell the story Henry.'

Henry, accustomed to his wife's interfering, went on unfazed. 'Oh, Benjamin Jeffrey said. 'Granddaddy Cecil found it at a swamp, miles from here down the coast. He said he thought it was a ship that wrecked there over a hundred years ago and he only found it because there had been a recent bush fire which had exposed the timbers. Granddaddy was a keen duck shooter see and he was at the swamp on a shoot with two young nephews. When did he find the wreck? Ross asked Benjamin. Before the war, says he. What? 1930s? No, no. Before the First Word War. 1912, thereabouts. Have you been to the wreck site? Ross asked him. Oh, I've tried don't you worry. But I'll be blowed if I can find it.'

'What happened to all this ... *stuff?*' Jameson asked.

'Oh, it was all sold the day of the auction. There was even a cannon amongst the items. A small one. Made of bronze I do recall.'

'Benjamin Jeffrey, you said,' Jameson made a mental note.

'Yes, but he died about ten years after the auction.'

'So, it was listed as the Jeffrey Estate?'

'That's right.'

Jameson crashed through the cottage front door bursting with enthusiastic energy. Elspeth wasn't far behind him. 'Boy, are we onto something!' Andre was absorbed, reclining in an armchair studying the contents of the *Mackintosh's Quality Street* sweets tin on his laptop while Calvino and Claire played *Scrabble*. Three faces fixed on the pair.

Jameson started. 'Wait 'til you hear what we've found out.' Like verbal ping pong Elspeth and Jameson related the news.

'So, is anyone in a hurry to return to Hobart?' Jameson said.

Their audience was momentarily speechless. Calvin spoke first. 'Ah ... why's that?'

'You don't qualify for that question,' Jameson grinned. 'You're unemployed.'

'I can hang about a few more days,' Claire said.

'And I can get more days off with one phone call,' Jameson looked to Elspeth.

'I'm good for a couple of days,' she said.

Andre jumped to his feet, sitting the laptop on the table ready for business. 'If this means were getting serious, then I'm in. Because when you hear what I have just read you'll be most excited,' Andre's eyes actually sparkled. 'Very excited indeed.'

Jameson. 'Claire.'

'What?'

'Do me a favour and call the property owner and ask if we can extend our stay ... say ... another three nights.'

'Stay here?'

'Yes, Stanley can be our base. It's only an hour drive here, or an hour drive there, from here. If that makes sense.' Jameson turned to Andre. 'Andre. What have you unearthed?'

Minutes later they found some kind of sense out of the material from the tin. Andre already had the file open. He split the screen into photos and writings.

'I suggest we start at the end and work our back,' Elspeth suggested.

'You mean, who owned the chocolate tin last and collected together the scrapbook's contents.'

'Exactly.'

'That's exactly what I was up to when you walked in.' Andre nodded seriously. 'I have done handwriting analysis on Jane Foderingham who signed the Spanish prisoner letters, using a false name Jasmin Bradenham – working as overseer at the Parramatta women's prison – and Anwyn Blizzard of the robbery in Cadiz fame, we all agree is the same person.'

'Yep, got it,' Claire said. 'I think.'

'And as we will see, I believe the chocolate tin, as found at the garage sale by Jameson, belonged to Anwyn Blizzard's descendants,' Andre said. 'Anwyn has handed down the information she had, along with the half plaster cast to her children and so on ...'

'And the descendants have been adding to the collection since.'

'Up until the 1950s at least, when the trail goes cold.'

'Yes.'

Jameson said. 'How did the plaster artefact end up in the tin?'

Andre shook his head. 'Good question. First, we need to re-familiarize ourselves with the major players. Anwyn Blizzard, a comely thirty-nine-year-old fearless woman determined and toughened by a Moroccan prison, Captain Alexander Ramsay Fate, his First Mate Ambrose Smith and ship's cook Walter Grubb.'

'Walter was identified as the man found dead in the vault, didn't we read that somewhere?' Elspeth said.

'That's correct. And we have a major player in the game, Septimus Tilley, by all accounts an overweight forty-seven-year-old bookkeeper.'

'There's a few of them around,' Calvino laughed.

'Okay, so?'

'So, here's my theory. Captain Alexander Ramsay Fate had a soft spot for Anwyn, they were probably lovers. When she opted to live under a false name in Parramatta – she would have had her reasons – Fate has made a perfect miniature plaster copy of the petroglyph, under which he and a few others hid the gold ingots and the saint's bejewelled skull. He then made two neat fitting halves and gave one half to Septimus and one half to Anwyn under the pretext that if anything happened to him ...'

'Who? Fate?'

'Yes. If anything happened to him, like the Yankee whale captain who was to take him back to the *El Delfin* wreck site cheated on him or killed him, Anwyn would only have to find Septimus and together she and he could retrieve the gold later. However, at the last minute Septimus has decided to go along with Fate on the voyage, on the whaler *Siren*, to retrieve the gold. The ship we know was wrecked on Flinders' Island and Fate drowned along with all the others. Septimus was the only survivor.'

'But Anwyn would have known where the gold was hidden anyway, wouldn't she?'

'I'm not that certain,' Andre said. 'I'm thinking, for security reasons, Fate has stashed the gold for safe keeping with only a handful of helpers.'

'Thomas Mogg!' Claire grinned at a sepia photo of an older man in double-breasted sports jacket with a walking cane. 'What a name huh? Sounds like the name of a cat.'

'What?' Calvino said. 'Thomas?'

'No stupid. Mogg.'

Elspeth studied the photo on the screen. 'If I didn't know any better, I'd say that photo was taken here in Stanley. You can just make out a steep incline in the landscape that looks awfully like The Nut,' she said of the unique landmark.

'I think you're right El,' Jameson said.

'Now I think about it, I went to school with a Mogg,' Calvino announced. 'Who lived up the coast here. Terry, I think his name was. He was in boarding school in Hobart.'

'Yeh, I think Mogg's a common name up here.'

'There's a few photos with Stanley connections I've observed,' Andre said.

Elspeth had a thought. 'There's a local museum here in an old church I noticed.'

'Why didn't I think of that?' Andre berated himself. 'Of course. Perfect place to start.'

The Parish Hall for St Paul's Church was converted to a local museum and run by volunteers as charming as the building itself. Mary Wilmore was overwhelmed. Where in one day she may only have half a dozen visitors, this morning she was inundated with five at once. 'Fifteen dollars,' seventy-seven-year-old Mary smiled.

'Fifteen dollars!' Claire's jaw dropped open. 'It's not the Louvre.' Claire hadn't meant to sound rude and Mary tried not to look offended.

'That's for all of you my dear,' Mary said. 'Three dollars each.'

'Oh.'

The museum was a mix of old shop showcases crammed with locally donated items since its conception in 1973. Outwardly the collection was so eclectic yet localised that the museum could be mistaken for a well-stocked antique shop. In fact, there were too many items to display behind glass and many larger items like porcelain chamber sets sat on top of the cases.

The hexagonal ceiling was Baltic pine, painted cream. The moderate church-hall's stage, once the scene of amateur pantomime, was now dedicated to maritime history displays, where Andre and Jameson gravitated first.

'Have you lived here all your life?' Elspeth asked the volunteer.

'Yes, born and bred.'

'Thomas Mogg does that name ring a bell,' Elspeth then enquired. 'He lived here in the middle of the 19th century?'

'There were Moggs living here for generations. I can't say the name *Thomas* Mogg rings a bell, but we have an archive here that you are welcome to use.'

'Archive. Excellent.'

While the others inspected the exhibits, engrossed in the seaside village history, Elspeth was made comfortable in a back room where the entire history of Stanley and Circular Head, was stored neatly and efficiently in two Edwardian blackwood filing cabinets.

Claire joined her. 'Where to start, eh?'

Elspeth flipped through the files, A-Z. 'M-M-M for Mogg. Ah there you are, Mogg.' There appeared an entire Manilla folder on the Mogg family. 'Excellent.'

'Thomas Mogg ... there you are.'

'Too easy.'

'Thomas was licensee of an inn for several years. Sixteen years in fact. 1869 to 1885. There's another photo of him, looking very dapper too I must say. This photo is dated 1871 when he was sixty-six.' Elspeth read on. 'Oh, he died there at his inn in 1885.'

Claire. 'Where's the inn? Stanley?'

'No ... oh check this out, it's Hadspen.'

'Jesus, it wouldn't be the ...'

'Red Fox! Yes Claire. He owned the Red Fox.'

Claire poked her head around the door back into the museum. 'We're onto something here guys.'

'My my, you *are* interested in the area,' the museum volunteer stepped into the crowded back room, slightly bemused at her company. 'I'll fetch more chairs.'

Elspeth thanked the woman before adding, 'Do you mind if we take photos, make copies of these documents?'

'By all means, make yourselves at home. It's so nice to have visitors with such interest.'

While everyone sorted through the manila folder Andre walked fingers over the files in the cabinet. Back under 'M' he noted a leather-bound book not much larger than a prayer book, tied with a thin leather boot strap. 'Well, what have we here?'

'What have you got?' Jameson recognised the book as early 19th century immediately. 'Vellum too,' he said of the goatskin cover. 'Nice.'

Andre turned pages, respectful of the artefact's age. 'It's a diary.' A bookmark fell free with the archive reference number and in cursive script it read: '*Diary of Matron Violet Newham. Hobart Town 1818-1824, Sarah Island 1824-1833 New Norfolk 1833-1846 Stanley 1847-1868.*'

'Did you say Sarah Island?' Jameson asked, knowing how rare such material was from that short-lived settlement, known as Hell on Earth.

'Yes.'

'What's the Matron's name again?'

'Newham.'

'And that diary was with the Mogg file.'

'Yep.'

Elspeth studied a rather restricted family tree, attempted by an archive volunteer in the '70s by all accounts. 'Violet Newham, listed as matron.'

'That's her.'

'Well, she was Thomas Mogg's mother-in-law.'

'Okay. Now we seem to be getting somewhere.'

'Thomas Mogg married a servant girl Agnes (nee Newham) in 1824. She was with child. Mother and child died of complications at birth 1824. How sad.'

Andre multi-tasked, one of his assets. Listening to Elspeth and reading pages from the diary. 'This is fascinating, absolutely fascinating. The archive in Hobart should have a copy of this untapped historic wealth.' Andre read excerpts from Violet's daily life, when the name Thomas stood out from the page dated 1825. *Thomas has disgraced the family. He has disgraced the memory of Agnes' and their child, lost to Lord Jesus at birth.'*

'Wonder what he did?'

'I need to read this in its entirety, it's fascinating.'

'It could be a clue to the whereabouts of the gold,' Claire reminded them. 'After all this Mogg bloke owned the Red Fox Inn where the plaster mould was found.'

'Yeh right.'

'Hello,' Andre's eyes widened. 'What's this? 1826. Page after page is written in some kind of code.'

'Code?' Calvino leant across to take the diary. 'I was a Boy Scout, code's my forte. Pass it here.'

'Gently, gently Cal,' Andre was hesitant. 'It's nearly two hundred years old.'

'Gee Andy, that's older than you.'

'Cheeky sod.'

Back in the museum Mary Wilmore's voice sang with enthusiasm. More visitors. 'That'll be six dollars thank you.'

Claire recognised strong accents and peered through an opening in the doorway. Carefully closing the door, she turned to the others. 'Hey guys, you're not going to like this – two suits just arrived.'

Elspeth. 'Suits?'

'Yeh, like *Men in Black* kinda suits.'

Jameson rushed to the door. 'They aren't regular tourists. They look South American?'

Andre. 'Or Mexican?'

With the front door open a cool draught filtered through to the back room. Elspeth caught a familiar, yet subtle scent. 'That's the scent of aftershave I smelt lingering at Storm Bay after the break in,' she told Jameson.

'Are you sure?'

'I'd bet my life on it. Can't you smell the cloves with undertones of cedarwood?'

Calvino. 'That's impressive El.'

'Bastards.' Jameson stepped back to the door.

Elspeth grabbed Jameson's wrist. 'What do you think you're doing?'

'Confront the bastards.'

'That would not be a good idea. If they're off that Mexican ship then they are thugs, gangsters. They're probably armed.'

'Do you reckon they're following us?' Claire said.

'Seems like it.'

'How did they find us?' Calvino said.

'Don't know but we've gotta get out of here.'

Elspeth cast an urgent eye over the documents. 'What about this lot?'

Andre. 'We'll have to come back.'

Jameson closed the diary and slipped it into his pocket. Elspeth was horrified. 'Wh-what are you doing?'

'What's it look like?'

'You can't just take it. It belongs to the community.'

'I'm only borrowing it.'

'Jameson! No!'

'I'm with Jameson El,' Andre said, wary of rebuke. 'We'll return it once we've deciphered the code and copied everything.'

'Like the plaster artefact Jameson stole from Red Fox Inn.'

'I'm going to post that back when I get a chance.'

'Post it back,' Elspeth shook her head.

'Anonymously.'

'Stop arguing,' Claire and Calvino hissed from the back door. 'Hurry.'

Parked twenty metres down main street outside the Stanley Hotel, an orange-gold Mitsubishi ASX SUV stood out to Jameson as a hire car. In the back seat he recognised a silver sports bag. A narrow, metre-long and ominous shape. The others watched on.

Claire. 'What's Jameson doing?'

Jameson made a quick inspection around the vehicle before joining the others in the *Provedore 24*, Stanley's specialty grocer, a hundred metres away, and directly across the street from the museum. The five spread out in the confined yet delightfully stocked store with its narrow shelves of delicious locally crafted products, overwhelming the owner who noticed her visitors appeared more interested in what was happening outside the shop, than within.

'Is there anything I can help you with?' the owned asked. Andre bought a freshly baked sour dough loaf.

'Here they come,' Claire said. The five peered through the shop window. Even the shopkeeper stopped to watch two tall and solidly built men hurry from the museum. They stopped at the footpath and appeared to be urgently searching for someone.

'Friends of yours?' the woman asked, enjoying the sudden electricity of espionage occupying her peaceful life. A moment's tension filled the air as the men looked directly towards the provedore. All inside backed into shadows with the subtlety of a drunk uncle at a wedding. Even the shopkeeper was on edge. Suddenly the two foreigners returned towards their vehicle.

'Do you have a back entrance?' Jameson asked, his voice urgent.

'Back entrance,' Calvino's chest rose. 'Why should we hide from these guys? Why don't we just ...'

'Through here,' the woman directed Elspeth and Claire first. Andre hooked his extra-large sour dough under his arm and plucked his change off the counter. Jameson and Calvino followed. Jameson smiled to the shopkeeper. 'You've never seen us, okay,'

The woman winked. 'Seen who?'

From the lane behind the provedore, they could just make out the SUV. The two men were circling the vehicle. They were far from happy.

'What's their problem?' Elspeth asked.

Jameson held up an ice cream stick broken into splinters. 'What's that?'

Andre recognised the trick immediately. 'You didn't?'

'Sure did.'

Calvino. 'Did what?'

Andre answered for Jameson. 'He gave the beggars a flat tire. The old *stick a match in the valve* trick.'

'Really? Excellent.'

Jameson grinned ear to ear. 'Not just one tire, I managed three.'

'No! Good work,' Claire slapped Jameson on the back. 'That'll slow 'em down.'

Back at the cottage Calvino was confident, running a keen eye over the coded pages. 'This is boy scout stuff.'

Claire was first at the sour dough; slicing the warm crust, she spread it liberally with butter then vegemite. 'It looks all googlichooks to me,' she said of the code, her mouth full.

'That's the idea,' Andre said.

'They, or she, has made up a code, breaking each cipher word into five letters,' Calvino explained. 'And to start with, our crafty Matron has reset the alphabet.'

'How do you mean, reset the alphabet?'

'Take a hat, drop twenty-six individual pieces of paper into the hat, each marked with one letter, then you pick them out randomly one at a time. So if 'M' comes out first it replaces the first letter of the alphabet, letter 'A'. Then if 'Q' is plucked out next, well that would replace the letter 'B' and so on until you have A-Z.'

'But all the coded words are five letters.'

'Yes, so let's say the message is ... *meet me at the cemetery*, before coded it would read.'

And Calvino scribbled the words in groups of five letters on a scrap of notepaper. *Meetm eatth eceme tery.*

'The last word is only four letters,' Claire noted.

'Glad you asked. You choose one letter, any letter, as a fill in to make it appear 5 letters. Say 'e' Then the cipher would be meetm eatth eceme terye. The last letter is just a throw in, easily deleted when the full message is decoded. Once the message is written in this way, you then exchange the letters for the cipher corresponding letters, pulled from the hat, and bingo. You have a coded message.'

'Or in our case a coded diary.'

'There's a bit of work to do here then.'

'Yes, there is,' Calvino said. 'But you'll find once you understand the most common two, three and four letter words used in the English language, its becomes easy.'

'Words like ...?'

'The, and, at, of, have, but, from, that ...'

'I get the picture.'

Calvino studied the diary's coded pages. The others peered over his shoulder. 'Hey, I need space alright. I can't concentrate with you all gawking.'

'Fair enough,' Jameson said. 'How much time do you need?'

'Coupla hours at least.'

'Fine.' Jameson dared to take his mind off gold briefly. He flicked the pages of his new acquisition, Mrs Beeton's antique cookbook. 'I'll start organising dinner,' he volunteered. Not because he particularly wanted to but because he knew he was the best cook in the town. 'What do you guys fancy?'

'Seafood,' Claire called out from the bathroom. 'We're in a fishing village for Christ's sake.'

'Perfect.'

With Calvino busy with the diary, Andre returned to the photos on his laptop. 'I'll arrange these photos in some sort of consistent order.'

Hursey Seafood on Alexander Terrace, fifty metres from the fishing boat docks, is Stanley's fresh seafood go to. 'Crays are in season,' Jameson acknowledged the huge aquarium in the foyer full of what some call rock lobster. However, the price was worthy of such a delicacy. Elspeth, Claire and Jameson settled for blue eye trevalla instead; Tasmania's premier fish trawled at depths of forty to five-hundred metres. A firm white fleshed fish versatile in the kitchen and adored by all aficionados of the fish dinner. Claire's belly rumbled.

'How are you going to cook it?'

Jameson watched the two large fillets being wrapped in paper. He knew his fish and there was no end of recipes for this delicacy. But a recipe in his recently purchased old cook book had caught his eye. 'I saw a recipe in Mrs Beeton's for fish and dill pie with shallots.'

'Yum.' Claire didn't realise it, but she was salivating. 'Can we have chips?'

Jameson had cooked his double-fried Kennebecs for Claire dozens of times and had to confess, they were bloody good. 'Chips with pie? Why not?'

'And salad,' Elspeth said, leading them out of the shop and to the only supermarket five minutes' walk away.

'Done it,' Calvino finally read a coherent line and sat back in his seat. '*July 29th, 1825*' he read aloud to Andre, his only company the past hour and forty minutes.

This date alone had Andre take notice. 'Really. Where's it say that?'

Calvino pointed out the pattern of words where the numerals that formed the date were spelt out in letters. In other words, *July twenty-ninth, eighteen twenty-five.*

Calvino had Andre's undivided attention. He read on the few words he had decoded. '*Thomas has returned from the wreck site with the skull of Saint Adamo Abate ...*'

'What?' Andre thought Calvino was up to his old tricks.

Calvino repeated the sentence. '*Thomas has returned from the wreck site with the skull of Saint Adamo Abate ...*'

'Where's it say that?'

'Here.' Calvino underlined his notes in pencil.

'Where's it say *Saint Adamo Abate?*'

'Jesus Andre, right there. Why? Don't yer believe me?'

Andre leant in to face Calvino, one hand each on the arms of his armchair. 'Calvino, look me in the eye and tell me you aren't pulling my leg.'

'I'm not pulling your leg, right?'

Convinced Calvino was telling the truth he straightened, 'This is amazing. Bloody amazing. Read on.'

'Ah ... *Thomas has returned from the wreck site with the skull of Saint Adamo Abate but no gold. I am worried. The head of such a sacred person terrifies me. I fear the devil afoot in my sleep.*'

'Oh my god, this is far bigger than I could ever have imagined. Brilliant work Calvino.'

'What's brilliant?' Jameson, Elspeth and Claire filed back into the cottage. 'Have you cracked it?'

'He sure has.' Jameson had never seen Andre so excited.

'I told yer I would.'

'He's actually found written reference to Saint Adamo Abate,' Andre gushed.

'What?'

'Read on.'

Calvino re-read what he had so far.

'This's crazy.'

'Amazing.'

'Amazing? It's bloody brilliant. At last something we can sink our teeth into to. Something tangible.'

'Who's this Thomas again?'

'Thomas Mogg remember,' Claire said. 'The son-in-law and a bit of a loser by all accounts.'

'He's mentioned earlier in the diary,' Andre said. 'He was the one born at sea.'

'Where?'

'Indian Ocean, in 1805 on the voyage from Plymouth to NSW.' Andre's photographic memory never ceased to amaze. 'Thomas's father was a soldier in the 88th Regiment of Foot sent to New South Wales. Later the family were re-stationed at Hobart Town's Anglesea Barracks in 1815. Thomas was given a good education in the army and signed up as a soldier when he was 17. He married a servant girl ... ah ...'

'Agnes.'

'Yes, that's her. Agnes. Agnes, nee Newham, two years later.'

'Agnes Newham, that's the matron's daughter?'

'Yes. Agnes and Thomas's newborn child died of complications at birth. So, by 1825 Thomas was twenty years old and already an old man in many ways, with convictions for drunkenness on duty. In 1825 he was discharged from the army for insolent behaviour.'

'That's amazing detective work.'

'I've managed so far to cross reference many facts with emigration and army records,' Andre added.

Jameson studied the coded sentences. 'Well done Cal, keep up the good work.'

Elspeth. 'Where are you at?'

Calvino pointed to the first page.

Jameson. 'How much time do you need?'

'Maybe another hour.'

While Andre continued with names, dates and events in an extensive Google search online, Calvino deciphered the coded pages. Jameson paced about impatiently. He checked Calvino's notes. 'Christ Cal, your scrawl is harder to read than the coded stuff.'

'Okay,' Elspeth could barely hide her excitement. 'What were the last entries again in the diary, before matron used code?'

'Here,' Jameson read Andre's notes. 'We do know that only a handful of the *El Delfin* crew knew where the gold was buried.'

'How do you know this again?'

'Matron Violet Newham wrote it in her diary,' Andre said.

Claire. 'Ah yes.'

'Where does this matron come into it again?'

'To answer that I need to explain the connection between the matron and Septimus Tilley, the now forty-eight-year-old bookkeeper,' Andre said. 'He survived the wreck of the *Siren* and was eventually rescued by sealers who sailed him across to Port Dalrymple, now called Launceston. It is late 1814. He is ultimately accused of being one of the crew on the stolen *El Delfin* wrecked on the west coast, who did not report to the authorities about the disaster and is charged with piracy in Cadiz. He is sentenced to fourteen years hard labour and sent to Hobart Town. Fourteen years is tough. But he keeps schtum and settles in.'

'Schtum?'

'Keeps quiet. After four years' hard labour, he is put to work as a bookkeeper and in 1822 is transferred to Sarah Island, a new penal settlement on Macquarie Harbour, west Van Diemen's Land. By now, as a prison bookkeeper, he has some freedom.'

'Like what?'

'Well, he's not locked in a cell with the other poor devils who are doing hard labour hauling logs through freezing waters for one thing. He would be able to free range the island as it was near impossible to escape anyhow.'

'Free range. I like that analogy.'

'Here he meets the prison Matron, Violet Newham. The same matron who kept a diary.'

'This is how we know so much?'

'Exactly.'

'By now it's 1825 and certain mitigating circumstances speed things up.'

'Oh, what's that?'

'Well, Septimus knows where the gold is hidden. He was there with Fate at the time. He was waiting for his release. But then, out of nowhere he learns that the *El Delfin's* first mate, Ambrose Smith, also survived the *Siren* shipwreck on Flinders Island.'

'Where has this Ambrose been all this time?'

'He's been in gaol in Sydney, but is set to be released. The pressure's on as Septimus, now 56, knows that Ambrose will go directly to retrieve the gold.'

'Jesus,' Calvino scratched his head. 'You couldn't write this crap in a mystery novel, could yer?'

'Yes, well ... so, Septimus has no choice but to confide in the Matron, the woman he has befriended over the years at Sarah Island. She in turn enlists the aid of her son-in-law, a soldier in Hobart Town, Thomas Mogg. Mogg couldn't do it alone and he recruited another acquaintance very familiar with the West Coast, Percy Stagg, who circumnavigated Van Diemen's Land with none other than the explorer James Kelly in the whale longboat, *Elizabeth*, back in 1815.'

'So, who got there first?'

'When Mogg and Stagg arrived – they sailed in Stagg's ketch, *Salty* – they were told by a small party of prospectors on the coast that there had been another man seen in the area with ... wait for it ... three pack mules.'

'That'd be Ambrose?'

'Three mules?'

'Yes.'

Calvino. 'Why three?'

'Think about it.'

'To haul gold.'

'Clever boy.'

'Ambrose Smith did indeed beat the others to the petroglyphs but storms over the past decade had shifted sand, exposing previously undiscovered petroglyphs and burying others.'

'Guys! Guys!' Jameson flipped through notes and footnotes. 'Matron says here, in the coded pages, that her son-in-law returned with the skull and no gold. I put it to you that the gold is still behind the petroglyph, in a deep hole well hidden, we just didn't look properly the first time.'

Elspeth. 'This guy Captain Fate who initiated stealing the gold in Cadiz was a Royal Engineer in the British Army was he not?'

'Yes.'

'So, he would be the ideal man to rig up some engineered hiding place for the gold. He wouldn't just throw it in a hole, it can be presumed that he hid it well.'

Calvin was like a big kid. 'Made some booby traps and stuff d'yer mean?'

Elspeth. 'You've been watching too much *Tomb Raider.*'

'Well,' Calvino said in his own defence. 'It's what people do, isn't it, booby trap treasure.'

'In the movies, Boy Scout, yes,' Jameson said.

'I don't believe the gold is in its original place,' Andre said.

'Oh.'

'No, I believe that Mogg and Stagg reburied it because they knew Ambrose was sniffing about. I also put it to you they re-hid it and that Mogg ripped off his mother-in-law, Matron Violet Newham. But he gave the bejewelled skull to her to appease her.'

'But the skull's priceless.'

'Exactly. I reckon they were spooked by its presence.'

'Superstitious?'

'Exactly.'

Jameson. 'Andre. What do we know about this Percy Stagg? Could there be a clue there if the gold was moved?'

Andre checked his notes. 'About James Kelly's crewman. Percy Stagg,' he read out loud. 'Born to James Stagg and Nancy Stagg (nee Baker) in Manchester in 1796. Sailed to NSW in 1810 as emigrants, free settlers. From the age of 16 years, in 1812, Percy worked with the sandalwood trade, even sailing on one occasion to India. In 1814 he was in Hobart Town and the following year he met James Kelly the explorer, and circumnavigated Van Diemen's land in the open whaleboat *Elizabeth.* They officially discovered Port Davey, Port Macquarie, Sarah Island etc. So, he knew the West Coast well. Percy became a master mariner and traded the coastal ports in his ketch,

Salty. He married Susanna Managua, the only child of Herbert and Agnes Managua and they had eleven children.'

'Only eleven?' Claire puffed out her cheeks.

Calvino shot Claire a salacious grin. 'No Netflix in those days.'

'Is there any note of wealth in his later years?' Jameson asked Andre. 'Like he may have found gold?'

'Outwardly? No.'

'For peace of mind I'm going back to the petroglyph and checking it thoroughly,' Jameson said. 'At the worst, we'll know for certain if it was actually hidden there by Captain Fate in the first place.'

'Yes, there'd be some clue, surely.'

'That's a point.'

'I agree,' Elspeth said. 'We should find out if it actually existed.'

Claire's stomach growled reminding her of her own survival. 'Guys, it's six already. Can we start cooking ... Jam? I'll start washing the spuds.'

Next morning...

It was barely eight o'clock. Andre's older model Mitsubishi van, now more dirt road brown than white, drove south-west once more, easing down Arthur River Road and into the small community of Arthur River.

The usually quiet little town was alive with activity.

'What the hell?'

Heavy machinery, clearly brought in from Launceston or Hobart, was busy at the estuary. Finding somewhere to park was problematic. Andre pulled in at the Arthur River Cruises carpark and the group hurried along the foreshore towards the activity on the northern side of the estuary where they joined a dozen or so spectators. Catching sight of old Bob Mundy leaning on his walking stick watching the activity, Jameson rushed ahead. 'What's happening Bob?'

'Hey there, yer back already.' Bob pushed his fisherman's beanie back to scratch his forehead. 'Jameson ain't it?'

'Yes.'

'Contractors moved in at the crack o' dawn,' Bob said, his eyes hidden behind smudged, cheap shades. 'Making all this 'ere racket with that crane and semi-trailer. Got a deal with National Parks they say, to remove them logs.'

Jameson watched on in silence for a moment considering the contractors' task ahead. The estuary shoreline here was strewn with trunks of blackwood, myrtle, eucalyptus, sassafras and Huon pine all washed down river over the decades, and now turned to driftwood scattered and stacked amongst the rocky shoreline. It was an unusual and awesome sight, an act of nature, like a graveyard for the wilderness.

As Elspeth, Andre, Calvino and Claire joined them, a truck-mounted telescopic crane raised six massive tree trunks in one hit, chained at the centre. Finding their equilibrium, they swayed menacingly like some drunken sailor on the deck of a listing ship before being dumped like skittles onto a semi-trailer flat tray.

'What on earth are they going to do with it?'

'Dunno really,' Bob muttered. 'Word is they wanna use it in craftwork. It *is* good timber mind, there's even a bit o' Huon in there,' Bob said of the valuable Huon pine. 'But it seems a bit over the top to me.' Bob's eyes sparkled when he saw Elspeth. 'You back to find the treasure love, eh?'

Elspeth politely smiled before turning to Jameson. 'Let's not waste time, let's get to Sundown Point and prove your theory right or wrong and get back to Stanley.'

'Why are yer back 'ere anyways?' Bob asked no one in particular.

'Ah ... we just wanted to check something out down the road.'

'So yer headin' back through 'ere again then?'

'Yes, in an hour or so I guess.'

'Good, you'll be ready for a cuppa about then, call in on the way through if you have time. You're most welcome.'

Bob watched the *treasure hunters'* van cross the narrow single lane bridge heading south before crossing the road to his home. Daughter Sandra, he knew, would have his breakfast ready by now.

'I suppose that would make good craft wood,' Claire said of the contractors. 'There'd be a few bucks worth there, eh?'

'Sure,' Elspeth said. 'But it seems a pity, it's been there for years. It's a part of the landscape.'

'Some bureaucrat making a buck probably.'

Twenty minutes later. Sundown Point, home of the Aboriginal petroglyphs...

Indigenous elders, Wayne and Kev, sat around a small orderly campfire at the edge of the car park. A brew steamed in a billy, the same way it bubbled and boiled every other day. The two men recognised their cousin's and fellow elder Ted Lanyard's visitors, from two evenings before.

'Ted about?' Jameson asked.

'No mate,' Wayne, the skinnier of the two, smiled back. 'He'll come along later I reckon.' Wayne fanned smoke from his eyes, turning his head this way and that.

'We just want to take some more photos of the petroglyphs,' Elspeth said, holding up her mobile. 'If that's okay?'

'Sure love, go for it.'

The small silver coin tangled amongst Kev's wiry black chest hairs and dangling around the man's neck caught Jameson's eye. It was not so much the coin but the portrait of Spain's Ferdinand VII that stood out. 'Where did you get that coin?' Jameson asked.

'This?' Kev pinched the coin between forefinger and thumb. 'Found it.'

'Really? Do you mind if I ask where?'

'I found it 'ere actually. Years ago, wasn't it Wayne?'

'Yeah mate.'

'Do you mind if I have a look at it?'

'Sure mate.'

The leather strap, worn and black with wear, wasn't leaving Kev's neck any time soon. In fact he told Jameson he'd been wearing it for ten years at least. 'In the shower, to bed, everywhere mate. Where I go it goes.'

'It's his lucky charm,' Wayne chuckled. Jameson leant forward for closer inspection, catching a whiff of black tea on the man's breath.

'Where exactly did you find it?'

'In them dunes, a long, long time ago.'

'Spanish?' Andre asked Jameson as they left the two elders to their brew.

'Yep. 1810 four *reale* piece.'

'Hmm. Very interesting.'

'Calvino,' Jameson took his friend by the wrist. 'Keep an eye out. Make sure they don't follow.'

'What will I do if they do?'

'You'll think of something.'

With an ocean coastline so untamed it was no problem finding a two-metre staff of solid driftwood to prise the petroglyph from its mudstone foundation; after all it had been loosened days earlier. Andre, Jameson and Claire eased the metre-wide disc of solid stone into a vertical position before wheeling it to one side. Where it lay the sand was compact, almost cement like. Jameson tapped it with his knuckles. The responding sound was subtle, but ...

'That sounds a bit dull.' Jameson knocked harder. 'If I didn't know any better guys, I'd say it's hollow under there.' The realisation that they may have missed a vital clue two days earlier had everyone on edge. Jameson fetched up a fist-sized rock.

Elspeth. 'What are you doing?'

No answer. Jameson brought the rock down hard. *Now* it sounded hollow. Excitement mounted. Claire found another rock and together she and Jameson alternated blows. A crack appeared. Immediately a fissure parted exposing a hand sized gap. The excitement was palpable. No one said a word. Jameson tore at the thirty-centimetre crust covering the hollow. With some effort the dried clumps reinforced with weed roots broke apart.

Calvino appeared at the run. 'Guys, they're stirring.'

'Well go and delay them.'

'How?'

'I don't know.'

'Ask them if they know anything about car engines,' Andre suggested.

'What?'

'Jesus!' Jameson clawed enough compacted sand away to peer inside the opening. 'Go Cal,' he ordered over his shoulder. 'You'll think of something.'

Elspeth, Claire and Andre crowded about the soccer ball sized hole. 'What can you see?'

'Nothing ... yet.' Jameson pounded his rock around the edges, widening the opening, pulling out vegetation. Suddenly the sides of the lid caved in. 'Christ!'

'What?'

The hole was wide and deep, about the width of an ATM, before exposing a much larger cave in the mudstone, the size of a large bedroom. Jameson crawled inside where he could eventually stand tall, with head room to spare. He shone his mobile torch in a wide arc, searching the natural contours of the cavern. His voice resonated back. 'Nothing.'

'You serious?'

Three sets of eyes peered hopefully into the dark emptiness. Jameson's voice echoed his disappointment. 'There's nothing here. Not a damned thing.'

'What's that?' Claire pointed to a small disc at Jameson's feet, its dull bronze sheen barely catching the light.

Jameson retrieved the object. He recognised it immediately. 'George the third halfpenny,' he said, his words echoing around the empty space. 'He rubbed it clean with forefinger and thumb. '1806.'

Claire slumped back against the rock-faced embankment. 'You are kiddin' me. A bloody halfpenny?'

Elspeth studied the coin while Jameson rechecked the hole using the driftwood staff to pound the cave floor double checking it was solid, looking for any other clues. Nothing. Except a shredded rag, stained violet blue. 'What's that?' Andre asked.

Jameson passed him the cloth. 'Possibly a piece of a bullion bag,' Jameson suggested. Andre recognised the calico material and tiny match-head sized nuggets of indigo, otherwise nothing.

'You know what finding this coin means?' Elspeth said. 'Don't you?'

'Yes,' Andre joined Claire leaning against the rock. 'It proves there *was* something hidden here ...'

'And some cheeky sod left us a calling card,' Claire held up the coin.

'So, the whole venture's been a wild goose chase – the gold was retrieved in 1815.'

'I'm not convinced,' Jameson said. 'We need to finish the coded diary.'

'Guys!' Calvino called out from the rise in the dune nearest the carpark, frantically waving his arms. Without a second to spare the metre diameter disc rolled back into position with a dull thud. Elspeth stepped back to frame her shot, making out she was busy photographing, while Wayne and Ted's happy faces appeared over the sand dune and, with mugs of tea in hand, they saluted their visitors.

An hour and ten minutes after passing through Arthur River, Andre returned, driving the Mitsubishi back across the narrow one lane bridge. He squinted through the windscreen into the sun, still low in the sky. 'Now what?' From the bridge they noted more machinery. If there had been a dozen spectators watching the contractors before, now the crowd had doubled. And there was excitement in the tight-knit community. Andre pulled over near as possible.

'They've found a shipwreck,' a woman rushed to the new arrivals, gushing with excitement.

'A shipwreck?'

'It was hidden under all them old logs,' another shouted. Jameson led the rush, following the trail of crushed button grass where the machinery had flattened the landscape. The logs on the north side of the estuary had been mostly removed and a local bobcat excavator now manoeuvred into position, digging into the sandbar where Jameson and the others now recognised rotting ship timbers. It appeared the vessel had wrecked out in deeper water and what remained of her port side had washed ashore, probably in a storm, many years ago. There was no remaining superstructure, no sign of masts or rigging, but Jameson and Andre agreed it was early 19th century, possibly around eighty feet by twenty-five, and the most likely scenario was that she broke up well before this area was settled, therefore not recorded in the local folklore. Then, over the years, the remains weathered and jumbled with the driftwood trees and became a part of the landscape.

But there was no denying it, the town had treasure fever.

Elspeth was furious. 'Stop ... stop this nonsense immediately. This is an archaeological site.'

Her calls were lost over the sound of crashing surf. She turned to Jameson who was mesmerised by the unique discovery ... Could this be HMS *Sting*? Was this the *El Delfin*?

'Jameson! Help me stop this madness.' As these distraught words passed Elspeth's lips, the bobcat rolled forward, crushing rotted timbers, scooping out a half tonne of compressed wet sand like it was spooning ice cream at a parlour, and with the finesse of the proverbial bull in the china shop.

Jameson and Elspeth charged forward. 'Hey,' Jameson yelled up to the driver. 'What do you think you're doing?' Elspeth stepped in front of the bobcat. Andre, Claire and Calvino joined them.

'Get outa the way,' the driver was a big lad, forty, wearing a wife-beater singlet tucked into boxer shorts accentuating a generous beer gut. His muddy Blundstone boot squashed the brake. 'Move it,' he barked over the motor and surf.

Jameson stared the driver down and tried to keep calm. 'What are you doing man? This is an archaeological discovery. This is history. This needs to be excavated by professionals.'

'Just doing what I've bein' paid for,' the big bloke grumbled back. 'Now get outa me way.'

Andre caught trouble in his peripheral. He saw two men in dustcoats and safety helmets conversed with other men. They weren't local, he was certain of that. In fact, they looked awfully familiar. At fifty metres distant he cleaned his glasses with his handkerchief, replaced them on his nose and squinted. Calvino watched on. 'Hey, isn't that the blokes from Stanley? At the museum?'

'Christ yes! Jameson,' Andre snatched at Jameson's elbow, while Elspeth was joined by Claire, at the bobcat bucket. The driver crunched gears, dropped the clutch and the cat lurched forward before he braked again. Enough to make the two women skip backwards.

'Hey!' Jameson shook Andre's hand free and leapt onto the bobcat step. He clutched the frame reaching in to manhandle the driver, a gorilla of a man. At the same moment Elspeth saw artefacts amongst the excavated sand in the bucket; predominantly shredded patinated copper sheathing from the ship's hull. She reached in to snatch a shard of pottery and what appeared to be bone. The commotion attracted the attention of the two men in hard hats. They started forward.

'Ah ... Jammo,' Andre warned Jameson. But Jameson was preoccupied with his brewing altercation.

On the brink of the embankment the locals spoiled for a fight. On one hand they rooted for the bobcat driver, a local character called Bear. On the other hand, the likes of Bob Mundy and the more respectable locals, weren't too keen on out-of-towners simply bulldozing what was potentially a valuable piece of their history, a discovery potentially good for tourism. And Bob knew Bear only too well. He poked his daughter Sandra in the back with his walking stick. 'For Christ's sake Sandy, get down there.'

Bear rose from the seat and instantly filled the cabin. Jameson suddenly questioned his own bravado. He took one step backwards, but stood his ground.

'Leave it,' Elspeth cried out.

Jameson stood firm, grinding his teeth, balling his fists. Bear jumped from the step, remarkably fit for an overweight forty-year-old. He snatched Jameson by his shirt front.

'You wanna piece o' me?' he barked in Jameson's face. 'Eh?' Jameson was planning his next move. 'Well?'

'Bear!' Sandra shouted at the man. 'Bear! Leave it.'

Bear said nothing. He held Jameson tight. His eyes narrowed. He wanted blood. Behind them the two hard hats approached.

'Bear ... not now,' Sandra pushed in between them. 'I-said-leave-it!' Sandra shoved Bear in the chest. The bobcat driver used his one fistful of shirt to shove Jameson backwards.

'Go,' Sandra ordered Jameson. She turned to Elspeth. 'It's best you all leave.'

Elspeth pocketed her souvenirs from the bucket, recognised the approaching trouble and tipped her head to Jameson. 'Let's go.'

Jameson, obstinate as ever, stared down the gorilla. 'We can't just let them trash this site El.'

Elspeth acknowledged what Andre and Calvino already knew. The men in hard hats were the guys from Stanley. 'Jameson, trust me, we're leaving.'

'El ...'

'*Now* Jameson!'

Mexican cartel boss Maya Hidalgo's head of security, Jorge Diaz, was bemused by the sudden appearance of the troublesome *gringos* from Hobart. First that business in Stanley and now here they were acting like environmentalists blocking progress. By the time he and accomplice Emiliano reached the bobcat they had escaped over the embankment. But Jorge had been amongst the small community long enough to recognise the old man with the walking stick who lived two hundred metres away in the weatherboard home on the upper side of the road out of town. After all, he had seen him sitting on his balcony more than once.

'He's got a bloody nerve,' Bob stood on his veranda eyeing the two thugs heading his way. 'Get in the house,' he ordered Jameson and the others.

'It's alright Bob,' Jameson started. He was angry. Angry at the intruders and angry at himself. He had lost face. 'We can handle this.'

Bob liked his new friends. And Jameson had spunk. But now wasn't the time. 'I said, get-in-the-house.'

Elspeth. 'For god's sake Jameson, do as you're told for once.' Jameson groaned.

Bob followed everyone inside as the two men crossed the road. The old man left the front door ajar and disappeared into the lounge room. Jameson watched Bob fetch the double-barrelled shotgun from the mantle. He wrenched open a bureau drawer, pulled two cartridges from a box, snapped the barrel open and rammed one into each barrel.

'Ah, Bob,' Jameson said anxiously. 'What's the plan mate?'

Bob snapped the barrels shut. Said nothing. Stepped back onto the veranda. Now he spoke as the intruders mounted the steps.

'Not a step further.'

The old man's voice had turned deep and ugly. Bob had to acknowledge, the two men were calm.

'Ah, senor. We are not here to cause trouble,' the taller, better looking one, late forties, had a heavy Spanish accent.

'I don't give a rat's arse. Back off. Get off me property. Now!' And to prove his muscle, Bob pulled back the left hammer.

'Be careful old man. You might ... ah ... how you say? Injure someone.'

'How about I injure you? Now move it.'

'We just want to talk to your friends inside,' Emiliano insisted. 'This is all, si?' Bob jerked the shotgun, re-aiming at Emiliano. Now he sensed the hint of a quiver in the man's voice. *At least one was worried.*

'They're preoccupied,' Bob spat.

'Preoccupied? What this mean?'

'Busy. Savvy? Now bugger off.'

The two Mexicans backed away a few steps before spreading out on the front garden. Smelling trouble Bob oscillated the gun. 'I said bugger off.'

Jorge Diaz was not easily intimidated. 'What is this to you, old man? We want to ask a few questions of your friends. Nothing more.'

'I won't tell yer again.'

Emiliano reached behind his coat. Bob didn't hesitate. He fired a warning shot between the two men gouging a deep hole in his lawn, showering the intruders with dirt and grass.

'Cuidado ... careful!' Jorge put his hands up, palms exposed. Bob pulled back the right hammer. But the shot could not have been better timed. Sergeant Dean Lark pulled the police issue Ford Ranger off the bitumen, parking on the verge of the gravel in front of Bob Mundy's house. He had just driven in from the nearest police station at Smithton forty-seven minutes away, under orders to investigate the discovery of a mystery ship in the sand and unprofessional behaviour. And now, here he was in time to catch his long-time friend Bob, threatening strangers with a shotgun.

'Everything alright here Bob?' Dean asked, closing the car door behind him and donning his officer's cap.

'No it ain't Dean. These here mongrels were givin' me grief.'

Jorge Diaz had heard enough to realise these two were associates. Old friends even. 'We were just leaving,' he told the policeman.

Dean was keen to learn more but also knew old Bob like the back of his hand. 'Bob? What say you?'

Bob scowled at the Mexicans. 'Yeh, they was just leavin'.'

Jorge and Emiliano made to leave when Dean asked, 'My guess is that you two are the contractors here to retrieve logs of forest wood.'

'Si.'

'Si? Spanish huh?'

'Mexicana.'

'Okay then.' Dean hooked a leg onto the second step placing his hands on his hips. 'You have papers I take it?'

'Si. In our vehicle.'

'Then I'll be down to inspect them shortly.' The policeman waited until they were out of earshot. 'Jesus Bob, what are you doing shooting at tourists? You haven't even got a licence for that cannon.'

'They're up to no good Dean. And they're found a shipwreck under that loose timber.'

'So I heard.'

'And they paid Bear a thousand bucks to excavate it.'

'Okay,' Dean watched the backs of the two Mexicans disappear over the embankment towards the shoreline. 'That's also what I heard. That's why I'm here.' Dean noticed the gathering at Bob's front door. 'My, you are a busy boy today. You've got visitors.' Jameson and Elspeth waved a greeting through the flywire.

'Treasure hunters,' Bob winked at the cop.

'Historians actually,' Elspeth was first onto the veranda. 'They are bulldozing an archaeological site,' she said urgently. 'You've got to stop them.'

'And you are?'

'Elspeth Poole. I'm assistant curator at the Tasmanian Museum. We have a major breach of the law underway at the shoreline.'

'Best I go see what's happening then. But I'd like to speak with you when I'm finished here.'

They sat about enjoying instant coffees, a huge pot of tea and Sandra's freshly baked tea cake. Andre connected his laptop to Sandra's Wi-Fi.

'Clearly they suspected all along there were the remains of a ship buried under that driftwood,' Jameson said, his mouth full of cake. 'That's why they got the contract to remove the timber. Who'd bother checking?'

'I agree,' Elspeth said.

'If that's the *El Delfin* it's all over for us,' Claire reached for another slice of cake.

The thin fragment of patinated copper Elspeth had retrieved from the bobcat bucket, they all conceded, was the same sheathing used on a ship's hull, found in Bob's shed.

'The pottery shard is from a salt glazed preserving jar,' Jameson said. 'Early 19th century. I'd bet my life on it.'

Claire looked to Elspeth. 'What do you think Miss Curator?'

'I'd put money on Jam's identification of glass and pottery any day of the week.'

'Thanks, El,' Jameson grinned. 'I love you too.'

Sandra clucked.

'But the bone?' Elspeth picked up the smooth polished rounded bone. 'It's almost like ivory.'

'That's because it is,' Andre was excited. He looked up from his computer screen. 'I've identified the wreck.'

'What! Really?'

'Yep. She is the *Montrose*, built in 1840 in Bremen in Germany and leased to a Lincolnshire company for Arctic whaling but with rich pickings to be found in the Southern Ocean she worked out of

Hobart Town for three years in 1846, before disappearing without trace off the north-west coast of Tasmania in 1849.'

Calvino. 'You reckon that's her?'

'Bet my life on it. She was reasonably small at eighty-nine feet by twenty-seven in the beam.'

Claire managed another mouthful of cake. 'And the ivory?'

Andre. 'That's whale ivory, a piece of sperm whale tooth. The *Montrose* was a whaler.'

Jameson took the bone from Elspeth, rolling it about in his fingers. 'I'd say you're right on the money.'

'I suggest we get back to Stanley and revisit our sources,' Andre suggested.

'What about the shipwreck?'

'Don't you worry,' Bob said. 'Dean's no fool. He'll run them Mexicans out o' town and secure that site for the right authorities.'

'That'll be Launceston's Victoria Museum, Bob,' Elspeth said. 'I'll make a call myself.'

'What about that cop?' Calvino asked. 'He wants to talk to us.'

'He'll have to wait,' Jameson wasn't so trusting. 'Tell him we had to go Bob. Thanks for morning tea Sandy.'

CHAPTER NINE

Retired florist Eve Shelley wore a wide brimmed straw hat and tight fawn shorts showing off snow white legs. She wore a floral cotton blouse tied at the front and thin leather gardening gloves. Eve enthusiastically trimmed the rose bushes in the front garden of her cottage.

'Eve,' Jameson smiled, stopping at the white picket gate. Elspeth was directly behind him.

'Oh hello, enjoying Stanley?'

'Absolutely. It's so pretty. Such a beautiful place to holiday.'

Eve sensed this meeting was no accident. 'Just passing by?' she hinted. 'Going down to the docks maybe?'

'Actually, we wanted to ask you something.'

'Oh! Did you now?'

'That plate ...'

'Off the old ship?'

'Yes. I don't suppose you'd like to sell it?'

'Oh, I don't think so. I'm quite fond of it.'

'I'll better the price of the similar plate you saw on the Antique Road Show,' Jameson said. 'Do you remember how much they valued it at?'

'Thirty pounds, I think. But it's not for sale.'

'Thirty pounds. That's about fifty dollars give or take. I'll double it, give you a hundred.' Jameson didn't mention the fact that the episode was most likely a six-year-old repeat, nor did he mention the word *inflation*. But he did throw in the extra spiel. 'Yours *is* damaged which affects the value.'

'I don't think so. As I said, I rather like it.'

Jameson didn't hesitate. 'A hundred and ten?'

'Sell it to them Eve,' Henry Shelley had heard everything and stepped from the cottage. Shih Tzus Cookie and Wiki skipped down the front steps following their master along the path.

'Now Henry,' Eve snipped her secateurs towards him in a playful threat. 'The plate is not yours to sell.'

'It's old and chipped and makes your Staffordshire dogs look cheap,' the retired public servant spoke of the antique porcelain dogs on the mantle.

'What's so special about that plate anyhow?' Eve asked. 'So special it makes you want it badly?'

'Oh,' Elspeth said. 'After you told us about the lost shipwreck, we became very interested and have actually been doing some research.'

'Oh, I see.'

'You said your father found it in the sand dunes,' Elspeth asked. 'Where exactly?'

'Can't say. My daddy was a little vague about it. But he did say it was at a remote spot, swampy in places near a river. Oh yes, he mentioned shifting sand banks and quicksand.'

'Yes,' Henry said. 'The beaches down the coast can be very dangerous. I've seen stray cattle on the beach caught in quicksand. They just sink and vanish, it's awful. There's nothing you can do to pull them out.'

Eve lopped a dead flower from a rose. 'What about that idiot fisherman from Melbourne, the one who lost his four-wheel drive?'

'Oh, yes. This chap drove along the water's edge at low tide and his car got stuck. Barely got out alive he did. He went to get help, and when he returned there was no trace of his vehicle.'

Eve. 'The sand swallowed the whole thing.'

Jameson. 'Crazy.'

Henry excused himself a moment. He whispered in Eve's ear. She smiled, nodded in capitulation. 'Tell you what,' Henry said. 'Shout us dinner at the Stanley Hotel and the plate's yours.'

Jameson didn't hesitate. 'Done.'

'Great, Eve and I love nothing more than a meal at the pub.'

With the evening pleasantly calm, they shared a table for seven on the pub balcony overlooking the bay, where Eve and Henry thoroughly enjoyed the company of their new acquaintances. Henry didn't hold back. Dozen oysters, ribeye steak with a side of rocket, parmesan and pear salad and chips. There was even talk of saving room for dessert. Eve was content with duck liver pate, chicken baked in filo pastry with camembert, no talk of dessert but a cheese platter was suggested. Jameson bought drinks at the bar. He was more than happy with the deal and content to buy their guests what they wanted, now that his latest acquisition was safe, wrapped in bubble wrap back at the cottage.

'We've been asking around and found more information on the whereabouts of the lost ship you're researching,' Henry said, his top lip already stained from the heavy peppery Heathcote Shiraz.

'Excellent.'

'We're certain it wasn't near Arthur River. It was further south.'

'But you don't know where exactly?' Elspeth asked.

Eve eyed Elspeth with more than inquisitive interest, her second glass of Bay of Fires sauvignon blanc giving her voice. 'Let's address the elephant in the room,' Eve said. 'Shall we?'

Elspeth. 'Elephant?'

'Why don't you just come out and tell us the truth, you're looking for the lost gold that was stolen from Cadiz, as the stories go, two hundred years ago.'

Jameson feigned surprise but Elspeth knew better. 'It's that obvious is it?'

'Well yes.'

'We are primarily historians,' Elspeth started.

Eve snorted. 'Yeh, right.'

'True. I am the assistant curator at the Tasmanian Museum.'

'Really?' Henry looked puzzled. 'I don't mean to sound rude, but isn't it against your ethics, I mean against museum policy for a curator to run about looking for treasure.'

'We're not looking for treasure!' Elspeth raised her voice and instantly regretted it. She leant closer, lowering her tone.

'It is true there are the rumours of missing gold bars but Jameson, Andre and myself *are* genuine researchers.'

'True,' Andre nodded vigorously, his mouth full of fried fish. 'We have even uncovered the diary of Violet Newham,' he managed to sound coherent. 'Mentioning more important facts like religious treasures from the Vatican, once stolen by Napoleon, also being involved with the missing ship.'

'Well,' Eve's lips rounded as she blew out her cheeks. 'That's new to me.'

Henry asked. 'Violet who?'

'Newham.'

'That's what I thought you said.' Henry forked his salad. 'Eve. Didn't you do a rub of a headstone for Violet Newham, here in the Stanley cemetery?'

'Yes, of course.'

'Eve and some friends started doing rubs with charcoal over tracing paper,' Henry informed the table. 'Rubs of the tombstones in poorer condition, for prosperity like.'

'It's a bit of a hobby,' Eve said.

Claire frowned. 'Rubs?'

'Yes, you cover the headstone with newsprint paper and use charcoal to rub over the paper giving you an exact facsimile of the inscription.'

Calvino. 'Cool.'

Henry. 'They're stored at the Stanley museum.'

'She's buried here then?' Andre said. 'This Violet Newham?'

'Yes, that's what I said.'

They stepped onto the footpath outside the circa 1847 Stanley Hotel and watched Eve and Henry Eddystone walk hand in hand home to their cottage. It was a perfect and still evening. Except for soft music tinkering from a speaker outside a cottage lounge bar across the street, there was not much other activity. Although it was past nine the remains of a warm summer day lingered. On the horizon clouds coasted lazily towards them. At the end of Church Street, a full moon lingered over historic Highfield House, built by the Van Diemen's Land Company in the early 1830s. The National Trust's homestead lorded over the township of Stanley and the gentle crescent bay of Godfrey's Beach, exposed to the wild seas of Bass Strait. Here, many past residents enjoyed ocean views from their eternal home at the southern end of the beach.

'Not too bad,' Jameson told the others, inspecting his Visa Card receipt. Dinner came in at sixty-five dollars a head. 'The plate cost me a hundred and thirty bucks. I'm happy with that.'

'I should hope so Jam,' Andre sounded envious. 'With its history and pedigree and in the right auction you'd get a grand, easy.'

Jameson. 'More.'

Calvino whistled. 'A grand!'

Claire yawned. 'Don't know about you guys but I'm exhausted, it's been a big day.'

'What?' Elspeth clearly had a second wind. 'You're not keen to visit the cemetery?'

Claire wasn't keen.

'Violet Newham awaits,' Jameson coaxed.

Andre. 'I'm in.'

'And it's a full moon. How could you say no Claire?'

Claire dawdled, scuffing her shoes like a spoilt nine-year-old, but by the end of the ten-minute walk to the cemetery she was refreshed.

'Remind me,' Claire said, last in and closing the white picket gate behind her. 'Who this Violet woman was again?' She spoke quietly, feeling the need for reverence in the presence of the dead.

'Violet Newham was the Matron on Sarah Island remember?' Elspeth said. 'Her son-in-law was Thomas Mogg the soldier she confided in about the gold.'

'Oh right.'

'Andre. 'He later owned the Red Fox Inn at Hadspen.'

'Got ya.'

The throaty hoot of an owl sounded from behind the closest of two Norfolk pines guarding the cemetery. 'Nice one Cal',' Jameson grinned. Calvino stepped from the cover of darkness.

'Not ones like the sound-track from a B grade horror movie, anyway,' Andre added.

'Okay you lot,' Elspeth took charge. 'Torches out. Spread out.'

There was not a mortal soul about. Had there been a passer-by they could be forgiven for thinking the cemetery was indeed haunted. Five *apparitions* – mobile phone torch lights held high – searched the headstones, casting their beams of light, oscillating and tilting as if hunting like lost souls looking for their respective grave sites.

'Found it!'

The others hurried to join Claire. 'Violet Newham, right?'

'Well done Claire.'

'Ah, so there you are,' Jameson spoke to the headstone. '*Sacred to the memory of Violet Newman*,' he read aloud. '*Who died at the age of 71 – 11ᵗʰ July 1874. Mother to Agnes Mogg – nee Newham – died 1824.*' They must be buried together.

'*May the Lord forgive me*,' Calvino read on. 'Forgive me for what?'

The chiselled sandstone grave was well weathered with lichen masking some of the inscription. Andre fetched a twig and scraped at the wording.

Though many seek, filled with greed
It's the Lord's words one should heed.
But Tis a saint, I ask for a pardon.
For disturbing your peace,
From the land of your decease.
Your crown alone resides in a casket
Guarded for eternity on that lonely islet.

'Is that for real?'

'Now that's weird.' Calvino wasn't a great fan of poetry, let alone amateurish verse from a long dead matron. They stood in silence a moment, each re-reading the inscription.

'This just keeps getting better and better,' Andre said.

Claire. 'Do you think she's trying to tell us something?'

'Absolutely,' Elspeth said respectfully, reading the inscription over and over.

Immediately the stone flooded with extra light. Andre's mobile snapped several shots.

'Asking a saint for a pardon,' Claire said. 'Do you reckon she is talking about one of the saint dudes from the Vatican?'

'You're quick Claire,' Jameson grinned.

'Claire,' Andre said. 'That's about the most sensible suggestion you've made this trip.'

'Are you being a smartarse too?'

'No, seriously. We know Mogg gave her the missing saint's skull.'

Calvino. 'This Saint bloke, what's his name again?'

'Saint Adamo Abate.'

'That's him.'

'And the Matron wasn't too pleased about it I shouldn't imagine,' Elspeth said. 'Being religious and superstitious.'

'No. Mogg and his mate re-stashed the gold bars, said they never found them, but they found the old skull with a few gemstones decorating it. They too are superstitious so passed it onto the step-mum.'

Elspeth read the verse aloud once more. '*But Tis a saint, I ask for a pardon. For disturbing your peace, From the land of your decease ...*'

Calvino. 'That'd be Italy huh?'

'Vatican State actually.'

'*Your crown alone resides in a casket. Guarded for eternity on that lonely islet.* So, what's that all about then?' Claire wondered aloud.

'Clearly our interesting matron reburied it,' Andre said.

'It could be anywhere.'

'What was that?' Calvino straightened. He panned his torch into the blackness. In the direction of what sounded awfully like a snapping twig. Headstones shifted shadows, ghouls disappeared, ghosts hid.

'What's what?'

'Didn't you hear it?'

'No. What?'

Another splintered branch had four more mobile phone beams follow the direction of Calvino's, like searchlights over London during the blitz. 'See that?' Claire said.

'No. What?'

'I saw it,' Jameson said in a whisper. With the approaching clouds blanketing the moon Jameson ventured forward into the dark. 'Who's there?'

In an impulse of bravado, Calvino joined Jameson. 'What did you see?'

'Dunno ... something. Something big.'

'There's wallaby shit on the ground Jam.' But Calvino's voice lacked conviction. 'A rabbit maybe?'

'Bloody big rabbit if it was.'

At the north-east perimeter, a wooden paling fence separated the consecrated land from bushland, leading steeply to the north-facing cliffs of the famous Stanley Nut. Jameson made it to the head high fence shining his light about. Nothing. Repositioning clouds allowed the moon to peep through briefly, painting the cliffs with a subtle luminescence. If there had been an intruder ...

'They could be hiding anywhere out there,' Elspeth said as they all had the same thought at the same time.

Jameson was first through their cottage door. It was ajar. Elspeth, Claire, Calvino and Andre followed.

'The bastards!'

'It was those Spanish dudes, right?' Claire said, stepping around her own backpack, its contents strewn across the floor.

'Mexicans actually.'

'Had to be.'

Andre pushed past Calvino, rushing into the laundry where he delved into the dirty washing. 'What?' Calvino shook his head. 'Frightened they nicked your undies?'

Andre ignored the comment, returning with his laptop. 'Thank god I hid this,' he said with a sense of achievement.

'Oh, good work Andre.'

'Anyone missing anything?' Jameson asked.

'Don't think so.'

Elspeth. 'What about your plate Jam?'

Jameson switched the light on in the cottage TV room. 'No!' The bubble wrap was on the floor. 'Bastards!' The Royal Navy plate was missing. 'Why?'

Elspeth picked Jameson's 1928 copy of Mrs Beeton's Household Management off the floor. 'Well at least they had no use for this.'

Claire stuffed spare clothes back into her knapsack. 'We need to call the cops.'

They received a recorded message for her perseverance ...

For an emergency, call 000, otherwise the Stanley Office will be open at 8AM.

'Brilliant.'

'I suggest we sleep on it,' Elspeth said. 'They may want to dust for prints so don't touch anything.'

Andre lay awake, staring at the ceiling in the dark. He couldn't sleep. Too many unanswered questions, and now the break-in. These people were dangerous. Having lain awake and wired since 5AM, Andre checked the time on his mobile. It was now nearly seven. He dressed and wandered off down Alexander Terrace towards the docks. The village was yet to wake. Andre was alone except for the ever-present gulls circling the docks. An old lady walked two tiny dogs. Passing the bakery sharpened his appetite where the fragrance of freshly baked bread travelled onto the footpath. The sign read *open at 7.30*. It was ten past. He knocked on the window and bought a loaf early, hot from the oven. Walking east after passing Hursey Seafoods Andre headed towards the breakwater of Stanley Harbour ... and stopped dead.

She was a magnificent sight. 1800 tons of sailing ship floated obediently in the harbour, moored to the man-made breakwater in all her maritime glory. Andre was enamoured, if not a little intimidated. He knew she was the Mexican tall ship *Il Corvo Nero* the moment he recognised the carved wooden figurehead: a black raven.

Andre edged forward carefully. Thirty metres closer there was sudden activity on board. Trying not to appear too suspicious, he stepped behind a docking ramp, peering around the corner. On board, animated crew appeared to be preparing to sail. Some crew members were looking in his direction. Andre took further cover from sight when he just heard a car approach from the township. It was the car the crew awaited.

Andre knew very little about autos, but he had recently read an article about electric cars and recognised the latest model Mercedes-Benz SUV speeding along the harbour road. Andre pushed his back against the dock ramp praying he would not be seen. The purring motor raced by and onto the dock where it stopped alongside the ship.

Keeping low, Andre watched a most attractive older woman step from the backseat. 'Well, I never,' Andre whispered to himself. The woman appeared with the two thugs Andre recognised from Arthur River. The woman was dressed all in black, her long shiny soot black hair coiffured into a chignon. Even from this distance her painted red lips captured the morning sun. She wore black jeans, tight to accentuate her slender figure, with a cream blouse under a black jacket with gold jewellery advertising her wealth. Andre fancied he had not seen such an attractive figure of her vintage in some time. The SUV doors slammed shut and a harness was craned from the ship. Within minutes the Mercedes had been hoisted on board and zipped into what Andre could only describe as a shiny black cocoon.

Andre hurried back to the cottage where the local cop, summoned by Claire, was standing inside the front door. He was not entirely enthusiastic.

'Backpackers,' Andre heard the uniform tell Jameson, Elspeth, Claire and Calvino in various stages of dress, and all standing in a semi-circle. Calvino was yawning.

'No way,' Claire barked. 'It was these two big dudes from Spain.'

'Mexico,' Jameson corrected.

'Look,' the cop said. 'Just because there's a Mexican tall ship in port doesn't make them your burglars.'

Elspeth. 'What ship?'

'He's right,' Andre stood behind the cop in the open doorway, short of breath. 'The *Il Corvo Nero*'s in dock here. I just saw it.'

'Really?'

'Really.'

'Well, there you go,' Elspeth said.

'They threatened us in Arthur River yesterday,' Jameson told the cop. 'And now they burgled our cottage.'

'What do you mean, threatened you?'

'Sergeant Dean Lark from Smithton knows all about our altercation,' Elspeth said.

'Larky!'

'You know him then?'

'Of course. What happened?'

Elspeth explained the situation of the previous day, omitting any unnecessary information, like seeking treasure.

'Look,' the Stanley policeman shrugged. 'Is there anything missing?'

'Well besides an old pewter plate, not much else that we can tell.'

This was of little interest to the cop. He decided to humour them, after all Stanley was pretty much a crime free village. 'All I can do is take down your details and file a report.'

'You're not going to arrest them,' Claire said naively.

'For what?'

'Try stalking.'

'Look, you can't prove a thing.' The policeman took out a note pad. He poised to write. 'Okay, names ...'

'You know what,' Claire stepped forward and made to close the front door. 'Forget it,' she said. 'Sorry I spoilt your morning.' Andre saw his queue and stepped inside hugging his warm bread. 'Goodbye,' Claire was cranky. She closed the door the moment the officer stepped outside.

'Go you!' Calvino laughed.

'Nice work Claire,' Jameson said.

'Now what?'

'Breakfast,' Andre held up the family sized, high-white tin loaf.

Claire's face brightened. 'I bags the crust, with butter and Vegemite!'

'Then I'm using the bathroom first,' Jameson slipped into the bathroom and locked the door before anyone had a chance to protest.

Jameson sat on the edge of the bath towelling his feet dry. He was deep in thought. Out in the kitchen he heard Andre telling the others about the Mexicans. *These were not people to tangle with,* he thought. *They were drug dealers on a big scale, and they were here in Tassie.* Jameson stared at the knots in the timber of the original pine floorboards of the bathroom. They were highly polished and the patterns intrigued him. He could make out faces, eyes – lots of eyes – he imagined dancing ballerinas, a wallaby in flight, he even fancied he made out a portrait of Elspeth in profile. Amazing natural designs. Suddenly the revelation hit him.

'Guys, guys! Jameson burst from the bathroom. 'We've been concentrating in the wrong place.'

'What do you mean?'

'We should be searching the Pieman River estuary,' he said of the wild untamed river a two-and-a-half-hour drive south of Arthur River. Etched into the bathroom floorboards Jameson had imagined a map of the Pieman Estuary. 'It came to me like the face of Jesus on a piece of toast,' he told the others.

'Jesus's face in a piece of toast,' Calvino laughed. 'Man, have you been smokin' something?'

'Seriously.'

Elspeth gave Jameson a little more credit. 'What did?'

Jameson tried to explain his revelation.

'Jesus,' Claire said. 'Jesus's face in the floorboards?'

'No Claire,' Elspeth said. 'The Pieman River Estuary.'

Jameson. 'Yes.'

Claire craned her neck to peer into the bathroom. She glanced at the floor. 'Yeh, right.'

While Claire and Calvino struggled with the analogy, Jameson had Andre open his file on the laptop. 'Now go to Google Maps,' Jameson was animated. 'Type in Pieman River.' The rich Indigo blue of the Southern Ocean was in harsh contrast of the various shades of green that denoted the wilderness of the west coast of Tasmania. Should Tasmania be the face of a clock, Pieman River sat at ten o'clock.

'Why here?' Elspeth wrapped both hands about a mug of coffee, blowing steam from the brew.

'Bob Mundy said his old man worked further south when he found the ship remains. Also, Eve Shelley said her father found the plate south of Arthur River.'

'Yes, but why Pieman?'

'Don't know. Call it sixth sense. Besides there aren't that many rivers to choose from.'

'Won't hurt to go see,' Andre was keen.

'It's a long drive from here.'

Claire. 'Then let's get a wriggle on.'

The bunched fist struck Jameson's lower gut like a wrecking ball. Exhaling a gasping breath, he doubled over groaning. There was no chance to defend himself, let alone retaliate. Jameson felt lightheaded. The pain was sharp and decisive. He thought he was about to faint, when all went dark.

Emiliano pulled the cloth satchel tight over Jameson's head, tying it off at the neck. His wrists were secured before him. He pushed his face close to Jameson's. 'Walk,' he ordered, frogmarching Jameson awkwardly, blindly, slipping over soccer ball sized rocks, Jameson was dragged waist deep into water before being tumbled unceremoniously onto the deck of the five metre Milan built Nouva, the *Il Corvo Nero's* tender. He lay centimetres from the triple Mercury outboards.

This was not good.

Jameson tried to work out what had gone so pear-shaped so quickly. While the others packed Andre's van, Jameson decided to return to the Stanley cemetery and snap more photos of the Matron's grave site in daylight. He had barely framed his first shot when he was attacked from behind.

Jameson felt it wisest to remain silent. Not to struggle. The swell in off Bass Strait rolled ashore, building momentum along the coast off Godfrey's Beach. Jameson knew he was being taken out to deep water, the bow hurdling white water before slamming into the trough of the next wave. Minutes passed. The water calmed and the speedboat thumped against something. The wharf? The Mexican tall ship? They must be at the Stanley docks on the opposite side of The Nut, Jameson guessed. Orders were exchanged in Spanish and Jameson felt the motor launch pendulum. They were being craned aboard the mother ship – the *Il Corvo Nero* – but not before grinding her hull against the jagged mussels along the breakwater.

The stern cabin was spacious, luxurious and gaudy. In Jameson's mind the red velvet upholstery and gilded furniture dictated the taste of the nouveau riche. The woman present, Jameson would learn later, Maya Hidalgo, had been raised as an orphan in a mountain village, until she married young at sixteen. Her first husband was shot and killed by drug dealers. Maya married a second time eight months later, to an ex-police commander turned trafficker, who was executed by hired assassins. She continued working for local gangsters, having several affairs with drug barons. By twenty she had climbed her way up the cartel ladder until she married Alejandro Hidalgo, the godfather and boss of bosses, ten years ago. Alejandra Hidalgo had been Mexico's most powerful cocaine dealer, until he too was gunned down in a public street in Mexico City. Wise to the world of drug trafficking, Maya surrounded herself with a small army of guards and, with her charisma as a beautiful woman, along with plenty of cash, Maya soon had the authorities in her pocket. Today she passed as an entrepreneur, yet her drug empire was as powerful as ever.

Nouveau riche maybe, Jameson recognised Flora Danica dinnerware, Porthault Jour de Paris tableware and glassware by the House of Beccaria; all world-class accessories for the wealthy. Maya had *some* taste.

Of particular interest to Jameson was the outlandish décor amongst the wealth. Skeletons and death seemed an ongoing theme, when Jameson remembered Mexico's macabre custom of celebrating death. *Dia de Muertos* or The Day of the Dead.

Decorated human skulls and even a full-sized skeleton were decorated in bright colours, in particular the orange marigold.

Maya studied Jameson. He was a little bedraggled by the treatment, but she liked what she saw. Fortunately for Jameson Maya was in one of her better moods.

'So, you're this treasure hunter Jameson Rowley huh?' Her English was excellent. Jameson didn't answer. 'What's the matter? Cat got your tongue?'

Emiliano slapped the back of Jameson's head. 'Speak.'

Jameson shot the thug a look before turning to Maya. 'What do you want?'

'What do you think?'

'There's no gold. It was found years ago.'

'Gold!' Maya pinched her lips and shrugged as if Jameson spoke of lead. 'What would I want with a few bars of gold? No, Mr Rowley, I want Saint Adamo Abate ... or at least his bejewelled head,' she smiled, caressing a pottery skull beside her with accentuated pearly white teeth, and a face of rich blue lapis lazuli inlay.

'The saint's skull?' With all this macabre in her life Jameson understood her interest. 'It belongs to the Vatican,' Jameson said without hesitation.

'So, it does exist then. Thank you for confirming that fact.' Maya sipped an iced tea through a stainless straw. 'Drink?' She pointed with her glass to a jug on the table, where Jameson now recognised his stolen chocolate tin. He didn't answer. 'Suit yourself.' Maya watched Jameson's searching eye. 'So there, I see you recognise the photos and letters ...'

'Which you stole from my friend's home.'

'He's not too smart, that friend of yours,' Maya tut-tutted. 'Hiding the tin under his bed.'

No answer.

'There's a photo in here which we have identified as the most likely place for the ship to have wrecked. But it has been torn in to two halves. All we need is the missing piece. I know you have it. Have a photo of it sent to us and you are free to go. It's as simple as that.'

'And if I don't?'

'We will be in deep water within the hour. Your body will never be found.'

Jameson swallowed hard. Mayo sent Emiliano to fetch Jorge Diaz, head of security aboard the *Nero*. Diaz, the suave dark haired and dangerous Mexican returned minutes later. He pressed Jameson own mobile into his bound hands. His grasp of English was basic. 'Call friends.'

Jameson weighed up the situation. He knew he was dealing with hard-core criminals. He tapped in his code and noted five missed calls, all from Elspeth. He called back.

Elspeth swiped her mobile.

'Where the hell are you?' her voice urgent.

They had finished packing the van, checked out of their Airbnb and were parked at the cemetery. 'I've been worried sick.'

Jameson explained the situation when Diaz's iron fist clamped his shoulder. 'Speaker,' he ordered. Elspeth's voice filled the cabin.

'On board the *Nero*! Are you serious?'

'Yes El, and they've got you on speaker phone.'

Elspeth went quiet a brief moment. In the background Andre and the others sat silently in the van. They heard every word. Elspeth's mind scrambled, trying to compute the seriousness of the situation.

'Alright,' Elspeth finally said calmly, trying hard not to betray her anxiety. 'What do they want?'

With the Pieman River as their destination Jameson sensed they had nothing to lose if Andre was to send the entire file to the ship. 'Tell Andre to send the file.'

'What?'

Jameson's deep sigh filled the van. 'They want the file El.'

'All of it?' Elspeth said without thinking.

'Yes woman,' Diaz shouted across the stateroom. 'All of eet.'

Elspeth froze. The voice was threatening. It was real. 'Jameson ...'

'Yes?'

'Are you okay?'

'Yes. I'm fine ...' Jameson's voice trailed off.

'Fine for now,' Diaz spat at the mobile. 'Now do as we say or your man, he feed fishes. Go to police, your man, he feed fishes, compri?'

Jameson looked to Maya. He held his mobile where Elspeth could hear him clearly. 'You'll set me free, right?' Jameson held up his tied wrists.

'Of course, once we have what we want.'

'Did you hear that El, don't stress, they'll set me free so send me the file asap.' Elspeth knew Jameson too well. He sounded worried. Very worried. Elspeth was terrified. She looked to Andre, nursing his laptop.

'There's no WIFI signal here,' Andre shrugged. 'We'll have to go to the pub, or the Post Office.'

'You guys packed already?' Jameson asked. Diaz twitched. His eyes narrowed. Jameson recognised the threat.

Elspeth frowned. 'Packed?'

'Yes, packed. Then if you are, you must drive to the Post Office and use the WIFI there.'

Elspeth looked into the worried faces of the others. *What on earth is he going on about?*

'What?'

'Go to the Post Office and send that file. Oh, and El.'

'Yes?'

'I hope you packed my Mrs Beeton's cookbook.'

Now Elspeth was really worried. 'Y-yes. I packed it.'

'Good. Cos I thought I'd cook those golden syrup dumplings for dessert tonight. I know how much you love them.'

If there was one dessert Elspeth could do without, it was golden syrup dumplings.

'Golden syrup dumplings?' Was this a cryptic message or was Jameson losing it?

'Yes, El, the one's you like. Mrs Beeton's recipe.'

'Stop your talking,' Maya said, angry.

'What's the email address then? Jameson asked. 'On board?' Jorge Diaz scribbled his address onto a slip of paper. Jameson read it over the phone.

'Give us a few minutes,' Elspeth said. 'While we go to the Post Office.'

'Call me the moment you send it.'

'There now,' Maya snatched his mobile and threw it onto the table. 'That wasn't so bad, was it?' Twisting about to face Jorge Diaz she ordered the ship underway.

'Ah ... you're about to sail?' If Jameson feared for his life earlier, now he was really worried.

No answer.

'You're going to cut me loose, right?' Jameson held up his bonded wrists. Diaz stared into Jameson's eyes. 'We'll see. Maybe you feed fishes.' The giant man chuckled. He bowed to clear the cabin door, followed by Emiliano. Instantly the bosun's whistle shrilled. Jameson heard the subtle thudding of feet on the teak deck above and the gentle vibration of the auxiliary diesel engine. The three-masted barque would set full sail once at sea.

On deck the tender remained tethered to the crane. Her lifting straps tightly fastened. As the tall ship drifted away from the dock the constraints threatened to damage the million-dollar speed boat. In the stern cabin Maya heard the panicked shouting. Something was amiss. With Jameson's wrists tied she locked her cabin door behind her and went to investigate.

Jameson didn't hesitate.

He rushed to the stern windows, managing to lift a latch on one of the windows. The ship was shifting away from the breakwater, but with his hands secured he feared he'd drown if he jumped. Jameson hurried back to the door. Thankfully his hands were restrained before him and not behind his back. With both hands, he tried the cabin door.

Locked.

On deck, order seemed to return. Jameson heard voices heading along the passage from the companionway leading back to the master cabin.

It was now or never.

Jameson shoved the diamond leadlight window wide. They were now twenty metres from the shore. Outside, Stanley's famous landmark, The Nut, loomed over the harbour. Jameson heard the key in the lock.

Mobile! My mobile!

Jameson reached the desk. Scooped up his phone and slipped it, two-handed, into his pocket the moment Maya walked into the cabin. For the briefest of seconds, they eyed each other, both surprised and indecisive. Maya screamed for Jorge. Jameson didn't hesitate. He charged the open window and dived headfirst, praying he would land in reasonably deep water. In all his haste he barely managed to take a breath.

The water was cold. *Damn freezing.*

With a five-metre drop Jameson plunged deep. Keeping his tied hands out in front he kicked for the surface. Gasping air he made out faces at the stern window, shouting curses in Spanish. Jameson rolled onto his back and swam to the breakwater where he immediately put the spiky barnacled mussels to good use, severing his ties.

A local waterside worker appeared at the edge of the pier. 'Jesus mate! You alright?' He climbed down fenders to reach Jameson. 'What the bloody hell are you up to?' the man grinned. 'Did you jump out the window or were you thrown out!' the man was incredulous.

'Long story.'

Another worker appeared and another and Jameson was hoisted aloft. By now the *Il Corvo Nero* was a hundred metres out. The bosun's whistle shrilled once more and sailors climbed up the ratlines and onto the yards. The Mexicans were setting full sail and they had a good breeze to make haste.

Jameson watched the ship head out to sea. He imagined they would have the file by now. The fact they had the original chocolate tin meant they hadn't achieved much, as the missing piece of photo Jameson had used as a bookmark for safe keeping, was in his latest book acquisition, Mrs Beeton's Home Management. And indexing Golden Syrup Dumplings.

He tried calling Elspeth. Reliable *Apple*, the company boasted a waterproof phone, and they were right on the money. Minutes passed. The van pulled up at the docks.

'Thank god.' Elspeth threw her arms around Jameson and was rewarded with a wet hug. 'What happened?'

Jameson explained.

'I sent the file,' Andre said.

'Doesn't matter. They have the tin. Where's my Mrs Beeton's?'

'Here,' Elspeth held the heavy tome in both hands. 'When did you hide this in there?' she asked, showing the torn photo.

'Before we left. I had it in my wallet to show Andre but ...'

'This is too much,' Claire said. 'We need to report this. You were kidnapped for god's sake.'

Jameson shrugged. 'Report to who? The local cop. Forget it.'

'I agree,' Andre said. 'If we hang about waiting on police reports and god knows what, we'll miss the boat ...'

'Literally.'

'No seriously. We need to get on the road.'

Calvino. 'I agree.'

'It's about four hours to Pieman's Estuary from here.'

'Then let's hit the road guys.'

While Jameson changed clothes, Andre examined the two halves of the photo, one an image on his laptop and the half bookmarking Mrs Beeton's book. 'I reckon this photo was taken in the fifties or the forties even,' Andre said. 'Probably with something like a Kodak Eastman autographic folding camera.'

'How's that?'

'Well, they were a popular camera in those days and the print looks about right.' Andre tapped in *Dolphin Cove* on Google Maps. 'There's no such place coming up,' he said.

'I could have told you that,' Jameson said pulling a rugby jumper over his six pack. 'Read the co-ordinates.'

'Of course. 41° 40'13" S.'

'And on the other piece?'

'144°.97'24"E.'

Claire. 'That's longitude huh?'

'Yep. Where's that take us?'

'Pieman River.'

'Exactly. Just like my premonition in the bathroom.'

'Hey guys,' Calvino had a sudden revelation, picking up the portion of photo with the crude hand-drawn map on the back. 'Dolphin Cove.'

'What of it? It doesn't exist.'

'No, but what if I told you the Italian word for Dolphin is El Delfin.'

'El Delfin! That's ...'

'That's the name of our ship ... *El Delfin.*'

'Certainly is.'

'So, whoever drew this map called the location Dolphin Cove. Clever.'

'If that's the case, then X marks the spot guys. According to Google Maps it's a small, unmarked bay with a sand bar on the south of the estuary.'

Arthur River had returned to its solitude since the *treasure hunt.* After a short stopover to say their farewells to Bob and Sandra Mundy, they drove the unsealed road south through the Tarkine on the western Norfolk Road, an unsealed four-wheel drive to Corinna.

Corinna, population five.

With the main attraction being the Tarkine Hotel, looking more like a colonial homestead in the wilderness than a hotel, it was surrounded by a veranda and tree ferns. The town was originally called Royenrine.

'Corinna is the Aboriginal word for a baby Tasmanian tiger,' Elspeth read aloud from her mobile linkup. 'Settled in the mid-1870s, Corinna is a remote historical mining settlement in Tasmania.' The unsealed rugged track spilled from the hills down to the river completely surrounded by Tasmania's wildest bushland, an ancient landscape and now world heritage.

Andre parked on the gravel in front of the hotel where the parking area fell away into the narrow, yet deep, Pieman River. Here, the river swept by in an eternal flow of tannin-stained fresh water.

'So how do we cross the river?' Calvino asked, casting an eye one hundred metres to the opposite riverbank. Here the road continued south.

'The car ferry,' Jameson alluded to the three vehicle punt pulled across the water by a steel cable.

'Great. So where is everyone?'

On cue, a voice appeared around the side of the hotel. 'You plan on crossing?'

Jameson wanted to say something like *well what do you think mate?* 'Ah, that's the plan, yes.'

'Sorry, but the punt's engine's buggered. We're waiting on a part to come down from Lonnie,' he said of Tasmania's northern capital, Launceston.

'You're kidding, aren't you?'

'No mate. Sorry. These things happen.'

Jameson turned to the others. 'Now what?'

'How long before the part gets here?' Elspeth asked.

'We're waiting confirmation that the part's in stock, but we should be up and running by early arvo.'

'Early arvo. It's midday now,' Claire said optimistically, looking at her watch.

'Early arvo tomorrow love.' The man, who introduced himself as Dick Swanston the manager and all-rounder, wiped his hands on his overalls. 'I have vacancies if yer want to stay the night. Or you can drive back north.'

With little option than to wait they checked into two rooms.

'Where yer headed, back to Hobart?' Dick asked, signing them in.

'Well, we are,' Elspeth said. 'But we want to visit the Pieman estuary first.'

'Then you'll need to purchase a Recreational Driver's Pass to drive in that area.'

'Oh?'

'Where do we get that?'

'Well, it's run by National Parks.'

'Oh. Where are they?'

'Their nearest office is at Arthur River.' Dick saw the anguish in his guests' faces. He loved the game. He waited to the count of five before adding cheerily, 'But you're in luck. They authorise me to sell yer a pass, right here.'

Jameson shook his head. This bloke was becoming tiresome.

Next day...

The engineer was late. A laid-back, short Peruvian bloke named Gus had little or no idea of urgency. For him the Corinna ferry breakdown was just another day at the office, albeit 249.3 kilometres away in *the bush*.

Dick was up for a fight but wisely kept his mouth shut. Otherwise, Gus would take even longer to repair the pulley system. He played assistant mechanic instead. Two hours later he donned the skipper's hat and made the ten-minute crossing with Elspeth, Jameson and the others sitting in the Mitsubishi.

'Ten minutes!' Jameson groaned. 'And we wasted a night.'

In fact, they had lost twenty-four hours, but at least they were on the southern side of the river. Once off the unsealed road, leading to the old mining town of Zeehan, and then west to the estuary, Andre engaged the four-wheel drive. 'First time I've used this.'

'Good thing you've got it,' Elspeth said, trying to steady herself. In the back, Andre's passengers tossed about in the cabin like Barbie dolls. It would be a slow drive to the coast.

The road crossed buttongrass plains, streams and myriad tannin-stained stony creeks, winding through spectacular rock formations and ancient Aboriginal heritage sites, before arriving at the south side of the Pieman River's estuary.

Calvino. 'Why's it called Pieman's anyway?'

'They say it was named after Alexander Pearce the cannibal convict who escaped Sarah Island in the 1820s,' Jameson said.

'What, like the Sweeney Todd dude barber who baked his customers in pies?' Claire said.

'Sort of. But there was also another convict, Thomas Kent, who was a pastry cook in Hobart Town nicknamed the Pieman. He too, once escaped from Sarah Island and is another contender for the title.'

The last kilometre to reach the coast seemed a continuous speed hump. Recent rains had furrowed the road, which uniquely, was 'sealed' with a white silica coating. This silica, mined from a local silica quarry, was spread over all the roads in this part of the wilderness. Finally, through the tall timbers of eucalypt, myrtle, pines and sassafras the Southern Ocean appeared.

'No!'

'Is that what I think it is?'

'You're kidding me.'

Andre at the wheel had seen the tall ship first. The others caught sight of the *Il Corvo Nero*. She was anchored in deeper water offshore. 'Are they for real?'

'Jesus! If we hadn't been delayed at Corinna.'

'Now what?'

Andre. 'Any ideas?'

Elspeth. 'You can bet your life they're watching out for us.'

For Jameson his recent encounter with the Mexican cartel was still raw. Their threat to throw him overboard out at sea had been a reality. He was wary, but more determined than ever to succeed.

'Get us as close to the beach as possible without being seen,' Jameson said. 'And we'll continue on foot.'

Crossing Violet Rivulet, Andre drove off-road before parking in secluded bushland two hundred metres from the shore. Armed with his latest model Minelab Equinox 600 Metal Detector, Jameson led the team to the dunes leading down to the beach. Here they had a kilometre stretch of sand terminating in a wide sandbar at the Pieman River estuary. With the heavy surf rolling in off the Southern Ocean, the tall ship was anchored a good kilometre out. 'Let's hope they don't see us,' Calvino said.

'And if they do?'

'Then we're in trouble.'

'South or north?' Claire asked, trying not to wet her shoes in the brown waters of Violet Rivulet.

'Dolphin Cove is about another three hundred metres past the end of the beach, to the south,' Elspeth said. She had copied the severed map halves onto her mobile along with Andre's file. 'At least the cove is in the opposite direction,' she added, looking back at the ship.

Nature's flotsam and jetsam were strewn along the beach as far as one could see. Thankfully man's detritus was scarce. Yet even here on the pristine coast of wild, untamed west Tasmania, the odd drink bottle or plastic fishing buoy attached to shredded nylon rope washed ashore, discarded or lost somewhere out on the vast Indian Ocean.

Jameson took in the beauty. To him it was easy to imagine the beach strewn with the cargo, passengers' belongings and the debris of a shattered centuries old sailing ship. Andre and Calvino stood by with shovels.

'What's that stink?' Claire was first to catch the stench of rotting flesh wafting towards them on the breeze. To the north, a dozen or so pilot whales had stranded some weeks earlier and nature was yet to complete its duty; that of ridding the beach of such putrefaction. Elspeth panned her binoculars from the tall ship back to the beach. The dead whales were several hundred metres away, but the stench reached them like an ill-omen.

'Why do they do that anyway?' Claire muttered through her blouse, pulled up over her nose.

'One theory,' Andre said, 'is if one whale is sick or dying its calls of distress can cause other whales in their group to follow it ashore, unintentionally stranding themselves.'

'Also, bad weather,' Elspeth said. 'Or their navigation gets confused, or hunting too close to shore or even old age can cause the beaching.'

Elspeth focussed on the carcasses, counting eleven. They all lay on one side, their black bodies appearing rusted like beached torpedoes where decomposition was well advanced. Their heads lay in shallow pools of tannin-stained water from the rivulet, or was the discolouring caused from spilt blood Elspeth wondered.

Readings on Jameson's metal detector were rare. On the ground, the so-named Dolphin Cove on the hand drawn map was merely a bite into the landscape. A bay no wider than a football oval, the years had eroded the landscape and remoulded it, but Jameson still felt confident. Behind the dunes was an expanse of tea tree swampland with razor grass and no doubt a breeding ground for snakes. It looked most uninviting. Fifty metres inland was the burnt-out trunk of a large tree.

'Could that be the burnt oak Bob talked about?'

'Dunno,' Calvino played with his plaited beard. 'Could be anything.'

'Yeh,' Claire agreed. 'A gum even.'

'It sort of has the stumps of two prongs.'

'I'll scan the dunes first then head around the perimeter of the swamp.' Jameson placed the headphones over his ears and tweaked the detector.

While the others searched for any clues, Jameson floated the detector methodically, careful to cover the entire area using an imagined grid, like he was mowing grass at the MCG.

An hour passed since arriving. 'Nothing,' Jameson sighed. 'Not even a bottle top.'

'Well at least the beach is unpolluted by man,' Elspeth said.

'Calvino found uniform timbers half buried in the sand,' Claire said. 'But Andre reckons it's modern.'

'Modern as in fifty years old,' Andre corrected.

Claire's skin wasn't handling the exposure. 'I need sun block guys.'

Elspeth sat on a boulder. 'There's just nothing here is there?'

Jameson was loath to agree. 'Maybe whoever drew that map was a little out with their co-ordinates.'

Elspeth looked to Jameson, her enthusiasm waning. 'Maybe it *is* just a wild goose chase.'

Jameson was loath to admit defeat. 'Maybe.'

Claire. 'Okay, let's head back.'

Elspeth scanned the ocean. The *Il Corvo Nero* was still anchored in deep water, riding the incoming swell. 'See anything?' Calvino asked her.

'Not really. Doesn't seem to be too much activity on board.'

Fifty metres from Violet Rivulet estuary Jameson caught a soft ping in his headset. He stopped, panning the detector search-coil over the area. The reading grew louder.

Andre joined him. 'What is it?'

'Dunno. Something. And something's better than nothing.'

'Five bucks it's a ring pull,' Calvino winked at Claire.

Jameson dug with a gardening scoop, shovelling the sand into a plastic vegetable strainer. He sifted, hovering the coil in ever-tightening circles. 'Huh! A button.' Jameson pinched the find between fingers and inspected the tiny brass dress piece with a coin magnifier. 'Well, there's no markings unfortunately, but it's not modern, I'll say that for certain.' In fact, Jameson had seen similar pieces in museums and suspected this to be late 18th century or at the least, early 19th century. He passed it to Andre who agreed.

'Well, that's a good sign,' Claire said. 'Isn't it?'

'I reckon.'

Jameson continued floating his detector low over the sand. Two metres north, another register. 'Huh, check this out.'

'What is it?'

'It's a bottle opener, made of some alloy.'

'Looks like some fisherman's lost his precious bottle opener.' The short-handled opener was complete including the paddle end, to lift caps off crown seal bottles.

'Can I see?' Andre took the opener. 'It still has its chain to hang around the neck.' Andre rubbed at the concretion build up to reveal the inscription ... *Ask for K.B. beer*, in bold pressed letters along the handle. 'That's Koenig brau beer,' Calvino recognised the name.

'And it's vintage,' Andre said. '1950s I'd say.'

'Hey guys,' Claire called out. 'Check this out.' Recent storms had uncovered large, milled timbers poking from button grass spilling down the side of a sand dune. 'That looks like ship timber to me.' The others gathered about Claire.

Elspeth. 'I think you're right.'

'Well spotted.'

'It certainly is, and my guess is it's oak,' Andre said, although the weather had bleached the timber grey. Calvino immediately shovelled sand down the dune face, exposing enough timber to identify a portion of ship's hull, although only a small section. Jameson scored instant pings through the headphones and was rewarded with a bronze bolt. The bolt was fastened tightly into the wood.

'Andre?' Jameson could barely contain his excitement. 'Andre, that bolt's exactly the same as the one Bob gave me.'

'I'd say you're right on the money.' Andre started shovelling. It was easy work with the loose sand collapsing down the dune face, but once again only a small portion of the ship exposed itself. 'It's like it has broken up into many smaller sections.'

'If I didn't know any better,' Claire said, 'I'd say it exploded. I've seen stuff like this in movies.'

'Movies huh!'

'No. Seriously.'

'You might have something there Claire,' Andre rubbed his chin in serious contemplation. 'But the ship hasn't exploded, someone has blown it asunder.'

The more they studied the shredded ends of the timbers the more Andre's theory appeared possible.

'But if it didn't explode,' Elspeth surmised, 'if the ship's powder magazine didn't explode by accident say, how could it be blown asunder, as you so quaintly put it Andre?'

'Salvagers Elspeth. Whoever took the photos back in the 1950s. I'm guessing the rumours are true.' Andre held up the vintage opener. 'In all likelihood the gold *was* found years ago.'

'But didn't we agree that the Matron's son-in-law and his mate found the gold and re-buried it, back in the 1820s?'

'And the dudes who were here in 1950 found the ship and dynamited it but didn't find anything,' Claire suggested.

'Stop!' Jameson said. 'You're doing my head in.'

Elspeth stiffened. Catching movement in the distance, she trained her binoculars on the activity. 'Hey guys, we have company.'

'What?'

Everyone faced north. Less than a kilometre away *Il Corvo Nero's* tender, the Nuova speed boat, had driven ashore where two dune buggies were being man-handled onto the beach.

'Do you think they've seen us?'

'Maybe.'

'Why else have they come ashore with buggies?'

Calvino borrowed the glasses. 'They're Honda Ranchers, those things rock man.'

'We need to make ourselves scarce.'

'They may not have seen us.' But as Jameson said this, the buggies, two men a piece, started along the beach at speed. In their direction.

'Follow me,' Jameson shouted. 'Keep your heads down.' Jameson was first up and over the dune and into the buttongrass. Bending low he ploughed through the wet, almost swampish moorland behind the sand dunes. 'We need to get to the van.'

Now they heard the motors, high revving buzzing approaching, like giant wasps. As they watched, hidden by vegetation, the buggies made a wide berth around the dead whales. Jameson and the others arrived at Violet Rivulet estuary. 'We're on the wrong side of the creek,' Jameson said. 'We'll have to go back onto the beach.'

'No way!'

'We have no choice.'

Stooped military style, Jameson led them back onto the beach where they crossed the shallow rust-coloured rivulet spilling into the sea. Looking south the buggies had arrived at the ship remains. 'They *must* have seen us.'

'Now what?'

'We need to get to the van and get out of here,' Andre said. 'That's what.'

Claire froze. 'No! They've seen us.'

The buggies turned sharply, heading straight towards them.

Calvino. 'Run!'

Jameson yelled to Andre. 'You get the girls back to the van. I'll distract them.'

'Girls! Don't patronise us,' Claire yelled back.

'Jameson,' Elspeth cried out. 'What are you planning?'

'I'll see you at the van.' Jameson was already running towards the sea.

'Wait!' Calvino took off after his friend.

'Let's do as he says,' Andre was more cautious. But Claire and Elspeth, out of sight in a dip in the landscape, were going nowhere.

Jameson didn't have a plan.

As he watched the buggies approach at speed, they steered towards the water's edge where the sand was firmer, gaining traction. Jameson twisted about, sprinting towards the whales. Behind him the whining motors grew louder. Calvino caught up on the run. 'What's the plan?'

'Don't have one.'

'Jesus!'

Suddenly they heard someone cry out. Animated shouting. Jameson looked over his shoulder. One buggy appeared stationary. The second made a wide U-turn. Calvino stopped alongside his friend, gulping breaths. Clearly, he was not fit. 'What's-going-on,' he gasped. But Jameson couldn't believe his luck. The first buggy was trapped in wet sand. As they watched on, the front end dipped sharply. The driver jumped free only to land knee deep also. The other passenger was disappearing with the buggy. Calvino wheezed. 'What's-going-on?'

'Quicksand,' Jameson grinned. 'It's lethal along this coast.'

'You're kidding.'

'No, I'm not.'

The buggy was slowly devoured by the beach. The passenger panicked and he too was caught trying to escape. Jameson and Calvino could hear their terrified cries for help. As they watched the second buggy held back. Someone threw the men a rope. By the time the two were dragged to safety only the buggy roll bars marked the spot.

'Quick Cal, keep moving, run!' Jameson started off.

'Run where?'

'Up the beach, divert them from the van.'

'But how can we ...'

The second buggy whined back to life.

'Run Cal, run.'

Leaving the two survivors their companions resumed the chase. The distance between them closed fast.

Jameson ran between carcasses of stinking whales. Calvino tried to keep up, but he was exhausted. 'Jam,' he shouted.

Jameson wheeled about. The buggy was only metres from Calvino. He recognised Emiliano from the ship. If Jameson didn't know any better, he'd say they were going to ram his friend. Jameson turned back. But out of his peripheral vision a figure appeared.

Claire!

Claire charged the buggy broadside. Screaming adrenalin, she carried a two-metre branch of driftwood ... and rushed forward like a pole-vaulter at the Olympics.

With the buggy two metres from Calvino Claire launched her lance. The solid limb speared between the front wheels and the tractor-sized rear wheels. Emiliano swerved sharply. The front right wheel plunged into a hole, bit the sand and the vehicle somersaulted. Calvino dived aside. Without seat belts Emiliano and his passenger were thrown. Jameson ducked to join Calvino as Emiliano cartwheeled by, landing heavily, ploughing into the rotted carcass of a pilot whale. The whale's side burst, and Emiliano was swallowed in the jellied putrefaction of a month-long dead animal. The stench was horrendous.

Emiliano's passenger wasn't so lucky. Landing on an awkward angle Jameson was certain he heard his neck break.

There was no time to hang about.

'That-was-awesome!' Jameson wrapped an arm around Claire's shoulder. Further along the beach the two quicksand survivors were on the run, in their direction. Closer by, Emiliano vomited before stripping off his clothes and running headfirst into the surf.

'Time to go guys,' Claire laughed anxiously.

Andre was more than impressed, yet cautious. 'We need to get out of here.'

'I won't argue with that.'

'Where now?'

'Guys, I need to get back to Hobart or I'll lose my job,' Claire said of her waitressing position at The Grand Chancellor.

Andre. 'Me too.'

Jameson. 'I didn't know you were waitressing.'

'Ha!' Andre laughed. 'No, I need to get back to Hobart too, I'm too old for this caper. This has proved fruitless. We gave it a good crack and besides, I don't like leaving home too long anyway.'

'Missing Cecil huh?' Elspeth said of Andre's pug.

'And him too.'

'Look,' Jameson suggested. 'We have to pass through Strahan on our way back to Hobart so let's have one last night there. It's a long drive otherwise. Break up the trip.'

Like Jameson, Elspeth still had a few days break available. 'I'll be in that,' Elspeth said.

Andre looked at Claire and Calvino. They looked back along the beach a kilometre away where the Mexicans were licking their wounds. 'Let's just get clear of here and discuss it in the van.'

'Good idea.'

'Hey,' Jameson said. 'I've got a fisherman mate in Strahan, Brad. He moved there years ago and took up professional fishing, he bought his own boat and all.' What Jameson didn't tell the others was that Brad was expecting them.

CHAPTER TEN

Strahan is the West Coast's most picturesque seaside village, nestled on the water's edge on the north side of Morse Bay, one bay of hundreds making up the greater Macquarie Harbour: a wilderness world heritage treasure six times the size of Sydney Harbour. Settled in the 1880s it was developed as a port for the early miners and timber-getters in the area. Later in the mid 1950s it was established as a fishing village for the commercial fishing industry.

Jameson's fisherman mate Bradley Champion was starved of company and hell bent on two things: they stay in his three-bedroom weather board home on Lynch Street overlooking the village and bay, and they discuss matters at the pub. The man loved a beer. He also wasn't taking no for an answer. After Jameson called ahead, they met at Regatta Point Tavern. Brad was in fine sprits, about three beers ahead of them.

'Go hard!' Brad cheered and swallowed his remaining half pint in one mouthful. After the past days they all needed a break. Finally, after several drinks and now sitting around a large table in the pub dining room, staring at the last piece of pepperoni pizza, Calvino talked about gold ingots, stolen jewels and sunken shipwrecks.

'You've been lookin' for what?' Brad was incredulous. 'Mate, that gold was found years ago.'

'You've heard about the lost gold then,' Claire said.

'Of course I have. Every man and his dog's heard about it.'

'So we figured,' Calvino said.

'Seriously mate,' Brad made to reach for the last piece of pizza when Claire plucked the limp wedge from the platter.

'If no one else's keen,' she said, the slice hovering before her open mouth, 'I'll have it.'

'Hmm. Where were we? Oh yeh, gold. That's old news guys. That gold was found by a local retiree and his missus, so they reckon.'

'Oh?'

'Josh knows all about 'em,' and Brad called out to old Josh Peters sitting at the bar with a pony of draught. 'Jock. Hey Jock.'

The old fisherman looked begrudgingly away from the afternoon races on the telly and craned his neck around like the hinges were rusty.

'What's the name o' that couple?' Brad asked. 'The ones who were supposed to have found that gold at Pieman's back in the fifties?'

Eighty-seven-year-old Jock eyed Elspeth, then Claire, before a smile revealed the fact that he had lost most of his teeth. 'Ingles ... Guy and Jackie Ingles.'

'That's them. They found an old wreck up near Pieman's, so the story goes, but ... well here's the weird thing, the couple went missing along with their motor launch ...'

'*Diligent*,' Jock said over his shoulder. 'The boat was called *Diligent*.' He may have turned back to the telly, but he had acute hearing.

'That's 'er, *Diligent*.

'Missing, you say?'

'Yer, not long after they supposedly found the gold. Then sometime later, Jock'll tell yer, the woman's body was found tangled in tree roots up near the Gordon River.'

'And her husband?'

'Never found 'im,' Jock muttered.

'What about the boat?'

'*Diligent*? She was a motor cruiser, a classy sixty-footer ...'

'Seventy-eight,' Jock called out.

'Seventy-eight-footer. They lived on her in Strahan here, didn't they Jock?'

Jock nodded. An advert came on the screen. Jock turned to face the out of towners, his beer near full in his hand. 'She were a beautiful thing, a gorgeous craft, if yer can call a boat gorgeous.'

Jameson asked. 'How's that?'

'Well, the MV *Diligent*, as I said, was seventy-eight-foot, wooden hull, eighteen foot in the beam, classic built, by Argos Brothers at their Prince o' Wales boatyard,' he thought a moment. '1947 I think she were launched. I was invited on board once. She had three staterooms and a grand saloon, that's what Guy Ingles liked to call it anyhow,' Jock had a chuckle to himself. 'A grand saloon. She had twin Perkins water-cooled diesels, state o' the art back them days.'

Elspeth. 'Sounds grand.'

'She were love.'

'Well,' Brad said, 'She was located, about a year ago actually, by fisheries doing water samples and stuff. It's in ten metres on a ledge and held tight by tree roots. A coupla feet more and she would have dropped off into deep water.'

'Deep water, how deep?'

'They reckon it gets to eighty metres in places.'

'Eighty metres! Hell.'

'What happened to them, this couple?'

'Dunno. Jock?'

'Some say they hit a submerged log.'

Calvino. 'And the gold?'

'Gold, treasure, pirates,' old Jock was back in action. He emptied his pony and banged the glass hard on the counter. 'You city people up 'ere lookin' for treasure. Christ. It were found long ago by them Ingles.'

'So where is it now?' Claire asked the old man.

'Buggered if I know love, some people reckon it's still on board the *Diligent*, others say the Ingles re-hid it upriver.'

'Oh Christ,' Claire said with a mouthful of pepperoni. 'Another wild goose chase! No thanks.'

Jameson. 'Well hasn't anyone dived on *Diligent*?'

'Jesus Christ boy,' Jock said. 'It's dangerous, what with the currents and the snags and visibility. It'd be suicide.'

Jameson shrugged, turning to face the others. 'It's gotta be worth a look at least. How hard could it be?'

'I can take yer to the wreck site in the mornin' if yer like?'

'Mate,' Jameson said. 'That'd be awesome. Have you got any diving gear? I didn't bring mine.'

'Absolutely, I've got a thermal spearfishing suit on board with hooker gear. No tanks but.'

'Perfect. Can we skip over to Sarah Island while we're at it? I'd like to show the guys.'

'Sure thing.' Brad eyed his empty glass. 'Tell yer what, I'll take some bevvies and you guys bring some tucker, and we'll have a picnic on the water.'

Claire was beside herself with excitement. The forest marched to the river's edge. Like an army stopped by the powerful river. There were no beaches, just the odd, narrow, pebbled landing, dropping away steeply into the unknown. Besides the abundant wildlife and what lurked in the frigid dark waters beneath them, there was no other sign of life anywhere.

'This is so cool,' Claire's voice echoed off the stillness from where she sat at the bow of Brad's fishing boat, *Grummet*, her legs dangling, her chin resting on the stainless steel rail. 'Anyone been to Disney Land?'

'Don't even think about comparing this to Disney Land,' Elspeth called back.

'Yeh but, I was just saying ... can't you imagine an elephant or ... or a dinosaur, coming out of those trees?'

The chorus came hard and fast. 'NO!'

'Jesus, you don't have to shout.'

Brad cut the motor, allowing the *Grummet* to drift to the river's edge at barely one knot. 'We're directly over the *Diligent* wreck site.'

'Directly?'

'Yeh, check the sonar.'

Jameson peered through the heavy underwater growth, tree roots, huge dead trees and nature's detritus. The blurred shape of the stern of a boat was quite discernible. 'How deep?'

'Thirty feet. She's caught on the edge of a ledge amongst tree roots and stuff. A few feet from plungin' into deep water.'

The current was strong. Brad allowed *Grummet* drift against overhanging forest and made fast to a sturdy tree branch to moor them securely.

'Grab the compressor from the deck locker will yer?' Brad asked Calvino.

Calvino jumped to it while Brad fetched the dive suit. Elspeth looked anxious. The venture sounded fun over a few beers yesterday, but now? She wasn't so confident.

'Are you sure this is a good idea?' Elspeth looked over the side into the unknown and uninviting territory.

'Yeh,' Jameson was always happy in the water. 'Why not?'

Elspeth had to concede that on the surface it looked friendly enough but ... 'I don't know if this is such a good idea on your own.'

'It's a virgin site El, no-one's ever dived her.'

'I understand, but ... what do you hope to find?'

'Don't know really ... a clue maybe. Or maybe gold,' Jameson said with a cheeky grin.

'Yer right,' Calvino scoffed, struggling to lift the compressor. Claire jumped to and gave him a hand.

'No seriously, at least I might be able to find why she sank. Both were drowned, weren't they?'

'Yer,' Brad said. 'The woman's body was found caught in tree roots a 'k' away down river, so I was told.'

'And her husband?'

'He's probably still down there,' Brad grinned. 'Standing at the helm with a beer in his hand.'

Claire's jaw dropped. 'Do you reckon?'

The others laughed at Claire's expense.

'Well, it's worth a reconn anyway.' Jameson and Brad were of similar build. The suit was a perfect fit. 'What's the visibility down there anyway, Brad?' Jameson asked.

Overhead was a clear blue sky. 'I'm only guessin' but I reckon it'll be clear enough at thirty feet, long as the sun stays out.'

'And we all know anything can happen with the weather here,' Andre said gloomily. 'Don't we?'

The sky *was* clear and blue, certainly, and the water deep and dark. Dark with miserable memories of the desperate convicted felons imprisoned at Macquarie Harbour's desolate penal colony all those years ago.

The air was still and the petrol fumes from the compressor cloying, hanging about the deck like some lost spirit. Jameson sat on the stern diving platform and felt the water before pulling on his gloves.

Andre. 'How's the water?'

'Bloody freezing.'

'Well, it is melted snow.'

Jameson checked his regulator connected to a fifteen-metre standard air hose, itself harnessed to Jameson's waist, where he also belted up lead weights. Brad connected a safety line as well. 'Tug twice, hard fast jerks, if you need to be pulled up asap. Got it?'

'Aye cap'n.'

'And you're gonna have to watch the current Jam, it'll pull like a bitch down there and you don't want to go gettin' snagged amongst all the dead trees and stuff.' Brad wasn't overly concerned – he knew Jameson well and knew he was a skilled diver.

'All good.' Jameson pulled on flippers and mask, giving Elspeth the thumbs up. Now that it had become a reality the others looked on nervously.

Jameson eased himself off the platform. And sank. Immediately submerging two meters. The current swept past him, an eternal and invisible force of nature. There would be no fighting it. It was certainly going to be a challenge. Jameson fastened onto the safety line, travelling a few metres before it reached the end of its tether. Looking out across the river, visibility was limited like a consommé du boeuf morphing to a blurred potage. Twisting about he found himself gaping into a wall of dead vegetation, a forest of dead trees, branches, jumbled tree roots and the intertwined underbelly of the wilderness above. A labyrinth of snags that demanded respect. Looking back towards the surface the midday sun was inviting. Jameson hovered below *Grummet's* red keel while ripples on the surface warped the trees overhanging the river. Beneath him, Jameson saw what remained of the MV *Diligent* with rays of sunlight, golden through the tannin-stained water, illuminating the overgrown wreck trapped in amongst strangling tree roots. The gnarly trunk of a massive moss-covered pine crushed the portside hull and Jameson wondered if the tree had crashed into the river after the wreck, or whether the tree was partly to blame for the accident. The sixty-five-year-old wreck lay on a thirty-degree angle in ten metres of water on a muddy ledge where a tangle of other rotted trees teetered over the edge, dropping away into an abyss of unknown depths. It would be a terrifying void in which to disappear. Jameson steadied his breathing as the haunting silence was only interrupted by the rattle of his regulator as he sucked air. Jameson checked his tether. If it came undone, he would be swept well away before he could surface.

Jameson collected his thoughts. *Do a reconn on the wreck and get out of here.*

Clawing tree root to tree root Jameson pulled himself over the wreckage, worming his way into a position to inspect the bow. It was a good thing he wasn't wearing tanks, Jameson thought, as it was now obvious how easy it would be to entangle in the maze of vegetation. Jameson steadied himself on the boat's forward rail, a chrome guard slippery with decades of slime. Now he could inspect the starboard bow where indeed, something large had breached the wooden hull. Otherwise, the timber was in good condition. Old Jock's words, back at the pub, replayed in Jameson's head.

'Some say they hit a submerged log.'

It looked like old Jock was right on the money. The current seemed to strengthen, and Jameson felt his body rise, almost horizontal. Progressing carefully, hand over hand, Jameson made his way to where the massive tree trunk had crushed the wreck some years ago. Now he had a clear view inside, and it was evident the current over six decades had washed the interior clean.

Diligent was just a shell. The interior walls of the three staterooms and the saloon were still in situ, but they were ravaged by time and the perpetual current. Jameson saw no sign of any artefacts – not even a plate or an old teacup. Any loose item appeared to have been swept away years ago. In fact, the damage to the hull was so great it wasn't difficult to swim inside. Heedful to maintain a metre of slack on the air hose, Jameson manoeuvred into the saloon. The cabin was the size of an average bedroom. Very little remained except for wall sconces that had held electric lamps, and the decaying chrome legs of a dining table bolted to the floor. Jameson recognised remains of a faux marble tabletop. Below deck the current was minimal. Jameson twisted onto his back, floating, weightless for a moment, his attention drawn to sunlight penetrating the saloon through a grimy Perspex skylight still in situ. It remarkably had survived. Jameson swam closer to inspect the portal when he noted what appeared to be writing scratched into the plastic. Jameson's first thought was of other sports divers exploring the wreck and vandalising the skylight by scratching their initials. Or was it a message for future explorers, like *Pete was here, 2019.*

Impossible.

Jameson was certain he was the first diver to dive this wreck. It was only recently discovered by accident, for starters. The writing was barely legible. Immediately Jameson felt a bristling shiver spark along his spine. He sensed the spirit of the dead. He was not alone. Jameson stared wide-eyed at the skylight. The words formed a sentence, a short line; terrifying yet poignant.

Jackie, I'm sorry. I love you.

Suddenly Jameson felt vulnerable. He sensed company from the afterlife.

Jackie, I'm sorry. I love you.

Jameson read the words over and over. Surely these words weren't written by the doomed skipper, Guy Ingles? Was the man trapped down here? It seemed so unlikely with the extensive hull damage. Yet the vessel had been wrecked nearly seventy years ago.

Keen to complete his reconnaissance and return to the surface, Jameson pulled gently on both the air hose and his safety line, reeling in enough rope to exit the damaged starboard hull on the riverbank side. The current dropped dramatically. Following the fallen tree roots Jameson swam beneath the embankment of the rainforest above. In places it was cavernous and really quite beautiful with shafts of sunlight spearing down through the entanglements and knots of long dead trees, the illumination enhancing hues of green, brown and gold. Jameson swam into tranquillity. Here beneath the overhang, he found an area of serenity the size of a small bedroom and for a moment Jameson was at peace with the world ...

Until ...

The creature slammed Jameson's face mask. He was totally ill-prepared. Gnashing teeth struck at the glass. Jameson lurched backwards, cracking his head against a rotted tree overhang. Biting hard on his regulator water leaked into his mouth. Jameson wanted to cough but restricted the urge. It all happened so quickly. So unexpectedly. The metre-long eel snaked away, back into its habitat. It too had been spooked.

Jameson needed to surface. Afraid to take a breath for fear of sucking in a lung full of water, Jameson swam back through the hull. Inside his panicked flippers stirred up silt. Within seconds Jameson was disorientated. Frantically groping about Jameson's glove snagged a sharp edge. The seal was pulled back and a rivulet of icy water leaked along his wrist. It felt like he had been slashed with a hot blade. Desperate for air Jameson had no choice but to kick away towards where he hoped the opening in the hull waited. Seconds passed. They felt like minutes. He swam back into the current and the silt washed away. The opening was directly ahead. Jameson torpedoed through the damaged hull and into the full river current. He snatched at the chrome rail and swept with the flow to the bow. Jameson was seconds from being dragged well down river. He clamped the bow rail. But the rusted bolts broke away like toffee. Jameson was immediately taken by the undertow. With lungs screaming for air Jameson managed two tight jerks on the safety line.

On deck Brad was already in rescue mode. One moment he had fed out all the safety line available and suddenly the line was being sucked away down river. Brad held fast. Jameson jerked to a halt. Now, finally, he managed to claw his way to the surface, fifteen metres downstream from the *Grummet*.

Back at the wreck site the eel, content it had frightened off the intruder, surveyed its territory. It made a cursory swim over its domain, gliding low over the riverbed where the silt was resettling, finally camouflaging once more the three shiny golden bricks – the sparkling golden bricks that glittered whenever the sun's bright rays hit them on occasion, when the sky above was clear, and the water smooth.

Jameson was hauled on board the *Grummet*. The others stood about, keen for a report, while Brad motored his fishing boat away from the shoreline. Elspeth recognised his alarm. 'I wish you wouldn't do that,' she said, kneeling beside him.

Jameson caught his breath. 'Do what?'

'Frighten me like that.'

Jameson loved diving. He was at home beneath the waves. But this last dive had spooked him. 'Sorry ... *Jackie, I'm sorry. I love you.*'

Elspeth straightened. 'What? Who's Jackie?' Elspeth crossed her arms looking fixedly down at Jameson who looked decidedly serious.

'What do you mean?'

'You just said, *Jackie, I'm sorry. I love you.*'

'I did?'

'Yes. So, who is this, Jackie?'

Jameson looked at Andre, Calvino, then to Claire, who also crossed her arms.

'You did say that dude,' Claire said. Calvino and Andre nodded.

Jameson stood groggily. 'I think Guy Ingles the skipper was trapped below deck when a log smashed into their boat.'

'Why?' Calvino asked, excited. 'Did yer see a skeleton?'

'No. Nothing like that.' Jameson explained the scratched words in the skylight.

'Oh Christ, how awful.'

'That sounds like his wife Jackie made it out and he was trapped.'

'Seems that way, then she drowned down river where she was found a kilometre away.'

'I hate to ask the obvious, Jam,' Calvino interrupted. 'But did you find any gold by chance?'

Jameson could only smile. He could have drowned down there. Suddenly he felt more philosophical. He peeled off his wet suit and the sun warmed his skin. He felt alive. But nothing had changed, had it, he asked himself? Throughout history mankind had, and would, always risk his life for gold.

Sarah Island. An hour later...

Brad cruised a kilometre offshore pointing out the old prison. 'Sarah Island,' Elspeth read aloud from her mobile for the benefit of Claire and Calvino who hardly even knew the historic island existed, 'is a former British colonial penal settlement at Macquarie Harbour, in the former colony of Van Diemen's Land, which we all now know as Tasmania, operated between 1822 and 1833. The settlement housed male convicts and some women. During its eleven years of operation, the penal colony achieved a reputation as one of the harshest penal settlements in the Australian colonies.'

'Sarah Island sounds too good for it,' Calvino said. 'Should 'ave been named Devil's Island.'

'Such a beautiful location,' Claire sighed.

'Not for the men incarcerated there.'

'It is surrounded by mountainous wilderness, hundreds of miles from the colony's other settlements,' Elspeth read on. 'Making escape near impossible.'

'It's a summer's day now,' Brad said. 'You should come here in winter. And the prisoners had to work in the water, sometimes up to their necks, carting logs from the Gordon River to here.'

'Lots of men drowned,' Andre said. 'And many died attempting to escape.'

'Then there's the only entrance by sea into this huge harbour,' Jameson added. 'The shallow and treacherous channel notoriously known as Hell's Gates, for obvious reasons.'

'That's more like it,' Calvino said. 'Hell's Gates.'

'I'll take you there first,' Brad offered. 'Give you an idea of just how remote this harbour is. There's a breakwater there nowadays, to stop the channel silting up. Sailing through the Gates from the ocean you've gotta steer for the breakwater then make a hard turn to port and follow the shoreline where it's deep water.'

'How deep?'

'Seventy feet thereabouts. It's not for the inexperienced and like Andre said, many have drowned there.'

It was sobering information.

After exploring the few remaining ruins on the eight-hectare island, Brad anchored a hundred metres offshore while Jameson fired up an electric bar-b-que on deck. Claire and Elspeth prepared salads. Andre, meanwhile, found a position under the wheelhouse roof where he could read his laptop screen more clearly in the shade.

'You like a bit of poetry?' Brad asked Andre, peering at the enlarged photo of the message on Matron Violet Newham's headstone.

'Some poetry, not all,' Andre said, when he realised their skipper was reading the inscription.

> *Though many seek, filled with greed*
> *It's the Lord's words one should heed.*
> *But Tis a saint, I ask for a pardon.*
> *For disturbing your peace,*
> *From the land of your decease.*
> *Your crown alone resides in a casket*
> *Guarded for eternity on that lonely islet.*

'This isn't really a poem,' Andre said. 'It's more a cryptic message on a tombstone at the Stanley cemetery.' Andre went on to explain the connection of the Sarah Island Matron, the shipwreck survivor and Sarah Island prisoner Septimus Tilley and their connection to the Vatican's jewelled skull of a saint. 'We suspect this inscription on the headstone is a clue to the whereabouts of the priceless skull.'

'Christ! A saint eh? Fascinating.' Bradley read the inscription over and over. 'Sarah Island you say?'

'Yes. This woman was buried in Stanley, but she was Matron here on Sarah Island for quite some time in the 1820s.'

'You know,' Brad said. 'There's only one *lonely islet* around here that fits the bill, don't yer?'

Waiting for the bar-b-que to heat Jameson was passing around beers when he heard the tail of Andre and Brad's conversation. 'Sorry? What was that?'

'The *lonely islet* yer lookin' for could only be Halliday Island,' Brad went on.

'Halliday Island?'

'Yes mate.' Bradley stabbed a finger at the tiny island about a kilometre south. 'That's Halliday there. That's where they buried the dead from Sarah Island.'

Andre looked at Jameson, their mouths wide. After what seemed ages to compute, Andre said, 'He's right ... *Your crown alone resides in a casket, Guarded for eternity on that lonely islet.*'

'El,' Jameson almost shouted. 'Where did Septimus Tilley die?'

'Here at Sarah Island, why?'

Jameson explained.

Elspeth joined him at the stern, gaping with renewed fascination across the still waters to the island, barely recognisable as an island, blending with the landscape as it did, with its wilderness backdrop. 'You're kidding. It's not possible ... is it?'

Claire. 'Of course it's possible.'

Calvino. 'What are you on about?'

'Well, the Matron would have prepared Septimus's body for burial.'

'True, her and the prison surgeon.'

'But as he died of a fever, possibly contagious, I suggest Septimus would have been embalmed post haste and buried quickly.'

'Giving the woman a brief chance alone to hide the saint's skull with the body.'

'But wouldn't that look a little suspicious,' Claire had a thought. 'Man with two heads? I mean, I remember you saying, they didn't waste wooden coffins on prisoners in those days.'

'What if she lopped Septimus's head off?' Calvino necked his beer with a morbid grin. 'And disposed of it, replacing the saint's skull on Septimus's shoulders before embalming him.'

'By god, it's possible.'

'Question,' Brad said.

'Shoot.'

'Why would she do that. Why wouldn't she simply retire, sell the gems and enjoy a life of luxury?'

'Huh! Glad you asked,' Elspeth said. 'Matron was fiercely religious. Haunted by what she had done with the saint's skull, and in a fit of guilt and mortal fear she decided the skull should be interred in consecrated ground.'

'She feared god?'

'Exactly.'

'So, you're all suggesting,' their skipper said, 'that the priceless skull of some great saint, bejewelled in gemstones, lies buried on that island?'

Jameson. 'We are indeed.'

'So,' Brad grinned like Captain Jack Sparrow. 'What are we going to do about it?'

'Weigh anchor captain,' Jameson chinked his stubby against Brad's. 'Let's rock on over to Halliday Island and check it out.'

'We have one problem,' Brad said.

'What?'

Brad pointed across the starboard bow. 'Here comes the *Harbour Master*.'

'Harbour Master?'

'That's the name of the Gordon River tour catamaran.'

As they looked on the red hulled tour company boat with over a hundred tourists on board headed directly for Sarah Island.

'So, we won't be messing around on Halliday any time soon,' Brad said. 'After they visit Sarah Island, they'll be sailing right past on their way up the Gordon River.'

'Yes,' Elspeth agreed. 'It's National Trust, Wilderness listed and not to mention World heritage.'

Jameson flipped the burgers on the flat grill. 'Looks like its beers and burgers guys, and we'll come back later.'

No one argued.

By late afternoon Brad nosed *Grummet* north, returning to Strahan when over his shoulder something caught his eye. 'Now there's a sight you don't see too often.' All on board looked over the stern. Their hearts sank.

'You kiddin' me?' Claire sighed.

Jameson studied the three-masted tall ship under full sail with a healthy blow behind her following in their wake a kilometre back. 'Got any glasses?' he asked Brad. The skipper passed binoculars. 'As I thought,' Jameson said, focussing hard. 'It's not our Mexican friends.'

'Then who is it?'

'If I had to wager a guess, I'd say it's *Amerigo Vespucci*, the Italians.'

'What are they doing here?'

Elspeth took the glasses from Jameson. 'Now that's a bit of a coincidence, don't you think?'

'It certainly is.'

Over beers at Regatta Hotel, they watched the Italian tall ship dock across the bay at the Strahan wharf, behind the catamaran, *Harbour Master.* 'Look at it will yer,' Brad grinned at the gathering sightseers. 'Looks like all o' Strahan's come out to welcome them.'

'I guess it's a big deal for the locals here,' Claire said.

The group studied the images on Andre's laptop one last time. Earlier, he had researched Halliday Island. There had been little information on the internet in regard to Macquarie Harbour's isle of the dead; but what Andre did find were photos taken in the late 1890s by a Government commissioned photographer, John Watt Beattie. Beattie's photos had proven invaluable in the past but one in particular, of the few taken on Halliday Island, had Andre's attention. It was a photo of a Huon-pine grave marker. The carved inscription was clear; *Sacred to the memory of Thomas Mauley, drowned in the waters of Macquarie Harbour. September 18th, 1826. May he rest in peace.*

'That wooden grave markers now in the Launceston Museum,' Jameson said. 'I've seen it. It's the only one known to have survived and I do believe it was Beattie who saved it for posterity a hundred and twenty odd years ago.'

'Well, there you go,' Andre said. 'Now archival records show that Thomas Mauley died only weeks before Septimus, so it stands to reason that his grave would be close to Septimus's if not directly next to it.'

'That's a long shot,' Calvino suggested.

'Not really. The British were a regimented lot. They were systematic with everything, including burials.'

'So, what are we looking for?'

'That tree in Beattie's photo. I've never seen a more gnarly old gum. And it was already ancient when Beattie took this photo. My bet is it's still there.'

'You reckon?'

'Yes, I do. The island is so remote, no one ever goes there. Why shouldn't it still be there?'

'I agree,' Claire said. 'It'd be easy to identify with that great dead branch shooting off at right-angles. It must be half a metre thick.'

Calvino. 'So, what if we do find that tree?'

'We locate where Thomas Mauley is buried.'

Elspeth. 'And then what?'

'We dig.'

Elspeth's jaw dropped open. 'Dig!'

'Only way to find out.'

'We can't dig. It's an archaeological site, not to mention a burial ground!' And to prove her point Elspeth tapped a finger on the computer image of the burial marker. 'Read the small print, *sacred to the memory of ...*'

Jameson could understand Elspeth being anxious. 'El works for the museum, guys. She shouldn't be seen with us ... not digging there, anyway. You can wait at Brad's joint El.'

Elspeth looked at five sets of eyes staring expectantly at her. 'You're not digging. Period!'

'Jesus El, how do you expect ...'

'Jameson Rowley! Read my lips. We-are-not-digging-up-someone's-grave ... especially on a heritage site.'

'Christ El,' Claire unconsciously shuffled closer to Jameson. 'We've come all this way, and for what?'

'It's against the law.'

'You've done worse,' Claire argued. 'Since when did you care?'

'It's sacrilegious!'

'When did you go to church last?' Jameson scoffed.

Elspeth remained obstinate. 'It's morally wrong!'

'We're investigating a rare historic event Elspeth,' Andre dared weigh into the discussion, albeit in a sympathetic tone. 'What could be morally wrong with that?'

'How about we vote on it,' Calvino suggested.

Brad. 'Aye.'

'Those, *for*?' Jameson asked without hesitation. Five hands pointed to the overhead fan. 'Against?' Elspeth scowled. 'Five against one,' Jameson said, and as if to rub salt into the wound he added dramatically. 'The *fors* win.'

Elspeth shot Jameson her rare, *I'll strangle you later*, look.

'Like Jam said El, you can stay at my joint.' Brad held out his flat key.

'I will.' Elspeth snatched the key and stormed off.

'Well,' Calvino said as the pub door swung shut behind Elspeth. 'That went well.'

Brad watched Elspeth storm across the car park onto the road where she had a kilometre walk to his renter overlooking the harbour. 'Drink up guys, it'll be dark in an hour. Now's a good time to slip out of the harbour.'

CHAPTER ELEVEN

'The Italians must'a notified Frank Blainey the town mayor that they were coming,' Brad said as he motored quietly past the Italian tall ship *Amerigo Vespucci*. On a deck lit with coloured lights, two dozen or more local dignitaries and businesspeople nibbled antipasto and drank Aperol Spritz at a welcoming cocktail party thrown by their Italian visitors.

A hundred metres up the hill overlooking the harbour, Elspeth sat on Brad's deck watching the fishing boat slip out of port, and listened to the laughter and joviality emanating from the cocktail party on the ship. She took the weather cover from a telescope fixed to a tripod on the deck and focussed on the tiny township. The seaside village was alive this evening. Most tourists were dispersing around the village seeking dinner at one of the two pubs or handful of eateries.

Brad motored discreetly out of Morse Bay, cruising on the still waters of the dark harbour. It was nearing eight in the evening by the time they anchored off Halliday Island where heavy cloud threatened rain, blanketing any moonlight.

Here they were at the edge of the wilderness. Even early evening the landscape was unquestionably of inescapable beauty, shaped by glaciers in the geological past. The forests of the Gordon River grew from the very edge of the dark waterway; an uninviting impenetrable wilderness leading into a dense rainforest. A bushland of ancient Huon pines, said to grow for up to three thousand years; thirty metre giants co-habiting with eucalyptus, sassafras and myrtle.

Desperate escapees from Sarah Island, some of the rare few to penetrate the wilderness, encountered dense rainforest and buttongrass moorlands, sharing the countryside with venomous snakes, Tasmanian devils and the now extinct thylacine, known as the Tasmanian tiger. It was, and still is, not a place for the faint hearted to wander.

Halliday Island was under a fine mist, like a spectre of gloom, Jameson fancied, portrayed in some cheap horror movie. Brad cut the motor and dropped anchor twenty metres out.

'How do we get ashore?' Claire asked gaping across the black stillness.

'Swim,' Brad said, trying to keep a straight face.

'What!'

Claire clearly had not registered the three-metre inflatable strapped to the wheelhouse roof.

Claire was first onto the rocks, hooking her hands onto her hips and stretching her back. 'It's really quite spooky.'

Andre and Calvino carried a shovel each. 'I feel like one of those gravediggers in that film,' Calvino said. 'What was it, those guys digging up bodies for medical research back in the old days in Edinburgh.'

'Burke and Hare.'

'That's it.'

'Only difference is Burke and Hare were digging up the recently deceased.'

Jameson and Brad, torches in hand, forged ahead, mounting the steep embankment, disappearing into the thick bushland of the tiny island. The others followed in the wake of torch light dancing up ahead, casting shadows and creating furtive demons in susceptible minds. With so few adult trees the gnarly gum wasn't that difficult to find.

'I reckon that's your tree Andre,' Jameson tilted his torch up and down the trunk.

'No doubt about it. Just look at it.'

'That tree's been dead for years,' Calvino said.

'So. Let's see.' Jameson circled the huge gum, trampling young ferns, to position himself roughly where Beattie the photographer would have positioned his camera in the 1890s. Finally, the remains of the half-a-metre thick, severed branch was now obvious from where he stood.

'That's it.'

Enthused, Andre held up a printout of Beattie's photo. Jameson panned his torch on the image. 'That's definitely it.'

Calvino, Brad and Claire joined them. 'So that means the grave site in that photo is ... where?' Calvino asked.

'At a guess, 'Jameson said. 'I'd say Claire's standing on it.'

'Jesus!' Claire started, jumping about like she'd stood on a jack jumper nest.

Andre made estimates, assessing the area with measured steps. 'I'd say Jameson is right. Where Claire was standing is where the marker was in this photo. Jam, shine your torch here please.' Jameson obliged. 'Look,' Andre said. 'You can see where the ground is slightly sunken. If that's not a sign of a gravesite I don't know what is.' Jameson and Brad floated torchlight across the immediate area and it was now clear there were several indentations in the undergrowth.

'Why are they sunken?' Claire asked, growing even more uncomfortable.

'Well,' Jameson said. 'As the bodies decompose and coffins rot the dirt caves in to fill the space.'

Claire stood as close to the tree as possible.

'Those indentations follow a pattern,' Andre said. 'Like graves have been dug systematically, side by side.'

'So, we're standing on the dead everywhere,' Claire looked positively pale in the reflective light.

'I'd say yer right on the money there Claire,' Calvino grinned with another of his trademark winks.

'Christ, I dunno about this,' Claire said in a soft and sudden reverent tone. 'Are we ... ah, are you guys really going to do this?'

Jameson didn't hesitate. 'Which side first? West or east?' he asked of the two graves either side of *Thomas Mauley*.

'Toss a coin,' Calvino suggested.

'No, go west young man,' Andre said. He was quite enjoying himself.

Jameson started digging to the west side of where they were certain Thomas Mauley was buried. With the coast of Tasmania here in the wilderness under frequent rain, the digging was relatively easy going, the rich soil moist and soft. Jameson shared the dig with Calvino. Twenty minutes later ...

'What's that?' Andre dropped to his knees at the grave's edge, pointing to something revealed by Calvino's last shovelful. 'Is that what I think it is?'

'It's a bone!'

Calvino seemed to suddenly realise the seriousness of what he was attempting. He distanced himself to the far end of the grave and crossed himself. 'Jesus!'

Elspeth watched an hour of television, *David Attenborough in Madagascar*, before helping herself to a Boag's Premium in Brad's fridge. There was little in the way of food, unless left-over lasagne or individually wrapped processed cheese slices were to your taste. A loud splash and laughter followed by an angry rebuke in Italian, echoed up the hillside from the wharf. Elspeth swung the telescope about.

Had someone fallen in the drink?

She twisted the focus. The dregs of the cocktail party were leaving but the gangway was crowded. It appeared some inebriate had thrown something heavy off the ship. Crew were busy with hooked poles groping at an object in the water. There was no urgency and Elspeth guessed it was not a drunk. Elspeth sipped her beer and watched intently. A dark shape glided across the water in the darkness of night five-hundred meters off the *Amerigo Vespucci* starboard. It was sleek, soundless and barely left a wake. Elspeth focussed on the mystery vessel.

No! Impossible ...

Elspeth pushed her eye hard to the viewing lens, tweaking the night lens 15.45 magnification until she fixed focus on the dark blur. Elspeth knew straight away it was the Mexicans. She recognised the sleek speedboat from Pieman's River. There appeared only two men on board, but it was hard to tell. But it was no coincidence that the vessel was headed out onto Macquarie Harbour, undoubtedly looking for Jameson. Elspeth panned the scope across the high-speed craft. The men were perched at the helm, when a third figure appeared from below. Elspeth's heart skipped. There was no mistaking, the man held an automatic rifle.

Jameson!

Elspeth called Jameson on her mobile. No answer. Claire. No answer. Andre, same. She had neither Calvino's nor Brad's numbers. She tried Jameson's again before remembering they would have all switched their mobiles off or to silent. Elspeth was about to call the local police when she had a more practical idea.

The body, now reduced to a frame of bones, had been buried without a casket, no doubt wrapped in canvas which had rotted away nearly two centuries ago. The bone proved to be the ribcage and the skull was in situ.

'There's no studded jewels in this bloke's skull,' Calvino said as reverently as possible. Assured they had dug the wrong grave, they started shovelling dirt back over the skeleton.

'Take two,' Jameson said swigging at his water bottle before spitting on his hands and pressing his shovel into the second gravesite with a heavy Blundstone boot. With Brad taking turns, the three were soon head height into the other pit.

Elspeth hurried up *Amerigo Vespucci's* gangway leaping onto the main deck into a knot of handsome Italian sailors in uniform. She looked desperate.

'Signora,' an officer broke away from his companions. 'Party finita, si.'

'I need to speak to the captain.'

'Captain!'

'Si, the capitano.'

'Signora, I ...'

'Capitano! You understand?'

'Si si, I understand, but the capitano ees ... how you say ... indisposed.'

'This is urgent. Get the captain. NOW!'

Elspeth's raised voice drew others on deck, amongst them Signore Orfeo De Luca who took one look at Elspeth; angry, distressed, impatient and beautiful.

'Signora, are you all right?' He spoke excellent English.

'Are you the captain?'

'No. I am Signore Orfeo De Luca, adviser to the Italian Ambassador here in Australia.'

Elspeth remembered the name and Jameson's experience on board this ship for breakfast days earlier. 'De Luca?'

'Si. And you are?'

'Elspeth Poole. You met my partner Jameson, the chef at the Hook, Line and Sinker Restaurant in Hobart.'

'Ah, si ... yes. Nice man. Good cook, yes.'

'Well he's in trouble.'

'Trouble? What kind of trouble?'

'He is ...' Elspeth paused. The deck was silent. All eyes were on her. 'Can we talk in private?'

'But of course.' De Luca led Elspeth to his cabin, insisting she sit.

'I believe you know all about Saint Adamo Abate?' Elspeth said.

De Luca's eyes narrowed. He was immediately wary. 'What of Saint Adamo Abate?' the adviser crossed himself as if the very name held power over him.

'Yes,' Elspeth read the man's face. 'Of course you do. I can see that. The missing bejewelled skull of your saint.'

'Yes. What of thees?'

'What would you say if I told you Jameson and some friends have discovered the whereabouts of the saint's skull and are at this very moment retrieving it?'

De Luca grew deadly serious. His face tightened and he gripped Elspeth by the arm. 'Do not treat me as a fool.'

'I am telling you the truth. Jameson's in danger ... they are ...'

De Luca held up a finger demanding silence. 'Wait.' He pushed a button on his desk top intercom. A woman's voice answered. 'Si?' Elspeth couldn't understand Italian, but she recognised an order. Seconds later an attractive older woman with light brown hair to her shoulders, sharp facial features and athletic body poured into a black leather jumpsuit, entered the cabin. She acknowledged De Luca. 'Signor.'

'English,' De Luca ordered for Elspeth's sake.

'Yes.'

'Miss Poole, this ees Signora Magdalena Kowalski. She ees with the Vatican Swiss Guard. You know the importance of thees, I believe.'

'Of course.'

'Senora Kowalski. Miss Poole, she has very important news to do with Saint Adamo Abate.'

Kowalski had not taken her eyes off Elspeth from the moment she entered De Luca's cabin. Now her eyes narrowed, and she looked positively challenging. Elspeth didn't hesitate. She told the tough Polish woman what she had told De Luca. 'And now the Mexicans know about it too,' Elspeth said.

'Mexicans?'

'Yes. Drug dealers.'

Kowalski twisted about to De Luca spitting vitriol in Italian. Elspeth recognised the name Maya Hidalgo.

'That's her, Maya Hidalgo,' Elspeth said. 'They're here in Strahan.'

'Here!'

'I just saw them.'

'So, they must have waited for *us* to enter Macquarie Harbour,' De Luca said. 'Then they sail in after dark. They would need a local pilot for thees things, I am theenkin.'

'And they are where, now, exactly?'

'They are on their way to intercept *Grummet*.'

'Grummet?'

'Brad's fishing boat. Brad's Jameson's friend. They have gone to Halliday Island, that's where the convict dead were buried two centuries ago.'

'So, what ees Saint Adamo Abate doing on thees island?' De Luca asked.

'Long story. We must hurry.'

De Luca sat on the edge of his cabin desk staring at Elspeth. He massaged his forehead, confused. 'How did the Mexicans find thees information in the first place? Can you answer thees?'

'They have been following us. They have these thugs who kidnapped Jameson and ...'

Kowalski. 'In Stanley, si?'

'Yes.' Elspeth's mouth dropped open. 'How did you know?'

De Luca floundered for words, he looked indecisive a moment.

'We have been following your progress also, signora.' Kowalski said in faulting English.

'You what?'

'Si, we follow you also.'

'But I must confess,' De Luca said, 'we had doubts you really would succeed. Now thees.'

Elspeth jumped to her feet. 'Well then? We're running out of time. I'll tell you all you need to know on the way.'

'How far is thees island?'

'Twenty minutes in a fast boat.'

Jameson had the last shift in the hole. 'Hear that?' He looked up at four pairs of eyes staring back. His shovel had made a hollowed thud. He tapped again. 'This one's got a coffin.'

Andre. 'That's a good sign.'

Claire. 'Good! Why?'

'Well, I'm guessing that the matron organised a coffin to hide her handiwork.'

'Hmm.'

'It could be *Thomas Mauley*,' Claire said.

'I don't think so,' Calvino said.

'Why's that?'

'Cos you're standing on him.'

'Bloody hell,' Claire skipped left. There seemed no way of avoiding standing on someone's grave.

Jameson managed to excavate around the casket, enough to fit a boot ether side. 'The moment of reckoning,' he said. He looked up at Claire whose face was subtly lit by reflected torch light from his mobile, beyond was darkness. Brad, Andre and Calvino also gaped down at him, their own faces all silhouetted. Jameson continued the theatrics.

'Headfirst huh?' he grinned, tapping his shovel to a hollowed thud on the wider end of the casket.

'Hurry up for god's sake,' Claire was anxious. Jameson brought the shovel to bear on the rotted lid of the coffin. The wood was too decayed to splinter. It broke like honeycomb. Jameson looked back to his partners in crime, prolonging the suspense, when he caught movement behind Claire in the night. 'Jesus!'

Claire jumped. 'What?'

'Is that a bat?'

The giant moth the size of a small bird was drawn to the light. It tangled in Claire's wild red hair. Waving manically, Claire dodged aside, lost her footing and slipped into the grave, crushing timber. The others broke into laughter.

'Jesus H Christ Jameson,' Claire cursed. Spitting dust, she tried to stand before realising she was lying amongst the bones of a large man. 'Oh, you're kiddin' me. No!' Claire clawed at the grave wall. 'Get me outa here. Serious. Now.'

Jameson suddenly froze. 'Hey guys!'

Up top the other three went deadly quiet, gaping open mouthed into the pit.

Brushing herself down Claire leant into the light. 'Is that what I think it is?'

'Bloody hell yeh.'

Beyond the honeycombed wood, behind the shredded and rotten canvas, several gemstones twinkled and blinked in the shifting torch light.

'You-have-gotta-be-kiddin'-me.' Calvino's mouth dropped open, mesmerised. Andre, ever the optimist, had been sceptical about the myth. Until now. *Myth!*

'It's no myth,' Andre said, his voice hoarse with emotion. He was barely audible.

'Well, I'll be buggered,' Brad fell back against the tree trunk pushing his beanie to the back of his head. 'You bastards were for real.'

'Can you lift it free?' Andre sounded suddenly urgent. 'Is it loose?'

Jameson propped his mobile torch to the side, freeing up his hands, when he noted missed calls from Elspeth. 'What's this?'

Claire. 'What's what?'

'I've got six missed calls from El.'

Claire looked at her own phone. 'Me too, I've got three.'

'Something's up.' Jameson looked up to where the excavated earth was piled chest high. 'Anyone else got missed calls from ...'

Where is everyone?

'Andre?' Jameson called out. 'Brad?'

'You look-een for this, amigo?' Jorge Diaz had Calvino secured by the back of his collar. Calvino struggled to breath. Jameson was struck speechless.

How on earth …

Jameson made to climb out but Diaz kicked his shoulder. 'Stay.' Jameson cursed, stubbornly resisting when Emiliano appeared next to Diaz. He pointed a Remington Arms Bushmaster automatic assault rifle at Andre and Brad who now showed themselves.

Diaz leant over the edge and, recognising the half buried jewelled relic, he shook his head, speechless a moment. Finally, he spoke.

'So, we did it amigos. We finally found the sacred relic.'

'We?' Jameson angered. 'We found the relic. Try *us*, arsehole. *We* found the relic.'

'Arsehole?' Diaz looked to Emiliano. 'What is thees arsehole?'

'Gilipollas,' a woman's voice answered for Emiliano. 'Douchbag, arsehole. Same in English.'

Maya Hidalgo's English was fluent, with a strong accent. She looked a goddess in her tight black leather – leather slacks and tight-fitting black leather jacket over a black silk blouse – and her gold jewellery accessories. Jameson noticed her raven black hair was tied back in a chignon with a solid gold hairpiece of the god Mama Quilla. Most likely the real deal and no doubt robbed from an Inca tomb.

'You are a brave man to name Diaz a gilipollas, very brave indeed.' Maya sat on her haunches, peering down at Jameson. Her voice purred. She held Jameson's gaze. There was something hypnotic about this most attractive, yet dangerous woman. If Jameson didn't know any better, he had the distinct sensation the cartel boss was flirting with him. 'Now pass me that skull, nice and slow.'

Diaz kicked dirt into the grave. Jameson jerked aside. 'Do it gilipollas. We will soon see who ees the arsehole.' Calvino was thrown against the spoil heap. 'I shoot this one first.' Diaz pounded the rifle butt into Calvino's stomach and he doubled over, groaning. Jameson hesitated. Diaz raised his rifle for another strike.

'Wait!' Jameson shouted. 'Here.'

Jameson reluctantly, yet carefully, passed up the relic to Maya while Emiliano watched on, his assault rifle pointed squarely at Brad, Calvino and Andre.

Maya Hidalgo was speechless. She barely breathed – the Saint Adamo Abate skull was a sacred relic to be revered, worshipped even, in a twisted sort of way. The missing flesh of centuries past had been moulded with wax in antiquity, allowing jewels to be studded into the skull, showing off the dead man's ecclesiastical status in life. The saint's bones, Maya knew only too well, would have been retrieved from catacombs and prepared for the Vatican in the 16th or 17th century. Diamonds, sapphires, rubies and emeralds adorned the Italian medieval Benedictine abbot's skull, the remains of a saint who lived during the tenth and eleventh centuries.

But these precious stones were nothing to the Ratnaraj Ruby nestled inside the articulated cranium. As the others watched, Maya spread a silk scarf on the ground before her, where she knelt. Then, with respect and reverence, she placed the skull, jaw first on the cloth. Using a handkerchief Maya brushed the dust and dirt from the skull, which was in remarkable condition considering its history. She unfastened four tiny gold latches, two either side, and with the greatest of care, she separated the cranium from the main skull.

The gasps were collective. Standing on the coffin Jameson and Claire had a worm's eye view. The world's largest recorded ruby was the size of a grapefruit. This extremely hard crystalized alumina, Jameson had read, only turned red when chromium was involved with its formation, millions of years ago.

The Ratnaraj Ruby lived up to its meaning, *The King of Precious Stones.*

Maya knew all there was to know of the legendary gem. Believed to have been found in East Africa, the pigeon blood red ruby of high clarity and brilliance boasted a twelve-rayed star. The star formed when titanium atoms were trapped within the corundum crystal. To the pious, these represented sulci, the crevices in the human brain. Hence the decision made all those centuries ago by Vatican priests, to enclose the ruby in the skull of the most revered saint.

Ecstatic with her acquisition, Maya replaced the ruby and wrapped the skull in the scarf. She would have to be vigilant, for she knew such treasure caused temptation, and the strongest of wills could succumb to greed at any cost, even human life. And she should know.

With the priceless reliquary under her arm Maya stood. She looked to Diaz and Emiliano. Clearly, they had pre-planned their next move. 'You know what to do,' Maya, resplendent in black, dissolved into the night towards the water's edge.

Diaz jerked his head to his partner. Emiliano yelled an order in Spanish brandishing the assault rifle, motioning the three above ground to stand at the grave's edge. 'In,' he ordered.

Calvino. 'No way.'

Emiliano raised his voice. 'I say, get in hole.'

'Bugger you man,' Brad yelled. 'If you're gonna shoot me yer better do it while I'm looking you in the eye, pal.'

'Do as he say,' Diaz shouted. Emiliano stepped forward poking the gun muzzle in Andre's back. But Jameson leapt up from the casket. He heaved a handful of dirt in the Mexican's face. The gunman wheeled to face him. Jameson raised the shovel to shield himself the moment the assassin squeezed off a few rounds. Sparks flew, metal on metal. The shovel went flying. Jameson braced for the worst. Andre dived for Emiliano's legs, tackling him to the ground as another dozen rounds shredded leaves overhead. Diaz went for his Glok, secured in the back of his trousers, when ... from across the still waters came the sound of an approaching outboard. Diaz stiffened. Maya called out from the shoreline. A kilometre northwest the spotlight from a fast-moving speed boat danced across the surface towards them.

'Vamos!' Diaz shouted. 'Go! Go!' The two Mexicans hurried to their speedboat hidden on the side of the island opposite to the approaching craft. Andre, Calvino and Brad dropped to their knees to hoist Jameson and Claire free. 'Who the hell's that?' Jameson yelled as the group were doused in shifting floodlight.

'Police?'

'No,' Brad said. 'The local cop hasn't got access to anything that powerful.'

On the opposite side of the island, they heard the throaty 1500 horsepower outboards start simultaneously. Maya was escaping. Jameson made to run through the trees after them, but Brad caught his arm. 'Don't be mad, they'll shred yer with bullets.'

Emiliano employed the Nouva's full throttle. The bow rose on acceleration and the skipper mastered a wide arc around the island before heading for Hell's Gates.

They drove blind. No lights.

'There!' Elspeth was the first to spy the sleek vessel. It skipped across the water in near total darkness. Immediately automatic gunfire exploded ... tenfold louder over the water.

All aboard the Italian speed boat took cover. But it was instantly clear *they* weren't the target. In the distance bullets ripped into *Grummet*. The hull splintered at the waterline. The escaping speed boat continued on, yet they fired magazine after magazine. A third burst of gunfire and finally a fourth eventually struck the fishing boat's diesel tank.

Elspeth saw sparks ...a lick of flame ... then a massive fireball mushroomed towards the clouds, illuminating Halliday Island and the five figures now waving frantically to be rescued at the water's edge.

'Bastards!' Brad waded out into the freezing water where his three-metre inflatable drifted out into deep water. He was screaming. 'Why? Bastards.'

Seconds later De Luca, Signora Magdalena Kowalski, two seamen and Elspeth motored to within five metres of the shore. De Luca, skippering the Riva Aquarama motor launch, turned hard to port creating a wash, allowing the craft to drift closer to take on passengers from the shallows. Thirty metres away another smaller explosion ignited the *Grummet's* auxiliary tank before she sank stern first in deep water off Halliday Island.

Blackness engulfed the ancient land once more.

'Jameson Rowley!' De Luca cried out.

'Jesus,' Claire said. 'It's the Italians.'

'Is anyone hurt?'

'We're all good.'

Jameson recognised Elspeth in the dim light off the dash. 'Elspeth! What the hell?'

No answer. As pleased as she was to see Jameson safe, Elspeth seethed.

While one sailor dropped waist deep over starboard to secure the motor cruiser, Jameson and the others climbed on board. The waterline rose noticeably. Andre, Calvino and Claire crammed together on the deck. Jameson squeezed next to Elspeth. But her reception was as cold as the water. Brad forced himself between the two sailors and Kowalski. De Luca acknowledged Jameson in the light from the helm dashboard. Grateful to be rescued, Jameson wasn't surprised De Luca was on board. 'Thanks,' he managed meekly.

'We have some talking to do my friend,' De Luca told Jameson over his shoulder. The sailor in the water reboarded. De Luca engaged gear. The motor launch lurched forward.

Jameson put his face close to Elspeth's. 'We found it El.'

'What?'

'We found the saint just where we thought.'

The revelation caught Elspeth by surprise. She softened. 'Really?'

'Yes. Really.'

'And?'

'We were jumped by the Mexicans.'

'*They've* got the skull of Saint Adamo Abate?'

'I'm afraid so.'

'Signor De Luca,' Elspeth called out, but the man was nosing the motor launch towards Strahan …

Brad wanted vengeance. 'Hey! Chase the bastards,' Brad shouted. 'What the hell are you doin'? Chase the bastards that sank my boat.'

'Signor,' De Luca sighed. 'Although I have twin V8 Chev motors this is a vintage boat made of mahogany.' De Luca looked across the massive harbour in the direction of the Mexican Nuova already kilometres away and dissolving into the night. 'We cannot catch them. We will return to Strahan and notify the authorities.'

'Jesus mate. They'll have a mother ship out past Hell's Gates. We can do this.' De Luca ignored Brad's demands. 'They're from a tall ship too aren't they?' Brad yelled out. 'Part of the Hobart Festival. Right?'

No answer.

'Bah, I know I'm right. So, they will be anchored off the coast.'

De Luca kept on course.

'Hey, I'm talkin' to you.'

Jameson. 'Drop it mate. We'll go into Strahan and get help. This is out of our hands now. This is a major international crime.'

But Brad was having none of it. 'Hey,' he said to Jameson, his voice barely audible over the motors. 'These are the Eytie's you were talkin' about from the Vatican, right?'

Jameson shoulders sagged. 'Yes, but we can't catch them in this. You can see for yourself Brad …'

'Hey,' Brad persisted with De Luca, yelling out over the V8s. 'De Luca ain't it? We found Saint what's his name's skull.'

Elspeth had told De Luca most of the story prior to this point, but not everything. The handsome Italian diplomat wheeled about. 'You found what?'

'The skull mate. We actually *did* find your saint's skull and we saw the biggest ruby ever.'

De Luca fixed on Jameson. 'Ees thees true?'

'Yes.'

'Yes mate,' Brad went on. 'And it's bloody beautiful.'

De Luca looked at Jameson. 'Well?'

'I was about to tell you.'

'Gesù Cristo, in god's name. Why you not tell me sooner?'

Jameson shrugged. 'I was about to.'

De Luca had a quick word with Magdalena Kowalski before managing a sharp arc at speed, threatening to jettison those on the port side before pointing the bow towards the Southern Ocean. Brad smiled. Vengeance at last. 'Come forward,' De Luca ordered Brad. 'That was your boat they sank, si?'

'Yes mate. Bastards.'

'You local fish man, yes?'

'Absolutely.'

'Then here, take helm.'

'What?'

'You are skipper, si. You know thees water good?'

'Bloody oath. Like the back o' me hand.'

'Then here,' De Luca killed the bow lights. 'Take the helm, ees dark. I am driving blind.'

'Sensible man, your Eytie mate,' Brad told Jameson as Jameson joined him at the helm. Brad steered north into deeper water. 'We got a few islands to watch out for like Elizabeth on our port and then there's the Shag Islands and Bird Island north o' that before we approach Macquarie Heads.'

'You mean Hell's Gates?'

'Yep.' Brad took a peek over his shoulder checking out the passenger in the tight jumpsuit sitting quietly in the dark, her mind deep in thought. 'Who's the fox?'

Although De Luca was out of earshot, he read Brad's mind. 'That is my chief of security Signora Magdalena Kowalski.'

'Oh.'

'How you say in Engleesh, *you do not read book by cover.*'

'You can't tell a book by its cover.'

'Si, si.'

'I think he means hands off, Brad,' Jameson grinned.

Jameson's eyes had adjusted to the darkness. He hoped Brad knew what he was doing. It was now approaching 10PM and the quarter moon was almost overhead. Passing clouds afforded Brad the subtlest of light, a vague reflection of moonlight, almost like a path leading to Hell's Gates. Andre, Calvino and Claire sat huddled against the cold breeze in the stern. Kowalski and the two seamen were amidships.

'So, what do yer reckon that saint's head's worth?' Brad said. 'Million bucks?'

'It's priceless mate,' Jameson said. 'You could never sell it.'

'Well, what the bloody hell did we risk our lives for then, and my boat?'

'Sorry about *Grummet*, I really am.' Jameson fished for an answer. He looked to De Luca, now sitting next to Elspeth. They were deep in conversation, no doubt, Jameson thought, talking about the saint's skull. 'It was the thrill of discovery. The archaeology and all that.'

'Oh. What about the gold?'

'Christ knows. It would be nice if we did find it, that is if it existed at all.'

'Well, yer found the saint's head didn't yer? So why not the gold?'

Half an hour passed...

'There they are!' Brad cut back from full throttle. The Riva Aquarama slowed considerably, bow first before a backwash lifted the stern. De Luca replaced Jameson at the helm. 'Look straight ahead,' Brad told the Italian. It was difficult to see clearly; the dark shape of a three-masted ship against its black backdrop of headland. As they focussed soft light circled the portholes below deck. The Mexicans were keeping a low profile, but they were certainly anchored there, five-hundred-metres east from Hell's Gates and the harbour's only exit to the Southern Ocean.

'They *are* inside Macquarie Harbour,' De Luca was puzzled.

'Certainly are mate,' Brad said.

'They would've needed someone to pilot them in,' Jameson said.

'Yeh. We're about two kilometres away,' Brad said. 'We'll have to creep forward slowly if we're going to surprise them.' Brad turned to De Luca. 'What's the plan boss?'

'Plan?' De Luca, who was growing to enjoy the company of his Australian guests, had to concede he too had been impulsive. He looked to the two sailors under his command. Both men were armed only with side-arms. Signora Kowalski joined him. They conversed briefly in Italian before the Polish security guard finally acknowledged Brad and Jameson with a curt nod.

'Plan, you say. Well, I am Signor Orfeo De Luca, adviser to the Italian Embassy in Australia,' he crowed. 'I will board this *Il Corvo Nero* and demand the return of the head of Saint Adamo Abate in the name of the Vatican. In the name of Pope Francis himself.'

Brad smirked. 'You reckon?'

'Why you laugh?'

'Mate, they have automatic weapons. You saw what they did to my boat.'

'Si. But I have two marines. Both mens have pistols.'

'Brad's right,' Jameson agreed with Brad. 'They have machine guns. We could maybe sneak up on them.' Jameson suggested. But he wasn't feeling overconfident after the grave site incident. 'I have been on board, I know the layout.'

'You have been on thees sheep?'

'Yes.'

'How?'

'Long story.'

Elspeth felt decisively uncomfortable. Armed marines on their side or not, she was worried. She tried to find a mobile phone signal. Nothing. But she had had three missed calls from 'No Caller ID.'

With the Riva Aquarama's motors idling softly, the bosun's whistle from the deck of the Mexican tall ship echoed across the waters of a calm night. De Luca straightened. 'You hear that, si?'

Brad and Jameson agreed. Action was afoot. 'They're preparing to sail.'

'Damn it, they have what they came for,' Jameson said. 'And they're going to escape.'

'Ees now or nev-er.' De Luca shouldered Brad aside. 'Hold on.' Gripping the twin levers, De Luca thrust the throttles full speed ahead. With a throaty roar the two three-fifty horse-power inboards raised the bow.

Like a rearing stallion.

All on board snatched the safety rails. Within seconds they felt the wind in their hair, the adrenalin rush and a flush of uncertainty.

De Luca was charged. Uncertain of the shoreline, he flicked a chrome switch on the dash. The twenty million candlepower spotlight bolted to the bow arced to life. From the deck of the *Il Corvo Nero* it appeared a UFO sped towards them across the water. Panic on board the Mexican ship gave De Luca courage. Steering directly for amidships where the tender was preparing to be hoisted on board, the Italian still relied on the diplomatic approach.

Suddenly gunfire destroyed any ambitions of a safe boarding.

They were fifty metres away. Warning shots perhaps. But terrifying all the same. De Luca turned to port while the two armed sailors dropped to their knees returning small arms fire. They were useless against the automatic weapons, but effective enough to make most on board the *Il Corvo Nero* take cover.

The tall ship's sails unfurled.

Jameson heard them flop towards the deck. But with little breeze to fill them they hung like laundry. Immediately axillary engines fired to life ...

Meanwhile the Nuova was stranded. The tall ship's movement interfered with the crane. Screamed orders and anxious yelling fetched across the water.

Andre. 'What's happening?'

Brad. 'Their hoist for the tender's stuffed.'

Jameson and Elspeth recognised the feline figure of Maya Hidalgo. She stood in the stern of the Nuova, holding a parcel under one arm while steadying herself on a crane cable. Jorge Diaz and Emiliano appeared alongside. Diaz shouted orders but all was pandemonium.

Under diesel power the ship motored away while sporadic gunfire caused the Riva Aquarama to keep its distance.

'You can forget the diplomatic approach,' Jameson told De Luca. But the gunfire still seemed like warning shots. 'If they meant real harm, they would inflict it.'

'Maybe they're just bad shots,' Claire suggested.

'They're escaping,' Calvino said.

'This'll be good,' Brad ground his teeth. 'That channel is dangerous. If you don't know your tides it can be treacherous.'

'How did they enter in the first place?' Jameson wanted to know. 'Surely the pilot hasn't been out here today.'

'Maybe they fluked it.'

Minutes past. Beyond Hell's Gates the wild Southern Ocean's temperament revealed itself. The breeze stiffened. Within minutes it turned into a moderate wind. Blowing north to south the wind curled around the lighthouse before sweeping over the rocks and shoreline of some of the world's most dangerous and unpredictable coastline.

A third burst of gunfire peppering the water about the Riva Aquarama had De Luca pull further back, although he still suspected they were more deterrent warning shots than aiming to kill.

Struggling with decisions the Italian diplomat toyed with the idea of making a run for Strahan. Round up the authorities and somehow arrest the ship before she reached international waters.

But that would only be futile. All they could do was watch. The Mexican's luck held, strengthening like the wind. The sails filled. With a good blow in the canvas the helmsman headed for the channel and freedom. But it proved too much, too fast, too soon.

The shouts from the lookout reached all on board the Italian launch. Maya Hidalgo and Diaz, still trapped on board the abandoned speedboat, instantly cut loose from the crane. The Nouva dropped two metres back into the water. But she landed on an even keel. Although water washed over the sides, she soon settled. Diaz re-started the engines and quickly motored away from the ship before they were crushed. As the others watched on, Maya tumbled back into the stern seat while Diaz sped into the channel searching a safe passage for the ship.

Jameson. 'What's happening?'

'They're goin' to hit the rocks,' Brad cheered. 'That's what's happening.'

'Serious?'

'Bloody oath ...'

Brad's words were barely understood by all those around him when they heard the sickening squealing of steel plate being wrenched from the port bow. The ship juddered to a stop. To the Italians the outcome was clear. The steel plate concertinaed, exposing a hole the size of a car in the hull. Splintered decking scattered like skittles thrown into the air. Water flooded into the ship. She was doomed.

Jorge Diaz and Emiliano motored frantically back towards the stricken ship. With Diaz at the helm his first priority now was to save his boss, Maya Hidalgo. He headed towards the shoreline one hundred metres away. Maya looked terrified, panicked. Diaz had never seen her like this. Grasping the skull, she pushed her back into the stern sheets and prayed. Diaz raced between the shore and the stricken ship. But white water warned him surf was breaking on rocks nearby. Diaz turned sharply, a bad move. The speedboat's starboard bow caught a twisted sheet of steel plate below the waterline, unseen in the blackness of night. Like a water skier might mount a ramp, the Nuova scaled the plate, turned onto its cabin and crashed back into the choppy channel. No one resurfaced.

Elspeth and Claire watched on in horror. 'We better go help them.'

'Maybe that's not a good idea,' Andre said. 'Look.' As they watched the ship founder, dozens of silhouetted survivors could be seen scrambling along the bowsprit, where they easily dropped onto rocks like so many rats. No one noticed the trim all black figure swim into the shadows where she clambered up the rocks, unhurt but emptyhanded.

'There's too many of them,' Elspeth said.

'I agree – there's no guessing what they might do.'

'And they're armed.'

De Luca said nothing. Spinning the wheel of the slender craft he turned about and steered for Strahan.

CHAPTER TWELVE

Five hours later. First light...

Those Mexicans wanted by the law had fled inland. Little did they realise they were sealing their own fate. Other crew members took refuge in the holiday shacks in the area. Some were treated for minor injuries, mostly abrasions from the barnacled rocks. Many sheltered in the lighthouse where first aid was available. With nothing to hide they would seek asylum. Of Maya Hidalgo and her minders, there was no sign.

Waiting for sunup, no one had slept. With tours on the harbour cancelled for the morning, Jameson and the others returned to the scene at dawn on board the tour-company catamaran *Harbour Master*. Also on board was a search and rescue team of Italians put together by De Luca. The local police were first on the scene, with law enforcement back-up on its way from Queenstown to the east, and Zeehan to the north. De Luca was close by in the Riva Aquarama launch, Senora Kowalski at his side.

The once magnificent tall ship *Il Corvo Nero* was a sorry sight. She sat on the seabed in shallow water with the high tide slopping about the main deck. With stubborn clouds blocking the morning's sunlight, a certain gloom haunted the area.

Jameson, Elspeth, Claire, Andre, Brad and Calvino were ferried ashore in one of several Zodiacs. Here, they joined other volunteers scouring the shoreline for anything salvageable. The tide was high, and although the ocean beyond Hell's gates was choppy, the breakwater calmed the wreck site.

'Hey,' Calvino clambered awkwardly over rocks to the water's edge. Something had caught his eye. 'That's their speedboat isn't it?'

The others joined him. The Nuova's keel showed in two metres of water where she had flipped and sunk.

Jameson stripped to his shorts.

'What are you doing?'

'Don't know yet.'

Elspeth shook her head. Jameson took a deep breath and dived headfirst alongside the tender. After an exploratory dive he surfaced, took another breath and duck dived. Brad balanced on rocks next to Elspeth. 'You've got yourself a mad bastard there El.'

'Tell me about it.'

Jameson surfaced, trod water offering a wide grin only ... and dived a third time.

Nearly a minute and a half passed. By now he had drawn a gathering. Elspeth looked anxious, preparing to dive in after him. Immediately bubbles burst on the surface five metres from where he disappeared.

'Bingo!' he surfaced, spluttering. Swallowing water, Jameson snatched lungfuls of air. He struggled to swim one armed to the rocks, a bundle tucked under the other.

'Here.'

Calvino was closest. 'What is it?'

'Just take the bloody thing,' Jameson coughed. 'For Christ' sake.'

Calvino waded in, relieving Jameson of the water-soaked parcel. 'What is it?'

'Just don't drop it.'

Calvino dragged the waterlogged object onto a flat rock. The others climbed down to the water's edge.

'Well,' Claire said. 'What is it?'

'Someone's coat.'

Jameson climbed barefoot onto weathered boulders. 'Open it.'

'Oh Jesus!' Calvino exposed the skull of Saint Adamo Abate. Immediately clouds parted and the morning sun, low in the sky, illuminated the wreck site.

'It was just resting there,' Jameson had good reason to be pleased with himself. 'Wedged under the dash.'

This was the first time Elspeth had seen the treasured artefact. 'It's ... it's just, simply, stunning,' she sighed. 'I can hardly believe this is happening.'

'Me neither,' Claire tossed Jameson a beach towel.

Signor De Luca and Signora Kowalski watched from the embankment. The Italian diplomat shook his head gently, an irrepressible smile of admiration washing over him. He sent Kowalski to take charge. Moments later two dozen onlookers stood around an upturned Zodiac, where the treasured Vatican relic was afforded a short exhibition before being carefully wrapped in beach towels for its sojourn back to the *Amerigo Vespucci*. Finally, the missing head of the saint would be returned to its rightful owner.

'Any sign of those on board the *Nuova*?' De Luca asked Jameson. Jameson sighed and shook his head. The Italian diplomat looked at the gathering. The crew members waited instruction.

'How many survivors?' De Luca asked his officers.

'Twenty-three senor, five women and eighteen men.'

'See the men are taken back to Strahan aboard the *Harbour Master* and the women put on board the launch.' De Luca watched Kowalski stow the treasured skull aboard the launch, in a locker next to the helm. 'We leave as soon as they are on board. We have what we came for.'

De Luca joined Jameson towelling himself. Elspeth stood by. 'I cannot thank you enough. You have gone beyond the call of duty. I will personally recommend your actions to the Holy See.'

'What?' Calvino joined them. 'No reward?' Elspeth shot Calvino a filthy look.

The five women survivors on board looked exhausted. Only two understood some basic English. With their immediate futures uncertain they kept to themselves, saying very little, yet grateful to be rescued. A translator acknowledged, that with their employer missing and wanted by the authorities for questioning on illegal firearms charges at the very least, there was pressure to have the cartel members arrested and charged. There would be an inquiry, they were informed. Preliminary phone calls hinted the United States Embassy in Canberra was even suggesting they should be deported to America. If there was ever a chance to arrest these people, now was it. But for now there was no sign of the major players.

None of De Luca's crew took much notice of the trim older woman in the tight-fitting black and gold uniform of the *Il Corvo Nero* crew, with her hair hidden beneath a shawl.

Maya Hidalgo kept her head bowed for the half hour journey back to Strahan. She hoped that her crew member, whom she had robbed of her uniform and tied securely in a fisherman's hut back at the wreck site, would not be discovered before she escaped this miserable place.

But she had unfinished business.

The temptation to possess the Ratnaraj ruby was overwhelming. It possessed her like some demon conjured through a Ouija board. Ignored by the other female survivors on board, under her own orders, Maya sat, head down. She stared at the locker near the helm, where she knew the precious skull had been placed.

And waited to strike. It was as audacious as it was cunning.

No one expected the skull of Saint Adamo Abate, wrapped in beach towels and placed in a satchel on board the Italian launch, would vanish one last time. Placed by Signora Kowalski on the skipper's seat at the helm for a fleeting second, while the other women were disembarked, Maya took advantage of the scramble. She scooped the relic from the leather bag, wrapping it in her shawl. With a sudden rush of renewed confidence, Maya even took advantage of the handsome Italian sailor's offer to help her ashore; after all she was encumbered by the parcel under her arm.

But where to run?

Obsessed, possessed, Maya pushed into the scrum of tourists, media and other sightseers, where at least fifty people had hurried to the docks to catch a glimpse of the Mexican survivors.

Elspeth couldn't believe what she was witnessing. She disembarked the fast catamaran *Harbour Master* in time to catch one of the rescued crew members off the *Il Corvo Nero* wrap the relic in a shawl. It was such a casual manoeuvre that Elspeth thought the woman was authorised, that she was responsible for the priceless artefact. That is, until she watched the surreptitious exit from the launch to the dock.

Maya dissolved into the crowd.

'Jameson!'

Jameson whirled to Elspeth looking particularly incredulous, gaping at the onlookers on shore.

'Jameson.'

'What?'

'That crew member from off the *Nero* just walked away with the skull. I'm certain of it.'

'What? Who?'

'The tall slim older woman.' Elspeth pointed. 'There.'

Maya shoved away from the rear of the crowd. Jameson caught her profile. 'Jesus!'

'What is it?'

'That's the Mexican cartel boss ...'

'I knew it!' Elspeth raced down the gangway onto the dock. At the same time Kowalski had been observing Elspeth and she snapped her head towards the crowd and she spotted Maya. With the grace of a stalking panther the Polish guard vaulted onto the launch's bow, leapt from vessel onto the dock and using a bollard as a springboard, she launched herself after Elspeth.

'Stop her!' Elspeth yelled to the crowd.

Heads turned.

People parted and Elspeth thrust between them. Maya heard the commotion. There seemed nowhere to run. It was so unlike her – unplanned, a knee-jerk reaction. Desperate, she ran along the wharf. Kowalski saw Elspeth in pursuit, closing fast on Maya. But Maya was slowed by the precious artefact she so despairingly wanted. The athletic Pole sprang onto a loading platform. She planned to cut Maya off.

Claire's timing couldn't be better.

Claire shoved the toilet door open the second Elspeth threw herself at Maya, Maya slammed into the door. The parcel hit the concrete and skittled several metres. Kowalski dived from the platform and immediately the Mexican cartel boss was rugby-tackled to the ground by two beautiful women. The crowd cheered.

Claire stood in the lavatory doorway stunned, slowly realising how instrumental she had been in the capture of one of America's most wanted. De Luca's security swooped, the local constabulary arrived, and Elspeth and Kowalski finally released the raging fire cat. Senora Maya Hidalgo was dragged away, screaming obscenities in Spanish – cursing her captors and all those about her in a spectacular fall from grace.

'Now,' Claire said as she posed with Elspeth and Kowalski for photos. 'That's what I call *Girl Power!*'

That evening...

By nightfall Strahan had become a media hub. Journalists from Melbourne and Sydney, helicoptered in from Launceston airport, joined Tasmania's news crews all vying for interviews and in particular, footage of the Saint's ruby. De Luca allowed film crews into the *Amerigo Vespucci's* saloon, one studio at a time, before locking the priceless relic in a shipboard safe.

Celebrations were now in order. For the second evening in a row the local dignitaries turned out to enjoy the Italians' generosity. De Luca's *thank you* cocktail party on the main deck was attended by the township. So many in fact, a marquee was set up on the dock to accommodate the overflow. Strahan was in party mode. And Jameson, Elspeth, Andre, Claire and Calvino were guests of honour.

De Luca took the champagne bottle from the steward and insisted on filling their glasses himself. 'Will you look at your pol-eece inspector from 'obart,' De Luca whispered in Elspeth's ear as he filled her flute with bubbles. 'What you say in Engleesh? Idiota?'

'Wanker,' Jameson said, overhearing the Italian. Standing proudly with his hands held before him, Inspector Ray Wilson bathed in camera lights, proudly boasting to the world media how he was responsible for the custodian transfer of the evil Mexican drug cartel boss.'

'I personally will see the woman extradited to Sydney.' They heard him boast to the cameras.

De Luca shook his head slowly. 'He can have the cred-eet for all I care. We have Adamo Abate's remains intact, thees ees more important, si?'

Brad finally caught up with the group, a chilled Birra Moretti Premium frothing in his hand. 'Did yer hear the news?'

'No, what?'

'Search and rescue found the bodies of the two blokes that harassed us on the island.'

'Excellent.'

'Yer, washed up half a *k* away on the breakwater.'

'Good, then we know they didn't escape.'

'Well, saluté to that,' De Luca raised his glass. 'Thank you once again. Ees a pity though,' De Luca continued,'that one diamond ees missing.'

'Oh?' Elspeth looked bemused. 'Missing?'

'Si. But eet ees from behind the left ear. The, ah … wax, si, the wax ees missing, and one diamond, she ees gone. But we Italianos cannot be sad. We finally have the saint's bones together.'

Next Morning. Brad's House...

With the van packed it was time to drive back to Hobart when Elspeth's mobile chimed. 'It looks like the same *No Caller ID* who called when I couldn't get a signal the other night.' Elspeth swiped the screen. 'Hello, Elspeth Poole.'

'Elspeth … got yer at last mate. It's Teddy Lanyard 'ere.'

'Ted!'

'Yer, remember me, caretaker elder at Preminghana and Sundown Point?'

'Yes of course.' Elspeth mouthed *Ted* to the others, all watching on. 'Nice to hear from you.'

'Likewise love. I tried to find Andre's number but I musta deleted it or somethin' an' couldn't think of it, but then I remember you said yer worked at the museum in 'obart so I called them and … well …'ere we are. Mind you they didn't wanna give me yer number, that is, not until I told 'em about the find up 'ere at the petroglyphs and our connection. Not that I wanted to tell the buggers anythin' really. No first peoples want the museum up 'ere, not since them mongrels come 'ere in the 70s and sawed off one o' them carvin's to take to the museum.'

'I am sorry about that Ted, but it's a long time ago. Attitudes have changed.'

'Oh, it ain't your fault love.'

'Hold on a moment,' Elspeth said, 'I'm with the others, I'll put you on speaker phone. So, what's this find?'

Everyone listened.

'Well, I got talkin' to Wayne and Kev 'bout the lost treasure everyone keeps bangin' on about when ol' Wayne, 'e's much older than me, nearly seventy, 'e says Ted, that bloody treasure was found years ago. How long ago says I. Christ knows says 'e, it were found not long after the wreck o' that whitefella ship 'ere. How do yer know says I. Well, they found the bugger in a cave 'ere, dead like, just a skeleton but wearing whitefella clothes like old seaman, what was left of 'im.'

'How did Wayne know this?'

'Well Wayne says 'e was a lad, 'bout ten, when there was this bloody great storm what smashed up the coast 'ere. An' there was a bit of a landslide and a cave was exposed, a cave what no one knew about before. An' in the cave was this skeleton.'

'Really?'

'Yeh. Really.'

'And Wayne was ten you said, so its nearly sixty years ago? Say late 1950s?'

'Sounds 'bout right,' Ted said. 'I was too young ter remember.'

'Was there anything else in this cave? I mean how do you know the skeleton had anything to do with a lost treasure … or a shipwreck for that matter?'

'Well, we don't know really. But it just makes sense don't it. Ted also said there was shitloads, excuse me love, heaps o' blue stuff, like chalky rock in the cave with 'im like. Piles and piles and piles o' the stuff in bags, what was rotted. One o' the other elders told Wayne at the time 'e reckoned it was blue dye.'

'Dye?'

'Yer, Like what whitefellas coloured their clothes with in olden times.'

'Indigo,' Andre said quietly. 'Ted,' Andre called over the speaker phone. 'This is Andre.'

'Andre … mate. You are there. 'Ow's it's goin'?'

'Good my friend, really good to hear your voice. Tell me, what happened to the skeleton.'

'Oh the first peoples 'ere back in the 50s, they burnt it. Gave it a proper send-off they did, to keep them spirits happy.'

'Fair enough.'

'Does Wayne know where this cave is? I mean is it still there?'

'No, all caved in again. Sand dunes swallowed it up again 'e reckons.'

Andre struggled to gain speed in the Mitsubishi on the climb into the West Coast Ranges on the Lyell Highway. 'You know what I reckon,' he said, oblivious to the vehicles in his wake, desperate for an upcoming passing-lane.

'Well, I hope you have answers Andre,' Elspeth said, 'because the last few days are doing my head in.'

Claire. 'Me too.'

'Come on then,' Jameson said from the seat behind. 'Tell us what you're thinking.'

'There was never any treasure.'

Claire. 'What?'

'There was never any treasure. There were never any gold bars from the wrecked *El Delfin*.'

'And how'd yer work that out?' Calvino looked miffed.

Andre looked at Jameson in the rear view and saw in his friend's eyes that they were on the same page. 'Indigo huh?' Jameson said.

'Exactly. I've been giving this a lot of thought,' Andre said. 'We know from what documents we have that *El Delfin* stopped at the Ivory Coast in West Africa. The gold ingots were hot property; they more than likely were all stamped with the assayer's stamp of the Bank of Cadiz. Fate would have been keen to trade, get rid of the incriminating gold and buy merchandise to trade up, possibly in the East Indies where he could have traded for spices or tea. He had the means, the gold and the ship.'

'And what commodity in 1812 was worth trading for gold?' Jameson's question was really a statement. 'Indigo.'

'Exactly.'

If Calvino was confused before, he was now completely lost. 'What the bloody hell's indigo?'

'You explain Andre,' Jameson said. 'I'm sure you'll do a better job of it.'

'Well,' Andre started. 'Indigo is a rich blue dye, somewhere between the blue in a rainbow and violet, extracted from the leaves of the Indigofera plant, used primarily in textiles.'

Calvino. 'So, it *is* a dye huh, like Ted said?'

Jameson. 'Yes. It was popular around the globe, highly sought after and very valuable. However synthetic alternatives were invented and in use by the mid-nineteenth century. Today indigo is worth only a fraction of what it fetched when Fate and his crew invested in the commodity.'

'Assuming they did.'

'Yes.'

'The word indigo, by the way, is the Latin for India,' Jameson said. 'As it commonly came from India.'

Claire. 'So, you're suggesting when the ship as wrecked the indigo was stored in a cave.'

'Yes, well away from the water's edge.'

'Why didn't this Anwyn Blizzard woman know where it was hidden?'

'Maybe she was left to sort out the Vatican treasure.'

'Oh, I forgot about that.'

'Yes, well that was hidden separately, somewhere safe as well. Fate was terrified of repercussions in the afterlife. He sent the Vatican a letter letting them know where the sacred bones were hidden, remember.'

'Who made the plaster casts of the petroglyph then?' Calvino asked.

'Thomas Mogg, Matron's son-in-law,' Andre said. 'And Percy Stagg.'

'Who were they again?'

'They're the two who Matron sent to fetch the 'gold'. Remember Septimus Tilley, the prisoner on Sarah Island who was dying ...'

'And the bloke who had his own head swapped for the saint's head in the grave!'

'Yep. Well, he told Matron, on his dying bed, where the treasure was hidden.'

'Didn't he tell her it was indigo?'

'Apparently not. My guess is that they continued with the gold ingot story because it is a compact asset. The same value in indigo would be prohibitive to move about easily and would have had less appeal.'

'And the plaster casts?'

'Well, this is more guess work mind,' Andre said. 'But I reckon I'd be correct in suggesting, they discovered the indigo, still valuable in 1825, and, like I just said, when they realised how much there was and that they couldn't cart it all away immediately, they took what they could carry to Percy Stagg's ketch, *Salty*, leaving the rest for later.'

'Did they make the cast of the petroglyph and kept half each in case they were suspected, arrested or possibly robbed even?'

'Possibly. But a more likely scenario would be for one or the other to pass onto the next of kin in case of death. Which is exactly what happened, but I'll get to that. They have enjoyed moderate wealth for a short period, having told Matron there was no gold ...'

'But they found the saint's gem-studded skull with the indigo.'

'That's correct.'

'But everyone was superstitious, terrified of the skull, and Matron made certain it was buried in consecrated soil, on Halliday Island,' Elspeth said.

'I have another theory. I found a death notice for Percy Stagg, suspected drowned at sea. His body was never found. His ketch *Salty* was found abandoned on a beach south of where the indigo was hidden. It was not deemed suspicions. I'm suggesting he met with foul play. I'm suggesting Thomas Mogg had returned to Sundown Point, as it's called today, and moved the indigo to where it was later discovered by accident and ...'

'The cheeky bastard left us a halfpenny as a souvenir,' Calvino said.

'So, the skeleton in the indigo cave,' Elspeth said, 'was no other than Percy Stagg.'

'That's my theory anyway.'

'A few years later Mogg buys the Red Fox Inn. That's how the plaster cast wound up there. God knows how it got into the chimney.'

'Mogg hid it.'

'So, you're suggesting Mogg made a few trips back to the indigo, taking a mule load here, a mule load there,' Jameson said. 'Enough to buy the inn eventually.'

'That sounds about right.'

'So why didn't he take the lot? By the sounds of things there was still a lot left washed out in that storm.'

'Maybe he became ill, who knows.'

'Anwyn would have known all along that there was no gold. That it had been traded for indigo. But in her mind, who would go searching for tons of indigo?'

'Fair enough.'

CHAPTER THIRTEEN

Melanoma Cottage. Storm Bay. The following Sunday...

On the balcony overlooking Storm Bay, Bradley and Calvino necked fresh beers and watched the master at work. Six Wagyu Scotch Fillet steaks slowly bar-b-qued on the wood-fuelled barbie. Jameson was in his element. To his mind there was nothing more enjoyable than a barbie on the deck of Melanoma Cottage enjoying the water views and in the company of great friends. Brad, in the market for a new boat, was staying the night, having driven from Strahan to inspect the *Proud River*, a thirty-foot, fifteen-year-old fishing vessel.

Cheerful voices from Elspeth and Claire in the kitchen told Jameson Andre had arrived and moments later the table was set with salads. Andre joined them with a bottle of pinot noir.

'I have finally put together the missing pieces of the puzzle,' Andre said.

'Great.'

'I have worked out who originally owned the chocolate tin that started our little adventure.'

'Oh, and?'

'Well, I found out that the *Diligent* was registered to a Guy and Jackie Ingles from Sydney.'

'Yes, we knew that.'

'Yes, but Jackie's ancestor was none other than Anwyn Fotheringham. They came looking for what they thought was the gold. They had the letters and documents. They also met descendants of Stagg, back in the 50s.'

'The Ingles,' Jameson said.

'Yes, Guy and Jackie.'

'Now I remember. The garage sale in New Town where I bought the tin, the name on the letterbox was Ingles.'

Jameson forked a steak wrapped in prosciutto onto Brad's plate and waited until he piled on salads. 'So,' Jameson said, 'are you going to buy the *River Proud* or what?'

'I'd bloody well like to but he's asking 1.2 for it.'

'Is it worth 1.2?'

'Christ yeh Jam, but Jesus. I'm only getting 400,000 for *Grummet* from the insurance company. Do the sums mate.'

'Well, *Grummet* was a heap of shit.'

Brad was incredulous. 'Heap o' shit! You bastard. *Grummet* was my baby. She was reliable. I haven't got a means of employment now. Heap o' shit! How could you be so heartless?'

'Ah, you can get another job mate. Washing cars, do errands for nice old ladies. Or get a real job like pumping petrol or stacking shelves in the local bottle shop.'

Brad's eyes narrowed. He had been mates with Jameson a long time. *Was this the grog talking?* 'Are you serious?'

'Here,' Jameson plucked something from his pocket. 'If you're going to cry use this.' He passed Brad his handkerchief.

'I don't want yer hanky.'

'Here take it.'

'Bugger off. I've got me own.'

'Open it you silly bugger.' Brad took the red and white chequered handkerchief. 'Open it carefully.'

If Brad was suspicious, he was equally cautious. A moment later he held a sparkling stone the size of a large marble. 'What's this then?'

'What's it look like?'

Brad stared into the handkerchief for what seemed an unnaturally long time ...

When it twigged. 'No!'

'Yes.'

'Are you for real?'

'Bloody oath mate.'

Elspeth Claire, Calvino and Andre who knew all about Jameson's gesture joined them.

'Jesus Jam,' Brad was flushed with the excitement. 'What ... how?'

'It was a little loose when I retrieved the treasured skull under water, and it sort of fell off.'

'Ha!' Brad laughed. 'Fell off, yeh right.'

'Well, let's say it was like a loose tooth.'

'Christ mate. What's it worth?'

'El did a little Googling and she came up with an estimate of nine hundred to a mill', thereabouts.'

Brad whistled. 'That's brilliant mate. Good for you. What are you goin' to do with it?'

'Not me mate, you. You're going to buy that boat.'

EPILOGUE

Yes, Jameson did return the plaster artefact back to the Red Fox Inn in Hadspen and Elspeth made certain the Matron's diary was returned to the Stanley Museum, albeit after it was digitally filed at the Tasmanian museum.

And the Vatican returned Adamo Abate's head back to the saint's remains, minus one diamond.

. . .

Van Diemen's Land. A short history...

Until the dawn of the nineteenth century the island of Tasmania, then known to the European world as Van Diemen' s Land, was a forgotten land, a land roamed by tribes of Aborigines living in harmony with nature. It is estimated somewhere between 3,000 to 15,000 Palawa people called the island home at the time of European settlement in 1803. Appallingly, that was about to change.

These people had crossed into Tasmania at least 40,000 years ago. Archaeological evidence excavated in the South-West's Warren Cave in 1990 has been dated to 34,000 years, making Tasmanian Aborigines the world's southern-most population during the Pleistocene epoch.

Tasmania was connected to the mainland by a land bridge during the last glacial period but sea level rise following the last ice age, some 8000 years ago, separated these Aborigines from their mainland counterparts.

The first recorded European visitor is Abel Janszoon Tasman, a Dutch seafarer and merchant in the service of the Dutch East India Company, who is credited as the first known explorer to reach the southern islands, including New Zealand, in two separate voyages, 1642 and 1644. Tasman named the island Van Diemen's Land after the governor of the Dutch East Indies. Interestingly the expedition did not encounter any Aborigines when they landed.

However, a French exploratory expedition, under Marion Dufresne, did encounter the Aborigines the day he rowed ashore in 1772. At first, they were friendly. It was only when a second longboat was dispatched to join him on the beach that the natives grew anxious and responded by throwing stones and spears. Musket shots were fired and regrettably one native was killed and several wounded. It would be twenty years later before another European ship explored the region.

The French returned almost a generation later and animosities were either forgotten or forgiven. Bruni d'Entrecasteaux's visit in 1792-3 and Nicolas Baudin in 1802 both enjoyed friendly encounters.

Meanwhile from the 1790s the northernmost tribes on Van Diemen's Land encountered the sealers, a violent and determined group of piratical characters making a living by trading in sealskins from the Bass Strait Islands. Many of these men were escaped convicts from Port Jackson or whalers who had abandoned ship for a castaway lifestyle. Their treatment of Aboriginal women was abhorrent; kidnapping them for their sealing skills and forcing them to gratify their 'companionship' urges. Many were kept tied up and treated like dogs. Many of the Aboriginal men were murdered by sealers.

British settlement and domination was not far off.

In December 1798, ten years after the first fleet arrived to settle New South Wales, Mathew Flinders and George Bass sailed to Van Diemen's Land's Frederick Henry Bay in their little colonial-built sloop *Norfolk*. They circumnavigated the southern island proving it was an island by exploring the strait between the mainland and Tasmania, which now bears the name Bass Strait. In the southern estuary, now known as the River Derwent, they sailed parallel along the seven-mile beach coastline believing the bay to be the one Abel Tasman chartered as Frederick Henry Bay, 156 years earlier in 1642. They did not, however, come ashore.

Four years later the French were prowling about the Pacific once more, spying on the British colony on behalf of Napoleon. The expedition of the French explorer, forty-eight-year-old Captain Nicolas Baudin, sailed into New South Wales' Port Jackson on board *Geographe* and *Naturaliste* in the summer of 1802. Like true gentlemen officers, the British entertained their enemy in Sydney Cove. Many of Baudin's crew suffered scurvy and were permitted recuperation time in the NSW sun, whilst the officers were entertained at Government House. But over roast wallaby, Madeira wine and rum the French bragged about erecting the tricolour on Van Diemen's Land shores, while recently there. (It is rumoured they imbibed too much of their host's hospitality)

They told of discovering Pittwater with its good anchorage, rich black soil, tall timbers, white freestone for building material and an endless source of fresh water. Why even Napoleon was keen to have a settlement here, they declared. After dinner this night the French officers showed off charts of Van Diemen's Land with areas coloured in gold and red denoting the proposed French settlements.

Among Baudin's crew, a young Louis Freycinet and Francois Peron had gone ashore in what is now known as Freycinet Peninsula, ostensibly to collect flowers and insect specimens. While there they planted a small provider garden of their own. Clearly, they planned to return or at least leave a food source for future expeditions.

When the gout-pained NSW Governor, Philip Gidley King, heard of this French boast he was furious and his response immediate. The southern island must be colonised and declared British for George III before the French did likewise for their emperor, Napoleon. Before the French even sailed out of Port Jackson, King sent a young lieutenant, Charles Robbins, in the small schooner *Cumberland* to seize King Island for King George III, under the French noses. To make a statement, Robbins claimed Port Philip next.

I don't think Tasmanians today realise just how close we were to being a French colony. We might all be speaking the French language and eating our daily baguettes. The local snails would probably taste alright too if we gave them a chance. Baudin's officers also sang the praises of the north coast of Van Diemen's Land, claiming the rich bounty of what would become Port Dalrymple, George Town and Launceston.

But with France's economy struggling through what would come to be known as the Napoleonic Wars, the French sailed for Europe and eventually Colonel Paterson was dispatched to settle this northern coast of Van Diemen's Land.

Tasmania could also very well have been Dutch for that matter. Abel Tasman anchored *Heemskerck* and *Zeehaen* offshore near Hobart on 1 December 1642. But the surf was up at Seven Mile Beach and the Dutch could not land, causing Tasman to send a strong swimmer, Master Carpenter Pieter Jacobsz, ashore to plant the flag of the Prince Frederik Hendrik, as a token gesture of Dutch possession.

Hobart Town finally settled.

To blight the French further, Governor King sent a young, albeit foolish, Lieutenant John Bowen to the Derwent estuary to claim southern Van Diemen's Land for King George III, arriving on board *Lady Nelson* and the whaler *Albion*, on 12 September 1803. He unwisely chose to settle on a marshy landing on the river's eastern shore.

Months later on 11 February 1804 Lieutenant Colonel David Collins was sent by King to join Bowen and establish a permanent settlement. He sailed aboard the grossly overcrowded 481-ton convict transport *Ocean*, captained by Captain John Mertho. Accompanying him was his chaplain, the Reverend Robert Knopwood, Lieutenant Edward Lord and 25 Royal Marines and 178 prisoners from Port Phillip.

Previously Collins had abandoned Port Phillip in Victoria, declaring the settlement as an unsuitable, sandy waterless wasteland. It's now called Melbourne.

On arrival in the estuary Collins was impressed with Pipeclay Lagoon and Pittwater on the shores of Storm Bay. But they were well south of Bowen's chosen site, which Collins had yet to inspect.

Knopwood was also impressed, writing glowing reports also in his diary where he noted the reedy shores abounded in the game precious to him as a sportsman and a lover of good living:

'We see a great number of wild fowl and one emu,' he wrote. *'Quails, bronze-wing pigeons and parrots. At 4 we returned to the party we left and got a great quantity of oysters. It appeared to me that the natives were much better supplied with fresh fish and birds than those at Port Phillip. Near the first lagoon which was large,*

more than 12 or 14 miles round, was a quantity of flax and very fine, ducks and teal, and I think woodcock was flushed.'

That was written the morning after they landed at Risdon Cove. The next day they encountered their first natives. A party of 17 appeared.

Knopwood wrote: *'They were well made, entirely naked; some of them had war weapons; they had a small boy with them about seven years old, and did not appear to flee from them.'*

But innocence was lost that day. Tragedy awaited these tall brown hunters with their ochre matted hair, carrying long thin spears and accompanied by their women wearing gleaming necklaces of shell and carrying woven baskets and stone hand axes. The sight of the tribe passing by on their way to find fresh hunting grounds panicked an ignorant Lieutenant Moore and his charge of uneducated marines. They fired a carronade loaded with canister shot into the tribe. It is not recorded accurately in the history books but there would have been many Aborigines wounded, if not fatalities.

Collins was rowed ashore at ten o'clock on the morning of 16 February and inspected Bowen's new settlement, basically a few tents. He was not happy. What he saw was a desolate repeat of Port Phillip Bay, from where he had just sailed; a land of marsh and brackish water, a miserable trickle only, could be gathered as soakage through the sands and into their sunken water barrels.

The next morning Collins, Reverend Knopwood, Collins' kinsman William Collins, two marine guards and a rowing crew, journeyed down river in search of a better location to start a settlement. En route several points and landmarks were charted and named, with Collins naming Sullivans Cove, after the Permanent Under Secretary to the Colonies, John Sullivan.

The natural and deep harbour was surrounded by tall timber growing back into the rolling foothills of a mountain they referred to as Table Mountain, due to its resemblance to the mountain at

Cape Town. This would be renamed Mount Wellington in honour of the famous Duke of Wellington, some years after he defeated Napoleon at Waterloo in 1815. Now in the 21st century Mount Wellington shares its name with the Aboriginal name, kunanyi.

The area appeared unsettled by the indigenous people. There were streams running east through the mountain forests of eucalypt and the tea-tree forests closer to the shore. Here the water filtered through reeds where bird life was prolific. The location for a settlement was idyllic.

Idyllic for the moment – it would not be too long before these fresh water rivulets ran with cholera and other pestilences of 'civilisation'.

The main stream poured into the harbour either side of a rocky outcrop, a sparsely timbered islet, which, at low tide, was linked to the shore by an isthmus, or a bar of sand.

Collins made a short walk that day into the woods with Knopwood and immediately recognised the area as suitable for the new settlement. The water ran deep and swift through the forest and was clear, cool and sweet in the height of summer. Timber and stone, lime and clay were all there in abundance. The soil was black and rich and ideal for corn, which Collins preferred to grow. The islet, which he named Hunter Island, would prove ideal for unloading stores and also protection of their precious supplies.

(Captain John Hunter was Second Captain of the First Fleet and governor of New South Wales from 1795 until 1800.)

Reverent Knopwood wrote in his diary:

> 'The Lieut.-Governor, Collins and myself went to examine a plain on the S.W. side of the river, the plain extensive and continual run of water which is excellent, it comes from a lofty mountain, most resembling the Table Mountain at the Cape of Good Hope, the land is good, and the trees very excellent,

the plain is well calculated in every degree for settlement.'

Bowen must have felt supremely inadequate. He had arrived on the 12th of September. What on earth had he been doing for five months, swatting mosquitoes in the swamplands of an area now called Bowen's Park?

Within weeks a village of wattle and daub dwellings sprung up at Sullivans Cove, and a government 'house' was erected, mostly of canvas at this early stage, on the site now known as Franklin Square.

In 1807 the population swelled somewhat as the penal colony of Norfolk Island was abandoned and its residents sent to Hobart Town, as the new settlement was now referred. Unfortunately, soon they all faced famine. Some corn was grown in small gardens to supplement the meagre and rotting rations sent from Sydney Cove, like two-year-old salted pork and beef. Rice brought from India however was a staple.

Hunting parties were sent into the bush, with fowling piece, powder and shot making kangaroo reasonably plentiful in the diet. Even convicts were sent armed into the bushland to hunt. Many absconded, befriending Aborigines where possible. But the reckless shooting of natives at Risdon must have made the natives wary.

From this complex and sometimes troubled history the modern state of Tasmania developed.

ABOUT THE AUTHOR

Craig was born in Hobart and has traveled extensively giving him the experiences and escapades he so enjoys putting into print. This included working as a chef for a restaurant owned by Sydney underbelly figures in the early 70s and cooking in Darwin when cyclone Tracy destroyed the city. Life has been busy and interesting to say the least. In the 90s, Craig independently shot two feature films, a murder mystery set in Southern Tasmania which aired on television and a splatter comedy available online. He wrote, produced and directed both.

Having led a busy life operating his own restaurant, The Drunken Admiral, Craig decided to follow his passion of writing fiction. And with Tasmania's fascinating past he has plenty to write about.

Using Tasmania's history as a blank canvas Craig loves nothing more than to weave adventure, mystery and mayhem involving colorful characters from all walks of life. He has written 33 previous titles, five have been published. Many are historical dramas and others contemporary action thrillers.

Published works are Penmore Press, Arizona; *Silent from the Grave, 1814* and *Coral Moon*. Black Rose Writing, Texas; *Prisoners of Fate* and *On the Devil's Knee*.

He has a graphic designer son living in Melbourne and a restaurateur daughter in Hobart. Craig lives and works in Hobart.

NOTE FROM THE AUTHOR

Word-of-mouth is crucial for any author to succeed. If you enjoyed *The Vatican Ruby*, please leave a review online—anywhere you are able. Even if it's just a sentence or two. It would make all the difference and would be very much appreciated.

Thanks!
Craig Godfrey

We hope you enjoyed reading this title from:

BLACK ROSE
writing™

www.blackrosewriting.com

Subscribe to our mailing list – *The Rosevine* – and receive **FREE** books, daily deals, and stay current with news about upcoming releases and our hottest authors.
Scan the QR code below to sign up.

Already a subscriber? Please accept a sincere thank you for being a fan of Black Rose Writing authors.

View other Black Rose Writing titles at www.blackrosewriting.com/books and use promo code **PRINT** to receive a **20% discount** when purchasing.

www.ingramcontent.com/pod-product-compliance
Lightning Source LLC
Chambersburg PA
CBHW010729100726
47899CB00009B/2986